JACK L. CHALKER

THE RUN TO CHAOS KEEP

Book Two of THE QUINTARA MARATHON

ACE BOOKS, NEW YORK

THE RUN TO CHAOS KEEP

An Ace Book / published by arrangement with
the author

PRINTING HISTORY
Ace hardcover edition / May 1991
Ace paperback edition / May 1992

ISBN: 0-441-69348-2

Ace Books are published by The Berkley Publishing Group,
200 Madison Avenue, New York, New York 10016.
The name ''ACE'' and the ''A'' logo
are trademarks belonging to Charter Communications, Inc.

PRINTED IN THE UNITED STATES OF AMERICA

10 9 8 7 6 5 4 3 2 1

Jack L. Chalker's
THE QUINTARA MARATHON

Three unique empires—threatened
by the discovery of alternate life . . .

THE EXCHANGE are exploiters who consume the universe's resources through the powers of their cybernetic leaders.

THE MYCOHLIANS are parasitic beings who, like a virus, can invade and take over other life forms.

THE MIZLAPLAN are a brilliant, long-lived race who will use any means possible to spread the word of the Cosmic All.

These three empires, maintaining a delicate balance of power, have very little in common—except a strange, recurring legend of a horned demon. Now, a shocking discovery has changed their lives forever:

The discovery of two horned creatures, seemingly lifeless . . .

But they are most definitely alive.

THE QUINTARA MARATHON includes

THE DEMONS AT RAINBOW BRIDGE
THE RUN TO CHAOS KEEP
THE NINETY TRILLION FAUSTS

"CHALKER KNOWS HOW TO TELL A STORY . . . A MASTER!"

—*Fantasy and Science Fiction*

Ace Books by Jack L. Chalker

THE CHANGEWINDS SAGA

WHEN THE CHANGEWINDS BLOW
RIDERS OF THE WINDS
WAR OF THE MAELSTROM

THE QUINTARA MARATHON

BOOK ONE: THE DEMONS AT RAINBOW BRIDGE
BOOK TWO: THE RUN TO CHAOS KEEP
BOOK THREE: THE NINETY TRILLION FAUSTS

AUTHOR'S NOTE

When writing the three volumes of *The Quintara Marathon,* I immediately ran into the problem of representing nonverbal communications. In the book we have various characters and creatures, some of whom communicate in whole or in part directly with the mind of another. When added to internalized dialogue, this began to make for a page that was both confusing and typographically unwieldy.

The late George O. Smith, when faced with this problem, decided that the easiest way to resolve this was to use a different dialogue delimiter so that the reader would instantly know which communications were verbal and which were mind-to-mind. I have often marveled that others never took up this practice, but it seems practical here and throughout *The Quintara Marathon.* Thus, to alert you, text delimited by opposing carets, or "arrows" as they are sometimes called (e.g. <*Watch out on your left!*>), is telepathic or mind-to-mind dialogue throughout this book, joining the traditional "Watch out!" for verbal communications and *Better watch out* (no delimiters) for internalized dialogue. It might jar right at the start, but as, every once in a while, all sorts of furious dialogue flies in all directions, I think you'll find it remarkably easy to get used to, and certainly preferable to the alternatives.

Jack L. Chalker

*For the late
Catherine "C.L." Moore,
who showed us how it's done
over fifty years ago.*

THE RUN TO
CHAOS KEEP

THE DEMONS
AT RAINBOW BRIDGE

An ANGUISHED, GHOSTLY SPECTRE TRAPPED IN Hell had summoned them to this remote place, and, worst of all, it was a collect call.

"All ships . . . any ships . . . Exchange registry . . . This is Research Vessel Wabaugh. *Coordinates based on special map frontier zone one one four eight two stroke five. Coordinates are Rainbow Bridge. Send assistance fast. They're all dead. They're all in there with the demons and they're all dead. Only one left. Can't leave. Approach with extreme caution! Power adequate for maintenance only. Any Exchange registry. Approach with caution. Demons at Rainbow Bridge! Coordinates . . ."*

The blue and green world below them looked so tranquil, so placid, that it seemed as if nothing could disturb its quiet beauty, but they were an Arm of the gods of the Mizlaplan, a holy gathering in Inquisition assembly, and they had already risked much to get this far.

Although, by treaty, the Mizlaplanian survival suit was officially categorized as "gold in color," that was simply to get around different racial perceptions of color. The suits were

3

not shiny, but rather dull, more a darker shade of yellow with just a bit of orange than golden. The form-fitted suits, customized for each individual, differed only in detail from those used by the other two great empires, the Mycohl and the Exchange, but for color, of course. Captain Gun Roh Chin, master of the Mizlaplanian freighter *Faith of Gorusu,* graduate of the Naval Institute, now an Instrument of the Arm of the Holy Inquisition, looked at them all in their fairly bright suits and wished that the diplomats had insisted on charcoal; he felt like a beacon in the damned thing, or a very good target. They had been forced into this desolate and isolated frontier sector of space on orders; to get here, they had been forced to cross Mycohlian space at its narrowest point, and, narrow or not, were two empires away from home and doubly illegal.

Even though Chin timed his drop and his thrust perfectly, it took him close to thirty precious minutes to maneuver up to the Exchange ship, and, when he did, he found it with beacons and running lights off and no sign of power.

The ship was an impressive sight nonetheless, framed against the blue-green and white backdrop of the planet below; clearly a research and supply, rather than military, vessel, it floated suspended between the planet and the stars, looking very, very lonely.

"It doesn't look damaged," Krisha the Holy Mendoro, the dark beauty who was both priestess and Arm security officer, noted, trying to see what detail she could. "I am telepathically scanning, and I get nothing at all."

"Nor I," added Savin the Holy Peshwa, who was a powerful empath. Empaths often received things at far greater distance than telepaths, although, in both cases, they weren't expecting to feel or monitor anything intelligible—just some sign that there was life aboard. "It feels like a dead ship."

Savin was a Mesok, a huge humanoid creature with a hard, rubbery reptilian skin, nasty yellow eyes like some giant cat's, with big, bony hands whose fingers and toes ended in suckers at their tips, and big, bony, dish-like ears that seemed glued onto the top of his angular head. He was a fearsome-looking one, all green and black, with enormous teeth that showed even with his mouth closed, and his very sight was intimidating as a vision of Hell. There wasn't one of them who didn't give prayers of thanks every time they looked at him that he was on their side.

Manya the Holy Szin looked up from her instrument cluster. "It *is* a dead ship," she told them. "No power levels at all. Even the emergencies have been drained. Only the broadcast emergency transponder, which is opposite the planet's surface, shows any energy at all. It is inert. No life forms, no internal power. We will have to cut through an airlock just to board her."

Manya, the science officer of the Arm, was a Gnoll—short, squat, barrel-chested gnomes with snake-like forked tongues, huge pointed ears that stuck up on both sides of their heads, and with gray skin like an elephant's hide and twice as tough. But they and Terrans could eat the same foods, tended to share a liking for sweets, had similar biological systems, and weren't as far apart in the evolutionary way as they seemed on the surface.

"You're certain of that, Manya?" Morok pressed her. "No life, no internal power? It can't just be shielded?"

Morok the Holy Ladue was tall, frail-looking, and quite bird-like in appearance, his tiny hands at the end of the long, leathery wings that could actually be used to fly—in the right gravity and environment—and the leader of the Arm. Still, there was also something reptilian about him, at least subjectively to Terrans, and this came across in his constant cool, seemingly dispassionate manner.

"No. If there were any attempts at shielding of that sort then the shields themselves would register," the science officer replied. "There is nothing alive aboard. Even its computers are out."

"*Somebody* survived whatever it was," Krisha noted. "Somebody sent that message along with the distress beacon."

"Yes, but how long ago?" Gun Roh Chin asked her. "Many days, certainly. Perhaps longer. With life support down, they might not have been able to find a way to keep going. They might have lost hope after nobody came. They might have gone mad."

Savin's huge eyes scanned the surface of the research vessel. "Holiness—the escape pods are still intact as well. Not a one has been fired. Not even the ones away from the surface that show some trickle charge—enough to use manually."

"Yes? So?" Morok was more spooked than irritated. They all were.

"Holiness—at least a few near the transponder are almost certainly usable, power drain or not. They weren't used. The first implication is that whatever happened here happened very quickly and to everyone. Everyone but one. He, she, it— whatever—survived, possibly by being in the only place near the transponder that's still active, and was possibly only knocked out when everyone and everything else went. They would likely not have a huge crew on this sort of ship anyway. That person is not aboard now, or, if aboard, died there. Died there right next to a getaway system. Or got away without using the pods."

Gun Roh Chin nodded. "The pod would have taken him to the nearest survivable planet. We assume that they wouldn't assign races to this who couldn't survive down there, since the climate, atmosphere, and the like have measured safe for us. It would have taken our survivor to the surface, with enough supplies and shelter for a month or more. That means . . ."

"It means," Krisha finished for him, "that he chose to die, either horribly or by his own hand, rather than go down to that world."

"There is a shuttle missing," Morok noted. "I saw its empty nesting bay on the underside."

"Within range of whatever it was, though," Savin pointed out. "I would assume that the shuttle was on the surface with the main scientific party. Since whatever killed this ship came from down there, I think it highly unlikely that anyone there risked flying up here to get that survivor off. Or was able to."

"Do you want to board her?" Chin asked them.

"Yes," responded Morok, "but not now. If there is no life aboard, we must first determine if there is still life below."

"Well, there is surely *something* below," Manya commented. "The energy pattern on the ship clearly indicates that it took a jolt of almost inconceivable power, pure energy, from a point below on the surface. It shorted out all the systems, shorted the computers, and most likely electrocuted almost everyone. Our survivor was probably the only one in some sort of insulated situation and so did not get the full jolt."

"If I am to be electrocuted, I should rather know who is doing it to me, and why," Morok said in a flat, hollow tone.

"Take it down, Captain. Land at their camp below. Everyone check suits and weapons. Yes, again. *Now!*"

It wasn't difficult to find the camp below. It was a world covered with trees and seas, but the camp appeared to be the only sign of any animal life on it. There were a number of temporary, prefabricated structures down there as well as parabolic communications antennae all of which were easy to spot.

"A standard scientific field station, not much different than the way we would do it," Manya told them. "The only thing I cannot understand is that large—house, or building, or whatever it is. It is of a totally different design than the others and looks quite permanent. In fact, it almost looks as if it were tooled from a single, unimaginably huge quartz-like crystal."

"More likely the object under study," Morok guessed. "Is it the odd light or my eyes, or does that—thing—seem slightly different, almost as if it moved?"

"I have been plotting it," Manya reported. "It *does* change, somehow. Not really in mass or even dimensions, but subtly, in detail."

"Could it be alive?"

"It might be—but if it is, it is like nothing we know as life in any form. I simply do not know what it is, and I suspect that they didn't, either. That is why they are here."

"The base station has normal power," Chin noted. "Looks rather cozy, in fact. But we're not being scanned by anything I can detect. It's as if everybody down there is asleep. Ah—see! Their shuttle's there, in that clearing. I think I can put down close to it. No use in sneaking up. If anything's left alive down here, it certainly knows we're here by now and should come out and welcome us with open arms."

There was no welcoming committee. They put on their helmets, pressurized, and went out, even though all the instrumentation said that the air was perfectly safe and the temperature was quite pleasant. Until they knew more, none of them wanted to take anything for granted.

"Dead like the ship," Krisha said. "Nothing. I get nothing at all. Savin?"

"The same, although I do get some very odd intermittent sensations from the area of that object there. I can't really explain the sensation. It's not like anything I have ever experienced before. Whatever it is, I do not think it is directed at us."

"That will have to do for now," Morok told him. "Check out their shuttle first, then the prefabs, one at a time. Use caution, keep weapons drawn."

Gun Roh Chin took the shuttle. It wasn't difficult to enter, and, inside, he found it rather bizarrely arranged but nothing he could not have figured out. It was clearly not designed to be flown by humans, although there were two human-shaped seats in the rear. The rest he put down to different designs and a different shuttle design philosophy. Still, he could tell almost from the moment he entered that it was powered, fully charged, and could be operational with a few flicks of a few switches.

"Shuttle is perfect and operational," he reported through his helmet radio.

"Then it *could* have picked up our survivor," Morok came back.

"Unlikely. Without power up there, they'd have had to cut away the outer airlock faceplate to get to the manual controls. They didn't. This thing was here before and it's been here all the time."

"The square prefab! Come quickly!" Krisha shouted.

They were all there on the run as soon as they got their bearings, piling into the door and then stopping dead just inside.

"May the gods embrace their innocent souls and reincarnate them to a life of peace," Morok intoned.

Gun Roh Chin was not prayerful. Even protected from the stench by his suit, he *still* wanted to throw up.

Savin bent down over a bloody form. "Krisha, exobiology is not my strong point, but isn't the human heart mounted roughly in the central chest cavity?"

Krisha swallowed hard. "Yes, roughly. What . . . ?"

The huge Mesok grabbed a shock of white hair atop the head of a Terran corpse, its face locked in a horrible and grotesque death mask, and yanked it up unceremoniously so that the chest was exposed.

The central area of the chest had been literally torn open, as if by some wild creature, possibly, even probably, while the man had been still alive. They all caught their breaths, but Manya scurried over and began using her portable instruments to examine the awful-looking wound. Even the tough, fanatical Gnoll seemed a bit shaky, though.

"It . . . has been torn from his chest," she managed. "Several of the others have equivalent mutilations. Something with great strength just pushed them down, like a child's plaything, and either ripped or tore key organs out of them."

"How long have they been dead?" Morok asked her.

"Seven days at least. This happened at least seven days ago. The bodies are dried up and beginning decomposition."

Gun Roh Chin wanted to avoid the sight of the research party, its nice little lab smeared in red human blood, and Zalerian green, and gray, and purple, and other colors of other races who had been here. He walked over to the far side of the lab and began to examine a huge hole that had seemingly been smashed into the wall around what had once been a window. He pushed away where the debris had bent inward and looked out at the strange, slightly changing, translucent structure just beyond.

In the small administration hut there was much the same, only here the door had simply been kicked or blown in. Here, too, were apparently several armed security officers, and this apparently had been, along with a couple found outside, the only armed members of the party. Some had clearly gotten off a lot of shots, and they looked, even in their present condition, to be the kind who didn't miss.

Whatever had come out of that thing and killed them was hardly subtle; it had just come, on and on, oblivious to anything that they could do.

He had been around, seen hundreds of worlds and races, seen violence and cruelty as well as gentleness and good, but he had never seen anything like this.

"*Something big,*" Kelly Morgan had told him. Something perhaps *too* big, even for them.

Krisha called to him. "Captain, I hate to ask, but I need you. We've found the depository recordings and none of us can read the writing to tell which is which."

He returned to the ultimate horror scene, noting how peaceful and gentle this place was, how *quiet,* and re-entered the lab.

He scanned the cabinet full of small labeled cubes she'd found, then picked one out. "This is a good place to start," he told her. "It says 'Preliminary Report on Remote Autopsy of Unknown Forms.'"

"There's a player in the office over there," she told him. "And no bodies. The recording system is different than ours. I'm not certain I know how to work it."

He took it, went into the office, which looked as if it had just been left for a moment by its occupant, then found the small previewer machine. "It's not difficult," he told her. "It's just that instead of the full-blown presentation we get a small representation on the viewer plate, there. Switch your suit to translate standard Exchange."

The power was on; he simply turned on the machine, inserted the cube label side out, and pressed the large actuator touch switch.

Much of it was simply a dictated interim report to some superiors back home, probably a record copy, but the small, three-dimensional images it projected of the research materials told them something.

"Subject A is a male of the species, 2.4381 meters tall, weight estimated at two hundred forty to two hundred sixty-eight kilograms. It won't be possible to totally eliminate the material in which they are embedded without extraction from the estimations. Sorry. The main body surface area is very tough, very dense. The skin is at least 1.2 centimeters thick, more aptly described as a 'hide' than mere skin, and various vital areas seem further protected by bony plates at or very near the exterior. Both hands and feet are overly large in proportion to the body and are hairless, with that mottled texture consistent and the palms probably rock hard to the touch although they certainly bend and flex in the expected manner. The talons at the ends of the fingers are suited to ripping and tearing flesh, consistent with the teeth, which contain no herbivorous molars at all. They are true flesh-eating carnivores, no question."

"By the gods," Krisha intoned under her breath as the long-dead voice went on. "I am looking at the scans but they mean little to me."

"Or me," Chin agreed. "Manya?"

The Gnoll seemed to be trembling visibly, her eyes rapt on the small viewing plate, intoning prayer after prayer.

Krisha looked somewhat stricken herself and looked up at

Chin. "Her mind keeps saying 'Demons! Demons! They have awakened Hell personified.'"

"*Manya!*" Morok shouted at her.

The science officer seemed not to notice, then pointed a gnarled finger at the projection. "There! The full scan! Now they will pull back and restore it!"

The tiny figure, still a computerized diagram, now showed a full figure. Humanoid, big—bigger than Savin by a head—and, slowly, more and more detail was overlain as the voice continued to drone on with its observations.

"Oh, gods of eternity protect us!" Savin prayed. "Manya is right. Look! Look!"

Gun Roh Chin had to admit that even the hair on the back of his own neck seemed to be tingling as he saw what they had found.

The creature didn't look quite the way his own religious teachers had pictured them, but it was still clearly recognizable, from the small horns on its head to the dull red eyes, fanged mouth, even the cloven hooves.

There could be no question in his or anyone else's mind that he and they were looking at—not a representation, not an abstract estimation, and not someone's imagination, but a real, three-dimensional photograph of an actual, in the flesh, classical demon.

"There must have been bodies in that thing," Chin commented dryly, his feelings at the moment impossible to describe. "They thought they were dead. They put a lid on this because they knew the effect this sort of discovery would have on not just our religion or even the Mycohl's but their own myriad faiths as well."

They could see the scene now: these cold, pragmatic, utterly materialistic scientists with their faith firmly rooted in what could be seen, felt, touched, and demonstrated, excited by the discovery of what must have been a burial place, intact, for what might have been the galaxy's earliest space-faring civilization. They had poked, probed, scanned, and done everything they could for weeks, probably months, to learn what they could before physically attempting to disturb or remove the remains, just in case exposure to air or light might cause damage or deterioration.

Finally, though, they had all they could from their instruments, their data filling those recording cubes and probably being beamed back to the highest levels of the Exchange. Finally, there came the point where they could do no more without physically extracting the bodies from whatever sarcophagi they lay in.

And the sleepers had awakened and wreaked horrible vengeance on those who had defiled their tomb and disturbed their sleep.

"I almost hesitate to ask this," Gun Roh Chin said at last, his throat curiously and almost painfully dry, "because I'm not sure I want to know the answer, but it must be asked."

"Yes?" Morok responded, watching in added horror as a *second* scan was being dispassionately discussed on the tape.

"They were suspended, not dead. They were freed, awakened, whatever. They came out and they killed all these people and somehow also fried the ship up there. Then what?"

"Uh? What do you mean?"

"Where did they go next?"

At that moment there came a roaring noise from outside, and in their current mental shape all weapons snapped to ready and they ran out, leaving the recording playing.

Near both the research shuttle and their own, they could see another, differently designed shuttle landing.

"The Mycohl!" Chin swore. "I'd forgotten about them! Just what we really needed right now!"

"Weapons, everyone!" Krisha snapped, pulling her pistol. She looked around. "Captain—could our own people play that cube?"

"Uh—yes, I suppose so. If we can break diplomatic codes I see no reason why we couldn't view a standard cube. The machine can be purchased almost anywhere in the Exchange."

"Then take the cube and any other that might look related. Don't take too long! Manya—you are best equipped to check out our visitors. Go, but no shooting! Do not betray yourself. Let them go past you and wait until we attack. We might catch them all in a crossfire. Practice the telepathic shielding and in the name of the gods keep your emotions in check!"

The Gnoll was still horribly shaken by the sight on the viewer, but she was a professional, and her horror at the sight of a real demon was no greater than her hatred of the Mycohl. She also had a rather unique Talent of her own. It would be quite effective—if she could use her training to block out those of the enemy with other Talents that might betray her.

"There's too many to carry," the captain told Krisha. "The three I've picked, including the one we viewed, will have to do."

She nodded. "Stand back, then." She aimed her energy pistol at the entire library, including the machine, and fired. There was a crackling sound, and what the beam did not disintegrate it melted into unusable form. "Let them get any information out of *that*!" she sniffed.

She stiffened. "We are being telepathically scanned," she told them.

That meant nothing to Chin, who was a null, the oddest and rarest of Talents. Although possessing no Talent of his own, he was immune to those of any other, something not true even of his powerful comrades. He was equally immune to Krisha's telepathy, to Savin's empathic abilities, and even to Morok's powerful hypnotic abilities. Even Manya could not fool him, although her own Talent was unique to her species. Still, if Morok's mind were read, or Manya's, a Mycohl telepath would know he was here just as surely as if he were in full view.

Krisha's telepathic shields were automatically up. That didn't mean that someone of reasonable skill and power and the same Talent couldn't detect her presence, but it certainly meant that they could get nothing from her mind. Morok, Savin, and Manya had fallen back into the somewhat effective methods of chanting prayers, a technique that, with their practice and experience and Krisha's coaching, also left an enemy telepath not completely in the dark, but with far less information than would be useful. Telepathy, like any other form of communication, had its limits. Among them was its lack of directionality, which could be maintained by a practiced opponent varying amplitude as the mind-reader moved toward or away from them.

Still, if a telepath were good enough, and supported by others to gain the missing information, there was no real hiding. In case the Mycohlian *was* that good, Krisha was prepared to engage her counterpart mind-to-mind.

Morok's thin, clawed, four-fingered hand, so tiny in such a large creature, touched her shoulder, and she turned and looked up and into his strange, blood-red round eyes.

"You are the sword of the Arm," Morok told her softly. "So long as that sword is needed, you are but an extension of the whole, a tool of the gods, and Krisha neither exists nor is relevant. There is nothing else; you exist only to protect the whole. No other telepath may defeat you, no hypno bind you."

<They have a hypno! Watch it!>

The words came to her mind as she turned away; coming, she knew, not from the enemy telepath but from the mind of another being cautioned by that telepath.

<Gray shades of Valdus! One of 'em's just gone colder'n stone!> another, obviously an empath, just said.

<He's locked in the telepath to single-minded defense,> said a third mind. *<That's very good. Don't underestimate these fanatics, any of you! I want them! I want them located—now!>*

<They are all praying up an assemblage of saints,> the telepath remarked acidly. *<I cannot get a real fix, but most of them are ahead, probably in or near that main building. There is another, but it is both closer and less distinct. They are very good at prepared defense. At the moment I can only say that the telepath is most likely Terran. The rest—unclear.>*

<We'll take no chances,> the leader told them. *<Desreth, go find them.>*

"They are sending someone named Desreth to find us," Krisha reported. "I get no clear image of who or what it is from their minds and nothing from this other at all. Whatever it is, it is a null. They are not taking nearly the precautions to block themselves, but are blocked where it counts. Two Terrans, a male and a female, the former their leader and I presume a hypno. The telepath is a race I do not know but seems large and very grotesque to me. It sees differently than we and depends on other senses more, but thinks in a standard linear pattern. The other is another unfamiliar race and more dangerous, because it can think fully in a form my inadequate mind cannot sort, nor does it see as we see. I can get only occasional flashes of anything close to normal. The null—somehow they have blocked it out."

<Tobrush—watch our back!> the leader commanded. *<I am most worried about that loose one somewhere. The rest of you cover the two exits to that main building. We may have caught the rest of them inside.>*

Manya had circled around from the main building to a point

where she could view both the newcomers and the building which held her comrades. The Mycohl leader was a tall Terran male dressed in the rust-red color of his Empire, tough and muscular, big without any fat, his muscles showing admirably through his skintight suit. He had a cold arrogance that unnerved her; the manner that she had seen before only in ''wild'' hypnos, whose power over others deluded them into a sense of near godlike ego.

The second was a strange Terran female, also quite muscular, medium height, with the cold yet subtle moves of a jungle animal. There was something, too, wrong with her face; at first Manya had thought that the woman was just superficially Terran and was actually some other race. Now she realized that the Mycohlian woman might once have been a beauty, but her face was twisted and scarred. With the Gnoll's inability to appreciate the real differences in Terrans without careful study, she thought that this woman somehow resembled Krisha in the essentials—a dark, evil Krisha, a poisonous distillation of all that was sinful in a young woman's soul.

The third member of the red-clad team was a large creature with a glistening, undulating black body, supported on six impossibly thin legs that appeared to terminate in soft pincers, its face a set of ugly mandibles and large, oval yellow and brown segmented eyes on short, independent stalks. The fourth, about the size of the third, was mostly encased in a gnarled, spiral-like shell of dirty beige, covered with a mass of writhing, thick hairs that seemed to act like tentacles— *thousands* of tentacles!

But the fifth—it was the one that struck some terror into her. It alone wore no environment suit, nor did it need one. Essentially a metallic cube, gunmetal gray with occasional streaks of dull bronze, supported on six long, pointed legs, it appeared to shift its shape in some kind of fluid manner as needed. She knew that sort, all right—*Corithian!* Machine-like, artificially created life of some long-gone civilization, able to change itself into whatever was required or ooze out whatever appendage it needed, it had not only the ancestry of a machine but the soul and morals of one, too. By the time the concentrated full-power firing of the rest of the team's guns had immobilized it, the rest of that crew of evil would have them!

Instinctively she knew she had to betray herself, at least a little, to give warning. Her mouthpiece was live, and, into it, she said, simply, "Corithian coming!"

The strange, shelled creature with the countless hair-like tentacles suddenly whirled as if on a single wheel, and two stalked eyes suddenly seemed to grow out of the shell and look in her direction. Obviously this one was the telepath.

"Behind us!" it rasped aloud, in an eerie voice that seemed to send chills through Manya. "Female, can't get more of a fix with that prayer screen. She just warned her congregation of Desreth, though, by radio."

The leader stopped, turned, and stared back into the jungle. "Can you see her?"

"No, and I cannot understand why I cannot," the telepath responded.

The leader chuckled dryly. "Maybe it's a vegetable. Spray the entire area, full sweep. We might get lucky."

Manya didn't wait. She opened up on the large creature using her own weapon on wide spread and started moving. Betraying her gnome-like, almost hunchbacked appearance and bulk, Gnolls could move pretty fast when they had to.

The attack caused the Mycohlian team to flatten, and by the time they opened fire, Manya had managed to move around all the way to the parked shuttles. The Mycohl, Manya had seen, had made a major sloppy mistake in landing closest to the camp and leaving their shuttle door open. If they fired in any sort of lethal concentration where they *knew* she should be, they might just blow the inside of their own craft.

The leader stood, fury clear on his face. *"Kalia! Get that creature!"* he snapped at the woman. "Tobrush—cover her! If a telepath and an empath can't root that creature out, we don't deserve to be here!" He turned to the insectoid creature. "Robakuk—you keep those doors *sealed*! I'm moving up to go in behind Desreth. Join me as soon as you secure our backs. Let us do this quickly! We are in enemy territory without authority—but so are they. It will be easier to explain this if we alone are left to testify!"

It had taken more guts than sense to get the Mycohl to this point.

They were a new crew, fresh from training and testing, out in a little ship in the middle of nowhere, performing routine

picket duty. All of them understood that they were on proba-
tion; all also understood that the alternatives to performing well
and impressing their superiors were worse than death in the
harsh, Darwinian system of the Mycohl.

There was Josef, their big, handsome Terran captain, sport-
ing his traditional ensign's big black mustache, absolute
monarch of a flea-speck of a picket ship and subordinate to just
about everyone else, his swagger reinforced by his inborn
talent as a hypno that had solved many problems on his way to
even this point, and who, because of that fact, was yet to be
tested in a situation where that power was not a deciding factor.

Here was Kalia, whom he'd met while working on an
undercover mission to salvage the great feast and carnival of
his Lord Squazos from sabotage by jealous rivals. Kalia, who
had risen from the bottom, the lowest *droi* classes of her hive,
with an intelligence born of experience, not formal education,
determined to show that she was even more ruthless and deadly
than any man, her body a finely tuned mass of muscles that
most men could only dream of, her once-beautiful face
disfigured by a horrible scar gained in that harsh growing-up
that she refused to have removed. Josef's sergeant and as much
a weapon as any on the picket ship under his command, she
was a powerful empath. She was also illiterate and ignorant of
almost anything not directly related to her job, but at that job
she was superb.

With them were the *Thion* Robakuk, whose powerful telekinetic abilities allowed him to move objects almost as large as,
and heavier than, he was by sheer force of will, whose race
bore more than a passing, if coincidental, resemblance to a
common Terran housefly, only wingless and as large as Josef,
and the *Julki* Tobrush, whose snail-like appearance was totally
deceiving in that he was neither shelled nor slow; the "shell"
was actually a thick organ that served as hide and from which
it could create and exude its countless hair-like tentacles that
could act either independently or in concert to perform the
finest manual tasks, and which could also secrete and even
inject an enormous variety of natural toxins and other useful
substances. Tobrush was a powerful telepath, a *very* strong one.

The final member of the team, and the one even they had to
admit as a group they understood the least, was Desreth the
Corithian. Most of the time it just sat there, usually looking like

a meter-and-a-half lump of dull silver; rounded, looking like nothing so much as an oval sculpture of a beetle not quite finished, it was by preference impassive and none too social. None of the Mycohl had ever really understood why the Corithians, who needed nothing obvious from anyone, participated in the Empire at all, but they did, and quite well. Descendants of an ancient robotic race, they had evolved, or perhaps evolved themselves, into a bizarre form where they could repair themselves, protect themselves, and form themselves into whatever was required. Legend said they could not be killed, which, like most legends, was wrong. But they were damned hard to kill, and had to be crushed, dissolved, or melted almost completely.

They were all ambitious—at least all save Desreth, whose motives were always incomprehensible—but they were also aware of how low they were on the Imperial ladder even though already higher than any had ever expected to be. They were on picket duty—routine guard duty, about the most basic and dull activity the Empire required, and in an area not likely to get them into serious trouble.

They were, then, perhaps the worst group to suddenly detect an incursion by a Mizlaplanian ship into Mycohl space and take up pursuit as they discovered, to their amazement, that the invader was making its way across their space toward the Exchange boundary. Interstellar treaty prohibited a chase beyond their boundaries, but Josef had been unable to catch the Holy Scow and had proceeded anyway. Technically, the incursion was an act of war, since their picket ship was a military one on a military mission, and diplomats would have attacks on all sides when they learned of it. Josef was content to let the diplomats fight their battles; he was determined to find out what would cause a Mizlaplanian ship to take such an inexplicable series of actions. If it achieved some wonderful result, all would be forgiven. If it flopped, he'd placed them all in deep shit.

The Three Empires each controlled nearly equal segments of the galaxy; each was of roughly equal size, each of relatively equal power, and each could most likely destroy another if it were willing to itself be destroyed and leave everything else to the third. For this reason, Josef understood, he was entirely on his own, and any failures would be laid to him alone.

And still he had followed that Mizlaplanian ship, followed it to a remote solar system off the maps and on the frontier, where the quarry stopped and he could now catch up and see what was so important that they would risk at least as much as he.

"They're not achieving orbit!" Tobrush reported. "They're detaching a shuttle on the fly and accelerating out-system!"

That pig of a Holy Captain has read my mind! Josef thought angrily to himself. Then aloud he said, "Then he knows, or at least guesses, that we are here."

"We could catch it and cut them off!" Kalia exclaimed excitedly. "I should like to be the one. I have never blown up a spaceship before."

"And you won't now, either! Not yet, anyway. I'm not worried about that massive hunk of metal and synthetics. It won't go far because it *does* have to come in and pick them up—or abandon them. Either is perfectly acceptable to us. We will get him after—if time and circumstances permit. We might waste several hours before we found and destroyed it, giving them time down there."

"So what?" the human woman responded. "Whatever they learn will die with them."

"Do you think they don't know that? That their gamble has failed? They are fanatics. They will die before they will be taken by us, and they know negotiations are useless. If they find nothing of hope, I would expect them to destroy or damage anything that might be of use to us. I have no intention of giving them that opportunity. I want everyone ready in full survival suit and battle gear. I'm going to put this thing close to that Exchange ship and we are going to see just what is going on there."

"All of us are going?" Robakuk asked, more excited than nervous.

"This ship is fully capable of maintaining itself, flying itself, defending itself, or, if need be, destroying itself to keep from enemy hands. There is nothing that freighter could do to it except present it with an automatic target. Those Mizlaplan shuttles can hold up to nine people depending on the races involved, and the races involved are unknown as of now. I do know that I am not going to underestimate that captain. Full gear—we all go. And don't get cocky or overconfident. These people are fanatics who will gladly die if they could take one of us with them, and they are *not* stupid or ill-equipped. Many of them are probably priests, but don't let that fool you. Almost all the priests they let loose like this are Talents and they're trained and they're good. And, most of all, they are going to be there ahead of us. If it were *us* in *their* situation, with them coming in on top of us but we have the same kind of lead, what would *we* do?"

"Traps and ambushes," Kalia responded. "The only chance they've got is if they can wipe us out."

"Agreed, and while it's on unknown ground for both of us, they will know it better than we having been there first."

"I would recommend ordering the ship in standby, with partial shutdown of all but our monitoring codes," Tobrush put in. "It's tempting to have it close at hand, but if the Exchange shows up while we're down there we're in no better shape than they are. If the Exchange shows up first weak and curious but unsuspecting, we can fight our way out. If it shows up in strength, we can then try and talk our way out."

"All right. Agreed. Desreth, you've been very quiet."

"I have been considering the odds that the Exchange is already here," the Corithian responded.

"Huh?"

"If they *did* show up first, they would have detected at least the Mizlaplanian ship before they themselves would be detected. They might well wonder what a Mizlaplanian ship was doing so far from home that it was willing to risk crossing Mycohl to answer a distress signal. In that case, they would lay back and monitor just as we and the Mizlaplanians are doing, until they see what happens. It would be the pragmatic thing, since both of us are now only rather lamely within the law. If we started shooting at one another or going where we have no right going—namely down to the planet—we would then be committing not a rescue mission but overt illegal acts within their territory."

He didn't like that. "What do the rest of you think? Is the Exchange that devious?"

"They are," Tobrush responded. "Yet I doubt the scenario. The Exchange in strength would have intercepted both of us by now and told us just where to go or else, keeping us well away from that place. They would only lay off in weakness, where they might fear either of us might eliminate them just to save our honor. In that case, they are irrelevant.''

"I would prefer they not be around, strong or weak," the captain responded. "Still, it would be interesting, would it not? A three-way battle to the death on a planet alien to all. It would be a magnificent challenge. I should like to think we would win such a battle.''

"Agh! Priests and scientists and traders," Kalia scoffed. "It would not even be a contest.''

Josef whirled around. "I told you not to underestimate these people!'' he snapped angrily. "Do that and you die and take the rest of us with you! I don't care if those Mizlaplanians believe their souls will become gods by eating grass and rolling in the mud and howling at the stars! One on one, in a real fight, they are most certainly our counterparts. No common freighter captain that I know would have detected us, let alone pulled that maneuver, and he did it coolly, knowing the odds. No matter what the vessel, they wouldn't send amateurs on a mission like this, and they are no amateurs. Any more stupid bravado like that and I will leave any of you who think that way here with the ship!''

They didn't really quite believe that anyone, particularly the Mizlaplanians, could be close to their equals, but they shut up because they wanted to go and to prove it.

This is where the greenness of the crew begins to show, Josef thought sourly. *And, damn it, I'm as green at this sort of thing as they are.*

Kalia moved silently and swiftly toward the Mizlaplanian creature somewhere among the shuttles. Her empathic sense gave her a fair idea of the quarry's location, but was not exact. Tobrush glided around to the other side, trying to get a telepathic fix, but while the large, snail-like creature was amazingly quick, almost as if it had wheels under that shell, it was not terribly limber and couldn't crouch down or climb over as she could. Evolution had provided the Julki with all the defenses its race needed on its home world, but Julkis had not been dependent on climbing, hiding, and sheer stealth to survive as had Kalia's.

Two eyestalks emerged from the Julki's shell, each extending more than a meter, and it looked around in obvious puzzlement. Unable to conceal its presence, even if protected by the Mycohl shuttle, Tobrush called, "I do not understand. It is *here*. I can *hear* it, even *smell* it—but I see nothing! Is it some tiny thing? Its telepathic defenses are good—my mind fills with the meaningless babble of its prayers, yet I can get no self-image. I have never encountered anything like this before."

Kalia remained silent, moving cat-like among the shadows cast by the shuttlecraft, then still, but she, too, was confused and confusion could mean swift death. Her sense of the Mizlaplanian creature was as strong as Tobrush's, although thankfully an empath didn't have to put up with those prayers. The creature they sought was indeed here, somewhere, and quite close. She could feel the quarry's tension, its mixture of apprehension and—disgust, perhaps, for them. She could also feel its almost fanatical hatred, so complete, so absolute, that it unnerved her a bit to know that it was there.

But where? She peered out from the shadows beneath the overhang of the Mizlaplanian shuttle, her field of vision easily covering one side of the space between it and the Mycohl shuttlecraft, and knew that Tobrush had the opposite field of vision. Between them, there was simply no place for anything to hide, and the metallic walls of the shuttles gave little concealment except at the ends, and the doors were shut tight. Both the telepath and the empath were certain that their quarry was outside, and was effectively trapped in the corridor between the two shuttles, yet—*there was nothing there!*

<Great Suza! Is the thing invisible?> she wondered, frustrated.

Maybe it was, although she had never heard of such a thing. A fighter had to be a pragmatist; if it was there and they couldn't see it, then go from there and figure how it was possible later.

Kalia could not read thoughts, but Tobrush could read hers. <Invisible is not invulnerable or it would not need to become invisible,> she reasoned. <Tobrush, keep your end covered. Snake some tendrils along the ground that would snare someone coming out your way. When you are ready, give me a sign, and I will open up with a wide spray along the whole corridor, keeping it above ground level. Either it will be driven to you or it will be caught in my pattern.>

"Any time!" she heard the Julki call, and almost immediately she opened up with her pistol at wide stun, stepping out quickly as she did so.

Manya had not survived all these years to be taken now by such a maneuver. As soon as Kalia opened up, she brought her own pistol up, knowing that the creature at the far end wouldn't chance those eyestalks against a wide beam and that the girl firing the pistol would, quite naturally, follow the beam and its results with her gaze. Against the Mizlaplanian shuttle, she was not really in Kalia's field of vision when the shooting started, and Kalia had to step out in order to cover the full corridor.

Kalia felt the emotions in her quarry rise and took that as confirmation of her plan, stepping out to cover the rest of the field of fire, and suddenly she felt the power of a tremendous blow, as if something very hard and very dense had struck her, sending her down and reeling.

"I see it!" Tobrush cried. "A little Terranoid in yellow!"

It was too late. By the time the Julki could emerge and bring its own weapon to bear, the sight of the fleeing Mizlaplanian was gone, and Kalia's limp body was the only thing in sight. Worse, Tobrush dared not go to his comrade's aid; that would have left the Julki exposed to fire from wherever this golden prayermonger was now.

"We've got a problem," it reported to Josef by radio. "Kalia's down and the thing's escaped! Watch your back! It appears to be able to make itself invisible."

"That's all we need!" Josef shot back. "We're set to crash this little party up here. We'll be back to help as soon as we can. Is she still alive?"

"Yes. It wasn't a full blow, considering the circumstances. Still, I do not know how badly she is hurt and I can't follow up yet without exposing myself. Do what you must, but if I were this creature I wouldn't still be here, I'd be closing in on you now."

Manya, however, had no intention of getting that close in, although she did want to cover her own team's back. The Talent she had, unique to her race, wouldn't fool a Corithian for a nanosecond. A variation of the same sort of mental Talents governing telepaths, empaths, hypnos, and the rest, it was hardly invisibility and would fool no machine. The wide field she could broadcast on the t-bands could convince any creature who received on those bands that she was not there, but anyone unable to receive those bands saw her clearly, even a null like Gun Roh Chin. To a Corithian, she would be totally exposed and an easy target.

She made for the cover of the buildings, which helped her protective abilities. Movement, particularly at normal or faster speeds, weakened the clouding power, as had been clear when Tobrush had spotted her making her break. It was a useful and essentially automatic defense under stress, but it had extreme limits, and while she'd more than once wished that the gods had extended that power a bit, she knew the limits precisely.

She could see them now, ready to strike. She couldn't really tell what the giant bug, as Robakuk seemed to her, could or would do in all this. The forward legs had a specially designed full power rifle it could easily fire for effect, but it seemed somewhat exposed, the pulpy, undulating black body so soft and vulnerable. The thing surely had a Talent that made it more valuable than just being able to stand there like a statue and stare at the laboratory building.

The Corithian, looking now somewhat like a smooth, silvery crab-like creature, appeared ready to charge the far door. As soon as it did, the big man would go through the back, firing as he entered, since his pistol wouldn't have much effect in a wide spray on his metallic ally. Krisha and Savin would be able to sense this Josef, but the Corithian they could only anticipate secondhand, from the big man's own mind. It was clear that the plan was to let the Corithian act at its own pace; Josef would follow, thereby not betraying the moment.

Suddenly Desreth took off toward the door with surprising acceleration and hit it full on. The door collapsed inward, and only a second or so behind, Josef crashed through the rear and Manya could hear the sound of firing inside.

It stopped almost as quickly.

Inside, Josef crouched warily, fearing traps, but he already suspected that he'd bruised his shoulder for nothing. There was a damned *hole* in the back of the thing you could almost pilot a shuttle through!

"They have escaped," Desreth said needlessly, scuttling over to the hole. "We have made a central error in not totally circumnavigating the structure first."

"We were short, thanks to that rear guard," Josef grumbled,

getting up, holstering his pistol, then rubbing his right shoulder and flexing it. "Besides, you sure they just didn't blow that out while we were setting up?"

"Lieutenant, you should examine this hole in the wall," the Corithian said in that strange, almost electronic monotone of its race. "The section is collapsed inward."

For the first time, Josef was aware of the sight and smell of the decomposing corpses. He went up to one, a race he didn't know, and could see no signs of any blood or blood-like fluid although its exoskeletal skin had been literally crushed, but there was a fair amount of black and yellow mold on and around the wounds and natural openings.

"They've been dead a long time," he commented, thinking. He looked over at the hole in the wall. "Something came in, right through the wall, and just wiped up the place with them."

"So it appears," Desreth agreed. "The records appear to have been methodically destroyed as well, but there are no bodies in the records section. The Mizlaplanians clearly did that, after taking what they thought was important. I had not thought that sort capable of such subtlety. I shall not underestimate them again."

Josef moved cautiously to the hole in the wall and looked out, expecting shots to be fired, but there were none. Very carefully, he looked out and saw that the hole was in a direct line to the other, far more alien, structure behind.

"I wish we'd gotten here first," he muttered. "Or at least that we'd had time enough to tie into those records on the ship. What could do this and not be destroyed itself?"

"Something like a Corithian, perhaps," Desreth suggested, "only larger. Perhaps much larger. Larger and savage, since most of these bodies appear to have no weapons at all, suggesting that they are scientists and that they had no idea that there was anything dangerous here."

"Robakuk?" Josef called through the intercom. "Can you see any sign of the enemy?"

"None. I have monitored your conversation and moved to a point where I can view the escape area. Unless they are all invisible like their rear guard, they are not there."

Manya did not know their language, but she had the idea from their reactions. They'd all gone out, probably through the hole in the wall. She remembered the layout of the camp and realized that if their Talents could no longer pinpoint her Mizlaplanian team, then there was only one place they could have gone.

She didn't like it, but she knew that, as soon as she could do so without being observed, she had to get in there as well.

Josef was coming to the same opinion. "Clearly these scientists were here studying that structure, and that's where whatever got them came from. Still, that's the only logical place the Mizlaplanians could have escaped to with our placement. Tobrush? Can you do a telepathic sweep?"

"Only one now—the same one," the Julki responded. "Up your way somewhere."

"How is Kalia?"

"Coming around. She has some nasty burns but I was able to treat them with my own secretions and with the medical kit from the shuttle. The enemy shot of necessity had to be on wide beam to get her at all, so what energy pierced her suit caused damage only to the external areas. She will not be at maximum efficiency, but she will not have much pain or major disability, although she will probably be slowed and stiff for a while."

"Maybe she should stay at the shuttle," Josef responded. "I don't like the idea of that other one skulking about here. We could be left without a way off this cursed dirtball. The rest of us are going to have to go into that building or whatever it is up there. That's where *they* went."

"I am not impaired!" Kalia snapped angrily. "Our automatic systems protect our shuttle as well as I could, and you know that!"

"You will follow orders—*Sergeant*," Josef came back.

"You cannot order me left behind!" she protested. "I am entitled to the one who did this to me! I want to disassemble that one, very slowly, to see if I can find out how she did it!"

"Come if you must," the leader sighed, "but if your injuries cause us any problems, you will wish that the shot had killed you." He paused a moment. "Full suits, everyone. We don't know what's in there. If whatever hit this place is still there, then the Mizlaplanians will be the least of our problems. Tobrush, Kalia, bring extra energy packs and medikits and meet us here as soon as possible."

"Understood," the Julki responded.

"Do you want Desreth and me to cover the entrance?"

Robakuk asked. "We could make certain that the enemy still around here does not get through."

"No. Just keep everyone else covered until we can gather and move up. Leave the entrance unguarded for now."

"What?" The Thion was confused. "But the enemy will get through!"

"I certainly hope so. I'd rather have them all in front of me than be caught in a crossfire. If we can't nail her out here, then we'll nail her inside. Understood?"

"Understood."

"And, all of you, listen up!" Josef continued. "I want those who haven't seen the inside of this place to all see it first before we move up. Use your respirators or the smell will get to you." He sighed and looked back out at the odd, quartz-like structure that seemed subtly to shift as he watched. "Just what I really needed to add to all this. All of us have to go in that one lousy entrance. If we aren't ambushed and picked off going in, then they're all dead in there."

"Have you considered the implications of going in?" Desreth asked him. "If they are all dead, then whatever did this is in there, waiting for us as well. If they are not dead, they are waiting to kill us all in an automatic trap."

Josef nodded and sighed. "Yes, I know, but we have no choice. We have violated a frontier border, engaged in a hostile action, all without authority, and at the cost of one injury we've done *nothing* to them, nor even learned what in the Mirkhem Hive is going on here. Better to die quickly here, than return empty-handed and as ignorant as we came and die slowly and painfully to soothe diplomatic feelings."

THE
QUINTARA
MARATHON

IF THE SHOT KALIA HAD TAKEN HAD BEEN BASIcally a chest shot, then Josef could imagine what she looked like under the rust-red environment suit she wore. If she'd kept the scar on her face as a matter of pride and protection, the shot that felled her should settle any remaining questions.

Almost half her face, the right side, which already had the scar, was a mass of charred flesh, through which the huge, ugly scar stood out even bolder. Most of her already short hair had been burned away, and what hadn't, on the left side, was white. Even her left eyebrow was gone, and, when the wrecked flesh was ready to come off, it wouldn't improve things. Her right side had gone from being cruel and somewhat disfigured to being literally monstrous; her left was basically untouched. The left profile would still show something of her old beauty; a right profile would be of some ugly thing, almost as if two different creatures had been joined together. She appeared to move her right arm and hand with difficulty, and only when she had to.

"Are you certain you are up to this?" Josef asked her point-blank.

''The left eye seems all right—I must have closed it in reflex action,'' she responded. ''I am left-handed, and have been as repaired as I can in the field. My legs remain in good shape. I am a soldier of the Mycohl, ready to do my duty until death. You have already stated that death is our most likely outcome. I choose not to be the one left here for sacrifice. If we were in battle, I would be expected to press on with whatever I had left. Failure is death. I choose to live until it is my time.''

He nodded. It was what he expected. Still, he had to ask, ''Have you seen yourself?''

She nodded. ''In the shuttle. A soldier bears the wounds of battle as the medals of courage.''

Although a good hospital and modern medicine back home could make her perfect once more, he knew she would never consent to cosmetic rebuilding, just as she'd refused to have that damned scar fixed even before she was in the military with its tradition of wearing your wounds. That scar had liberated her from a short, unhappy life as slave and prostitute, and he wasn't sure if she'd be happy until experience wiped all traces of her former beauty from her. He caught her eye, although she always tried to avoid his, and caught her before she could do anything about it.

''You feel no effects from the wound,'' he told her in a firm, steady voice. ''You are as good as you ever were.''

He sighed and let his control of her go. ''All right, then. Tobrush—give me a scan. You, too, Kalia.''

The telepath and the empath surveyed the scene for a full circle. ''Nothing,'' they both said, almost in unison.

The officer nodded. ''All right, then. We can assume that our back shooter has made it up and in there while we were here. That means we can count on at least one ambusher right from the start.''

''Let me go in first, then!'' Kalia pleaded. ''I will draw her fire and locate her, and perhaps I can get her if she makes a try for you.''

''You and Desreth will go in together, one to each side. Kalia, the reason you were shot was your left-handedness, which caused you to have to walk out and then turn before you could fire. This time, take the right side. If it's too overpowering in there, get back out and tell us. Otherwise, Tobrush and I will come in one minute later. Robakuk will cover our rear just in case, then enter as soon as he is satisfied. Understood?''

Robakuk looked up at the gaping, jagged entrance to the structure beyond them. "Any idea yet what that thing *is*?" he asked.

"Too busy to do much research," Tobrush responded. "Not that it matters. Every instrument and scan I've tried on the thing returns impossible and inconsistent readings. We can't even accurately *measure* the thing the way it keeps shifting. I also get very odd sensations when I attempt a telepathic scan of the thing. I cannot read anyone inside it, but that might just be a result of the field or whatever it is that protects it and causes these anomalous readings. And yet, somehow, I sense a *presence,* almost as if the thing were alive, but on some level that I cannot comprehend."

"I feel it, too," Kalia agreed. "Have you thought that perhaps it *is* some great beast, and that we are proposing to rush right into its open mouth?"

"Unlikely," Tobrush responded. "These scientists were here for quite some time. If any of them had been eaten, I suspect that this camp would have been modified a great deal. Also, one does not build a walkway, complete with lights, into something's belly. In fact, those are power cables running along the walk and inside. They were doing work in there."

"Did you get *anything* from the Holy Horrors before they cut and ran?" Josef pressed. "Any idea of what they might have found in those records to explain what happened here?"

"Nothing much made sense unless they could not avoid it," the telepath replied. "They were *very* well trained and had a hypno with them. The hypno was the only one I could get much of anything from, and it was all that mumbled mess about angels and demigods and demons."

"The demons were probably thoughts of us," Josef chuckled. "You know that in *their* cosmology demons are the creatures of pure evil. You've all seen what that carnage in there looked like. It's easy to see them seeing their vision of demons doing just that."

"Now that you mention it—that *is* very odd," the Julki commented, thinking. "Stray thoughts here and there in the thick of busy times aren't usually worth much, but more than once, from more than one of them, I got a concept that could only translate as 'demon house.'"

"More of their babble!" Robakuk snorted.

"No, I don't think so," Josef put in. "It's easy for us to make fun of them, but let's not forget that they run an interstellar empire and they do it very efficiently and with a fair sophistication towards technology. They may be insane, but they are *not* stupid! That was a good team they had down here, too—well-trained, effective."

"It beat the living shit out of us and made us look like incompetents and fools," Kalia spat. "That I will grant."

"Are you seriously suggesting that they were thinking objectively of that thing as a demon house?" Tobrush asked him.

Josef shook his head. "Forget it. We'll know when we go in, and there is no more reason to delay this and quite a bit of reason not to. I'd much rather fight it out with the Mizzies inside there than be caught sitting here when an Exchange fleet shows up. Check equipment, everybody! Here we go!"

The building or whatever it was didn't look any less weird up close. Like some monstrous quartz crystal or the great tooth of some incomprehensibly huge monster lying on its side, half buried in old rock, it lay there, shifting now and again without actually moving in a way none of them could quite reconcile, its jagged, hollowed-out end drawing them in.

The door was some sort of energy barrier that kept the elements out but did not impede deliberate entry. It was deep inside the thing, and only the still-operating lights of the doomed scientific expedition illuminated the scene, even though the walls themselves seemed to have a slight luminescent glow.

Guns drawn, flanking the entrance, Josef nodded to Kalia and Desreth, and they went in, the darkness of the "door" quickly swallowing them.

It was a very long two minutes until Josef, on Kalia's side, and Tobrush on Desreth's, entered. Not a sound had been heard, not a single light seen inside.

He was surprised to find the interior fairly well if indirectly lit by a stronger glow from inside the walls, if that's what they were. The entryway was a small chamber, somewhat rounded, as was everything inside, made of the same translucent material as the exterior. It seemed to him as if the thing had been cast as a single solid, then hollowed out by some kind of tremendous heat so that pillars oozed from ceiling to floor and passages melted into the bottom surface. The opaque, sort of pinkish off-white of everything seemed totally plastic, as if everything was the inside of some monstrous, unnatural soft-rock cavern.

He went to Kalia and crouched low. "Anything?" he whispered.

"Some voices echoing ahead," she whispered back. "They sound like they are coming from pretty far in, but it is impossible to say just where they are or how far they come from. This is a *very* strange place."

He nodded. "What about readings? Anything empathic?"

"The field from this building is far stronger inside here. It overwhelms any strength I might have."

Tobrush, motioned over, had the same report. "Too much interference. I have never experienced this before."

"Well, if we can't get a read on *them,* then *they* can't get a reading on *us,* either," Josef reasoned. He stopped suddenly, raising a hand for silence. From somewhere deep inside he *could* hear voices, now and again.

"We'll wait for Robakuk and then advance using the same system, only we won't have any more long delays," he told them.

"The interference may make them useless, but I've been tuned on their intercom frequency," Tobrush told them. "If we get close enough, I can tie in the translator and perhaps find what they are saying."

"Let's just kill them and be done with it!" Kalia snapped.

Josef shook his head, then turned briefly to see Robakuk enter and come toward them, then turned back. "No. No one is to fire unless we are discovered. Got that, everyone? No one. Not unless I give the order. We don't know what we're heading into in there. If we can learn something from their comments, all the better."

"They are being too unguarded, too casual," Kalia pointed out.

"You suspect a trap?"

"Don't you?"

"I'm not so sure. If they were going to lay a trap for us, this would be the place to do it. Plenty of cover and we all had to come through there."

"True," Robakuk agreed, "but they also know we're here

and bound to come in after them. If their rear guard is here, they are well prepared. If not, then her absence would make them even more wary.''

''You're all talking like any of this makes sense,'' the officer commented dryly. ''Well, let's go find out. Weapons for stun except mine. If I get a crack at the hypno I want him out for good. Otherwise, if we can take some alive, all the better. On kill only if absolutely unavoidable. We need to know what they learned back there. *After* that, you can do with them what you will. *Understood?*''

They all assented except Kalia, who finally agreed as well when she realized that he was about to use his own powers on her once more.

''Not a word on the com after we start in,'' Tobrush warned. ''If I tune to them, they'll be tuned to us as well, so set your coms now for receive only and use physical signals. Understood?''

''Everybody make those adjustments now. And turn back to full capability on our channel as soon as things start happening,'' he said. ''All right—Kalia, Desreth—positions. One room at a time. I have a feeling that this is very like a cave, and we'll be moving from chamber to chamber.''

He was right about the cavern analogy, although it was a strangely artificial one. He just couldn't shake the idea that he was inside a real dwelling, perhaps a research station of some sort, or even a crashed and half-buried ship of some unknown and probably ancient race much like that derelict in orbit above them. Still, what kind of a lab or ship or even dwelling was it that had no furniture, no instruments, nothing but empty room after empty room?

The only thing he'd ever seen, once in his youth, that had any correspondence with this place—elaborate, built with much planning and effort, yet with nothing but empty chambers— had been . . .

A noble family's mausoleum.

The more he thought about that, the more the place, in spite of its eerie lighting, lack of corners or straight lines, and its somewhat melted look, took on more and more the cast of an as yet unused, or at least unfilled, family tomb.

Kalia and Desreth moved through an oval corridor—yet another one—and suddenly both stopped. Kalia turned and, with hand gestures, indicated that the next chamber was not at all empty, nor did it contain just the dead.

Tobrush glided up close to them, as silent as the Julki could be, tendrils extended, and began making small adjustments on its suit external control system. Suddenly voices came to all of them in their own tongue. The translator wasn't a hundred percent accurate and it made everybody sound like Desreth, but it certainly did work.

Morok's head moved back and forth on its long, thin neck in Stargin agitation. "How could *anyone, anything* do something like this?"

"The two demons were there, encased," Manya said, pointing to the shattered stalagmite-like extrusions that had to be what they had seen on the preview cubes. "The scientists would proceed with extreme caution and the luxury of time. It might have been weeks, even months, before they got to attempting to cut them out of there, or even decide whether or not to do so. When they did, they undid the work of the angels who created this place and liberated the evil, who repaid the favor by killing everyone and everything they saw."

"You no longer think this is a demon structure, then?" Morok asked.

"Doubtful. Why would they encase and imprison themselves? No, these must have been among the most terrible of all demons, whose power and cruelty surpassed all others. They could not be killed, for who can kill a demon? The only recourse was to create this place and encase them in this material from which they would have to stand there for millennia, trapped, held, out of harm's way, on this remote world. Then the Exchange came along and in its ignorance undid the work of the Warriors of the Gods."

Gun Roh Chin looked around at the carnage. "Where are they, then?"

"Huh? What? It is obvious. Demons are not bound by the laws of our plane! They are on the supernatural plane, where they can move unseen from world to world instantly with the power of thought as it says in the ancient books. Probably seeing how things had changed in the eons since they were imprisoned here before plotting ultimate evil. They have made their sacrifices here!"

Gun Roh Chin examined a corpse. He wasn't sure what sort of creature it had been, and that was disturbing. There wasn't enough left of it to even make more than a slight guess, and bones were all over. Bones that looked, well, *gnawed* upon.

"Maybe they woke up hungry," he suggested. "These people weren't sacrificed. They were slaughtered and eaten. There were no signs of anything being eaten or gnawed in the bodies back at the camp. They were simply ruthlessly murdered, their ship also attacked and rendered inactive, so they couldn't go for help. First they were like wild animals, unreasoning, savage, gorging. Then they began to think, and plan, and act on that planning. They activated weapons, possibly defensive weapons aboard here, to get the ship, which might have threatened them. The ones outside, though, they just took on without much concern. By that time, they knew that the people here couldn't hurt them and were vulnerable."

"Aboard? What do you mean, 'aboard,' Captain?" Morok pressed him.

"Aboard this ship, for that's what I think it is. Some sort of transport. Whatever it carried, it already disgorged, for all the chambers we've seen are empty. Then, on the way back, something happened. It crashed here, well off its flight plan, in the middle of nowhere even to them. The crew, probably just those two, took the only means of survival possible. They put themselves into some sort of suspended animation in the hopes that one day someone would discover and rescue them. The ship still had power, just not enough for transport. It's maintained them, protected them, and kept them essentially above ground and the forces of nature ever since they crashed— perhaps thousands, even a million years. Until they *were* rescued, not by their own kind, but by these hapless souls. The effect of the long animation—who knows what it would do to them or anyone else? They emerged savage, animals, mad, and starving. Later, they regained their senses, if not their sanity. They needed to buy time and saw these others as aliens, invaders. They eliminated them."

"You sound like the Exchange!" Manya snapped in disgust. "They were imprisoned here! Demons! *Real* demons! If they were as you say, where are they? They could no more get off with this so-called ship of yours now than before. Castaways from some ancient supercivilization such as you postulate would not kill everyone. They would try and learn who these people were and something about them. They would go through the records.''

"She's got you there, Captain," Morok agreed.

"Not necessarily. Look at this place! It's a completely different sort of technology, a completely different approach than we have known from *any* race. The fact that they recognized the research ship for what it was and could find and destroy it shows that they knew as much as they needed to know. We have no evidence that everyone was killed off the bat, or even that everyone here was killed, since we don't know how many people were here. If they also had Talents, perhaps telepathy, they wouldn't need anything else. With this level of technology, it's even possible that the ship itself had been monitoring and told them all they needed to know.''

"It begs the major question," Manya retorted. *"Where did they go if not into the other plane?"*

Suddenly Krisha's voice came over the suit intercom. *"Forty-one B,"* it said simply.

They immediately gave the mental instruction to their suit controllers to switch frequencies.

"Company," Krisha reported. "The Mycohl five, just outside the entryway. Slow and easy, move towards cover in the rear.''

Inside the corridor, Josef and the others heard the numeric code, then silence.

"They made us," he said quietly. "Attack at will.''

Desreth moved forward first, and was immediately met by concentrated fire, all at maximum. Seeing no immediate cover, the Corithian pulled back almost as fast as it entered.

"They have at least two sentinels with weapons trained at maximum on the corridor," it reported. "I fear damage before I can get to effective cover. They have placed their people well.''

"Let me try it!" Kalia said eagerly. "I do not need the amount of cover Desreth does.''

"You would not get in before they killed you," the Corithian told her. "It took them less than three seconds to concentrate both weapons fully on me and match my movements, and, by now, the others are in position as well.''

Josef scratched his chin and thought about the situation.

"We wait—a little while. This was the only way in, and it's the only way out through this maze. If it wasn't for the scientists' power cable we wouldn't have found our own way here. Since we chased them in, it's unlikely they did anything else themselves, so they're stuck. Tobrush, find their current frequency. They'll change often, but if we can get something, we'll take what we can get. Desreth, probe them at five-minute intervals. I don't want them to get comfortable, and, sooner or later, they'll realize that they will have to come to us. Let *them* walk into *us*. We have the exit at our backs, not them."

That thought hadn't escaped the Mizlaplanians, who had retreated to the chamber exit in back of the grand chamber, except for Krisha and Savin, who had good cover behind instruments and debris at the far corners, allowing concentrated fire on anyone entering from the front.

"We can't stay here," Gun Roh Chin pointed out, glad nonetheless to be away from the chamber of horrors inside. "It's a complete standoff, only we hold the wrong door at our backs."

"Any suggestions?" Morok asked, his own thoughts echoing the captain's.

"There appears to be considerably more of this structure further on. Probably all empty chambers, of course, but you can never tell. I suspect that if there was anything of real interest back there, though, the Exchange team would have found it."

"That does not improve matters," Morok responded glumly.

"It might, if it's the same sort of labyrinth we saw coming in. We did what they did—we followed the cable. There were other corridors, though, and other branches. It's quite possible that some bypass this central chamber."

"You mean we could flank them, I think the term is? Yes, perhaps. But that assumes that some of them *do* go around, and that we can figure out the route without any guides."

Chin looked back out at the chamber. "How wide can this thing be, anyway? Long, yes—I'd say we were in the buried section already, although I don't feel the angle. But width? That chamber—it's easily three-quarters of the width of the structure, if I'm any judge."

"The captain is correct on that point," Manya hissed. "The gods will correctly guide the resolute. Besides, if we hesitate too long, then *they* will also think of it."

The captain looked at the team leader. "You want me to try and reconnoiter the side passages?"

"No," Morok responded, thinking. "If we get lost in here, we get lost together. Under the circumstances, there is more weakness in separation than any other course. If we are correct and they have sent someone the other way, we will have an advantage. If we get all the way around, then the circumstances here will be reversed. It is time to leave this remnant of the Darkness and make a run for home. Others can use what we have to consider future courses of action. We can do no more." He peered anxiously out into the chamber, and one of the Mycohl threw a reckless shot in his direction. It missed, but the point was well taken. "We have to find a way to get Savin and Krisha back with us."

"I will go," Manya told him.

"The Corithian can see you clearly," Chin reminded her.

"Then there are four blind ones and one with sight. If you go, all five can see. With your permission, Holiness?"

"Go, Manya," Morok told her, and she barely hesitated.

Manya was not completely without cover, and the distance from entrance to exit was wide. She moved behind a large pillar that reached from ceiling down to the floor and turned toward Krisha. "In! In!" she shouted, then turned and shouted the same aloud to Savin, her deep, raspy voice creating eerie echoes through the chamber. "I will cover you!"

Krisha broke first, and even as shots started coming her way Manya opened up on the entrance, firing shots in rapid succession. She had little hope of hitting anything, but it might well keep any of them from getting a good enough look to score a hit.

"They're retreating!" Josef snapped. "Something's up! Robakuk! Maybe it's time you gave them some nightmares to think about. The rest—in behind the cover!"

The black Thion moved cautiously to where its huge eyes could take in the chamber. Manya's shots were wild; only a lucky shot would cause him any real damage.

Suddenly, on the floor of the great chamber littered with bodies, *some of those bodies twitched, stirred, and began rising off the floor, some leaving entrails and limbs stuck to the floor as they rose!*

Manya stood suddenly, transfixed by the horror advancing

on her, and she screamed. Krisha, almost inside and safe, froze when she, too, saw the gruesome advance, and Savin was also taken aback.

"*Stop it and get in here!*" Gun Roh Chin shouted. "They've got a levitator with them! That fifth one we couldn't figure out—a *levitator*! That's all it is!"

It wasn't his comments but the sudden near misses coming all around them that spurred them into action. They got back in fast, before the oncoming Mycohl team could get into positions giving them full coverage of the exit opening.

"Come on!" Morok shouted. "Everyone move back—*together*! They can keep themselves under cover and be on us! Best we get back where it doesn't have anything to use!"

Krisha shivered. "If ever I doubt the purity of evil inside each Mycohl, no matter how much like us they appear, I will remember this moment!"

They moved back into the recesses of the demon structure until they came to another chamber with branches.

"Left!" Gun Roh Chin told them.

"But what if it is not the way back?" Morok asked him, uncertain as to the logic of another race on this sort of thing.

"It's as good a choice as any. All are equally likely to be right, or wrong," the captain replied. "We know *they* will be coming right through here! We can't stand here—let's *move*!"

They turned sharply left and took the first rounded corridor that seemed to angle back toward the entrance, then stopped, and all aimed their weapons at the entrance once more, just in case the pursuers came the wrong way. For a very long time there was no sound at all except their own slight movements and breathing.

Finally, Morok bent low and whispered to the captain, "Why left? Why were you so certain?"

Gun Roh Chin shrugged. "I wasn't. But we know that their leader is a Terran, and that means that the odds are about nine to one that he's right-handed. Right-handed Terrans tend to turn right when making a choice."

The Stargin was taken aback. "I—uh, you are a most unusual man, Captain."

Chin shrugged. "Might I suggest, Holiness, that we might as well not wait here any longer? Let's see if we can get around them and either ambush them or get out of this foul place. If they want to waste time exploring for us back here, well and good. Let's be somewhere else.''

"Very well. Manya, take the point ahead. Krisha, back her up. Savin, you guard the rear but do not hang back too far. Keep us always in sight.''

The fierce-looking Mesok nodded.

Morok's eyes looked down on Gun Roh Chin's impassive features. "After you, Captain.''

The captain opened his utility pouch, removed a cigar, bit off the end, and stuck it, unlit, in his mouth. Then he followed the women.

Of all the ones who converged on the tiny, isolated world of death, the Exploiter Team of the Exchange was the only one legally entitled to be there.

They were an odd crew, even for the vast Empire called simply the Exchange, ruled by a hidden race no one had ever seen, which bought, sold, and exploited worlds, people, and assets with abandon.

Fresh off a much-needed and profitable mission that might have enriched them all, they had answered a distress call intercepted by sheer chance, and had come not merely to help but, possibly, to salvage.

The star-shaped Durquist almost draped himself over his instruments, then said, "There is nothing alive on that ship. Nothing at all.''

The Durquist—the term described the race, not the individual, but all of them used only it, to everyone else's confusion—was shaped like a five-pointed star around a central orifice that looked very much like a huge set of jet-black human lips, behind which, mostly invisible to the onlooker, were row after row of sharp-pointed teeth. Brain, stomach, all the internal organs were clustered somehow inside that hard center. From it emerged the arms—fluid, sucker-clad, able to stretch and twist and bend in almost infinite ways, yet with incredibly powerful muscles. The Durquist's eyes were a stalked pair on either side of the mouth; this allowed the creature to assume almost any posture, from walking upright on any two arms of its choice and looking weirdly humanoid from a distance, or walking on any combination of four.

"Scan the colony,'' Modra Stryke instructed him. "I want to

know if anything's alive anywhere here." She paused and shook her head. "What in God's name could have happened here?"

Stryke was Terran in origin, a dark beauty in perfect physical shape, with flaming red hair and a hard-bitten demeanor that masked her highly emotional real self. A strong empath, she was married to the team bankroll, and, therefore, the boss, on her last field mission before returning and settling down to a less risky and more comfort-lined life with her husband, whose firm bought and sold futures in worlds as others sold stock.

<*Gives you the creeps, doesn't it?*> Grysta commented to Jimmy McCray.

"It's the dunes world all over again," the telepath swore under his breath, not really replying to the parasitic creature on his back. "This smells really bad."

McCray was a sandy-haired, craggy-faced Irishman who was no less Irish by being born thousands of light-years from a land he'd never seen save in legends. He believed in legends, and in curses, for he bore one that, for being so small, was an enormously heavy weight on his mind and soul. This was Grysta, a tiny, furry parasite called a Morgh that was firmly embedded in his back most of the time and which required him in order to see and hear the outside world, as well as for nourishment. Through tendrils into his nervous system, she could cause him pleasure or pain, and spoke to him and him alone through direct neural link.

"It is even worse than it looks," the Durquist reported. "I do not scan any living forms below, but I scan not one but *three* parked shuttles."

Tris Lankur rushed to the command screens. "Put them up, Durquist. Full enlargement."

The ship's captain, Lankur was outwardly a Terran male; large, muscular, with light brown skin and curly black hair. He was also a walking dead man; a man who'd loved Modra and who had not been able to accept her marriage to another. He had blown some of his brains out, and the medical wizards of the Exchange had given him another, artificial brain that governed him to a great degree. He was a cymol, a living creature with a synthetic brain that could mock Terran behavior and personality, but which was far more alien to all of them than Modra was alien to the Durquist.

McCray, Lankur, and Stryke all suddenly gathered around the screen.

"What the hell?" Tris Lankur exclaimed, frowning. "The brown rectangular one there is from the orbital vessel. It's similar to ours. That dull gray oval one, though—that's Mizlaplan! And the black one that's kind of beetle-shaped—that's Mycohlian!"

"They had a bloody interstellar *convention* down there," McCray commented.

"I read no higher form anomalies below, either," the Durquist reported. "And if those are foreign shuttles, where are their base ships? And what the hell are they doing here in the first place?"

"That's easy enough," Lankur replied. "They're here, someplace. Either automated or with a standby skeleton crew, watching us from out there someplace. Or chasing each other. I can't see those two groups in particular having any sort of friendly arrangement."

"You think the winner's getting ready to jump us?" McCray asked. "I mean, what if them bastard heathen Mycohl jumped the research ship and camped down there 'cause they were onto something real important and stuck all out here in the middle of nowhere? The Holy Joes get wind of it and figure on an ambush—or vice versa. You said yourself they're all pretty close by here, all crunched together."

"Yes, but this is *our* territory, damn them!" Modra Stryke responded, feeling oddly angry about the sight. "And if they're here to get something, they have to pick it up and run. More of our people will be here in just a few days."

"Aye, and the winner of their free-for-all will be all set to prove that they came here in response to a legitimate distress signal, found everybody already dead—whether they did or not—and the colony abandoned. Then they'll stake their own claim on it and there'll be hell to pay," McCray theorized. "I'm no patriot, and I'm not keen for a fight, but how many of our people would be represented on a thing like this? Forty, fifty in the ship, maybe half as many down? It sticks in my craw that if we just sit they might just get away with it."

<Another way to try and commit suicide, Jimmy?>

Modra looked around at them. "McCray's right. This is *our* space, *our* territory. And if anybody's going to put in a claim on a planet so important it would tempt in both of our enemies just to get it from us, it's going to be us."

"As an officer of the Exchange I've *got* to investigate," Tris Lankur reminded them. "As a member of this team, my presence is as good as all of us for our own claims. I *have* to go down. The rest of you could lay off and give me what cover you can."

Modra Stryke shook her head firmly in the negative. "Oh, no, Tris. No offense intended, but, God help me, you're a dead man. You look like Tris and talk like Tris and mostly act like Tris but we have no idea what you have in your head or whose marching orders you follow in a pinch. The Exchange thought this was so important they didn't even put it up for bids. They kept it, and kept it quiet, too. As far as I'm concerned, that doesn't put you squarely on the Team's side in this. Uh-uh. We go down *as a team.* Same as always."

"I hate to keep bringing up nasty and inconvenient things," the Durquist put in, "but all evidence seems to indicate that whatever hit that ship did so from the planet's surface, not from space. And no matter if the Mizlaplan and Mycohl both have ships down there—*I am registering no known life forms on the surface, either!* I think that suggests several prudent courses of action."

Tris Lankur nodded. "All right, then, if it's a full team job, then we have to approach it that way. For one thing, we don't land where they did. I'd much rather come in from the other side if there's any sort of clearing, even if it means a little walk. Tran will drop the I.P. inside the camp but will then withdraw. I'd like to keep this ship in orbit for a lot of reasons, and I'm not really nervous about attack from enemy vessels—even if one of them *did* do all this, hitting us as well in our own territory would make it impossible to explain. I *am* concerned that nothing from down there does to this ship what it did to the research vessel. We'll drop a relay beacon here so we can be in touch, then Tran will lay off and out but within range, so he can come in quick and dirty if need be. Understood?"

"Agreed," Modra responded. "Full packs and equipment, too. Durquist, any last bad news?"

"I am trying to figure out what that structure or outcrop or whatever it is down there is," the Durquist responded. "It has rather—bizarre—properties, and is certainly what these people were studying.''

''Well, I don't care what it is right now,'' Tris told him. ''I think we'd better get suited up and ready and drop that beacon and get down there as fast as we can. It's going to be almost dark by the time we get into that camp, and I don't want any nasty surprises just in case that thing's masking our instruments or has a Mycohl military team inside it just waiting for us.''

Back in the ready area, Jimmy McCray was surprised to see Molly come in and start rummaging around. ''What are you doing here? You can't come with us on this.''

''Where you go, I go,'' she told him. ''Besides, Molly did what Bigbrains couldn't. Molly got funny suit. Molly go with Jimmy.''

This was the last of the team, as it were, although only nominally. Of all the creatures that made up the Three Empires, Molly was almost, but not quite, unique, for her race was artificial, and she'd been born in some remote laboratory, a genetically engineered impossibility designed specifically, in her case, to allow lonely sailors of Terran and Terranoid races to have safe and superior sex. Her skin was a pale pastel blue; her lips, even her hair, a darker blue. From just above the hips up, she was in every way an exotic, sexual Terran woman with all of the physical attributes exaggerated, save for the two tiny horns protruding from her hair just above the scalp line. At the hips, short, thick curly blue hair extended down to a pair of thick but equine-like legs terminating in broad hooves, and she had a long, silky equine tail emerging from the small of her back and going down to her knee.

A broadcast empath designed to inspire passion in the paying customers, she had a mind that worked so strangely even telepaths like McCray couldn't really follow her thoughts, but they were very basic thoughts on the whole, almost like a small child's. No one was certain what mental limits were put on syns like her, but, to ensure that no syn would ever develop ambitions, the designers had omitted thumbs.

Jimmy McCray had rescued her in a moment of pity and found himself her keeper and ward as a result. Unable to reconcile slavery with his Irish soul, and mindful of his own condition, he'd married her to give her legal status, but it was without passion and certainly without consummation. Grysta would have no others ahead of her.

And so Molly was here, because she had no place else to be.

The fact was, she *did* have an environment suit, although she couldn't manage to do much with it other than exist on the automatic systems. She had to; you couldn't go into space on anything less than a capital ship without one.

<Order her to shut up and stay here!> Grysta snapped. *<She's just gonna get us both killed.>*

For once he agreed with his unwanted mate. "No, Molly! It's too dangerous! This isn't like being off the Hot Plant."

Molly stared at him. "Jimmy say Molly free girl?"

"Yes, but—"

"Didn't Jimmy say back there that Molly part of team?"

"All right, damn it, but I didn't—"

"Then Molly go," she responded with total finality in her voice.

"Molly," Modra put in sweetly, trying to be kind. "There might be a lot of bad people down there. Shooting and killing. We're afraid you might do something because of that that might get some of *us* killed."

"Molly had lots'a bad men in life. Molly not as dumb as folks think!"

Modra looked around. "Tris? Durquist?"

"I don't like it, but we can lose what little light we have arguing with her," Tris Lankur pointed out. "Either somebody's got to club her into unconsciousness or she's going to go."

"I agree," the Durquist sighed. "Molly, if you come, you must be a full member of the team. You must be very quiet and do exactly as we say, no matter whether you agree with it or not. You must obey us instantly because we have done this before and you have not."

"Molly understand. Molly also know rest of you had first time sometime, right?"

Modra Stryke sighed. "Give it up, Jimmy, and help her into her suit."

Molly *had* been very good and very cautious, and she was strong as an ox, which allowed Lankur and the Durquist to bring some extra equipment and supplies along.

They had landed about four kilometers northwest of the camp and trekked in. It wasn't an easy walk, but compared to some of the worlds they had been on, it was almost absurdly simple, and they arrived at the camp just at sunset, then fanned out to find out as much as they could.

"Stay away from entering or even touching the foreign shuttles," Lankur warned them. "We want to know if anybody's aboard, dead or alive, but nothing more. They're almost certainly booby-trapped."

The grisly scene of carnage that had shocked and baffled the Mizlaplanians had no less effect on them. More, in some ways, because all of them were *their* people, Exchange citizens.

"There's been a fight here, too," Modra noted. "See some of the searing on the exterior walls there? Whichever of them was here first fought at least a brief battle with whoever came second."

"No signs of foreign dead, though," the Durquist noted, a bit shaken to discover that some of the original victims of the carnage had been Durquists as well. He felt as if he were looking at his own end. "None of the victims we found were shot, and all the clothing and equipment here appears to be ours. I did an entire surface scan."

Tris Lankur stood in front of a huge cabinet in the administration hut that had clearly been filled with the accumulated scientific recordings made there. "Maybe nobody shot these folks, but somebody shot the data," he noted. "I bet there isn't a single intelligible or salvageable data cartridge there. Somebody wanted to make sure that we had as little to go on as possible."

"Or, more likely, whoever was here first didn't want the newcomers to know what they were in for," the Durquist said from behind him. "And they did a very nice job of that, too."

"I wouldn't worry so much about them," Modra replied. "There are surely tons of materials on the ship in safely insulated interior regions, or maybe already sent back to the Exchange. That vandalism is just senseless."

Jimmy McCray, still in the research prefab, turned and surveyed the lab, with its twisted, wrecked bodies and dried blood of a half-dozen races all over everything. "And *this* makes *sense*?"

Molly had been more shaken by the gruesome sights than

she wanted to let on, still fearing they'd send her back up. She wandered over to where a huge hole had been made in the side of the building and looked out.

"Whoever do this thing don't like doors," she noted.

McCray went over to her and looked at the huge inward burst and through the hole. "No, my dear, you're absolutely right. Whatever monstrosity came through came right through here—everything's bent inwards. And if they came on a straight line, then . . ." She followed his eyes as they looked at the bizarre structure not too far up on the bluff.

Molly frowned thoughtfully, something she rarely did. "Jimmy, you think that be somebody's house? They maybe not like be broken into."

He stared at her in surprise. "You might just have something there, darlin'." He suddenly paused. "Huh. Gettin' pretty dark in here. I think either I better find the lights or I'm gonna be spooked right to Jesus."

"Somebody already got lights on," she said, pointing.

In the near darkness, the huge alien structure was definitely glowing, although slightly.

"There's no two ways around it," Tris Lankur told them, shining his light on various signs of a fight leading from the camp up toward the thing embedded in the bluff. "We either camp here and wait for something to happen or we go up and see just what the hell that thing is, with the likelihood that either *it* will kill us or that it contains both whatever did all this and two very mean and fully armed foreign crews."

<I vote to stay here!>

"Shush, Grysta. You don't get a vote in this."

"Alas," the Durquist sighed, "I fear he's right."

Modra looked around in the near total darkness. "I think I'd rather take my chances up there than spend the night in this morgue," she said. "And I don't see how waiting until morning will help us. I think we call into Tran, make our report, then go in. Funny. I'm feeling remarkably wide awake for somebody who's walking right into death."

<Shit!> Grysta swore.

"You can always hop off now," Jimmy McCray suggested hopefully.

"Team to *Widowmaker,* team to *Widowmaker,*" Tris called. "Do you read me, Tran?"

"Coming in fine," Trannon Kose responded. "I wish I were down there with you."

"I wish *I* was up there and *you* were down here," the Durquist commented sourly.

Quickly but thoroughly, Lankur made his report on their findings, which would supplement and detail the recordings of their intercom communications automatically registered on the ship.

"People go in there and they don't come out, or so it seems," Lankur concluded. "As a result, I recommend that nobody, repeat, nobody, follow us in. At least not until experts have recovered the data on those cartridges and know exactly what they are facing. Instead, I recommend active quarantine of the planet until they are a lot more confident and I also recommend a military sweep of this system. If the foreign ships are hiding out in there, they could probably learn a lot from them."

"Affirmative, Tris. You sound like you don't think you're coming out, either."

"I don't know. None of us do. But—come in briefly and blow up the foreign and base camp shuttles as soon as we go in. Understand? Blow them up. Make them unable to fly. If anybody *except* us comes out of there, I don't want them getting off this hellhole. But you blow them and then back right off. You understand? Come in, blow, and withdraw. Then you wait, either for us or for reinforcements."

"Understood. Take care, all of you. I should very much hate having to break in another team."

"You can bloody well afford the best, Trannon Kose," Jimmy shot back. "If we don't come out of there, you get the whole bloody payment!"

Kose was silent for a moment, then responded, "I hadn't thought of that, McCray. Now I *know* I'll see you again. The way you've been, you'd come back from the grave to claim that money before you'd let me have it all."

"All right," Lankur sighed. "We'll keep our monitors on, but since we're not getting even carrier signals from the Mycohl or Mizlaplanians, the odds are pretty good that ours won't carry, either.'' He drew a deep breath. ''All right, everybody—let's see what the hell this is all about.''

They walked up the well-worn path in the eerie darkness.

''Place feel real strange,'' Molly commented as they neared. it.

Modra nodded. ''I feel it, too. Something on the empathic band, but not like anything I've ever felt before. It's almost as if that was some kind of new life form rather than a structure. Something somehow *alive,* yet so different, so alien, it's like nothing we know.''

<I knew it! It's some kind of gigantic stone beast and we're walking right into its stomach!> Grysta cried to Jimmy McCray.

Jimmy tried to ignore that comment as he did most others, but damned if it didn't echo his own dark thoughts. He could sense secondhand what they were feeling by scanning their thoughts, but scanning the object produced nothing except the creeps. ''Nothing on my wavelengths,'' he told them.

''The glow is very low-level energy,'' the Durquist reported. ''Essentially a trickle charge through the thing almost too low to measure at all. The stuff, whatever it is, must be built to glow. It might even be simply radiating back absorbed sunlight.''

Standing at the end of the thing, they could see where someone, presumably the scientific team, had laid down a plastic carpet up to what had to be the entrance. It looked dirty and well-trod.

''Well, if anybody thinks it's going to eat us, I think that should disprove at least that much,'' Lankur noted. ''From the looks of this and the data modules and equipment, I'd say our people have been going in and out of here for a long time.''

''Strange how it seems to change, somehow, every time you look at it,'' Modra commented. ''And yet, you can't ever catch it in the act.''

''Weapons on full lethal except Molly,'' Lankur stated flatly. ''Don't give anything or anybody a chance to pick you off first. Check equipment, then report.''

Molly didn't even draw her pistol. She doubted if she could harm anything, even something trying to kill her. The fear of death, or the unknown, didn't enter into her mind. To the syn, it was always ''now.''

"Okay, everyone. Let's go in," Tris Lankur said in a flat, yet determined voice.

The eerie, opaque, creamy-colored walls seemed almost to be dissolving about them, although intellectually they all knew that it was really just some sort of design feature of some mind alien to each and every one of them.

"Keep your suit lights on," Lankur warned them. "We get to depending on this place and suddenly something cuts the power. On your guard."

"We may be nuts but we aren't dumb," Jimmy McCray muttered in reply.

"I'm going through that entrance there," the cymol said, pointing. "Durquist—left. McCray, right. I'll go through the middle, you two follow on my signal or if I open fire."

He crouched down and let the other two get into position, then checked and double-checked his rifle, took a deep breath, and charged into the nearly heart-shaped opening.

For a moment there was silence, then Tris Lankur's voice came, "It's all right. Come on in. There's nothing alive here . . . now. Modra, come on up with us if your stomach will take it. It's worse than the base camp. Molly, you were bothered by that scene. I'm not real sure you should even see this."

That brought them all in a hurry, Molly, somewhat indignant at the patronizing, charging right through. She, and the others, stopped dead just behind Tris Lankur as they entered the chamber, though, transfixed, as he seemed to be, by the scene.

Everywhere there was blood. Red blood, green blood, blue blood, all the colors of the rainbow, smeared all over in such a pattern that it seemed as if some mad artist had been loosed inside.

The chamber was huge, far larger than could be accounted for by the apparent size of the "house" or whatever it was, with the slightly rounded floor characteristic of the rest of the place, and in the center were the remains of what had once obviously been two pillars rising from floor to ceiling, although it appeared to need no support—which was good, since much of the pillars was now gone, shattered, mixed in with the blood.

It was Lankar who moved first, walking over to the closest remains of what might have once been a living creature. The heaps of bone, flesh, and muscle were so mangled and distorted that it wasn't even possible from just looking to tell the racial origin of any of the remains.

Lankur approached the bloody, twisted lump cautiously, almost as if he expected it to come alive in some hideous form and leap upon him, even though cymols were supposed to be immune to fear and imagination's tricks and that thing was through ever leaping anywhere.

"It's been *gnawed*," he said hoarsely. "Who—whatever did this, it indiscriminately tore up and gnawed on every one of them. It was a blood feast, without any sense of reason at all. The ones back at the camp were just sadistically murdered—not these. What in *hell* did they set loose in here?"

The Durquist moved next, over to Lankur's right and near the pillar. "It was our doing, whatever it was," he noted. "This is—*was*—a Durquist. Mangled, but ungnawed. Whatever it was knew not to eat a Durquist."

Of all the known creatures, the Durquist was the only one whose flesh had proven toxic to any living thing that consumed even a small part of it.

Modra Stryke walked carefully across the remains of carnage and up to the base of the shattered pillar nearest the Durquist. She was shaken, certainly, by the sight, but she was also a pro. She could be sick later.

"There appears to have been some kind of hollow center in the pillars," she noted. "The rubble isn't quite enough for solid posts of that thickness and height." She stooped down and picked up two shards, not randomly chosen but selected for their obvious difference.

"Look at this," she said, holding one shard in each hand. "The one here is better than ten centimeters thick. This one, though, is very thin, very fragile—a few millimeters, no more."

The Durquist's stalked eyes turned away from the sight of his dead relation to the contents of her hand. "Interesting. Two enclosures, then, one inside the other. The outer thick, perhaps for protection and support, the inner—a capsule? You suppose that whatever it was was in some sort of capsule, suspended, and then the pillar was poured from the top down, over it, to seal it in?"

"Yeah, but what was inside the thing?" McCray asked, looking nervously around. "And where is it now?"

"Not here," Durquist responded. "Not now. Whatever it was was *big*. Look at the teeth marks here. And those really nasty marks there—what could make them? Fangs?"

"Their weapons seem to be still here," Tris Lankur noted. "I found a few. Small stuff but it should still have been adequate to have stopped just about anything *I* know."

"If they had a chance to use 'em," Jimmy put in.

"They did. You can see the marks on the walls all around you, and at least the one pistol I just checked is totally discharged. It's a near certainty that whatever it was wasn't invisible, or faster than lightning, and there were a fair number of people here. Whatever it was got hit all right. Got hit—and kept on coming. And it was *fast*. There wasn't even the obvious element of surprise implicit in the base camp attack. I—uh-oh."

"What's the matter?" Modra asked, tensing.

Lankur kneeled down before another mass of mangled flesh, then reached out and began peeling parts of it away. Modra, even McCray, found themselves averting their eyes. "What the hell you doin', cymol?" Jimmy asked.

"You said it right," Lankur responded. "I am and this is all that's left of another. *Jesus!* The skull's been *crushed*!" There was a sickening popping sound. "Ah! Got it!"

"What the hell are you doing, Tris?" Modra almost screamed. It was like a dead man loose in a slaughterhouse.

"Sorry to be so ghoulish," he responded, "but I got what I was looking for. Maybe damaged, maybe not. Hard to tell until I connect up."

They all turned in spite of themselves and saw that he was now standing, holding something that resembled a crudely shaped lump of some dull, lead-colored material to which small bits of organic matter still clung.

"I have one of these in my head," he told them. "Different size and shape, probably different capacity, but something like this just the same. Odd—never actually *saw* one before."

"That—that's the cymol part?" Modra asked weakly, wondering if in fact she *could* wait until later.

He nodded. "It's inert—now. No thought, no life left in it.

But if its recording function is intact, I might well be able to learn just what happened here."

"You want to take it back to the ship?" she asked hopefully.

"I think I want to try it here. But—uh, sorry. Let's move back into one of the earlier chambers."

They got no argument, even from the Durquist, and when they entered the antechamber they found Molly already there, looking like she'd just puked.

Lankur unlatched the small case he wore on his belt, did something, and the case opened to reveal a dull metallic checkerboard surface. He removed a cable, stuck one end on the box, where it seemed to stick like glue, then reached up and removed a small section of hair and possibly skull. Modra watched in horrified fascination, unsure whether this sight was worse or not as bad as the one in the other room.

"This won't take long. Not at the speed I can operate in that direct mode," he told them, sticking the other end of the cable into the space in his skull.

Somehow they all expected him to assume some trance-like state, but he seemed much the same, eyes darting to each of them, face nearly expressionless. After a minute, perhaps less, he sighed and said, "It *is* badly damaged. I can't believe the kind of strength this would take. I don't have it all, but I think I have enough. I can tell you just what was inside there, and a little of what happened right at the end."

"The demon message was correct, no matter how mad the fellow was," Tris Lankur told them. "About three months ago, a scout discovered this world and this place, the only artificial structure on it. The scout didn't enter but *did* send in a probe, and got back pictures of that central chamber in its original state. You were right, Modra—two bodies, one in each pillar, sort of like giant stalagmite sarcophagi, each containing the body of a demon."

"Demon? What do you mean, 'demon'?" Jimmy McCray asked him.

"Just what I said. It was always theorized that we'd find at least the remains of them sooner or later. Hundreds of worlds, hundreds of races, and two out of three of them have demons. Even some water-breathing and silicon-based races have demons. Changed, altered, filtered through countless generations of legend, superstition, and racial viewpoints, but demons all the same. Tall, bipedal creatures—the one looked to be two and a half meters easy, the other maybe two—with horns, blazing, fiery eyes, ugly expressions, fangs, cloven hooves, pointed tails—the whole business. Ugly as sin and twice as fearsome-looking. My old Islamic grandfather would have recognized them in an instant, as would your Catholic priest, McCray, or your high priestess, Modra. Even you would have known them instantly, Durquist, although they look considerably more humanoid than your people's version.''

''Demons,'' the Durquist mused. ''*Xotha,* in my mother tongue, which is, by the way, the exact same word as ours for 'evil' but for the inflection that makes it refer to a living thing rather than a concept. The universal personification of evil—except to the Mycohl, who have them in place of demigods or angels or whatever.''

Tris Lankur nodded. ''It was long theorized that such memories couldn't have arisen independently, even on early worlds like Mother Earth where cultures and religions were so different, let alone on worlds that had no creature in any way resembling them on their planets. An early, brutal, interstellar race that made such an impression that ancient cultures preserved their memory in legend and myth.''

''Some impression,'' Jimmy McCray muttered. ''The personification of evil.''

Lankur shrugged. ''Well, you saw the other room,'' he noted. ''I'd say that they more than lived up to their reputation.''

''*They* did *that*?'' Modra asked, incredulously. ''Just *two* of them did all *that*?''

Lankur nodded. ''Just two. And two who'd been probably in some kind of suspended animation for thousands upon thousands of years.''

''The two—a set?'' the Durquist asked him.

He nodded. ''Yes, a male and a female. Conventionally bisexual, racially, although his organ looked big and half bone. Their females had to be really tough, I suspect, or have no pain nerves in the vaginal area. Probably both.''

''The story now appears obvious,'' the Durquist said. ''As far as it goes, anyway. Such a discovery had the Exchange rush their best scientific team here, along with a military guard ship

to keep everybody else out, both entrepreneur and Mycohlian.
Then they tested, poked, probed, and eventually would come to
extracting the pair from their tombs. When they broke the seals,
the two awoke and—well, fulfilled expectations. But how did
they also cream the naval frigate?''

"That's not in here," Tris told them. "It must have
happened either after they did this or simultaneously. I played
back the end scene frame by frame and it's still not really clear.
Too much disorientation and shock, too much damage. But it
appears they only cut through the base of the female—that was
the one on the left—and suddenly this whole place lit up. I get
a picture of the light being much brighter all of a sudden, and
a kind of pulsing, almost like this building was some kind of
living organism. It's like—well, maybe examining a bacterium
under high magnification. Fluids moved, tiny things pulsed and
flexed—I'd say this place *is* alive, somehow.''

Jimmy McCray looked nervously around. "Jonah all over.
And we walked right into the fucking whale's *stomach*!''

"Artificial life," the cymol responded. "No offense, Molly,
but you're an example of the earlier stages that this represents.
They grew and designed artificial life as their housing, as their
machines, everything. It probably thinks, even anticipates.
Don't worry—I *think* I know what happened. I think they cut
a little too high. I think they were going to cut just a little of the
female's right leg, at least if my figures are correct. It triggered
the defensive mode of this place. It revived the pair and
shattered the external casings, which kept her from being
sliced, and at the same time it automatically reacted against
everything that could be perceived as a threat. That means it
has the power to shoot and take out even a warship in high
orbit.''

"You mean—this—*place*—did that to them in there?"
Modra asked, growing more and more nervous by the second.

"No," replied the cymol. "Not this place.''

*The cutting laser was having trouble with the substance,
even though it could cut through the toughest known alloys. It
did slice, but not cleanly, nor easily, nor particularly straight.
It began to get jagged, and the robot saw stopped a moment
and said, "Warning! I cannot guarantee that I can get through*

without raising the angle. This has the potential of cutting into specimen.''

Professor Makokah, a Brudak, flaired its umbra in frustration. "What do you think?"

The Durquist, a female of high rank, snorted. "Too bad, but we have to get them out of there. She won't feel a thing. My instruments show she's been dead a mere three quarters of a million standard years, more or less."

"Any chance of better luck with the male?" asked Juria, a matronly-looking human cymol who was the theoretical official in charge.

"Negative," the robot responded. "The problem is the thickness of the base and the nature of the material. I am the finest precision cutting tool we have. Something catches and twists the beam but does not weaken it, and their interior chambers give almost no latitude at all, being, as you noted, form-fitted. The tolerances built into me should be adequate, but they are not. My own abilities do not foresee a way to prevent loss of at least most of the foot."

Juria sighed. "My computations do not see any way out. The drill knows what it talks about. We shall have to accept the damage or leave them there."

"Very well," the professor responded. "Proceed, then. The anticipated damage is rather minor compared to the value of an actual autopsy."

The drill turned itself back on, and in that moment the walls, floor, and ceiling of the chamber suddenly burst into illumination, but they no longer had the hard, quartz-like appearance and texture. Rather it seemed almost as if there was a tremendous network of transparent veins and arteries, cells and other objects, suddenly alive, suddenly moving, like some great beast.

The drill, programmed to stop at any unusual occurrence, shut down, and the people in the room were still gaping, in shock and wonder, when the two pillars burst at the center with a loud double explosion that both deafened them and nearly knocked them down.

Great demon figures stepped out, and from their backs spread large, barbed, leathery wings. They did not step out as if suddenly revived, nor were they groggy, fearful, or even, apparently curious.

The only two words Tris Lankur could come up with were imperious, *and, somehow,* arrogant.

The guards' weapons came up, and even as Juria shouted, ''No! Don't shoot them!'' the pair made incredible leaps on the nearest living things and began to use razor-sharp claws and fangs and great strength to tear head from body and limb from limb. The soldiers hesitated for fear of killing others, but when they saw the ferocity of the demons, they opened up, pouring every bit of their charges dead into the two attacking monsters.

The demons appeared to find the shots, sufficient to vaporize part of the inert drill, mildly irritating, and immediately went after the soldiers, falling upon them and making of them very quick work.

Several of the team members, including the cymol, started to make for the exit, but, to their horror, the wide, ovoid opening through which they had come suddenly shut, as if it were more valve than door, trapping them inside!

It did not take the demons long to finish them off at that point, going next for the cymol, whose memory and sensors became disoriented, then failed, but not, as first suspected, of immediate damage.

As the first demon, the male, touched her, there was a sudden shock, a sudden opening of receptors, and some kind of contact, somehow, was made between the cymol computer in her head and whatever that thing was. There was a sudden, tremendous surge in her head, like contact with the Guardians themselves but with a difference; with a strange, terrible alienness about it, and crude, terribly crude, without regard for what it might do to her. She felt the contents of her cymol capsule being written out, copied, somehow, but the two-way contact fed her such a totally alien stream of incomprehensible thoughts and images that she could not grab hold of them, nor make any sense of them, even as her cymol half tried to do so.

Then, suddenly, that cymol brain assembled something—a thought, a concept, a distorted and meaningless misinterpretation based on overload—who could tell. It said:

''The Quintara—they still run!''
Then all was blackness.

''I wish I could show them to you,'' Tris Lankur told them. ''Alive, animated, they are like nothing I've ever seen before, even though they are in every sense the classical demon. It's not just the size and strength and form, it's something else, something *inside* them, that radiates out from them with every look, every gesture, every move. Almost the way . . . well, that an entomologist might look at a collection of insects. Only, no, even *that* doesn't convey it. Maybe . . . the way he'd look at a collection of *common* insects, of no particular interest. The kind even an entomologist wouldn't hesitate to step on without another thought. It's not even viciousness—they're so damned smugly superior for that. But it *is* power. Incredible power.''

For a moment, there was silence, and he asked, ''Any questions?''

''Yeah,'' Molly said, voice trembling slightly. ''What the hell we still *doin'* in here?''

''She's got a point,'' the Durquist noted. ''On a strictly pragmatic level, our current weapons aren't even a match for the soldiers, not really, and we have no idea how far back this thing goes. They certainly didn't go out onto the surface—we'd have detected them as life forms, at least—and they didn't just spread their wings and fly off into space. Whatever they are, I refuse to renounce the laws of physics. That happened days ago in there. They were certain to be hungry—pardon—with three quarters of a million years between supper and breakfast, but one would suspect that by now they would have at least a passing interest in lunch.''

''I'm afraid it makes no difference,'' Tris Lankur commented. ''If this thing is alive, it's monitoring us right now. If it's got armaments capable of what we know it has, then we're no safer up there than we are down here right inside it. In other words, if it wants us, there's not a damned thing in creation that can stop it.''

Jimmy McCray let out a long breath. ''Well, that sort of says it all, doesn't it? Kept around like mice in a snake case until the snake gets hungry. And if we try and leave, it can bloody well just blow our ship to Kingdom Come.''

''Wait a minute! Wait a minute! This thing's got us all spooked!'' Modra snapped at them. ''There's no evidence that we're anything of the sort. It did nothing to the scout's probe, nor to the people here until they made a decision that would have harmed one of the owners. It didn't just shoot us out of the sky when we arrived, so it isn't in defensive mode all the time even now, and maybe it can't use all that stuff on its own initiative. Maybe, just maybe, it had to be directed to shoot.''

''A telepathic link to machinery?'' Jimmy McCray scratched his chin thoughtfully. ''Well, it's been attempted for centuries, but I don't know that it's ever been done or can be.''

''I think she is right,'' the Durquist put in. ''Consider that all prior attempts have been to link people to machines. This isn't a machine—not in the sense we think of it. It's no more a machine than Molly there is a machine, and they found a way to induce broadcast empathy in Molly. If the Exchange knows how to do *that*, who knows what sorts of creatures with what sorts of powers they're producing or at least working on right now? And, if the Exchange can do that much, how much of a stretch is it to imagine that a technology that could create a station or base or whatever it is like this couldn't design in telepathic abilities as well?''

''You make me feel like some kind'a space suit or somethin','' Molly responded sorrowfully.

''No offense meant, I assure you,'' the Durquist responded.

''Well, Grysta just pointed out to me that it's no skin off us,'' Jimmy commented. ''We've done the job, right? We answered the call, inspected the deed, didn't disturb the evidence much, and it's now up to us to make our report for other, wiser heads to follow up and then head home to collect on our successful mission. Personally, I don't give a damn *where* those demons are, so long as they're not near me.''

Tris Lankur thought about it, then nodded and put away his equipment. ''All right. Your little companion is a hundred percent right as far as my own obligations are concerned. Still, I hate like hell to turn this over to anybody else after we beam the report. After all, a claim's a claim and salvage law is still the law.''

''You mean—claim this place as salvage?'' Modra was appalled by the idea. ''But—that would mean some of us would have to stay here until the salvage claim was registered.''

''We'll have to stay in the area, anyway, until somebody else gets here,'' Lankur pointed out. ''You can bet that the Mycohl are headed this way as well. They *had* to pick up that call. If we're here, they won't get the claim—they'll be blamed for it if they try anything straightaway. Only if we aren't here and can't file a report can they get in under the same salvage.''

"Well," the Durquist sighed, "if we are stuck, and we are, and if we are targets anywhere, which we are, I suggest that we are much more comfortable targets aboard *Widowmaker*.''

"Agreed," responded McCray, and the others nodded. "Let's get out of this accursed place."

They picked up their gear and started back the way they came, Molly, in this case, taking the enthusiastic lead.

They walked for some time, from chamber to chamber, but there was no sign of the entrance.

"Wait a minute! We've gone much further than we did coming in," McCray commented. "We must have taken a wrong turn."

"Impossible!" Lankur snapped. "It was a straight line and we retraced exactly. Trust me."

Molly suddenly stopped after hearing this. "Uh-oh! I got bad feelin' 'bout this. *Real* bad."

"The instruments aren't working right in here," Modra said, "so I can't say for sure, but I think you're right, McCray."

"Press on for a little," the cymol urged them. "It's this place. It's got us all spooked."

But after a half hour or more and chamber after chamber, even Tris Lankur had to admit that things weren't right.

"Who'd have thought this thing was this *huge*?" Modra said more than asked.

"A tesseract," the Durquist mumbled. "We're in a real, live tesseract!"

"A what?" Molly asked, looking totally confused.

<A what?> Grysta echoed to Jimmy.

"A what?" asked McCray.

"A tesseract. Purely theoretical, of course. Or was. A structure of some sort built in a shape or form that intersects more than the usual dimensions. The plaything of mathematicians for centuries. Any structure, even us, exists in the three obvious dimensions plus time. A tesseract is folded so that it goes through more dimensions than just those. That's how this place seems larger on the inside than on the outside and why it appears to change its dimensions now and again. It seems larger because it *is* larger. The rest of it is folded through other dimensions we can't perceive. But, since we're inside, we're carrying our own dimensional perceptions with us, so nothing appears to change—it's just a lot roomier. One wonders what a pair of *anything* needs a place this big *for.*"

"Maybe they don't," Lankur responded. "If you're right, and everything says that you are, if this *is* a true tesseract, it might just be that all these rooms are necessary only because they're needed to create just the right folds. Who on our side knows how to build one of these things? What's needed to be included to maintain structural integrity? A tesseract must be potentially incredibly unstable."

"I think I get what you mean, sort of," Modra said, sounding like she really didn't. "But if I follow you at all, then the front door might still be wide open. We might just have taken a wrong turn into some other dimension or something."

"Possible, but unlikely," Lankur replied. "The scout probe got in and out in a straight line, and that team was here for months and never had a problem. Unless . . . Hmmm . . . Perhaps it was triggered to switch when the place activated. Become a one-way door."

"In which case it's probable that the owners are indeed still inside," the Durquist noted uneasily.

"No, they can talk with the place, remember? They can open the door any time they want and have an illuminated roadmap and complete directions. No, you have to ask why they'd *want* to go out the front door."

"To get outside, I assume," the Durquist noted.

"To what? A world of trees and oceans, totally deserted, and all creation inevitably bearing down on them? Uh-uh. But maybe you only have one exit at a time. If this thing folds through space and time, they might not even *need* spaceships. I'm sure they had plenty of time to read the chronograph in this thing and all the other data and they know how long it's been. And if *I* woke up under those conditions, the first thing I'd try to find out is what happened to the rest of my people. What's home like? And that . . . uh-oh. Now *there's* a wrinkle I hadn't considered."

"What's one more in a furrowed brow?" McCray asked sourly.

"They got a complete readout of the cymol data from that dead cymol back there. Not enough for military secrets or stuff like that, but it's a good bet that they know pretty much what we know. They know about the Three Empires, about the various races, the systems, that sort of thing.''

"Three quarters of a million years ago my ancestors were slithering through the jungle marshes in a constant search for food and worshiping our sun," the Durquist noted, "and probably communicating in grunts and whistles. I suspect that your ancestors were not that much more advanced. Even the Guardians themselves were an interstellar civilization within the last hundred thousand years. A civilization this high and this pervasive a quarter of a million years ago would either be gods of the universe by now or they are extinct, at least until that pair breeds. Hmmm . . . I wonder how many children they have, and how quickly?''

"I wonder about that last enigmatic thought that the cymol got," Tris Lankur responded. "The Quintara—they still run. Suppose, somehow, it was a last analytical gasp. A warning, in hopes another cymol would do as I did? If these demons are the Quintara . . . well, you see what I mean.''

"They *can't* still be around!" Modra asserted. "It's got to be just some garbage. After all, she *was* being torn to pieces at the time. Even a cymol is bound to be a teensy bit less than clear under those conditions. Like the Durquist said—if they were around, and were at this level that long ago, as is probable by the demon legends, then we'd know.''

"That pair of demons was around a quarter of a million years," Tris Lankur pointed out. "And we didn't know about *them* until recently.''

"What do you—oh! I see! How many more are there out there? Sleepers? Sleepers who now can be awakened. Oh, my God!''

"The front door was open," Tris Lankur noted. "I assumed that the back door is now open. All we have to do is find it.''

"And go where?" McCray asked.

The cymol shrugged. "Anywhere. Anywhere but here.''

"And then what?''

"I don't know. We'll find out when we get there. We can't stay here. We'll run out of food and water eventually, and then power as well. As for me—they've got at least a four-day head start.''

All the others suddenly started and stared at him. "You intend to pursue?" the Durquist asked.

"If I can. Things will have changed in all this time. They, too, have to eat—that's obvious. And drink, presumably. The preliminary reports said they were carbon-based life forms, fairly standard for all the extraordinary abilities and immunities they showed. I think they can be tracked. And, of course, I doubt if it would even *occur* to them that any one of the likes of *us* would give chase. After all this time, I don't think they'll be in a hurry, and subtlety isn't their strong suit."

"And then what?" McCray pressed. "Suppose you catch them? Your pistol's useless. Your strength's no match for them, and they at least know a little more of the stashes along the route than you do. You're going to wind up in a loincloth with a homemade spear stalking them in their own element. The odds of you catching up to them, let alone catching them, are remote. And, if you do, the best you can do is be dessert."

Tris Lankur looked at the telepath squarely. "McCray, did you see any Mizlaplan bodies around? Any Mycohl? No. And neither did I. There was nothing in here that recently died." He stopped, stooped down, then picked up something off the floor. He examined it, then showed it to them.

"A cigar butt?" Modra responded, looking at the curiosity.

"Yes. A cigar butt. Not dried out, either. The tobacco is still moist in the unsmoked part. That small yellow band there near the end tells me that it was a Mizlaplanian who smoked it."

"I didn't know any of them had *any* bad habits," McCray commented dryly.

"One of the foreign teams landed, found what we found, and probably also still had use of the recordings back in the office. They know what was here and what was done. The second team surprised them and they had to fight, eventually taking refuge inside this thing, whatever it is. The newcomers, maybe fearing a trap, maybe just out of good sense, didn't pursue right away. They went back, found probably the recordings that the first group watched and saw them, too. Then they destroyed them, in the hopes that nobody could or would follow them soon. Then they, too, came up here and came in. I don't think the second group found the first one. In this sort of place, it would be nearly impossible for *everybody* to miss and I can't believe they're all lousy shots."

"One can imagine what being faced with live, real demons would do to the Mizlaplanians," the Durquist noted. "It would be like their angels suddenly face to face with the physical forces of Hell itself. No force other than death itself would prevent them giving chase, no matter how hopeless it seemed.''

"And the Mycohl venerate the demon figure as a kind of demigod," Tris Lankur pointed out. "Although, to be fair, they are about as deep-down religious as the average Exchange citizen, which is to say, not much. But if they followed the Mizlaplanians in, and found them gone, what were they going to do? Go on a hunt, or camp out by the front door until the Exchange came in and, at best, arrested them? They had no choice—and they at least have some reason to believe that, of all three systems, these demons will be more favorably disposed to them than to the other two.''

"They're probably all dead," McCray pointed out.

"Probably. But what if they're not? What if this back door opens right into some ancient base world of the demons' civilization? What if these two are all that's left? Think of the knowledge, and power, represented here. No, go camp out front for a few weeks or come with me.''

Modra shook her head in wonder. "I don't think we have a choice. If there *is* a back door to someplace else, perhaps another world, perhaps another dimension, as the evidence, over logic, seems to suggest, I'd rather go there than camp out here and hope against hope that somebody will come in and rescue us. If there is only one exit, you take it.''

"Consider the possibility, though, that it does *not* lead directly to them, but rather to intermediate stops," the Durquist chipped in. "Perhaps a great number of intermediate stops. A tesseract is a rather odd thing. That would mean that we would be in both a chase, and a race, with two teams of mortal enemies, to catch up with representatives of an ancient race we might be powerless to do anything to. All the time the three teams would be going not only after the same unholy end, but fighting each other every step of the way. And we are already behind, perhaps half a day, perhaps more. One feels the firm bounds of reality slipping madly away in this, particularly when such an insane race as we propose is in fact the more desirable course!''

Jimmy McCray gave a wan smile and looked at each of the others in turn, then said, "Hurry! Hurry! Hurry! Step right up, ladies, gentlemen, others, those of all races and creeds and nationalities! Three highly trained teams are about to set out on a racecourse blindfolded, where they will attempt to murder one another in their quest to catch creatures that will certainly eat the winners! Yes, indeed, beings of all races! Don't dare miss—*The Quintara Marathon*!''

    <*Shut up, Jimmy!*> snapped Grysta.

LIMBO
IS FOR
LOSERS

JOSEF WAS NOT PLEASED.

"We had them right there!" he shouted, his voice echoing off the vast death chamber. "Right there! And we lost them!"

"There are a great many ways to go from the next chamber," Kalia pointed out. "There is simply no way to know which one they chose, and we do not have enough force to explore all of them."

Desreth projected two stalks from its body which seemed to flow out of it and into their shape. "Their tactics are clear," it said in its monotone. "They could not get through us, but if they retreat they gain nothing except risking being lost in the bowels of this place. Clearly they are attempting to find a passage leading in back of us, to the entrance once again. Then they either flank us or they simply leave."

Josef nodded. He looked around the chamber and said, "I wish we had some time to really take a look at this mess, but I agree. The best course is not to pursue, since we risk getting trapped ourselves or lost. Our best course right now is to retreat and recall the ship. We will blow up the other shuttles on the ground, leaving them trapped here, and then return. I believe that mind scans will reveal that we were justified in coming, and if we must suffer for some of our failures, then it is our due."

"Agreed," Tobrush replied. "It is relatively clear what happened, if we can believe the overheard Mizlaplanian conversation. Two creatures that they in their fanatical fervor see as demons were here in suspended animation. The scientists tried to cut them out, accidentally revived them, and paid for it. Although I would prefer to know where those creatures are now, and just what they did look like, I believe *not* knowing makes a well-ordered retreat mandatory, and with all speed."

Josef nodded. "All right—same system as we came in. Kalia, Desreth, to either side. Just follow the cable, and watch the side exits on the chambers as we go. We don't want any nasty surprises."

Even with curiosity unsatisfied, it was still something of a relief to get out of that chamber of horrors. They proceeded back, methodically, as they had come in, pausing now and again to listen for voices, but there was nothing but silence. Still, the way back seemed interminably longer than the way in.

"This is the fourth chamber we've passed through," Tobrush noted worriedly. "We only passed through three coming in."

"You must be mistaken," the leader responded. "We're still following the scientists' power cable."

"The Julki is correct," Desreth put in. "We are not going back the way we came in."

Two more chambers without a sign of an exit convinced even Josef. "How is it possible, though? There are no cable junctions!"

"There is one remote explanation," Tobrush said. The Julki extended one of its tentacles and emitted a chemical spray that was jet black. It traced a design on the floor near the cable, then withdrew it. "Now let us proceed on."

Another corridor, another small chamber, then another corridor, then they emerged again into a small chamber and stopped, all of them staring.

Tobrush's black design was unmistakably on the floor.

Kalia ran back to the corridor and peered back in the direction from which they'd come. It wasn't a very long corridor; despite a slight bend, she could essentially see where it opened up once more. "Impossible!" she snapped. "There is not enough of a curve in this short distance for us to circle around!"

"I agree," Desreth put in. "At best a six- or seven-degree curve. We have been going essentially in a straight line and we have wound up where we began."

"It is almost as if this thing was trying to keep us here," Kalia breathed, looking around nervously.

"Doubtful," Tobrush responded. "The only possible explanation is that this structure is the first concrete example we have ever seen of a tesseract. That would explain why it never quite looked the same from the outside."

"A what?" Kalia asked.

"We, all of us, regardless of our racial origins, experience things in three concrete dimensions—length, width, depth—and a fourth, time," Tobrush explained. "The tesseract is a theoretical mathematical construct that exists in all of those dimensions but also others simultaneously. We were not designed to perceive those dimensions and so we do not, but they act upon us here all the same. We have not been passing through the same space. Instead, we have been passing through other unseen and unperceived dimensions in which this thing also exists, and, folded through them, we are winding up pretty close to where we start."

"You want to explain that more slowly and clearly?" Josef pressed.

"Each of these chambers and corridors intersects all of the other chambers and corridors in the place through dimensions we cannot perceive. We have walked through a realm we cannot comprehend and so was invisible to us until we reached a point where that other realm intersected with something that would."

"I do not quite understand," said the usually quiet Robakuk, "but I admit the effect. If this is so, although it makes me dizzy to attempt to think upon it, then why did it not affect the scientists who must have been coming in and out for months?"

"Perhaps it was stable then," Tobrush replied. "Relatively so, anyway. Think of our own ship. We do not so much fly it as it flies us. It has its own computerized brain and instrumentation that is far faster and better at its job than we could be flying manually. This structure might well have a similar governor. When the scientists came in, the structure's first object was to study them and perceive a threat, but to maintain stability in the route to the passengers. Eventually the research team goes to dig out the passengers and that now constitutes a threat. An initial defense mechanism might then be to turn this on, so that those who threaten are trapped."

"But the passengers got out," Josef noted. "We saw the results."

"Precisely. Either they can see and persist in more dimensions than we, which is a distinct possibility, or they know the one route to get out. Either that, or the ship, obedient to them, stabilizes as needed—the most likely scenario."

That made them all a bit nervous. "Then, we're trapped inside here, too?" Kalia asked. "Inside a building that can think and considers us threats?"

"Possibly. If we keep going in a straight line, I believe we will be trapped. The old concepts have no more validity in here now. We might need to go back to go forward, to go down to climb, to turn left to go straight. If we do not threaten the structure or any of its inhabitants, providing they are still here, then one of these faces, at least, will intersect with the entrance."

They all thought of the scenes of carnage. "You think there's a possibility we'll meet other—inhabitants?" Josef asked.

"Doubtful," the Julki replied, "although there might well be living quarters or a whole city in this sort of thing. I doubt if they are still here, though—why allow us in if they were? Why not finish us?"

"But, if they are not outside, and they are not in here," Desreth said, "then they must be someplace else. A third place. Might this be not merely a building but some sort of transport system? If it can fold and refold inside itself to warp space, why not in normal space as well? Think of a vehicle one could build and keep in one spot, yet which allows anyone to literally walk between worlds countless light-years apart, through dimensions that circumvent the normal rules."

Josef stared at the Corithian for a moment. "You mean," he said at last, "that this thing might actually take us somewhere else? Another world?"

"Another galaxy, even," Tobrush told him. "Space, time,

everything might be bent through and come out in any fashion.''

''Assuming I believe this fantastic crap for a moment, it wouldn't be unplanned. Not these people. If this is a transportation system, it's a hell of a ways beyond anything we know. I don't care if they're demons, devils, or ancient gods, as far above us as we are above a blade of grass, they won't do things for no reason. If in fact this goes somewhere, it won't be just anywhere and it won't be random.''

''Hmmm . . . Yes,'' Tobrush said after a moment. ''I see your point. Considering how they regarded and treated the people here, do we *want* to go where this will take us?''

Kalia looked at them in disgust and shook her head. ''It sure beats stayin' here,'' she said.

Josef took a deep breath. ''All right, then—we go. Same system, only this time we go off this damned cable. We'll try it, at least for a while, because there seems nothing else to do. Remember, though, that there's still that pack of Holy Ones stuck looking for an exit just like we are.''

Kalia suddenly drew her pistol and whirled at one of the corridor exits. They all froze, and Josef whispered, ''What's wrong?''

''Voices. From down there.''

''All right, then,'' the leader told them, ''why don't we go that way and see just who we bump into?''

In and out, back and forth, they crisscrossed the seemingly endless labyrinth inside the demon structure, often hearing voices, occasionally seeing things move well in the distance, only to find nothing when they got there. It was getting very discouraging, but no less tense.

''We've been here before,'' Gun Roh Chin noted, pointing to the floor. ''But we're not alone.''

Next to the chalk mark he'd made on the wall was a black design in some unknown substance.

''Look! Over here is another of their marks!'' Krisha called, pointing to another possible route. ''And over *there* another of ours. And here—a third mark, perhaps? It seems some sort of marking pen.''

They went over and looked at the odd pen marking.

"Definitely not ours or theirs," Chin agreed. "One of the original scientists' marks, perhaps?"

"Either that or—how many people are wandering around in this hellish place, anyway?" Morok wondered.

"I admit that, seeing all these marks, I almost believe someone from the Exchange has set up an admissions booth and is selling tickets. They *would* do it, too," Gun Roh Chin commented sourly, crouching down to examine the markings. "Wait a minute, here. . . . Wait a minute!" He got back up and looked around the entire chamber. "Six possible entry-ways into this chamber, see? And five of them have one sort of marking or another, some several. Only one, there, bears no mark."

"But, Captain, that's the one through which we just entered," Morok noted.

"Perhaps. Is it, really? I wonder. Let me mark it here, then we go through it."

They waited for him to draw his mark, then wearily set out along a path they were all, even the captain, certain they'd just traversed. This was getting very old very fast.

The next chamber, however, had far more markings than could possibly be accounted for by their short absence. Two, however, were totally unmarked, and Chin went first to one and peered in, then the other. "This one," he told them.

"How can you be so certain?" Morok asked him.

"The lighting's different down at the end. I'm certain of it!"

And it was. When they reached the end of the corridor this time, they passed through an energy barrier much like the one at the entrance to the structure through which they'd come, and were suddenly outside the labyrinth, although still within and surrounded by the hollowed-out quartz-like core.

"We have done it!" Savin shouted in an expression of joy and relief that sounded to most of them like a dangerous beast after a kill. "We're back at the entrance!"

"Are we? I wonder . . . ." the captain responded. "Where is the walkway? Where is the power cable?" He turned, pulled his pistol, and began walking straight down the center toward the opening beyond. The others followed, and soon they were back in open air.

Before them stretched a vast plain, flat and featureless as far as the eye could see. The rock was hard, gray, and featureless, as was in fact the sky, which seemed a vast sea of light gray in the twilight through which nothing appeared to shine.

Savin started to see if he could scratch into the rock with the heel of his boot, but Gun Roh Chin told him to stop it. "Examine the area. No marks at all. Either we're here first, or someone else had the same idea I did. Walk *very* carefully; make no marks at all that you can avoid. Sooner or later, if only by trial and error, the others will find their way here, unless there are alternate destinations for this thing. It would be best for us if *they* thought that they were the first here, too."

Krisha looked around at the vast, colorless nothingness. "But what good does that do us, Captain? There's no cover!"

"Yes, and all directions look the same," Manya noted. "My suit compass shows no reading—it just keeps going around and around. The heat and humidity are at oppressive levels, yet there is no sign of erosion or runoff of any kind in this hard rock, implying that it does not rain, at least in this region."

Morok walked out and away from the exit to the demon structure, examining the ground with the kind of gaze he normally reserved for his hypno Talent. Finally he stopped, then bent over and examined the ground more closely. Finally, he got up and turned back to them. "There are marks. Very faint, but marks most certainly."

He walked out a bit more, then did the same. "Yes, definitely."

"Then the Mycohl are already here?" Manya asked, concerned.

"I think not. They would either be careful to make no such marks or they would make far different marks than these. Examine them, all of you. Some are just single marks, but one or two are clearly slight crescents." He stepped to the next set. "From the stride, I'd say between two and three meters tall. I thought it was just one, but there is a third mark, a bit smaller, with this set, almost overlapping the left large one. Two, then—one a bit smaller and lighter than the other."

Manya was on her knees and examining the marks as if they were specimens. "Oddly shaped. One would almost say like the sort of marks the horses from the Holy Retreat would make, only the sets do not indicate a quadruped. I—" She suddenly seemed stricken, then got up quickly and backed away from the area of the marks as if she expected them to suddenly come alive and bite her. "Cloven hooves! The two demons!"

"Here is your other plane," Gun Roh Chin said with some satisfaction. "If in fact it isn't simply some other world. Morok, bless the gods that your people are such keen trackers. I would have missed these for sure." He turned back to the demon structure, which looked curiously the same, sticking partway into the rock, the only thing to break the landscape at all. "The reason they weren't stranded on that world for lack of transport is that transport was at hand. They don't need spaceships."

"I don't know how it is done, but clearly you were correct in that part, Captain," Morok agreed. "However, it certainly was not a crash, was it? Then, why the pair in suspension in the center, and why, when they did awake, did they take the trouble to ensure that no one currently there survived or got away, yet failed to lock their own transport front door?"

"I can imagine a lot of diabolical reasons!" Manya snapped.

"Or, it may be that they just didn't care," Gun Roh Chin suggested. "The chamber business, horrible as it was, we must put down to some aftereffects of the awakening. These are a violent people with a very mean origin; in an unthinking state, they might well be vicious. Or, it might just be that they still weren't thinking so straight after and forgot the details. In any event, we are here, and they went that way, and I thought that we were trying to find out about them. Most Holy One, I defer to your natural tracking abilities, but should we not follow the trail?"

"I say we remain here for now!" Manya put in. "We can use the demons' house as cover, set up an effective ambush. When the rest emerge, we can mow the devil worshipers down like grain!"

"No," Morok responded. "We don't know how long anyone else will take to get here, or if they *will* get here, although I am more inclined now to think that they will. We have only sufficient food reserves for a week at best, water twice that. I am already down to an eighty-one percent charge thanks to the fighting back there. Some of you who did more firing have less. We simply cannot afford the time. Indeed, if there is no source of edible food and water ahead, we might well perish anyway, leaving only that Corithian abomination alive to go on.''

''I would bet on water,'' the captain told him. ''Probably food as well. The demons are carbon-based life, carnivores, warm-blooded, and they exist most comfortably in environments close to those we consider comfortable as well. I saw a lot of random slaughter back there but no sign of really methodical search. I'd say that this pair took little or nothing with it. Power will be a problem, although if we get to some point where we have direct and real sunlight, we'll have a crack at at least maintenance level recharge. If *they* can survive, *we* can survive. But, I agree, time is running out, and if there is somewhere in this desolation where we can find cover and camp, we will all need some rest.''

''You speak as if demons require the things of flesh and blood!'' Manya rasped. ''They are not creatures of our universe but of another, darker one! Now they have sacrificed for their energy and gorged on the flesh of their sacrifices for strength.''

Morok raised a hand. ''*These* demons appear more bound to our sort of limitations than one might expect. For now, I agree with the captain.'' He looked up at the sky. ''No way to tell if this is dawn, dusk, mid-day, or midnight, but we must assume the worst. I prefer to be out of sight of this place in case it gets very dark, though. Come, let us make haste. Patrol formation, but relaxed. Krisha, you take the point; Savin, you take the rear. If any threat comes, I think it will be from our back in any event. There is no way to tell how old these markings are, but from the condition of the bodies and the amount of time it took us to receive and act on the distress call, it may well be weeks. We are going where they went, but I do not expect them just ahead of us.''

Modra Stryke looked around the bleak landscape and sighed. ''This has got to be the flattest, dullest piece of nothing in the entire universe.''

''Aye, Limbo,'' Jimmy McCray responded, staring into the nothingness. ''But where is our Virgil?''

''What?''

''Dante.''

''I beg your pardon?''

"Dante. Ancient writer from the even more ancient home of our ancestors—yours and mine, anyway. He wrote a book once, a thousand years or so ago, give or take a century or two. Walked right into Hell he did, in that book, all the way to Satan's throne and beyond. They still make all the good little Catholic lads read the thing, sort of as an example."

The Durquist was unimpressed. "I rather doubt that some primitive book based upon some ancient, localized religious cult has any bearing here."

"Religious cult indeed!" McCray sniffed. "That's the trouble with all this interstellar civilization. Overrun with all you heathen, it is. The first place that primitive fellow hit when he went to Hell was a gray, dull, featureless sort of place called Limbo. Went into several languages of Old Earth as a legitimate word—a place of nothingness, neither here nor there. We are following demons, right? Against all our better instincts, and no matter how we explain them, that's what we're doing. Walking to Hell just like that old fellow, and look at the first place we come to! Limbo it is, if it's anything at all. The rest of Hell is for the evil ones of the world. Limbo, though, is for the heathen and the losers."

"I should think, then, that we should be over our heads in people," the Durquist commented acidly.

"Point taken," McCray replied. "Yet I am still struck by the similarities here. If this holds up, there are nine more worlds to go, all without divine protection, each one a worse horror than the one before."

"I'm not sure I can imagine a worse horror than this nothingness," Modra commented. "It's so—*bleak*."

Tris Lankur examined the ground. "Well, we're not the first. The question is, after that maze, are we the last?"

<We'll sure be the last and getting more and more behind if we stay around here,> Grysta commented to Jimmy.

"Shut up, Grysta," he mumbled. "I'd rather be last than sandwiched in between Mizlaplanians and Mycohlians."

<Umph! Good point. I hadn't thought of that.>

Lankur stood and shook his head. "Can't tell from those marks, except that we're not first and everybody's going the same way." He straightened, then slowly turned three hundred and sixty degrees around, looking out at the horizon.

"May one ask what that was for?" the Durquist said with an amused tone.

"There's no curvature," Lankur told him. "Even without landmarks, light acts differently as it strikes a sphere the further away you get. There is a slight deflection."

"Too small for any but the finest instruments to see," the Durquist responded, then stopped. It had become routine to think of this creature as the same Tris Lankur they'd always known, but that was a fraud, a masquerade, for whatever had been made out of Lankur's parts. "You can see that and measure that by eye?"

The cymol nodded. "That's not the important thing. The important fact is that this place is dead flat. Either we're on a massive polished mesa, or on some artificial structure, or this world is in fact flat."

McCray noticed Modra give a slight shiver, and read her thoughts as a telepath could.

<Oh, God! I don't know whether I can take this! I . . .>

He tuned out. The basic flood of thoughts surrounding the kernel were anything but logical or rational. She still blamed herself for Tris's condition, and rightly so in McCray's estimation, but he was glad that *she* was the empath. He was picking up enough of Modra's inner turmoil from what he could read of Molly's mind.

"She close to fall to little pieces," Molly whispered to him, and he nodded. He was still unsure just how intelligent Molly really was, since her mind worked in ways too alien and twisted for him to comprehend, but she, too, was an empath, and working the clubs had given her a practical knowledge of troubled souls.

Jimmy, too, worried about Modra as the tensions and pressures increased, and he knew the Durquist shared those concerns. Only Lankur, with the soul of a machine, seemed oblivious to the problem. Feigning emotions was not the same as having them, or, perhaps, understanding them.

<We might have to do something about her,> Grysta commented.

"Not until we have to," he responded in a low voice. "We keep our aces in the hole."

<Aw! You never let me have any fun!>

"Look who's talking," he muttered sourly. Aloud, he said,

"So, shouldn't we get started? Who knows how long this light will last?"

"Started, yes, although cautiously," Lankur responded. "If this place is in fact flat, and without cover, then if we get close enough to see someone ahead, they'll be able to see us as well. Suits on minimum power, stay close and on voice, and go easy on the food and *very* easy on the water. I'm not sure we'd like eating what these Quintara eat, even their scraps—you saw the bodies—and they might know a water source we can't tap." He paused. "Last chance to check out of this. I'll be willing to bet you that you can get out the exit in that place now, particularly if we're the last ones. The odds are very good that just re-entering that entrance there would reset the thing."

<C'mon, Jimmy, let's go and leave that cymol freak to his programming!>

Jimmy just shook his head, although she couldn't see it. Ahead was probably a quick and ugly death; back there was the same, only real, real slow. He knew she could force him back and wasn't doing so; possibly she knew it might be the last straw for him, but, more likely, she just wasn't at all certain they wouldn't be wandering around in there forever.

"I admit to being increasingly intrigued," the Durquist commented. "I still think you should return, Modra, now that it's likely you can."

She whirled and stared at them, an angry, almost dangerous expression on her face. "I will not desert my team! We've been all through this! Let's move!"

Seeing that it was impossible to convince her, even by coming right out and saying it, that their concern was less for her than for her value in a desperate situation, they set out.

Trekking through the vast nothingness was not only boring and additionally wearing for that, it left each of them alone with their thoughts and plenty of time to do nothing but brood. Normally Jimmy McCray could shut the others out, but his power was most likely their first, and perhaps only, line of defense, and that meant that he had to have most of his shields down and allow the thoughts of the others to pour in.

Not Lankur, at least, but Jimmy wondered again just what *was* going on in the mind of that machine in a man's body. Molly was almost as unnerving, if only for what little seemed to be going on inside that pretty head. She didn't even appear to be bored, or curious, or apprehensive; about the only thing he could grab onto in her mind was irritation at picking up the dark moods of the others. Unlike Modra, Molly had never learned how to shut off the empathic powers. Perhaps she wasn't designed to do so. In any event, the depression of the others was getting to her, making her moody and irritable as well.

The Durquist's thoughts were difficult to sift through and sort out; the internal point of view was simply too different and too alien. Still, it was clear that the star-shaped creature was very uncomfortable, walking with its centered "face" up on four of its five points, its eyes extended and looking in more than one direction at the same time—disconcerting to a Terran in its own right—and apparently wondering if the lure of this possible demon technology was worth all this.

Modra, however, was turning internal suffering almost into a new art form. Until now she'd sort of lived in a half-fantasy, deliberately forgetting most of the time that the fellow over there wasn't really Tris, but that was gone now. She kept reliving that night all over again, that terrible hospital experience, even her last talk with him before he'd blown his brains out, putting herself through massive pain.

Grysta sensed his own mood from all this and said, <*You're gonna have to tune 'em out, Jimmy, no matter what. They'll drive you nuts otherwise.*>

"Maybe," he replied very softly. "We're the newcomers on this team, so maybe I'm not seeing the full picture, but it's really odd about Stryke. She thinks of the old, dead Tris Lankur all the time, but never once about the husband she married instead of him. All this time and I never once even had a clear picture of the fellow in my mind. If she loved Tris all that much, why the hell did she marry some other bloke? She had to know he loved her, too—she's an empath!"

<*People do stupid things all the time for reasons that seem real smart when they do them. You've done your share, too. That's why we're stuck with that factory-built wooden-head over there.*>

He looked over at Molly. "It's possible I did her no favor, but I would do it again, which is more than I can say about going down once again to a certain world run by furry worms."

<If you keep talking like that, I'm not going to speak to you any more.>

"Promises, promises."

A bit farther on, Tris Lankur called another rest period. "Anybody see any differences after all this way?" he asked them.

"None. Not even the light seems to have changed," the Durquist replied.

He nodded. "Right. It's *exactly* the same."

"I find the marks in the rock even more disturbing," the Durquist told him. "True, there are a number of folks ahead of us, but there are no other marks."

They all looked at the star-shaped creature. "Huh?"

"No other marks. No sign that anyone has ever been here before. No cross-trails, nothing. The marks we follow are recent, but they are also consistent. It is as if we—and the foreign teams, and even our demons—are the first to ever come across here. If these conditions are constants, it's not as inviolate as a vacuum, but it would take centuries, perhaps millennia, to really see any changes here. The implication is that we, all of us, are the first people to ever cross this place."

"They could be walking all over somewhere else," McCray suggested. "We don't know how big this bloody flat really is."

"I think not. If the demon structure is indeed some kind of means of interstellar travel, as it seems to be, there should have been *some* marks *somewhere* right around the thing, at least. There weren't. It was the only reason that the very slight traces of the others on this hard rock could be seen at all. It makes no sense. *Nothing* about this makes any sense. Why were those two in suspension back there? And why just those two? What could all those other chambers possibly be for? Why kill everyone there and leave the door open, when it is obvious to the most primitive simpleton that others would inevitably follow? What, and where, is this place? And why?"

Tris Lankur nodded. "I keep wishing we'd looked in that lab ship. Not just for the records there, but I keep asking myself if we'd find their transmitter switched on and a recording of the distress signal."

Jimmy McCray looked up at the cymol. "What?"

"There are two teams up ahead. Clearly versions of the sort of thing we do, only as the Mizlaplan and the Mycohl have

them. Have you considered what the Mizlaplanians must have
risked to get here? Across at least sixty light-years of Mycohl?
Or the fact that the Mycohl commander, whoever it is, put his,
her, or its whole team's neck in a noose even tighter than the
Mizzies did by following it up? What are the odds of that
message getting to a full team, and only a team—not a
freighter, or a cruiser, or a free-lancer, or anybody else—from
each of the Three Empires? We think we're chasing all of
them—you said we were sort of racing them, McCray. I just
can't shake the nasty suspicion that maybe instead we're being
led by the nose.''

"By who?" McCray asked him. "These Quintara?"

"Probably, since it's clearly their show. That one demon—
when he got the cymol, for just a moment, impossibly, their
minds were linked. That big one *read out the data in her mind*
before it killed her, and, for a very brief moment, she got
something from him. Something that didn't fully scan, but it
gave us their name. In that moment before she died, she got
from his mind enough to understand who they were and what
the hell was going on. That information, save only the one
statement, wasn't stored—or wasn't permitted to be stored. To
do that—selectively erase—without any mechanisms, without
anything like an interface—means tremendous power and great
intelligence.''

"They could just be ensuring that they have a decent food
supply trotting along after them," Jimmy suggested.

"They will choke on me," the Durquist commented. "If I
have to go, that is a noble way to do so."

"The Durquist's right," Lankur replied. "Unless they're
omnipotent, which is not the evidence, they couldn't know just
who or what would respond. Not precisely. If it was food, they
wouldn't want a Durquist, another cymol, or even a syn in their
hoard, and who knows *what* the other two teams are composed
of? I'm pretty sure that, if we were led into this, it was pot luck
for us. They neither wanted nor knew who would show
up—but they wanted one from the Exchange and we were
elected because we were the closest ship.''

"Yeah, but all that wanderin' around inside the bloody
building or whatever it is . . ." McCray said. "What was *that*
for?''

"Maybe to make sure we were the right ones," Lankur

replied. "If, as we assume, there's some kind of controller, some sort of computer or similar thing, inside that structure, it would have been left with a loose set of definitions based on what the male demon took from the cymol's mind. When it finally decided we'd do, it let us out here. If we'd been wrong, I'm pretty sure we'd have found ourselves back outside on that world again."

"You make these violent barbarians sound like high plotters," the Durquist noted. "We're not even certain that those horrors built that place. It might well have imprisoned them."

"In which case we're the coppers," Jimmy added, nodding. "And the others, too. The warden's recruited us as havin' the best chance to catch them and make the collar."

"If so, I find that oddly less than reassuring," the Durquist noted. "Tris's vision basically says that we have no power over them, but they have vast power over us, and they know the territory we now aimlessly wander through, with the teams having a vested interest in eliminating each other as much as these demons. It *would,* however, explain why they killed everyone so brutally but didn't shut the door. They couldn't, because they didn't control the door."

"Stuff and nonsense!" McCray shot back. "What sort of a prison depends on only bars, as it were? The governing computer had control of the doors—we agree on that. Yet these blokes had no hesitation about walking outside, and were able to do so, then bumping off everybody including, somehow, the ship in orbit, then they walked *back in* to their jail and were permitted to go out the other door? I've had experience with a lot of alien thinking, but no warder who thought like that would have ever risen high enough to build that sort of place."

"I suppose you're right," Tris Lankur sighed. "Still, it was a theory that *almost* explained it." He turned. "Modra, you've been—" He broke the sentence abruptly, seeing her, stretched out on the rock, out like a light.

"I suppose no matter how far behind we are, we have to get some sleep," he said at last.

"Well, if it's any consolation, *they* will, too," the Durquist said. "Indeed, having been ahead of us all along, they're probably all asleep right now. I suggest that to face them, let alone the Quintara and these riddles and enigmas, as tired as we are, is suicide anyway."

Tris Lankur sighed and nodded. "All right. I'll take the watch. Everybody else get some sleep. Here is as good a place as any—and about the same as anyplace else."

"What about you?" McCray asked him. "You going to wake us in shifts?"

The captain paused for a moment, then said, "I only require rest, not sleep. There's just no sense in forcing anyone who requires sleep to miss it. Go ahead. Sleep solidly as long as you need. It'll give us an advantage over any of the others, who will have to rotate guards."

The others didn't respond to this, another example of just how different this seemingly personable man really was. But, meditation on that fact could wait; as tired as they were, sleep came first.

Morok gazed into the distant nothingness. "I may just be very tired," he said hesitatingly, "but I would swear that there was something out there, near what might be considered the horizon in another place. Off to the right."

They all stopped and strained to see, popping in their magnifiers, and Krisha scanned it, and a couple of them *did* think they saw some form off in the distance, while Gun Roh Chin and Krisha saw nothing. Possibly the others saw something because they wanted to see something; still, Morok's eyes were far better than any of theirs, and, tired and deadened by the monotony, anything he saw could not be easily dismissed.

"The trail goes straight," Savin noted. "Still, it might bend around later. You want me to check it out, Holiness?"

"Take Krisha with you. I know we're all in, but we can't take any risks if something might be there. Keep checking visually. If you get closer and still see nothing, do not press on but come immediately back. We have no idea if there is anyone behind us and I dislike splitting our forces, particularly with no cover, for very long."

Krisha inwardly groaned but had no choice but to obey. Although she was in excellent shape and worked at it, as an involuntary late-ordination priestess, she didn't have the advantage the other clerics had of genetic-engineered perfection, and she knew that even they were tired.

Gun Roh Chin, who was neither a cleric nor anywhere close

to physically perfect, sensed Krisha's dilemma. "Holiness, I agree to a point, but I think Savin can handle it alone. His empathic powers can sense if anyone's there, and, no offense, if we are set upon I'd like at least one of the military-trained people with us. We can open a channel on one suit and Savin can keep in touch by radio."

"Savin?"

"I can handle it, Holiness."

"Very well, then. Go now. Fall back to the default channel; if anyone's trying to listen in, they could find any other channel anyway, and that is the cleanest signal."

Krisha's eyes met the captain's, and he could see in them the gratitude for getting her out of that.

The rest of them settled down wearily on the smooth rock "floor" of the place while Savin bounded off.

Gun Roh Chin looked in his pouch. Five cigars left. He was loath to smoke any of them now, since they might well be the last he'd ever see, but pragmatism won out. Better to enjoy one now than to die, perhaps, with its destiny unfulfilled.

"I'll take the watch," he told them. "The rest of you try and get some sleep. I'll awaken you in a flash if I hear anything from Savin or we have any visitors."

Morok didn't object. "Two-hour watches, though, Captain. You select the next one up, and so on. I shouldn't think Savin will be away more than four hours, but if he finds nothing, then we should all get *some* rest."

Chin got up wearily and walked about a dozen paces from the rest, then sat down again. "Savin? Radio check. The others are getting some rest."

"Check is fine," Savin reported. "Wish I could get some rest. Nothing yet, but I am really beginning to believe that something *is* there. It's simply a very long ways, and distances in this place are deceiving."

"Very well. If you need to rest, do so. No use in you getting so tired you either can't get there or can't get back."

And that was that. He reached into the pouch, took out one of the cigars the others hated and despised so much, bit off the end, then lit the other with the old battered lighter he kept with him. He certainly was no tobacco addict, going as long as he did between cigars on the whole, but there was something about being surrounded by clerics, compelled by the strange powers of the Mizlaplanian masters to not sin themselves and resist it elsewhere, that made him want to smoke. That perversity in his nature was one of the countless reasons why he was pretty sure he'd never rise much above his present station no matter how many incarnations he might undergo.

The smoke rose almost straight up, and much of it just seemed to hang there. No breeze at all. Even the systems in his old, clunking freighter cleaned and refreshed the air. A flat world of complete nothingness. Not even the light seemed to vary. It *had* to be artificial; some sort of transition zone for the ancient demon transport system. All in perfect working order after how many thousands, or tens of thousands, of years? What *minds* they must have had, to have this command over dimensions undreamed-of and create their machines so that they never broke down or wore out!

It was difficult to reconcile such a people with the scenes of carnage back at that camp and in that chamber, or the brutishness of smashing right through a wall to murder all inside. It seemed impossible to conceive of ones like that creating and building all this.

Thanks to an intellectual father and an occupation that left him with a lot of very dull free time, he'd delved deeply into the history of his own people, both the subculture from which his direct ancestors had come and the whole of Terra's fragmented subcultures.

He'd been quite surprised to find that the demon was in almost all of them. Not quite the same look, of course, but always evil, often cunning but vicious, and quite often with an ugly face and many times with horns just like those in the recordings they'd seen. Even when not evil, they tended to be the representatives, the angels, as it were, of the gods of darkness, death, and destruction, as if they were some ancient vestigial memory of some prehistoric common reality. The Jewish, Moslem, and Christian faiths, still practiced on many of the Terran-settled worlds of the secular Exchange, all had demons looking damned near *exactly* like what was on those recordings. It made him wonder if in fact all those ancient tales weren't truths; that these demon creatures had visited and perhaps been around Old Earth in ancient times, possibly in the central area where all those faiths grew up, and earning so terrible a reputation that the tales of them, and the fear of them, spread, bent, distorted, and twisted, to much of the rest of Earth's ancient cultures.

The demons in the faith of the Mizlaplan weren't that much different from the ones in the recordings, either. Not in appearance or reputation. He'd been startled to learn at the Academy that many races that had nothing at all in common with Terrans, some not even bipedal, also had demon myths. Again, they were distorted, the tales filtering down through alien minds and alien points of view, but they were nonetheless recognizable. The Church, in fact, gave it as a primary proof of the existence of the Lords of Hell.

He knew the same was true for the Mycohl. There, however, the demon figure had a place of honor, representing raw power and will. He always supposed that it was because those who ruled by fear, selfishness, and brutality would naturally respect the ones who epitomized and perhaps legitimized what they were doing. Each of those ruling Lords had their own personal demon and made sacrifices to it. He'd been wondering what would happen if any of that Mycohl team actually came face to face with one of these creatures. Would they fall down and worship it, or willingly give themselves to it as sacrifices, or would they shoot and run like hell the same way he would?

One bunch emulates the demons while the other bunches make them the core of all that is bad. It was a fascinating idea, now that the existence of demons was proven true. It implied that these people had once visited many, if not most, of the worlds harboring sentient life, and had earned their reputations by deeds so vile that they came to personify evil.

And, like damned fools, we're chasing them, he thought, shaking his head in wonder. They appeared from their pictures to be the products of a particularly nasty home world, yet, in their own way, they didn't look any more fearsome than, say, Savin, whose own people had a very nasty history and were only brought into the fellowship of civilization by their conquest and absorption into the Mizlaplan.

There was movement out of the corner of his eye and he whirled, adrenaline pumping.

"I'm sorry," Krisha whispered, "I didn't mean to startle you. I just couldn't sleep. Too tired I think."

He waited until his heart was out of his throat and back down in his chest where it belonged. "That's all right," he managed. "I just got too deeply lost in my own thoughts."

She sat down facing him and crossed her legs. "I want to thank you for getting me out of that. I'm certain I would have collapsed halfway there."

"Oh, it's nothing. Morok, like all of us, tends to measure others by himself. It's bad enough when we Terrans do it to one another, but it's nearly impossible to remember the limits of other races. We seem so much alike under the different bodies, but those similarities are often superficial. We see differently, hear differently, have different physiologies and biochemistries, and we grew up on worlds whose cultures and even physical layouts are alien to ours. Morok can balance on a log no bigger around than your leg, and actually go to sleep on it without falling off once. Savin sees well into the infrared. Morok sees a nearly infinite number of levels of grayscale but has so limited color vision he couldn't comprehend how we see things. Manya, on the other hand, instinctively avoids anything colored violet or lavender, and her whole race is very near-sighted, yet can work close up on things we can barely see. You see what I mean? How can we, any of us, really keep in mind the strengths, let alone the limits, of the other?"

She sighed. "Well, I thank you anyway. It gets—very hard, sometimes. And this place doesn't help. With nothing to see, with no variations, your mind turns inward. I think I have relived, and brooded upon, every mistake in my life, over and over. Don't tell me not to—it happens anyway. I spend a lot of time doing it, and this place has just made it worse."

"Can't Morok's power help you with it? At least it would ease your mind."

"He can't. That would be interfering with my spiritual development. A hypno's power is limited on a telepath in any event, because we always know it's coming and, after, we can read in the hypno's mind not only that it was done but *what* was done. No, there is no way out for me."

Back at the retreat she had sought audience with the Grand Master, the Highest of High among mortals, and had pleaded with him:

"Master, I cannot continue to live like this! The agony is too much for me to bear!"

"It is not, child, for you are *bearing it, and you must live this*

way since you cannot live otherwise. No one can withdraw an ordination, not even the Holy One who ordained you. There is not power higher than the one which made you thus.''

"Then must I live in torment eternal to death? Is there no way to end it?''

"Your pain is self-induced, because you continue to fight, to resist, divine will and destiny. Only when you rejoice in being of the Chosen, when you no longer wish to be any other way—then and only then can it end.''

"Tired?'' the captain asked, breaking her reverie.

"Yes,'' she replied. *Oh, gods of mercy! I am so very, very tired!*

He didn't know what else to say to her. He never did. Even suicide was no answer; it never was for a believer in reincarnation. If she went on much longer like this, her mind would snap. Restrained even in madness by the power of the One who had made her thus, her own strong personality would crumble and extinguish and she'd become someone else; a one-dimensional fanatic, most likely, an angel incarnate without even a trace of Krisha, for whom there would be no questions at all, and who would make even Manya seem the soul of reasoned discourse. They stacked the deck on people like her, making that sort of outcome almost inevitable. She'd already held out far longer than most.

The others would rejoice when it happened; they'd give her a new name and do celebrations of thanksgiving that she had been purified.

He, alone, might find it difficult not to cry.

She was asleep now, and looking so tragically beautiful.

"Savin to watch.''

He flicked on his intercom. "This is Chin.''

"It's—it's—I can hardly describe it.''

"Is it another demon building?''

"Yes, but smaller, more basic than the other. The trail winds around to it. I can see some of the markings, but I'll need equipment to tell if everyone we've been following has passed. It has an elaborate, ornate entrance, unlike the other, and slightly removed from the structure, so that the gate of solid stone stands before rather than as a part of the building.''

"Well, don't go in it!'' the captain instructed him. "Remain there, use what's available for cover, and get some rest. I'm going to let everyone here rest a bit more, too. I doubt if there is anyone between us and it, and there's a good field for seeing anyone coming from the rear. We need rest before tackling any more.''

"I—I agree. But I'm not too certain I want to be too near this thing.''

"Why? Trouble?''

"It—it's the gate. There are *words* etched in the stone!''

"Nothing you could read, surely. What do they look like?''

"That's just it! I *can* read them! They're in the Mesok tongue! My native tongue!''

Gun Roh Chin suddenly felt wide awake and a little chilled. "Wait a minute! That's not possible!''

"I swear it by all the gods and souls of my ancestors!''

"Etched in stone? In *Mesok*? What's it say?''

"The closest translation I can give you into Standard is—'All who enter this place enter without hope.' ''

Oh, great! the captain thought, a sinking feeling growing in the pit of his stomach. *There goes my own chance to sleep.*

GUARDIANS
OF THE
SECOND CIRCLE

UPON THAT DESOLATE, FEATURELESS LAND OF unchanging gray, the small party stood before the great gates of the sole structure they had seen since leaving the first. The second was in many ways like the first: some great single crystal of unknown composition that seemed to change before your very eyes in ever so subtle ways, thrusting upward from its place embedded in the otherwise polished rock floor. It was, however, smaller, and thinner, than the one that had extruded into the known universe through which they had entered this eerie plane, giving some hope that there weren't endless chambers within.

In front of it was erected a great ceremonial gate which appeared to be made of some marble-like rock, so finely polished they could see their reflections in it. Two massive rounded columns rose up on either side, then bent seamlessly in until they joined at an arch in the top center. From the inside of the columns and arch, a thinner, flat panel extended from the arch and from the sides, creating a smaller, rectangular entry-way rounded at the top to match the angle of the arch above. It was on this panel, above the opening, that the words were carved, perfectly, and inlaid with what appeared to be solid, polished, gleaming gold.

"Why, it's in no Mesok tongue," Krisha commented, a bit awestruck. "It is in Hindi!"

"No, it is in Torguil, the language of my ancestors," Morok maintained. "Savin's translation, though, is fairly close."

"It is a demon trick!" Manya rasped. "I see it in my mother tongue, as you all see it in your own!"

"Not quite," said Gun Roh Chin. "It's nothing but a line of very small golden dots arranged in squares. I read nothing in New Mandarin, which gives me a thought." He turned to Krisha. "Scan that thing, right where it is, as if it were a living creature," he instructed. "See if you get anything."

She tried. "A headache," she responded. "I cannot keep on it for any length of time."

He nodded. "Savin? Morok? Try your own powers on those words, right where you see them."

Morok looked up, concentrated, then his long legs buckled and he caught himself just before he fell. "Vertigo," he said needlessly.

"Static, like a de-tuned transceiver," Savin told him. "There was a real burst when Morok almost fell just now."

"It's some sort of broadcast device on the neural band," the captain replied, feeling a theory confirmed. "The difference in most Talen's is nothing more than sensitivity to one or another part of that band, but the frequencies aren't that far off. The message it is actually broadcasting is in a purely holographic form; your minds change it into the writing of your native tongues. It's quite clever. I know that a great deal of research has gone into trying to manufacture just such a device, in all three empires. Even ones without Talents would get the message; only ones like myself, who are essentially crippled, unable to even receive or send or otherwise use those bands, see nothing but what is really there."

"I've tried to block it out, but I cannot," Krisha told him.

"Its band is too broad, beyond the mere telepathic limits. Still, its purpose is clear. It means 'Keep Out' in everybody's language."

Morok studied the ground. "Well, *they* went in."

"Naturally. People who erect the signs perforce exclude themselves," Manya noted sourly.

"There is something else," Savin said, hesitating a bit. "Come over here—about twenty meters to the left."

They followed him, more curious than apprehensive now that one mystery had been at least rationalized. They looked where Savin pointed and Morok gave a noise halfway between a squawk and a gurgle that passed for a Stargin gasp. "A trail! Leading *away*!"

Savin nodded. "It just—starts. Nothing leads from the structure to it, or from anywhere else. Notice something else, too, Holiness. You've been studying our trail since the start."

"Similar to the markings we've been following—only there are many more, over a larger area. Strange . . . if I didn't know better, I'd swear that the main markings were the ones we've been following all along."

Manya ran her basic equipment over them. "The Holy Gods and Their Mighty Angels be with us! They *are* the same marks! See? You can see the demon strides easily here, and the pair are the same!"

Krisha shook her head. "You mean those are the same tracks? And our own? That, somehow, we've come two days' march in a *circle*? That's not possible! I admit we could easily have gone in a circle for all the landmarks, but *that* is not the demon structure from which we came!"

Gun Roh Chin nodded thoughtfully. "Nonetheless, the conclusion is hard to avoid. We're dealing here with a totally different set of rules, even if things seem similar. Some of the similarity might be due entirely to what our own bodies and minds are designed to perceive. The fact that the trail emerges out of nothing, away from this new structure, indicates that we did indeed emerge at some other point, but came to this one."

"But why didn't we just then see this thing behind us at that point, then?" Manya asked him.

"I have no idea, Manya. How did we get from that Exchange world to this one?" He got up and looked back at the new structure with its warning gate. "If this is some other universe, then the natural course of things we take for granted might not all apply. Certainly some do—we have gravity at a manageable level, and air, and suspended water. Better to ask why the demons, who know this place and its rules, didn't just double back as well. This sounds totally insane, I know, but we have left conventional wisdom behind."

''How can we cope without the anchor of natural law?''
Morok asked him, disturbed.

''Don't ask me how—divine intervention, maybe, if you
want to think that—but I am convinced that logic is not out the
window with the rest. Logic demands that any such place have
natural laws and rules that are consistent. I fall back again on
the records we saw, that the demons are carbon-based life, and
not that radically different than a number of races we know,
except, perhaps, in the head and the spirit. Their major
advantage over us is that they know the rules, but our
advantage is that the rules cannot deviate radically from what
we know without causing them as much of a problem as it does
us. It is a matter, then, of deducing those differences.''

Krisha looked at him. ''Captain, you remember what we
talked about? About the physiological differences even between us?''

''Yes?''

''Suppose—just suppose—there *is* a difference. Just as the
two of us can't see into the infrared, and others of us either
cannot see colors or perceive them differently, perhaps these
demons can see things we cannot. Things native to this
environment. There might be things all around us that none of
us are equipped to perceive and which even our instruments
have no way to detect.''

He nodded. ''I've thought of that, and it's most likely true,
but their primary perspective overlaps ours, it's clear. We can't
worry about what we cannot see, hear, feel, or touch. We can
only trust that the situation is mutual, in which case the price is
that things are pretty boring to us. I am more concerned with
getting the rules straight.''

''Such as, Captain?'' Morok prodded.

''Logic suggests that we did not go in a circle, at least not in
practical terms. Most likely it is a spiral. The demon houses
angle down, suggesting some sort of descent. Somehow, we
could not get that short distance between there and here without
walking around—and, most importantly, neither could they.
Now, what did they—and we—have to do to get to this point?
We had to walk around anti-clockwise—*to the left*. Somehow,
under the strange rules of this place, left is down, right is up.
How we can perceive the old, upward, trail is a mystery to me,
but I would wager that if we refused entry there, as the sign

suggests, and continued on, we'd walk around again, two days, to this very spot. If we retrace, going right to do so, we'd wind up back where we came in. It's important. It means that, even if we lose the trail, we know the general way to go."

"I am feeling dizzy once again, but not from that *thing*," Morok said. "Still, I have been around a long while and have traveled far. I've seen races that were clearly intelligent, industrious, and totally incomprehensible, who spent all their days creating bizarre structures they never used, who had no languages as we understood them yet somehow communicated with each other, and who would act in ways one could only consider erratic and insane—except that they were consistent. How can someone converse with, let alone convert, creatures so alien that they have no apparent common mental ground with any known race? If whole peoples can be thus, then why not some demonic universe? There is no alternative but to accept your theory as a working hypothesis, Captain—until it fails, if it does."

"That is all we can do," replied Gun Roh Chin. "However, Holiness, if my theory on dimensional directionality is correct, we have problems. There are a *lot* more marks over there than can be accounted for with just our passage. I particularly dislike that series of nicks, three and then three, as if sharp metal points had dug into the rock. Nothing we or the demons did accounts for them."

"The Corithian!" Manya gasped. "It had six such legs when I saw it!"

Chin nodded. "And that means we've got our Mycohlians behind us, and not very far behind, either, I'd wager."

"I was also concerned with the extra pair of prints similar to the demons', only smaller, with a shorter stride," Savin noted. "Over there, to one side. The forward scuff is definitely hard and rounded, like hooves, but I know of no hoofed races other than demons that are also two-legged. Do we have another demon behind us? Perhaps joined with their worshipers?"

"I have no idea," the captain said honestly. "All I know is, if we stay here, we're going to have very unpleasant company once more. We can either try and set up an ambush here, using this place for cover—after all, they *have* to come here—or do we go through?"

"I say nail them right here!" Savin exclaimed forcefully.

"We have cover. They have none at all. There might not be another spot this ideal."

Morok considered it. "Don't forget that we'd be facing a pretty strong telepath, if Krisha is to be believed, and a Corithian as well. I'd like at least a full charge on the power packs before I fought a pitched battle, and we didn't get that here. And there's the matter of the smaller demon figure. I'd rather know more of *them* directly. No, for a good ambush I want better than even odds, and I doubt if we are even at that point in this place. Let us go through. Perhaps there will be someplace ahead to camp, to recharge, to wait for them, that gives us an edge. Right now our best edge is to remain in the lead. It allows *us* to pick the time and the place."

Gun Roh Chin turned and looked back up at the sign only he could not read. "Well, we are supposed to discard all hope at this point, but I haven't gotten to that point yet. Step up! Who will be the first to enter the upper Hells while still alive?"

"I'll lead," Krisha told them. "I have no fear of what might be in there." *I am in lower Hell already,* she added to herself.

The inside was pretty much the same as the first demon structure had been: the same indirect lighting emanating from the walls, the same melted plasticine texture to everything. They went from the outer chamber to the inner one with no sensation of going down, although from the angle they must have been descending and rather steeply, and stepped into a new grand chamber, only slightly smaller than the one they'd first encountered, but still pristine, unchanged, without bodies or gore.

Krisha stopped and stared at the center of the chamber, and the others all froze and gaped with the same sense of awe and terror.

"*The Evil Ones!*" Manya screamed, and raised her pistol, and it took both Chin and Savin to stay her hand.

"They're still in suspension!" Chin yelled at her. "You shoot them and we'll just get what they got back at the first one! You want that? Think, Manya! *Think!*"

She trembled, and they could tell her resolve was shaken, but it was more than a minute before they felt safe to let go of her.

It was as if they had stood there on slightly raised platforms, the male and the female, and allowed the strange material that made up the inside of the crystal structure to ooze down upon them, covering them and locking them eternally inside semi-transparent columns.

"Just like on the recordings," Morok managed, his twin hearts somewhere inside his rubbery beak.

Krisha nodded, mouth still partly open. "There is the enemy," she managed at last, her voice cracking, her throat impossibly dry.

"But not the enemy we chase," the captain reminded her.

Savin, for all his fierce looks, was equally stunned. "Evil," he muttered. "Impossible, pure evil. It beats inside my mind like a drum. Cold, horrible evil. Repulsion. Revulsion. Every dark emotion I have ever felt, magnified a thousand—no, a million times. Never in my studies, never in my wildest nightmares, could I conceive of an evil like this."

Chin was fascinated. "You feel that empathically? From them?"

Savin nodded. "I cannot conceive of how those scientists did not also feel it. Surely they, too, used empaths. Even now I fight an insane, driving urge to flee this place."

"Krisha, are you getting anything?" the captain asked her.

The telepath did not answer, but kept staring at the two figures as if in a trance.

<Unlock Us! You can do it! Unlock Us and worship Us and become Our priestess. We can free you as you can free Us. Our priestesses know no limits; their power is Our power, and, for them, there is no such thing as excess. Free Us and worship Us and We shall free you from the tyrants who did this terrible thing to you and aid you in revenging yourself against them all. Our time is coming once again. Soon We shall be free again to conquer and rule and reign no matter what you do. Free Us now and you shall reign over a multitude of worlds in Our name. Refuse and We shall be free soon in any event, but We shall keep you as you are, frozen in this state for eternity, allowed neither madness nor rebirth. Free Us! Free Us now, and you shall be High Priestess to the very stars!>

Gun Roh Chin suddenly grew concerned. "Morok! Get to her! If those things can send that kind of dread into Savin, they might be getting into Krisha's mind!"

<We are the gods of pleasure, the gods of passion. All that you desire We can give you, and things so wondrous your mind

*cannot even dream of them. Free Us! All you must do is free Us
and worship. Since the dawn of time We were, and to the end
of time We will be, and during all that time We have acted
according to Our own code. We are always honorable; We
always keep Our promises, enforce Our word and Our bond.
Even the legends of your own silly church admit that much. Do
your false gods answer all those prayers? You can do it. That
much of your curse We lift even here, trapped as We presently
are, but you must do it of your own free will. Only by that can
you prove yourself worthy to serve us. Your false gods are long
dead and gone. Your faith is enforced by carnival tricks. Free
Us and We shall make you more powerful than your false and
foolish gods. Free Us . . . free Us. . . .>*

"I cannot get through to her! Something is blocking me!"
Morok shouted.

Savin moved swiftly for so large a creature, grabbed Krisha,
whirled her around although she resisted, and, with a huge,
leathery fist, knocked her cold.

She went down like a suddenly empty sack collapsing to the
floor. Savin caught her, and picked her up as gently as he
could, and turned to the others. "We must get out of here, and
now! What I have done has enraged them so that I cannot stand
it much longer myself!"

"Yes, now!" Gun Roh Chin shouted. "Everybody! Get
by those living mummies up there and out the back way!
Quickly!"

They did not hesitate, and moved forward and around the
creatures on a run. They all felt it; even the captain felt
something, although he wasn't sure if it was real or merely his
own feelings reflecting what he'd seen and experienced. It
didn't matter. It didn't matter where this thing led them next,
either. Clearly they were not yet up to taking on demons, even
demons in amber.

As soon as Josef accepted that they weren't likely to catch
the Mizlaplanians, rest became the number one essential. He
had hoped to catch up to them, knowing that they couldn't be
that far ahead, and could hardly hide in this flat wasteland, but
he finally had to admit that there just wasn't much chance at
this stage. He would have to count on the fact that they, too,
would need to stop and rest, and that, being ahead, something

would eventually slow or stop them, allowing his people to close.

Tobrush sent hundreds of slender tendrils into the medical kit. "Kalia, remove your suit. I have limited knowledge of Terran anatomy but a burn is a burn, and the book says to keep treating it. Do you have any pain?"

"A little," she admitted. "Not as much as when I came to, and not nearly enough to lay me out. I am very stiff, though, on my whole side."

She deactivated the environment suit, which caused it to suddenly loosen, as if it were three or four sizes too large, allowing her to pull down the fasteners and essentially let it drop.

Although the burnt side of her face looked awful, Josef was unprepared for the red, flaking skin underneath the suit. She hadn't had any deflectors on when she'd been shot, since that would have slowed her down and limited her maneuverability somewhat, and the energy blast from the Mizlaplanian whatever it was had partly gone through the suit to bare skin. The suit itself was undamaged; it was simply the heat, which had been of sufficient strength to get through the normal insulation at that range.

He, frankly, couldn't understand how she could walk at all, let alone this far, and without complaint or collapse. The left arm and upper thigh had taken the most damage. They weren't the fatal, near disintegration, strength that she'd have gotten without the suit on at all, but those were pretty mean burns.

Well, there wasn't much he or anybody else could do about her now. In a way, seeing the damage and knowing what she'd done after it, he felt glad that she was on their side.

"You know, at any normal distance the suit would have prevented all but the head damage," Tobrush commented. "Even at stun or wide spray it would have done some, lesser, damage to the exposed skin on the face, but little else. That Holy Horror had her weapon on tight beam maximum and from a distance of probably no more than three meters. As it is, only the fact that she *was* using a tight beam and had a bad angle kept you from dying on the spot."

"Skip the lecture," Kalia responded, slurring her words slightly as if a bit drunk due to the damage to her face. "Just patch it up and I'll make it."

"Well, you survived what the medikit calls shock, which is apparently the real killer in such cases, and the medication and spray-on mediskin seems to have done quite well, so I suppose I guessed right," the Julki told her. "However, I am going to keep giving the series of injections and applying new mediskin until things settle to natural healing. According to the kit, if you lived this long you'll survive, but it recommends at least three weeks in a healing tank for this scale of burn."

"Fine. I'll just trot on over to the nearest hospital. Just do what you can."

"Yeah. She's too mean to die," Josef said, trying to sound jocular, although the extent of the burns really shook him. He wasn't sure if he could have walked back out of the shuttle after that, let alone get all the way here.

Kalia was a genuine psychopath, but she was *his* psychopath.

Although he felt uneasy about stopping, at least Desreth made it a full rest for everyone; the Corithian didn't seem to require sleep *or* rest, and seemed content to do virtually nothing for hours.

Sleeping was easy, even on the flat rock, but waking up was hard, even when as a result of a warning. Josef checked his chronometer first and saw he'd been out a bit under five hours; his body screamed at him that it was not enough. Still, Desreth couldn't be ignored. Better to be tired than dead.

"What's the problem?" he called.

"Others coming behind us. Small group, probably no larger than ours."

"How far off?"

"Estimate approximate. About one and a quarter hours at current speed. I can detect them only with my receptors on maximum range."

Kalia yawned and tried to shake herself awake. "Could it be the Holy Ones? Got behind us somehow?"

"Doubtful. The rock tracings have been most consistent," Desreth told her. "More likely it is a troubleshooting team from the Exchange. It was their territory and their personnel, after all. It was inevitable that they would show up sooner or later."

"Bad news for us," Tobrush commented. "That makes us the middle of the layer, with the fanatics ahead of us and the Exchange behind us, which is bad enough. Desreth, however, indirectly makes an equally telling point in that those people, if Exchange, are the ones with all the rules on their side.''

''The dead do not quibble over rules,'' Kalia spat.

''Perhaps not, but we are quite alone here and it is unlikely any more of our own forces will cross the border in our defense. On the other hand, we can only regard an Exchange team as the vanguard of many, many more. Consider: if this world were in our own territory, and we came upon the same scene with our own dead lying about, half the military of the Empire would be called down upon the spot. Unlike the prayermongers, if we take out the first Exchange group we will almost surely face a second, larger force, and a third, and so on, and most likely they would jump to the conclusion that the Mycohl were behind all of this. After all, does not the primary religion of our leaders venerate demon-like creatures? The distress call itself could be interpreted as signaling not an alien force but rather a Mycohl attack. 'Demons at Rainbow Bridge' and all that.''

Josef nodded. ''Tobrush is right. There's the threat of actual war over this. Damn! This is getting more complicated by the moment.'' He looked around. ''Get everything together! Let's move and move fast while we still can. It's possible that they haven't spotted us as yet, and if we can open up a little lead, we might be able to keep it that way for a while.'' He looked around. ''If there was just some damned cover around here we might be able to let them slip past us! Let *them* take out the Mizzies and us heroically coming to the rescue. For now, we just have to move.''

Josef liked to think that the superior training of the Mycohl military gave them an edge. Few of the enemy, whichever one, could double-time for so long with so little rest and very shortened rations.

About two hours of that and they came to a minor mystery.

''The tracks diverge,'' Robakuk noted. ''Most went off *that* way, and these two only go on.''

They looked around, but saw nothing but the same gray expanse as always. There seemed no reason for the sudden divergence, but Josef had no doubt which one to follow. ''The one to the left,'' he told them. ''That has to be the Mizzies, and they are our first priority here.''

"If the other two are with them, they might be circling around to catch us in a trap," Kalia pointed out.

"I can't believe they'd split their forces here on some off-chance of catching us. No—to the left. *Go!*"

After almost an hour, they saw the demon house and gate in the distance, and it energized them just to see *something* in this wasteland. Still, they approached with caution, widely spread apart, fearing that perhaps the team ahead of them was lurking there around and behind the gate and structure, waiting to pick them off against the glow of the sky and the flat plain without cover of any kind.

Kalia, for one, was mystified to discover that nobody was there, and, truth to tell, so were the others. "A perfect spot for it," Josef noted.

"Are you certain that invisible bitch isn't lurking back here for us?" Kalia asked, pistol out, nervous and ready to shoot at shadows.

"No," Tobrush replied. "I could at least hear that interminable praying and you could sense her, too, if you'd use your head. They are gone, and almost certainly through the gate."

"Perhaps the sign had something to do with it," Josef said nervously, pointing at the underhang below the arch.

The warning caused them the same initial fears that had struck the Mizlaplanians, but, as Gun Roh Chin had with the earlier group, Desreth was able to solve the mystery in a manner that at least made sense and kept things on a rational basis.

Josef thought a moment. "That thing, building or transport or whatever, interferes with the neural bands," he mused. "If we got up close and behind it, the team behind us might not detect our presence."

"Too risky," Tobrush responded. "They will certainly check out the entire structure as we did, and with the same caution. That would mean a firefight with no advantage to us. I don't think the situation favors our continued existence in that case." The military oaths and honor of the Mycohl military did not permit surrender, and that was understood from the start. You triumphed or you perished.

"Shit!" Kalia swore in frustration. "Ain't we ever gonna get to shoot *anybody*?"

"Patience, Kalia, the time will come," Josef soothed. "For now, Tobrush is right."

"That sign may be more than a mere warning," Robakuk noted. "The place could be filled with traps. I read it as 'Keep out—or else!' I don't know what the 'or else' is."

"Well, we can't stay *here*," Josef pointed out. "Okay, the same system we used before. Weapons out, Desreth and Tobrush in first. Kalia, you come in with me. Robakuk, rear guard, thirty seconds and in. Be extra careful and take nothing for granted! Even if there's no trap set by whatever made these things, *inside* that thing is an even better place for an ambush than here, and we don't want to get pinned down between the Mizzies and the Exchange, either."

There was no sign of a trap from either their enemies or the builders inside, just the expected entry chamber. They moved as before, a precision team, but when Tobrush and Desreth entered the second chamber, they could hear the Julki say, "Oh, my!"

"Tobrush? You all right?" Josef called, worried.

"Yes, I'm all right. But I think the rest of you had better get up here. Desreth says I'm not seeing things, but I need confirmation."

Josef and Kalia entered the chamber cautiously, then stopped, struck equally dumb for a moment by the sight of the two demons in suspension in the center of the chamber. Robakuk, coming in last, had no less a reaction, but Josef's professionalism snapped him out of it a bit. "Robakuk—keep back in the corridor. I don't want the Exchange walking in on us until we've had a chance to look at this."

"Uh—yes, at once, sir!"

"Not even as a hatchling have I ever believed in these things," Tobrush said in a distant tone. "Or anything else I couldn't see, hear, and feel."

"Are they *real*?" Josef wanted to know.

"Yes, sir," the Julki responded. "Nor are they comatose, at least not mentally. *They know we are here!*"

"Such *power*," Kalia sighed, and Josef was startled to see her fall to the floor and prostrate herself before the two figures and begin a low chanting prayer.

Desreth was clinical, as usual. "The subjects are definitely warm-blooded, carbon-based. The smaller of the pair is the female, indicating probable bisexuality of the race.''

The Julki made a noise unlike any they'd ever heard him make before.

''Tobrush? You all right?'' Josef asked, concerned. It didn't take a detective to figure out that this was pretty much what the Exchange had found in the first structure, and that a pair much like this one had gotten out and done all that destruction.

''They are speaking to me!'' the telepath responded. ''They are—powerful. Hard to think. Can't block them out!''

''Well, you're our medium! What are they saying?''

The Julki's body shivered, and it was clearly having real problems. Then Tobrush spoke, but the voice was not Tobrush but someone, *something* else, a kind of voice none of them had ever heard before, and one which, if coming through Tobrush, strained the creature's abilities.

''We welcome you, who are Our grandchildren,'' said the voice from the Julki.

''Who are you?'' Josef asked, not sure why he was shouting. They obviously could read minds.

''Before the universe was, We were,'' replied the voice. ''We were among those who created the universe and the worlds within, and planted the seeds that would become you all. Those whom you call the Mycohl, your masters, are Our children and Our guardians of the countless nests of worlds We designed. Our other children have, it seems, followed a rebellious path, but Our time is almost at hand once more, when, with the Faithful at Our side, We shall re-establish Our rule and reign over the whole of your galaxy and more, to the edges of Creation. Then shall the Faithful rule as gods over all the others, with power and glory undreamed-of.''

Josef felt a little uneasy, wondering what sort of speech the other demons had handed the Exchange scientists before wiping up the place with their broken remains.

''Those were unbelievers, followers of the rebellious ones,'' the demon voice responded, reading his mind. ''Had they been discovered and Our comrades freed by the Faithful, the result would have been very different.''

''Why did you kill all of them?'' Desreth asked. ''It seems—excessive.''

"Why not?" came the chilling reply. "The numbers of the unbelievers are like the stars; a few one way or the other matters not at all. In any case, it was practical; Our comrades did not at the time realize how powerless those creatures were."

"And what will you require of us if we follow you?" Josef pressed.

"Your worship and your faithfulness," came the response. "You have nothing else to give."

"Your claim to be the gods who created us all is suspect," Desreth noted in its flat monotone. "If in fact that cannot be shown, then we cannot trust your word as to the rest, including our own fates."

"Why do you doubt, Corithian?" the demon voice asked.

"First because, by asking, you show that you cannot read my thoughts," Desreth responded. "By any logic, a creation should have no secrets from the gods. Second, you are imprisoned, as, obviously, were the others. Who can imprison the gods?"

"There are things beyond your limited ability to comprehend," the demon responded, sounding, to Josef, a little bit pissed off. "We are the commanders of this station. By Our own choice and the necessity of remaining one with the station, We are here, sleeping until someone activates the station. Only Our mature grandchildren could reach, let alone activate, a station. When that happened, it placed in motion a chain of events leading to Our reclamation of Our rightful rule."

"I regret that I do not believe you," the Corithian responded. "You are not necessary to run this station; the first one we used required no operators. Nor would you place yourself in such a position that there was no emergency override to extricate you. The most telling argument, however, is that your own comrades, as you call them, passed through here and they chose not to liberate you. If your own people, imprisoned themselves, do not trust you free, then how can we be expected to do so?"

"*Fools! Worthless hunk of self-maintaining machinery! How* dare *you question Us?* Free Us and pledge your souls to Us and We will make you the vanguard, Our first priests and priestesses with power beyond your wildest imaginings! Those

who free and pledge themselves to Us will reign in Our names;
those who refuse shall be Our first sacrifice!''

There was a somewhat desperate tone to their pleading now,
something not lost on either Josef or Desreth and perhaps not
Robakuk as well. It was hard to tell just how much control
Tobrush retained.

''*Girl!* We shall make you the Goddess Kalia, and give you
power over all the world that used and abused you! You will
avenge yourself against all who caused you harm, and command your enemies to grovel and eat the dung of animals, and
all will worship you and sing your praises and your glory, even
the very Lord of your clan! All you need do is take out your
pistol and set it to narrow beam maximum and cut through the
columns above Our heads.''

Josef's hand went to his own pistol, and he made ready to
draw and fire, wondering if in fact he was faster than she.

Kalia's head came up, and she raised her torso up on her two
hands, but she did not reach for her pistol.

''Feel a pale shadow of what We offer you,'' the demon
voice said, and the woman's body stiffened for a moment, then
began an incredible, sensuous writhing, her face a picture of
absolute ecstasy. The empathic signals the demons were able to
impart even from their prison must have been incredible.

''Draw your pistol,'' cajoled the demon voice. ''Break Our
seals. Shoot anyone who might try to stop you, for they are not
worthy. Do it now, and you'll see that there is nothing which
you cannot have, nothing you cannot be, or do. Do it!''

''Sergeant!'' Josef snapped. ''You took an oath of obedience
to orders! If you break that oath now, you will be no more
trusted by *them* than you deserve, for you will have forfeited
your honor!''

He saw the longing in her face, saw her good hand go to the
pistol, then hesitate.

''Do not draw! *That's an order!* Move to Desreth and around
the pair!''

''A command of your gods supersedes any oaths or promises
to mere mortals!'' the demon voice responded. ''You are
relieved of all such oaths! Free us!''

She hesitated a moment, then tensed, and, just as slowly, her
hand moved away from the gun. Slowly, ever so slowly, she
moved toward the Corithian.

"Desreth! Get her out the back!" Josef commanded. He looked over at Tobrush, who seemed held there, and wondered if he had to leave the telepath.

Suddenly the Julki's body quivered and began to move, first toward the demons, then around them to the right of the pair.

"You join the others, sir! *I'll* make certain Tobrush gets out of here!" came Robakuk's voice behind him.

Realizing that the Julki was being moved by the telekinetic powers of the Thion, Josef gave a wry smile and a salute to the two demons, then made to join the others, even as Tobrush's demonic voice was screaming, *"You cannot do this! We command you to return! You will suffer in agony for all eternity for this!"*

For the first time since he was in his early teens, Jimmy McCray crossed himself as he stood before the gate.

"Abandon all hope, all you who would enter here," he read. "Not quite where it should be, nor as complete, but I'm a bit taken aback to see it here at all."

"Huh? What?" Tris Lankur responded. "Where do you see that?"

"Up there, above the gateway."

"There's nothing up there but some kind of gold dot pattern."

"I read the same thing in Durquist," said the Durquist. "Modra?"

"Just reads in standard Commercial to me. Kind of weird, like everything else."

"Obviously a holographic message, intended to be read by anybody," Lankur responded. "But you seem to know the passage, McCray."

"Indeed. The full thing—it's been a *very* long time—but, the full thing should read,

> *'Through me you pass into the woeful city;*
> *Through me you pass into eternal pain;*
> *Through me you pass through a people lost.*
> *It was justice moved my lofty Maker;*
> *Divine power brought me into being,*
> *The first love and the highest wisdom.*

Before me were created only things eternal.
And I endure for all time.
Abandon all hope, all you who enter here.'"

"More of this primitive poet?"

"He's lookin' less and less primitive as we go, although more the poet," the telepath responded. "If it holds, what we stand before is nothing less than the gates of Hell itself. The place where all the interestin' folks wind up, and where I half expected to wind up one day myself—but not like this, in a suit and still alive. Still and all, it's the very place you'd go if you were a demon, and the very place to go if you wanted one."

Modra Stryke stared at him and frowned. "You're not seriously suggesting that that's *Hell* in there, and that we're chasing real, live demons?"

"Either that, or somebody's gone to a whole lot of bother to make it seem so," McCray replied. "And I, for one, sure can't think of a motive for that."

"I think it's a bit difficult to swallow either explanation," the Durquist responded. "This is hardly a primitive age. It's the age of spaceships and interstellar, interracial empires, and technology so extreme that we deliberately limit it for fear it will overwhelm us. It is an age far removed from sun worship and glorified tree spirits. It's an age when we already know almost everything."

McCray looked around and swept the horizon with his hand. "That so? Then explain *this*!"

The Durquist was nonplussed. "Well, I said '*almost.*' Still, we've gone a long way, both in and out, and we haven't found a single god yet."

"But we found two devils," McCray shot back.

"Enough of that, you two!" Tris Lankur snapped. "I will grant you that we have stumbled on something totally new, something we don't understand, and the major reason we're here, other than investigating the thing, is to find out if our people somehow also triggered something nasty. That, in fact, is my main concern, the real reason I had to follow those two. The universe is still full of surprises, no matter what you say, Durquist, and the more we discover, the more we find we don't quite know. That's our *job,* remember? To find the nasty little surprises before they do major harm. Before it was always a new world, and was localized, at least. Now we've stumbled onto something big, maybe the biggest thing anybody's stumbled on in history. Big and as nasty and mean as anything any of us have ever faced before. At the very least a fourth empire, with technological powers we can't even come close to figuring, and a mind-set that doesn't seem to like any competition. But that's *all* it is, clear? That's *enough!*''

''I'll admit it must be a comfort not to have been brought up Catholic,'' McCray responded. ''For one thing, you didn't have to endure all those years of those bloody interminable catechism classes. I long ago abandoned the faith of my ancestors, but I can no longer shed the mind-set than I can my skin. And, as a rational man of the great technological now, I'm beginnin' more and more to see that those old priests and nuns got it close. Closer, at least, than any New Planet Survey I've ever been given.''

''Well, there's no use standing here arguing,'' Modra pointed out. ''From the traces, it looks like not only the demons but half of creation's been through here ahead of us, and *those* type of folks we *do* know. Having seen no bodies on the way, I assume they got here spaced enough that they haven't had another gun battle, or been set upon by monsters, or whatever, so we're still ahead of the game in following in their footsteps. Either we stand here and let them go on and wait for reinforcements that might or might not be able to follow us, and hope they come before our water and food run out, or we go.''

''The lady indeed has a point,'' Jimmy McCray admitted. ''Shall we ignore the sign and go on in?''

Modra nodded, but said, ''Uh, tell me, McCray—this Dante you keep spouting? How'd he wind up? At the end, I mean.''

''He made it all the way to Heaven, lass,'' the telepath replied. ''And then he got home and wrote his bloody epic.''

''Let's hope we come out the same way,'' she replied. ''You know any more about demons than that book?''

''Quite a bit,'' he admitted, ''although filtered through many years of total neglect. At the age of thirteen, demonology was far more fun than bein' an altar boy.''

They entered the first chamber.

<*I don't like this, Jimmy,*> Grysta noted. <*I feel something— like something's waking up.*>

He felt it too. "On your guard," he hissed. "Something's ahead."

Coming before the two demons had no less an effect on them than it had on the first two teams. For most of them, it was their first true visualization of creatures which, up to now, had been more loosely defined; Lankur had no problems replaying the recording from the other cymol and matching the scene rather exactly. For the second time in a matter of minutes, Jimmy McCray found himself crossing himself.

"I told you," the cymol said softly.

"They're aware of us," Jimmy warned. "I felt a probe just now."

"You mean they're *awake*?" the Durquist responded nervously.

<Don't resist Us, telepath. You cannot resist Us in the end, and it will only cause you additional strain.>

"Grysta! I am under mental attack!" McCray called in an unusually loud, somewhat panicky voice.

<Reinforcing, Jimmy. Hold on!>

The demons seemed suddenly taken aback, even a bit confused. *<He blocks Us! How can he possibly have that kind of power?>*

Even with Grysta amplifying his defenses, Jimmy was under severe strain from the concerted attack of the two most powerful telepaths he'd ever come up against. He wasn't at all sure he could hold out for long.

Something deep inside his mind welled up from a half-forgotten childhood, a combination of idly acquired half-knowledge and a strength in belief he'd felt he'd long abandoned.

<In the name of the Father, Son, and Holy Ghost, I command you to depart my mind! In the name of God, get out!>

To his utter amazement, the pressure lessened, although it was still there, still strong, still capable of attack if he let down his guard.

The demons seemed thoroughly confused and frantically sought to regroup.

<What are you that you can withstand and dare command Us?>

<An Irishman, you spawn of the Snake! We Irish have a way with snakes.>

The reference went completely past the demons. *<He is infected,>* said the female demon. *<He has a parasite which controls him! I read it in the minds of the others!>*

<To whom do We speak?> they asked him. *<To the host or the master?>*

All the old lore that he'd somehow absorbed during the times he'd sneaked into Father Donovan's private library seemed to come instantly to the fore.

<I am James McCray. What are your names, demons?>

They didn't answer, which fit. To know the name of a lesser demon was to have some control over it, or so the old books had maintained.

"You all right, McCray?" Lankur asked.

He nodded. "I think so, Cap. Me and the boys, here, are just havin' a little get-acquainted session."

"Who are they?"

"Well, they're not too polite and they won't give me their names, but as to *what* they are—oh, you wouldn't believe me if I told you."

<I am Astaroah,> said the male demon at last, *<and My companion is Tahovah.>*

McCray smiled, feeling more confident, although he whispered, "Keep me blocks up, Grysta, girl." To the demons he sent, *<Now, strictly telepath-to-telepath, you and I know that those aren't your real names. We can't really lie convincingly, even to each other, can we?>*

They were mighty strong telepaths, though, clearly not limited to the conscious band and unfazed by the reflexive blocking systems that Modra and the Durquist, at least, had implemented the moment they'd been warned.

Frustrated at their inability to get McCray, the demons turned their attention to Modra, without letting up much of the pressure on the telepath as well. The empath was suddenly filled with monstrous, overwhelming waves of despair, as if all the pain inside her, all the guilt she had carried and brooded upon, was suddenly amplified a thousand times. She gave a sudden sob and moaned horribly, dropping to her knees.

"McCray! Tell them to stop it! They're *killing* her!" Lankur shouted, even as the Durquist moved near the stricken woman to aid her or prevent her from doing harm.

<In the name of God Almighty, who made even this dismal place, I command you depart from that woman!>

The demon laughed. *<Your puny God has no hold on us here! Free Us, and let Us into your mind, or she shall be beyond helping! Even now she is sunk so deep she reaches for her gun. Shoot Us—or herself. It is your choice, telepath!>*

"Stop that!" Molly shouted at the demons. "You hurt her bad! You stop that now!"

Frankly, they had forgotten about Molly, the poor syn who was along for the ride. Forgotten, too, that she also was an empath.

Molly walked forward on her two hoofed feet and faced the demons. "You look like me, but you *bad* inside!"

Jimmy, for the life of him, couldn't figure out why the hell the same waves of terrible despair didn't fell Molly as well. Maybe, just maybe, the demons couldn't use anything that wasn't already there, and Molly was too simple and childlike to have those things within her that were being amplified. Until now, she'd never actually *seen* a demon, nor had any real concept of what they looked like; to her, the creatures seemed just another kind of syn, the evil sort. Although they really looked nothing like her, the somewhat goat-like lower half and the tiny horns *did* make her seem some kind of opposite of what was inside the pillars.

Molly turned to Modra and laid her long, four-fingered right hand on the sobbing woman's head. Slowly, Modra seemed to grow calmer, more in control, almost as if Molly were drawing the hostile empathic waves striking the Terran woman into her own self, where they were harmlessly dissipated. Modra now stared only into Molly's eyes and as she slowly got to her feet a strange smile and sweet expression replaced the pain on her face.

<Holy shit! Modra looks like a love-struck kid!> Grysta commented.

"Shut up, Grysta!" Jimmy snapped. "I need all your concentration right now."

Lankur was as confused as the others—including the demons—but he was, as always, in full control of himself. "Durquist! Lead them past these bastards and out the back! McCray! You think you can make it past them?"

"I'll make it," he responded. *<Hail Mary, full of grace,*

blessed art thou among women, and blessed be the fruit of thy womb, Jesus. . . !>

Slowly he edged his way around the pillars.

The demons were suddenly driven to near panic. *<Wait! We will talk fairly and with no other tricks! Come back!>*

<Sorry, you black-hearted bastards,> Jimmy shot back as he went past. *<Stand there and rot in your plastic prison for another ten thousand years like you deserve!>*

As soon as he was down the corridor and into the next chamber he felt the pressure lift so completely it was as if someone or something had thrown a switch. Tris Lankur saw his relief and asked, "How are you feeling?"

"Sweatin' like a stuck pig, but I think we showed 'em!" the telepath replied. "How's Modra?" He shot a probe to the empath's mind and got back such a tangle of confusion he didn't try long. *Sweet Jesus! Modra's turned on hotter than a neutron star!* he realized suddenly. *And she's got the hots for Molly!*

Molly turned, assuming that he'd know, and smiled at him with a look of complete and utter satisfaction. "It what I do, Jimmy. It the *only* thing I do. Did I do right?"

He sighed. "Yeah, Molly, you did right, as complicated as it might be until that wears off. Durquist? You all right?"

"Indeed. I had some very odd feelings in my head and body in there, as if they were trying to figure a way in, but they did not, and there's no ill effects. I suggest we move out of here to wherever this takes us, though, before we get any more nasty surprises."

<Nobody asked if I was all right,> Grysta said grumpily. *<I got such a* headache *you wouldn't believe!>*

"Yes, let's get out of here," Jimmy agreed. "Those were strictly lesser type demons, and we were almost corned beef from *them*. If they'd gotten out of there, we wouldn't have had a prayer. And, just think, if this thing works out as it has, everyone we meet from now on will be stronger and more powerful!"

"Well, I hope you're wrong," Lankur told him. "Still, we have to find someplace out of here, and now. Preferably someplace with water and food and a lot of direct light so we can recharge the suits."

They moved down the next corridor and suddenly found themselves outside once more.

The sound was almost deafening, like the moaning of countless millions of lost and damned souls all around them and echoing here and there and back and forth and swirling around. The only thing that kept it to a mere unpleasant roar was the even greater sound of torrential rainfall. They all pulled on their helmets to keep as dry as possible.

Lankur had his wish for water, but light and food were nowhere to be seen.

The rain was so dense it was nearly impossible to see. "Which way?" the Durquist asked.

"Left, me boy!" Jimmy McCray came back. "The ancient word in one of the old tongues of my world was *sinister,* and, around here, that seems just the way to go!"

DEATH AND REDEMPTION IN HELL

"**G**ET HER VISOR DOWN!" GUN ROH CHIN snapped as the rain and noise engulfed the Mizlaplanian party.

"In and on automatic," Manya responded. "She's had quite a shock to her system, though. It is difficult to say when she will come around."

"Yes, we need a telepath to get to her, and she's our telepath," Morok agreed. "By the gods! This place is going to eat up power!"

"If we don't move away from here, we might well get a telepath, only not ours," Savin noted. "If the Mycohl are behind us, they're likely to release that pair without even being coerced."

"Good point," Morok agreed. "We'll have to continue to carry Krisha, though. Can you manage it, Savin?"

"Yes, she is as light as grass leaves. But where do we go?"

Morok looked over at Gun Roh Chin. "Captain? Any suggestions?"

Chin was looking all around in the gloom and until questioned seemed lost to the others. "Oh, sorry, Holiness. I was trying to figure out where those screams and moans were coming from. What did you ask for?"

"We've got to move, Gunny! Before the Mycohl come along and release those *things*."

"Hmph! I doubt if even the Mycohl will be that stupid. They saw what we saw, and from what I know of them, volunteering to be eaten alive by your gods isn't in their required rituals. Still, you are right. We must get away from this point, and find shelter if we can. I think we can safely assume we won't be following any tracks for a while in this stuff, but clearly we go left. Let me scan the terrain."

A mental command, and his faceplate came alive with a series of markings plotting the immediate vicinity. "Well, it's not level, anyway, and there seems to be some vegetation on the rises, but it's going to be a long walk in the muck. Location transponders on, everyone, if you haven't switched on already. Be careful of any dips—form a single file, so if anyone suddenly finds themselves either in a quagmire or a raging stream or river, we might be able to get to them without going in ourselves. This ground is already far too saturated to absorb water, and it has to be going somewhere."

Morok wasn't the only one to check his suit energy levels. About five days' worth, if major demands weren't placed on the system beyond this, assuming no opportunity for a recharge. Without power, they would be at the mercy of the elements, without backup air, without major supplies, tools like the terrain scanner, communications, defenses, or weapons. Spare energy packs didn't weigh much, but had some bulk. Who would have thought when they explored the camp that they would need more than one? Certainly they would have taken spares before entering that first demon station, had they not been chased in at gunpoint. They had never needed spares for a preliminary investigation before, and he'd gone strictly by the book. That still did not leave the Lord High Inquisitor without a sense of guilt. It all was on his responsibility, no matter what.

They walked for a while, most needing some reinforcing power lift from the suit to manage in the deep, thick, black mud.

On top of it all, the place stank, the captain noted glumly, although both Savin and Manya had remarked on how pleasant it smelled. It only reinforced his lesson on their basic differences.

He was tempted to completely seal his suit and go on air purification, which wouldn't drain much power, being mostly a mechanical system, but that would also shut out much of the sounds of the place. As horrendous as the noise was, it fascinated him.

"I wonder if it rains like this here constantly?" Morok mused. "It seems an entire ocean unloads upon us."

"Doubtful, or this place would already have eroded as smooth as a ball," Manya responded. "We simply do not know enough about this place to draw conclusions beyond that, however. It might stop at any moment. It might rain only once in a hundred years like this, but for a week."

"Cheery thought, that last," Morok commented.

"Well, if we can get through this mess, I believe it will probably be about the same distance around to the next station," the captain put in. "That could take some time in this stuff, but well within our power and supply limits."

"Are you certain that there *is* another 'station,' as you call it?" Savin asked. "There was no other station on the world where we came in."

"That was either an end point, which looks doubtful from the world's nature and location, or a mistaken end point. The thing was undoubtedly built or grown elsewhere, if it's a crystal of some kind, and then transported to its end spot, as they all were, using these interdimensional pathways. It is possible that they were going to do something on that world and halted for some reason before it was done. It was, after all, well within the comfort and life zones of most carbon-based forms. Whatever, it's the end of that spur line. We're now on that same spur going backwards. Our big problem is going to be when we intersect a main line and have to choose which station to use. I believe that all the stations are enormous single crystals, hollow inside and coated with something internally, and that each is probably tuned to a specific destination by means of oscillation by some hidden power supply. It's ingenious in its own right, and totally bypasses the tricks we must pull with artificial wormholes and temporal distortion fields to effectively bypass light's speed limit."

"They certainly pick destinations that only demons could love," Morok noted.

"Maybe they didn't pick them. Maybe they have to go

where the laws of interdimensionality, whatever they are, allow them to go. Then, again, this system's been in place for who knows how many thousands or tens of thousands of years. This might have been a veritable paradise the last time anyone visited it. Or, its ecosystem might have been destabilized and altered horribly by the demons themselves doing whatever they once did here.''

"Ever the rationalist!" Manya snapped. "Not even coming face to face with demons has shaken you. We are in the Underworld, the Nether Worlds, the regions of Upper Hell in the plane where demons reign!''

"If that's true," Chin responded, "then we're all going to die here and be trapped eternally. 'Surrender all hope,' remember? The demons I've seen are carbon-based, warm-blooded life forms that eat and breathe and probably breed, considering the two sexes. They are a major life form, that's all, on a very advanced level, like the Guardians of the Exchange and the Mycohl race from which their Empire gets its name." *And the Holy Angels of the Mizlaplan as well,* he added silently, thankful during that thought that Krisha was still out.

"Indeed? And so what is your current theory, Captain Rationalist?''

"I think that in the distant past there was a war," he said honestly. "I think this group was so much crueler, so vile, that the others banded together in ancient times to defeat them. For some reason—possibly mercy, probably something more pragmatic—the demon race wasn't exterminated but rather locked away in their own continuum. Possibly that was the Mycohl's fault—they might well have sided with the demons initially, then pulled back when they saw they weren't equal partners. That would explain why that Empire still has them as objects of admiration. Shared goals and attitudes, but not shared fates.''

Morok was fascinated by this. "And what of the first station, the one that got us inside?''

"Somehow, one of the entryways to our plane got missed. As I say, it was probably a mistake or a failure, possibly too new to be on the records. That was the one the Exchange found as it expanded, and inadvertently set two of them free. Reading in their minds that those people represented an ancient enemy, the Guardians, they didn't push like those two back there to be freed. That alone implies that they can somehow be stopped, or even killed. When they were chopped out of there, they went on a rampage so that no signal that they were free could reach the Guardians until they were well away.''

"Highly rational," Manya snorted, "but it begs two questions at least. They were discovered *months* before they were freed—the size of the camp shows that. Word had to already reach those Guardians, whatever they are, that two of the ancient enemies had been found in one of their machines. Why, then, did the Guardians do nothing at all to ensure that they remained sealed? Why, particularly, did they allow a relatively defenseless expedition to go there and risk freeing the demon folk—without even a warning or at least supplying a means of defense? Second, where are those two freed demons going in such a hurry, and what purpose can they have that they would not even stop to free their companions?''

"I don't know," Chin admitted. "But as to a possible answer, I think I can provide a theory. We know the parasitic Mycohl still exist, but probably as a shadow of their former selves. Not even the people of the Exchange really know what a Guardian is. Nobody ever communicates with them except through the cymols, and the cymols are programmed like any sophisticated machine no matter how they appear. What if the Guardians no longer exist? Even some within the Exchange really believe that. What if they died out or became so ancient they no longer function? What if the cymols are actually in contact only with a library and maintenance computer? It's quite possible that all this was so ancient in time that even the Guardians, or their computer, now thinks this race mere legends. As to the other question—that's what we're here to find out.''

Chin took another step forward, then fell back on his rear end as a chunk of ground broke away under him and toppled into a roaring river below. "Hold it! We've got a problem!" he shouted.

"Are you all right?" Morok called to him.

"All safe but my dignity," he responded. "I'm going to have to slide backwards a bit to be safe, though.''

"Do you need a hand?" the Stargin asked.

"No! Stay back, just be still. I'll manage. *Oof!* I'm all right, now. I almost fell into that thing, though, and who knows where I'd have wound up before I stopped?''

Picking himself up and approaching again, more cautiously, he turned on his night beam and radar system and saw a massive, swollen river, black with the mud it was washing away, churning and bubbling and rushing on into the dark at breakneck speed.

''We are not going to get across *that* without flying,'' Morok noted glumly.

''*They* got across,'' Gun Roh Chin said flatly, ''and they didn't fly on those leathery wings in this weather and in this atmosphere, either. That means that there is a crossing point somewhere.''

Savin surveyed the torrent. ''Possibly—but where?''

''Where else? To the left! And watch it! This thing could twist and bend at any point, and there are bound to be feeder streams. Stay at least three or four meters in from the bank, and keep it in mind always!''

After more than two hours moving along the river's edge, however, even the captain began to wonder if he'd been wrong this time. Now, though, their route was not only straight, but up, and more dangerous because of it. Although the slope soon became bare rock, simply because all of the soil had been washed from it, the slope was increasingly steep and slippery, and water was running off it in all directions.

Suddenly his locator indicated a change, slightly to the right, near the river now dangerously far below. It appeared to be a ledge, nearly flat, with large boulders or perhaps structures on it. Too tired and too worried to go farther, Chin made for it and guided them to it.

At first glance it did appear to be just a jumble of huge, oddly shaped rocks, but on closer examination it proved to be some sort of deliberate arrangement. The rocky slope appeared sedimentary, its layered appearance much like shale or slate, but these great rocks were igneous, granite-like formations. Great pillars, now weathered into grotesque forms of their original selves, had been arranged by someone into a circular shape perhaps twelve meters across the arc, then sunk deep into the existing rock, and had been joined by capstones at one time. Not all the pillars still stood, and only two or three capstones, but the original look of the place was clear.

In the center was a smaller area, with five pillars much like the outer ring only shorter, and capped by a single stone that once had a well-defined shape but which now looked like some ancient version of a misshapen pillow. Unlike the outer ring, though, the important thing was that the single inner capstone still stood, water rushing off its twisted top in all directions forming almost a curtain, yet not going inside. Instead, a nearly imperceptible slope and channels carried it away, out of the structure, out beyond the ledge, to collect and plunge into the river now perhaps a hundred meters below.

"Want me to check it out?" Manya asked them.

"No need," the captain replied tiredly. "I think there is nowhere else we can expect to find even *that* much shelter, and we need it badly. Any demons or other horrors left behind by whatever ancient people built it had better be prepared to fight me for a spot."

It wasn't very high, which was one reason it had weathered better than the outer ring. The captain was not very tall, and he had to stoop to enter. Even Manya, the shortest of them, was barely able to get in without a lot of effort, and, as for Savin and Morok, they had to crawl under. With Krisha's limp body between them, there was barely enough room for all of them, and it was damp and smelly and ugly looking, but the rain, blocked a bit by the hillside and channeled by the slope, didn't get in to them, save when an occasional gust of wind would bring a brief spray or shower.

"Gunny, neither you nor Savin has had any sleep in more than two days," Morok noted. "I am so contorted here that I might as well lie on the stone here and keep watch. Manya, you will relieve me. If anyone else approaches, you'll know. I intend to fire first and *then* raise an alarm."

"I will not argue with you for a moment, Holiness," the captain responded, suddenly feeling the full, crushing weight of just how tired he really was. Within minutes, he was so sound asleep he was dead to *any* universe or world.

Morok leaned more on his faith than his reason to get through the next few hours. Lying there, staring out into the tremendous, steady rain, listening to the roar of the downpour, the echoing answering roar of the river below, and, through it all, those eerie, incessant screams, shrieks, and moans that seemed even louder in this ancient place, it was difficult for him to remain with the intellectual explanations, theories, and rationalizations of the captain which he *much* preferred, and far easier to believe that Manya was indeed correct: that this was Hell, and those were the shrieks and agonized moans of the eternally damned.

Krisha came out of her dark, dreamless near coma with a sudden rush, as if she were immersed in water and fighting to reach the surface before she drowned.

When she did, the sudden onrush of awful sounds and equally unpleasant smells frightened her for a moment, and she tried to raise her head. Doing so brought dizziness and a headache that was beyond belief, and she sank back down again and hesitantly reached out with her mind.

Touching first the sleeping minds of those nearest her and then Morok, she smiled and gave a sigh of relief.

I'm alive! She rejoiced in the realization, and in that moment she found the peace and joy and love that only the Blessed shared. Gone, totally vanished, was the self-pity, the doubt, the horrible inner pain with which she'd lived most of her adult life. It all seemed so ugly, so—*trivial.* So much joy flooded her that she felt tears coming to her eyes. She prayed thanks to the gods for making her a priestess of the One True Faith, awed by the way they had cared so much about her to manipulate her to this point—and to have demons as the instruments of her cleansing and her salvation!

She had become as the First Mother, cleansed of sin, beyond the ability of anyone or anything to tempt her.

The demons had entered her and overwhelmed her ability to block, throwing aside all her resistance as if she had no power at all, and they had probed down to the very core of her soul. One by one they dredged up and cataloged her sins, both the ones she had committed before her ordination and the ones she lusted after in her mind during those subsequent years of suffering. And, one by one, they had tempted her with the ability to actually do every one.

They had offered her great power: the power to reign over vast numbers of people as a goddess of sin and lust, to be adored and worshiped by all, to indulge her every fantasy and whim. More, they had sent visions making her body feel what those sensations would be like, to know raw power and no limits upon it.

And, as only a telepath could know, she understood that they would have done what they offered to her. And although she knew that no power in her universe could undo the restrictions of ordination, she also knew that here, in the demons' universe, right then and there, in the presence of the demons, she could in fact have broken them. She had raised and armed her pistol just to test it out, and she *knew* at that instant that she could have done it, could have freed them, committing what had to be the ultimate sin, and at that moment her soul would have gone to them, and she would have become their goddess, their anointed one, and built temples in their name, and ruled over vast numbers of worlds for countless centuries to come.

Not even Savin could have knocked her out fast enough to keep her from shooting, although he would never believe that. In that moment of mind-link with the demons, she was also linked to the other minds in the chamber, Savin's included, and while the Mesok's action was mostly unthinking reflex, she had just enough warning.

In that ever-so-brief microsecond of ultimate decision, she had made it. *Better to die a humble chattel slave within the blessing of the gods than to reign in the depravity and evil of Hell!*

And in that same split second, it was as if all of the darkness and sinful thoughts and pain within her flowed out of her, back and into the demons. Having seen the pettiness and insignificance of all her old lusts and desires, she no longer wanted any of them. Having freely refused all that sin could offer, temptation was no longer possible.

For the first time, she realized she was in her environment suit. She gave the mental command to switch to control from auto, then set the com channel for Morok only, so as not to wake the others.

"Holy Father, I am awake," she told him.

Morok was so startled he almost started shooting. Then, realizing who it was, he switched to local response. "Child, I am squeezed in here too tight to turn around, but I feel joy that you are back with us. Shall I awaken one of the others to see to you?"

"No, Holiness, I am fine. A bad headache and a little dizziness, but I think I can get a pill out of my emergency kit without awakening anyone else."

"I'm afraid Savin doesn't know his own strength. Manya says that it was a miracle that your jaw wasn't broken. Even so, I'm afraid you've lost or chipped some teeth, and you're going to have a very bad bruise for a while."

"So *that's* what that is!" She rolled her tongue back against the top row of teeth and found quite a gap along the left front. "It is not fatal," she said casually. "Poor Savin, though, will probably not be convinced that he needs to feel no guilt at having done it."

Morok was surprised. "That does not sound like you at all," he noted.

"I must tell you all that happened," she said excitedly. "It is the most wonderful thing. . . ."

He listened with growing amazement at the way her mind had sorted it out; this was not like any forced cleansing he'd ever experienced before. There was none of the rigidity, fanaticism, or self-righteous egotism that almost always resulted from such things. Rather, it was as if she was as she said: the same person, only somehow cleansed of inner sin, with an almost childlike quality in her voice and attitude, and a humility that was the most striking difference of all. It was a quality which, frankly, he'd not seen before, not in his fellow priests, and particularly not in himself.

He wondered if it would last. It might, so long as she really believed that she had rejected the ultimate temptation. In a quieter, more restful time, if such a time ever came again, he would like to put her under and find out if her version was really the true one. If so, he might well have experienced the perfection of a true mortal saint, something very rare indeed in history and unique in his long experience.

Still, he was the leader of this Arm because of his mixture of faith and pragmatism, where sainthood might be a definite liability.

"Krisha?" he asked a bit hesitantly. "Could you still kill if you had to?"

"To defend the Arm and the Holy Faith I could," she answered, her total lack of hesitation in answering that or any other question being the most striking thing about her change. "Not for any other reason."

"How's your headache?"

"Better, My Lord," she responded. "The pill is taking effect, and I don't feel as dizzy as I did."

"Since you've been out all this time, I assume you don't feel sleepy."

"No, Holy One. I am wide awake, although perhaps not at my full capabilities."

"If you feel up to it, or when, I'd like you to assume the guard duty position so I may get some rest."

She wriggled out from between Manya and Savin, got out into the rain, then came back in beside him. "I feel capable of that. My! This is an ugly place!" She looked around. "What are those fearsome sounds? It sounds like a mighty throng of people in agony."

"Take from my mind the information and events leading us to this point," he told her. "That will tell you as much as we know."

She did so, and was amazed.

"What do you think about the debate between the captain and Manya?" he asked her, genuinely curious.

"The captain is a sweet man and one of our best, but his life is among the things of physical existence, not spiritual. My mind has been joined with the soldiers of the ultimate evil. These *are* the demons about which much has been preached; of that I have no doubt. That does not mean that the captain is totally wrong, within his limited view. Surely these are the worst of the dark powers, who were put away like this, after their break with the gods. As to the machines, all but the gods require them for some things. Have not even the forces of evil required rituals and sacrifices and cursed objects and formulae to work the ultimate dark powers upon people? Are not evil spells required formulae?"

"It is a good answer," he responded sleepily. "Now, if you can only determine how to kill one, we might just get out of this place. I know the rituals that banish them to Hell, but, all things considered, those are sort of academic right now."

Morok was silent for a while and she thought he'd sunk into sleep, but, suddenly, he called, "Krisha?"

"Yes, My Lord?"

"What made you, of all people, reject the ultimate temptation? If they were convinced that it was a true bargain, there are very, very few who could. Was it because you did not believe that they would honor their promises?''

''No, My Lord, I was and remain convinced that they would have, at least to the degree that they could. I remain unconvinced that they were as powerful in their own hierarchy as they made themselves out to be. Is it not written that Hell keeps all its bargains, but exacts the greatest price?''

''Yes, that is so.''

''When every desire, every craving or lust, that I had ever had was paraded before me, I suddenly realized the truth of what my teachers had told me: that every one was selfish, inward, for me and me alone. I had been blinded to the greater needs of others by this total selfishness. By following the Holy Way, billions upon billions of thinking creatures had achieved a society of peace, of plenty, and of selflessness; a society where giving was valued over all else. What the demons offered was taking, to the torment and suffering of the masses. They made me realize that my sins were the same as theirs, and came from their corruption. Up to now, my selfishness had harmed only me; now they proposed that it harm whole worlds. For what? For the selfish, temporary gratification of animal lusts? My own desires seemed trivial, even obscene when magnified thus. In the end, their way is corruption and slow death; ours leads to perfection and contentment. When I saw that what so pained me was like them, I was repulsed. I cast it out. I gave it back to them. I became free.''

He marveled at her response, and began to really believe that through descent into Hell she had become sanctified. Still, he couldn't help but wonder how helpful a saint would be in a gunfight.

''It is no use, Captain, I cannot make it up that slope in the rain,'' Desreth said flatly. ''It is simply too slippery, and the rock flakes off as I try and dig into it.''

Josef didn't like that at all. The Corithian was his primary weapon, his invincible warrior.

''Perhaps we can go around,'' Tobrush suggested. ''Find a better area.''

''In this mess? We'd be lost before we went half an hour without the river as a guide mark,'' he responded, ''and most likely be well off any possibility of finding the next station. Robakuk—can you lift him all the way?''

"Impossible, sir," the Thion responded. "Although weight isn't in and of itself a limiting factor, concentration and duration are. I can lift Desreth, or I can climb, but not both, and I do not believe I can get him up in stages, particularly as I can't totally see what I'm doing now. The instrumentation is of no value in a mental Talent; if I took the time to read it, even for a moment, I'd lose him. No, sir—under these conditions, it's beyond my limits."

Josef sighed. "Then, as much as I dislike it, Desreth, you will have to find your own way and catch us. You aren't limited by suit power as we are, but you have your com pack and can keep us located by the transponders. If you make the station first, hide and wait for us. Because of our position, I doubt if we can do the same for you, though. You will either have to beat us or catch us."

"Understood," the Corithian responded. "Go, before you are washed over or mired in the mud."

Tobrush looked no more able to climb than Desreth, but the Julki environment suit had provisions for extending massive quantities of the tendrils through openings in the suit if necessary. Secretions through the tendrils allowed it to gain a sure, sticky hold on the rocks; massed tendrils within the forward and rear parts of the suit allowed them to bunch and form like tentacles, giving the creature a grip. It was not the best of all solutions, but suit designers couldn't possibly imagine every situation.

Robakuk had no such problems. Special transfer pads at the base of his six legs, which had their own secretions, gave him a sure grip no matter what. An obvious problem, Thion suit designers had created transfer pads that could ooze the secretion to the feet of the suit while permitting nothing back in. That left Josef and Kalia to depend mostly on their own footing.

Tobrush lumbered steadily forward and up the rocks, but suddenly stopped. "Mizzies ahead! Not far! The telepath's on watch! Seems like the others are asleep, but they won't be in a minute."

A sudden blue-white blast from their right struck rock just above them and sent splinters flying down.

"Ledge, maybe ten meters up and twenty over!" Kalia shouted. "Some kind of rocks!"

"Keep down, everybody!" Josef cautioned. "Tobrush, can you scan their positions?"

"Yes. Some sort of primitive ruin. Excellent cover, but they are all bunched up. They have more cover from fallen stones, but they're not in the best of all positions. The river's at their back, and they're up against what's pretty close to a sheer wall. This is the only way out."

"No good, not in this foul weather," Josef replied. "They can wait us out and hope they get lucky with some shots, while we have to waste most of our power trying to dig them out. Sooner or later some smart godmonger's gonna figure out how to bring some of this rock down on us." He did an instrument scan. "Damn! Can't get above them, either, without allowing them too much time for clean shots. I'd try it in the clear, but with all this water and everything so slippery there's not a chance."

"They're wide awake and pretty well deployed now," Tobrush reported. "It would be murderous crossfire. That's about all I can get, though. I'd swear that telepath of theirs has increased her power by a huge factor. Either that or my brush with our friends back there has weakened mine. She's thrown a pretty fair block over all of them. I'm only getting intermittent images. I wish *I* could do that!"

"Can we go wide of them?" Josef asked.

"Don't think so," Kalia replied. "Check your scans. It's a dead drop over there and a waterfall comin' down. In back it looks almost straight up."

"I could get up there that way," Robakuk suggested. "The only danger is the waterfall, and the rock seems bowed in behind it. If I can withstand the water enough to get behind it, I could go right up."

"Yeah, but they'll know what you're gonna do," Kalia pointed out. "Just 'cause Hairy Brain over there can't cut it don't mean their telepath ain't readin' us loud and clear right now!"

"Won't matter," the Thion responded. "They can't shoot at me while I'm going up, and once I'm on top I can drop anything I like on them at will without their being able to even see me. *That* ought to flush them right into your guns no matter what.''

"All right—do it, then!" Josef snapped. "I don't want to be here like this any longer than I have to!"

Robakuk headed to the left and was quickly lost from sight.

"Yeah, and what happens if that overgrown dung fly falls to his death?" Kalia wanted to know. "Too bad he can't levitate himself!"

"Let him try first!" Josef snapped back, irritated. There was no way he was going to let those bastards get out of that trap of theirs if he could help it. If necessary, he'd go back and make a deal with those monsters in the station before he'd do that!

Tobrush surveyed the upward terrain with instruments. "I can't understand why they haven't tried to knock us off by firing at the outcrops above us."

"Don't give 'em no ideas!" Kalia warned sharply.

Josef looked up and surveyed the same section. "Because, if they miss, they give us a pile of rubble for cover right on their only exit," he replied, then stopped. "Now, that's a thought! It's dangerous, but if we can move back and aim correctly, we might be able to knock down that big overhang there. If it stays in one piece it's gonna just keep coming, but if it shatters when it hits the flat area . . . It's worth the risk, damn it!"

He ran the problem through the suit computer and it gave recommended places to be and points to shoot at to achieve the desired result. He had better than a sixty percent probability that it would fall right—and safely. The odds were almost even that it would come off in one piece and continue down, or that they themselves would still get swept over with it.

"Sending coordinates!" Josef called. "Get in position and let the suit computer do the aiming."

Up in the ruins, Krisha picked up the thought and reported, "They are going to shoot at the overhang to give them some cover, and some creature of theirs is climbing the sheer wall out of sight and range with the idea of getting above us."

Gun Roh Chin, still feeling the effects of the trek and the sleep, was amazed at her calmness and almost clinical clarity. Savin, the empath of the group, was equally startled at Krisha's total lack of fear and tension. *Must be some of Morok's hypno work,* he thought approvingly. Still, he wasn't at all certain that he'd ever know for sure, considering.

"I might be able to get over and foul that up," Manya suggested. "Krisha says that the Corithian isn't with them."

"They're on instruments, Manya!" Morok reminded her. "If they'd been in full battle gear the first time, you wouldn't be here. Your Talent doesn't extend to fooling a computer."

Manya said nothing for a while, but took her own measurements of the outcrop in question. "Let them do it," she said at last. "Tie in to my suit; everyone but Krisha, who'll keep the way covered and remind them we're still here."

"What do you have in mind?" Morok asked her.

"If Krisha can give us a signal when they start to shoot, we shoot, too. They'll free it, all right, but we'll deflect it a bit right onto them!"

"Krish, can you do it?" Morok called.

"No problem," she responded. "I'll send a signal through the suit link to you. If you're in position, Manya's system should do the rest."

The odd thing was, it *wasn't* a problem. Even she was amazed at her sudden clarity of mind and added power. Never before had she been able to so effectively manage so many things at once. She'd faced this telepathic creature out there before, on a mental level, but where before it had seemed equal in power to her, now it seemed far weaker, almost as if the Mycohlian's telepathic band was some kind of solid, physical thing that she could sense and deflect. She'd managed that for very short periods and with some disorientation, but never this long or this easily—and certainly not while also covering a range, checking instrument readings, and keeping tabs on the rest of the Arm. It was almost—*supernatural.*

Her reading of the Mycohl almost, but not quite, confirmed her preconceptions. That girl—she was all emotion, and the emotions she had were almost exclusively repugnant. Blind, unreasoning hatred, revenge—against nothing and everything— and an absolute worship of power. She liked—no, *loved*—to kill. So eaten up inside, she didn't have to go to Hell, she was already all those demons liked.

The man was almost the opposite, yet she could find the demons in him as well. Cold, cruel, yet intellectual; a man so self-centered that he viewed all others, even his own team members, as mere tools of his own aims. The kind of man who never did anyone a favor without ulterior motives.

The creature climbing the wall was about out of her range now, but she had gotten enough of a look into its mind to sort a little bit of it out. The thought patterns were strange, nearly impossible to follow, but at the core she recognized the demon once again. It thrived in tension and loved excitement, thrills, taking chances. Somehow she got the strangest idea that, to the thing, this business was *fun*.

Only the Mycohl telepath was closed to her, and then only with effort. She was certain, though, that if she ever got through those defenses she'd see the demon there, as well.

Not, to her surprise, that the demon wasn't in her own team as well. She hadn't noticed it before because she herself had been so full of it that she couldn't recognize it in others. Yet even Morok had that core of coldness within that not only drove him to this sort of position but which made him actually *enjoy* battle, enjoy exposing heretics, spies, and traitors, enjoy consigning them to punishment. At least he *knew* his own failings, but they were very much there and, in spite of some guilt, he didn't really want to get rid of them. Manya's self-righteousness and intolerance came from her egomania; her need to believe that whatever she thought or did was the will of the gods because she was entitled to it.

And Savin—there was an animalistic quality to Savin that she had always dismissed as part of his people's nature and upbringing, and perhaps it was. But, deep down, Savin loved instilling fear in those he dealt with beyond the Arm; he had tortured and killed in the name of the Church and he reflected on those experiences with fondness and nostalgia.

Only Gun Roh Chin remained as much of a cipher as ever, and she was thankful for that. She wouldn't like to find the demon in him; she felt closer to him than to any other person, but she had no lust for him. In some past or future incarnation, they might well have been or might yet be lovers, but for this life a platonic love was now more than enough for her.

"Mark to shoot!" she sent.

Almost simultaneously, the two separate groups began firing at the same rocky outcrop from different angles. The rock shuddered, reddened, then began to tilt forward.

Josef was almost too slow. "They're trying to deflect it!

Trajectory change! *Shoot!*'' Molkur's bones! That Mizzie bunch was *good*! Almost *too* good!

The rock mass, freed, began to slide down, and they kept the pressure on as the Mizlaplan team also adjusted. Fragments broke off and flew in all directions, one just missing Tobrush by the width of a tendril. It remained, however, essentially intact, and struck the flat region edge on, teetered for a moment on edge, then overturned and continued sliding on a thin curtain of water past the Mycohl and on down the hill.

"I begin to wonder if we aren't out of our league here," Tobrush commented worriedly.

"Well, there's still Robakuk!" Josef snapped, trying to avoid thoughts like that himself. "There's precious little they can do about *him*!"

That thought was on the minds of the Mizlaplanians as well. "If only this cursed rain would stop, or even let up," Morok grumbled. "The gravity's a bit more than I'd like, but the thermals are excellent, and with that cliff back there to get off of, I think I could climb that high."

"That's their TK man up there, too," Gun Roh Chin pointed out. "Has to be, if the hypno, telepath, and empath are all down here as Krisha says. If he gets his eyes on us he can bring these columns down all around us, maybe sweep us right off this rock."

"I'll nail him if he so much as sticks his ugly head over that ledge," Savin growled.

"He might not have to," Chin pointed out. "If he's got anything big and loose up there, or anything he can blast loose, he can add rocks of all sizes to this rain and do the same thing with little effort, no exposure, and the same effect."

Morok sighed. "I can try a flight, rain or not."

"You will *not*, Holiness!" the captain snapped. "First, you'd have to be out of your suit to use your wings, which means no protection. If he's up there by the time you can climb to that level—*if* you can get that high with this rain and added gravity driving you down—you'd be very little competition for his instruments, suit, and weapons. I realize that even Holy Law permits suicide under various conditions, but not under *these* conditions. We need you too much."

"Yes, but do you have any other suggestions?" Morok

asked him, secretly more than a little relieved to be talked out of it.

Savin looked up at the apparently sheer wall. "I might make a stab at climbing it. The thing's slightly concave; that, the winds, and the ledge keep the direct, driving rain off."

"I think I left my pitons in my other suit," the captain commented dryly. "Along with the rope and the null-gravity boots."

"I'm serious," the Mesok replied. "While we get along well enough in daylight, my people are basically nocturnals. I grew up in mountains, too. With the rain not as much of a factor, I think I can make my way up there. It's not nearly as smooth as you think it is. There are small bits of shale sticking out just about the whole way. I think I can make it."

"Talk about suicide!" Manya put in. "And the Mycohl creature has a good twenty-minute head start!"

"Won't matter," Savin told her. "He has a lot further to go than I do. Besides, what choice do we have?"

Gun Roh Chin surveyed the cliff with his human eyes and couldn't see how it might be done, but he said, "You're right. If you think you can do it, you must try. Everybody else, we must give the ones down here enough to do that they don't see Savin go up. And we must lose no more time debating."

"All right," Morok said hesitantly. "The gods be with you, Savin."

"Everybody!" the captain called. "Be ready. Shoot at any of that trio down there that so much as pokes a finger or a tentacle or whatever they've got into view!"

Savin put his huge, clawed hands together in a silent prayer, then surveyed the cliff. After a moment, he began climbing, and they began randomly shooting.

Below, Tobrush said, "Something's up. I can't tell what, though. There's none that can climb out of there as Robakuk could, though."

"Maybe they prayed some climbing gear into existence," Josef responded irritably. "After all this, I'd believe almost anything."

Kalia had different ideas. "If they're shooting at anything that moves, give them things to shoot at," she suggested. "If they're basically on automatic, they'll all go for any available target. That might be all the time I need."

"For what?" Josef asked her.

"There's a ton of rubble where that rock crashed down. Just not high enough or close enough to do us no good. If they're all firin' over *that* way, say, I can make it. Then we got a crossfire."

"No good," Tobrush told her. "As soon as you got the idea, their telepath knows it. They'll be waiting for you."

"Then get some guts and fire at the fucking telepath!" she snapped back. "They don't know where I'll be comin' from 'cause I don't know myself. All this shit looks the same, anyway. They won't have nothin' to use to lock onto me before I'm there. That means whoever draws me'll be in freehand mode, and I ain't too damn impressed with their freehand shootin'."

"I believe she thinks she's still a trifle underdone," Tobrush commented wryly. "Or perhaps she wants her right to match her left."

"Screw you, Turdface! If you hadn't hung back all scared to death at the shuttles, maybe you'd'a nailed that bitch and saved me the burn!"

"More likely fried instead of you," the Julki responded. "Please! I'm having a difficult enough time maintaining this block so at least *one* of us can keep thoughts secret."

"Shut up, both of you!" Josef snapped. "Robakuk, where are you?"

"Almost all the way," the Thion responded. "It's more difficult than I thought near the top. The water's just pouring over. I have to maneuver over and get up at the wrong point. Give me another fifteen minutes."

Josef turned back to Kalia. "Wait fifteen minutes and maybe what you suggest won't be necessary."

"Yeah? Even if he makes it, you're gonna have maybe five really mad and desperate professional guns comin' at us from the high ground, and who knows what they got they ain't showed yet? You *need* the crossfire and you know it."

"I don't want to lose anybody else, not after Desreth," he came back. "And we don't have a field hospital here."

"If they get out of there, it won't matter how many you got left," she responded.

He sighed. "All right. On your own head be the consequences if you blow this, though. Tobrush—concentrate all fire on the telepath; I'll do the same. They'll either have to come back at us to protect her or we'll bring those stones right down on her head.''

"Understood. By her, too, I assume. Give me your suit control.''

"Huh? Why?''

"I have an idea, and if I tell you, *they'll* have the idea.''

"All right,'' Josef agreed. He didn't like surrendering control of anything of his to anybody, but this seemed a special case.

Up at the ruins, Krisha called, ''They're going to try and get the girl across by opening up on us. I can't tell from where because it all looks the same. They're going to target me, so let them. Concentrate everything on keeping that girl from crossing. The telepath has something added planned, but I can't tell what. Be on guard and ready to shoot.''

"*Now!*'' Tobrush shouted, and both he and Josef raised just enough to get shots in toward the ruins as Kalia began a mad, low dash, firing wildly into the same place.

To Josef's own surprise, both he and Tobrush opened up not with powerful pulse shots but on wide beam stun, side to side. Even as he shot he realized how clever the Julki had been; they managed to cover almost the entire area. It wouldn't do a lot of real harm no matter who it hit at this distance, but it sure would keep them under cover and wild.

It was the first time the Mizlaplanians had been really caught napping. Expecting concentrated fire on Krisha, they'd opened up almost immediately, only to be hit by the wide beams. Manya felt her left side go slightly numb and it took her mind momentarily off shooting, even as her suit repulsors absorbed and deflected most of the energy. Gun Roh Chin found his suit shorting and had to withdraw completely behind a pillar and go to emergency backup, while Morok received the most glancing of blows but had his instrumentation blank out for a few seconds—more than enough.

Krisha had rolled out from under the rock as soon as she'd heard Tobrush's call, just in case a lucky shot might knock out one or more of the pillars holding up that ancient rock and bring it down upon her. Like Morok, she was caught completely by surprise, and as the suit switched primarily to protection, her sensors blanked for a critical second or two, making her fire wild.

Josef and Tobrush ducked back down. "Kalia, you all right?" the leader called.

"Perfect. That was real smart, Tobrush. All is forgiven. You know, I think I could work on one of those tall stones from here, one with the roof still on it. Might get somebody."

"Save your power!" Josef snapped. "We want to be able to do more than just throw rocks at them when they come out!"

At almost that moment, Robakuk reported, "I'm up top! It's not too bad up here, either, if you don't mind the rain. There's more ruins up here, plenty of stuff to toss down. There's old trails up here, too, either dug out of or worn into the rock. They're running streams at the moment, but they show a way to go that *somebody* liked and if this rain ever stops they'll be good for traveling."

Josef was pleased, feeling that things were suddenly going his way. "Any time you're ready, we're ready. We're in position."

"Be cautious!" Tobrush warned. "When we opened up, their telepath was as surprised as the others and there was an opening. I got only three minds—the telepath's, the hypno's, and the one Kalia couldn't see. We know there's also a null there, but they had an empath as well. I got a very odd, far more distant, signal from him, and while they all were aware of each other during our attack, none of them wondered or asked about him."

"Is he still there?" Josef asked, suddenly worried.

"Telepathy isn't directional," Tobrush reminded him. "I can't really tell the *where* of things, and can only sort who's thinking what when I can see them. But there is a difference in *amplitude* when someone's further away. It wasn't much, but experience tells me he's not with the others."

All along, Robakuk had to fight the instinctive urge to find some cover and just hold tight until the downpour stopped. Now on top of the hill, he felt the full force of the driving rains and winds.

The ruins ahead were *very* strange, but offered some shelter as well as, well, ammunition. These stones were in no better shape than the ones below, but, having been a more complex structure, it was harder to get the plan and the sense of them. There seemed to be concentric rings within rings, and in the gloom and rain it wasn't very difficult to imagine that some of the weathered, misshapen pillars were the remnants not of supports but of statues of weird and impossible creatures. It also wasn't difficult for the imagination to detect movement where there was none; the place had that kind of effect on him, and it made him nervous and jumpy in spite of himself, although he would never admit that to his comrades below.

He began looking around for loose stones. Unlike the one below, there did not seem to be any capstones here; it was just pillars, arranged almost like a round target, originally set only one or two meters apart and narrowing as you moved toward the center. Many were missing now, of course, but there wasn't nearly as much debris as he'd hoped, possibly because the rains or whatever other weather might have struck this exposed position had taken the lesser stuff over the side and into the river, while the larger pieces had been almost chemically bonded to the slate floor.

The Thion also had their own ancient demon legends, which didn't help matters a bit. The carvings and mental pictures of the creatures weren't very close to the real thing, filtered as they were through an entirely different physiology, but they'd always been fierce, huge, and bipedal in the legends. That last had caused the death of many spacefarers when the Thion world had been discovered; in the Thion mind, being a biped was synonymous with demonic powers. It didn't help that the Mycohl had a positive feeling toward demons, either; many had died before an accommodation had been reached.

Josef's voice came to him over the suit intercom. "Robakuk? What's the situation up there?"

"The ruins are very close to the edge, and the standing stones quite close together," he reported. "I am having to thread my way through them to the overhang." *What was that?*

He whirled, certain that something had moved within the rows of stones. It took half a minute before he was satisfied that nothing in fact was there. He turned, and shortly was in the center of the formation.

There was no doubt that the central area had once held a statue; part of it still stood, although aside from having two legs it was impossible to get any other details. In front of the statue was a great stone, clearly carved in some ancient times but now so misshapen that no one could have told its original shape. Even so, he knew from Mycohl customs that this must surely have been an altar to some long-forgotten deity. With the beating rain and the eerie screams and moans that had to be the wind but sounded like no wind ever heard, it was no wonder he was jumpy.

The ancient ruin didn't go all the way around, as the Thion discovered when he abruptly came very close to the ledge. It had once; you could see that it wasn't designed this way. Long ago the shale had been eaten away by the fierce weather and about twenty percent had almost certainly fallen into the river below. One day, perhaps soon, the overhang that was left would collapse and fall onto the other ruins below, perhaps taking them all eventually into that roaring canyon.

He attempted a peek over the edge and got several shots fired at him for his trouble. The big head turned and focused on a mass of rubble and broken stone. It quivered, then began to slowly rise perhaps a hair above the shale, then moved forward as if pushed by some earth-moving machine.

There was a sudden sound behind him, and he turned, the rock dropping just at the edge, a few pieces going off. Robakuk had just time enough to turn and see a huge figure in a golden suit looming monstrously against the ruins before the three quick pulse shots struck him and pushed the Thion's body over the edge instead.

The body missed the river and landed instead atop the inner capstone of the smaller ruins below, startling the ones who were there. Both Manya and Morok gave cries of alarm at the sight. The smoldering, crushed body of the Thion had landed on its back, and in after-death reflexes the huge legs kept lashing out at the sky and rain.

There was a sudden, brief rise of the shrieks and moans to a crescendo that equally unnerved them all, then things faded back to normal levels.

It was Krisha who recovered first. "Savin? Are you all right?"

"Fine here. I wish I could figure out some way to lift the rest of you up. Sorry about the silence, but I had to wait until the thing started to lift or throw something before I dared expose myself and shoot. Until it was concentrating on lifting and moving, if it had caught sight of me it could have lifted and pushed *me* around.''

''That's all right,'' she told him. ''Can you get around and above the others? We're in a bad situation here. That rock the thing moved is right at the edge and we're getting small bits and pieces falling now. That stuff could start coming down at any moment, with or without the rain.''

''I'll see what I can do. I acted as soon as I could.''

''I know. Without you we'd already be goners, but it's only half the job.''

Gun Roh Chin's pulse had come down to what he considered maybe three times normal. ''It's five to three now. One of them will have to target Savin, who might not be able to hit much but can make things mighty uncomfortable for them just shooting randomly down. If we could concentrate our fire on the other two, we might be on them before they could get off a solid series of shots.''

''Let's borrow their trick,'' Krisha suggested. ''Two of us could move forward blanketing them and maybe knocking out their instruments. The other two could shoot to kill, with Savin taking advantage of what we're doing down here to get some clear shots at the pair just down the hill. If the creature's concentration is broken in the attack, I may be able to engage it mind-to-mind and neutralize it.''

''I don't like that last part,'' Gun Roh Chin responded. ''You don't know anything about the creature, but it clearly knows Terrans. You might well have a far more powerful gun, but if *it* has all the ammunition, not only your mobility but your sanity is at risk. Don't take it on unless you absolutely must, but the rest of the plan is excellent.'' *Except that I'm getting much too old for this sort of thing,* he added to himself.

Slightly below, the Julki had no intention of engaging in a mental duel. ''That's the second time they've made the same mistake,'' Tobrush commented. ''Leaving their suit intercoms unencrypted.'' He fed the intercept in translation to the other two.

''Yes, but what can we do about it?'' Josef asked worriedly. ''We're outgunned and outflanked.''

Josef looked up at the cliff top. ''If *he* can shoot *me*, then *I* can shoot *him*,'' he noted. ''I suggest that you take a full sighting, sweeping the possible field of fire back and forth through which they have to come, then get down and let your gun go on automatic while you remain under cover. Kalia, do the same from your angle. I will target-sweep the cliff no matter what happens down here. When he shows, I should be able to get a lock on him before he gets a lock on me. If I get him, you two keep the pressure on and I will try and take advantage to cross. With luck, you might get one or two and that will slow them down or make them regroup. From that point we'll be able to effectively cover you, Tobrush, in coming across."

"Well, we don't have time to argue about it," Kalia snapped, "'cause I think they're about to come at us!"

THE
EYES
HAVE IT

"**H**OLY SHIT! WHAT THE HELL'S GOING *ON* UP there ahead?" Modra Stryke asked. She'd shaken off the effects of Molly's broadcast just enough to realize all that had happened and was trying to shake the rest out.

"Exactly what you said," Jimmy McCray responded. "We're too far away for many details, but from what I *can* pick up from here, the Holies are in deep dung and fighting their way out through inferior but very well positioned Mycohl forces, all taking place in Hell, of course, if that is indeed what this is."

"We are thus faced with an ethical conundrum," the Durquist commented, ignoring the attempted humor. "We are still far enough away that, with all that going on, they probably won't even notice us. We could just wait it out and deal with the survivors, whoever they are. Or, we are alternatively close enough to intervene if we decide right now—but on whose side? I've never found any of the Mycohl particularly nice folks, and the kind of ones who would come into our territory so boldly are probably of the worst sort. On the other hand, they aren't boring, which the Miz certainly are—and the kind that would try and get across Mycohl to us to check out a vague distress call about demons have to be absolutely sickening fanatics.''

''I'm satisfied that we've caught up,'' Tris Lankur said. ''If we can just stay close enough to find out the result without having anything turned on us, that'll be fine with me. Besides, we don't have the reserve power to afford to get into a fight.''

''I don't think they do, either,'' McCray told them. ''I'm only getting the Mycohl side of things, and that very limited, but I get the strong idea that they were no more prepared to get stuck on this idiots' railroad than we were. With these continuous fights, they have to be running pretty low. Also, the Mycohl leader's a hypno, and I'm not sure we want him in the group right now.''

''We always wanted a hypno in the team,'' Modra commented, ''but they all want too much of a share and they always want to run things.''

<If we hold back, maybe we can finish off the survivors and get their power packs,> Grysta suggested hopefully.

''Grysta just suggested we fall on the survivors and steal their power, as well as the dead, I presume.''

''No good,'' Tris Lankur told him. ''While the suits are all based on the same stolen design—*our* design, by the way—internally, they're very different. They'll loot their own dead for what's useful anyway, just as we'd better be prepared to do if any of us gets it.''

Modra sighed. ''You mean we get to stand here in this muck and pouring rain and watch bright flashes and hear a blow-by-blow from McCray?''

''Molly think that just fine,'' the syn commented.

<First time she and I have been in total agreement since she came aboard,> Grysta put in.

Jimmy McCray shrugged. ''I'll fight if I have to, but I'm not overflowing with a desire for action,'' he told them. ''Pick an ankle-deep section of stinking mud and relax, I suppose.''

''*Go!*''
The quartet came out blasting, the wide stun lighting up the whole hillside while rock flew from in front of and near the Mycohl shooters.

At the same time, Josef and Kalia opened up on automatic, shooting single full-strength pulses in a pattern going from the edge of the hill to the cliff and back again.

Manya took a glancing hit in her left thigh and stumbled; Gun Roh Chin caught her and forced her to her hands and knees, then went to a military crawl himself. The long-legged Morok took a number of great leaps between the shots and made it to the section of hillside below the flat; Krisha, realizing as Chin had that the automatic shots were a little high, went to the military crawl as well, pausing occasionally to shoot at the girl behind the rubble, keeping her down.

Morok, now a bit below, thought he pulled something when he landed, but managed to get forward to where he could almost see the two Mycohlians shooting from below the flat.

Tobrush picked up a sudden mental image of a very familiar shape and with a start realized that it was an image of a Julki. Swiveling, the telepath was struck by a beam before any defensive fire was possible, but Morok had forgotten that his was one of the pistols on wide stun; the Julki reeled and felt some numbness but wasn't otherwise hurt.

By the time Morok made the adjustment on his weapon, both of the Mycohl were taking shots at him, forcing a slight retreat.

At that moment, Savin opened up from the hilltop, three quick bursts coming around both Josef and Tobrush. That was enough for them. "Tobrush! Kalia!" Josef shouted. "Wide stun across! I'll shoot! We're both making the crossing *now*! It's our only chance!"

Atop the hill, Savin gave an ancestral, primal growl of victory and aimed for the pair as they started across.

Suddenly something struck him in the back, then came right through the suit, grinding into his internal organs. He stiffened and screamed in agony but did not immediately fall over, as whatever it was held him like a piece of meat on a skewer. Agonizingly painful but not yet fatal, Savin roared and struggled to grab at the thing that had bored through him, but found only a metallic tentacle so strong and supple it was beyond his strength to deal with.

"There is more than one way up a hill," said a toneless, metallic voice behind him, and then he was lifted into the air and held out over the edge of the ledge, and then the tentacle withdrew, leaving him to fall, still living, to the rock below.

The shock of the attack on Savin stunned Krisha, and for a few seconds she could only watch and cry out in horror as the Mesok fell to his death. Chin, giving cover fire and helping Manya, wasn't aware of the drama above but couldn't adequately cover Krisha's lack of shot, allowing Josef and Tobrush to come all the way across, beyond Krisha, and continue on up.

"Hurry, all of you—get up here before they regroup," Desreth called. "You have only a few seconds to get up to a point where you cannot be shot directly from below. I recommend no hesitancy."

The Corithian got no arguments from the trio below.

Morok had the only clear shot at them, but, raising up to do it, he felt a sudden severe pain in his right leg and fell back down, scrambling now to just keep hold of the wet rocks and keep from sliding all the way back to the bottom.

Less than three kilometers back, on the riverbank below, Jimmy McCray sighed. "That's it," he said flatly. "Battle's over, and now it's four to four again. *Ugh!* That Mycohl woman's ugly as sin!"

"No cracks now," Modra warned.

"Yeah? Wait'll you see her."

Tris Lankur got to his feet. "Let's move up," he told them. "I think it's time we cut ourselves in."

As they approached the hill, McCray warned, "They've made us."

"Which side?" Lankur asked.

"Both of them. *Man!* That Mizlaplanian telepath is *strong!* I know she's got us because I felt the probe, but I haven't got a one of them. Not one. The Mycohl on top, though, are fine. It particularly helps that both the non-telepaths up there are Terrans. Coming in strong as a radio signal. They have the Miz bunch pretty well trapped against the wall, unable to go up or down, and they're debating whether or not to keep it that way or press on now that they're in the lead."

Tris Lankur gave the mental command to his suit to turn on the all-frequency hail and auto translator. The last simply took his words and translated them into the two interstellar commerce languages of the other Empires.

"This is Captain Tris Lankur calling all foreign parties ahead of us. You are operating illegally in our territory and represent a substantial risk to ourselves and our interests here by your presence and particularly by your fighting. We demand to know your identities and your purpose and goals for being here."

There was a pause, and then Gun Roh Chin sent, "Are you really suggesting, Captain, that this is Exchange territory?"

"It was reached through a legally claimed Exchange world on the recognized frontier in Exchange space," Lankur replied. "Since the only way you could get here was by violating our frontier, this is in fact Exchange territory under all treaties."

"That would make all the demons citizens of the Exchange," the Durquist commented dryly, for local broadcast only. "Oh, dear. I never really thought about that."

A sudden, different voice broke in. The translator didn't really put any emotional emphasis on words and phrases no matter how the original sounded, but somehow the voice sounded a little meaner and more arrogant anyway.

"Lankur, you are a freebooting team with no governmental authority stuck here in this mess just like we are," Josef noted. "If we all get out of this, you might be able to file a proper complaint against us, but if you didn't, nobody would even miss you."

"Bravado," McCray commented. "While *his* telepath is feeding him the information on *us,* the fact is that he has no more idea than we do if there's an entire army division of our people somewhere behind us. On the other hand, he isn't above thinking that if he is the only survivor, then he'll have considerable control over how the diplomatic mess is managed no matter what the truth is."

"What are you proposing, Captain Lankur?" Gun Roh Chin asked him. "I'm afraid we are a bit indisposed at the moment."

"You met those *things* back there, and I notice that even the Mycohl didn't succumb to their promises and release them. This entire thing, and those demons or whatever you want to call them, pose a potential threat to all three empires and the stability we've achieved over the centuries. It's *us* versus *them.* Any more fighting and killing each other will just work to the demons' benefit. No matter who or what follows us, the odds of any of us getting out of here alive, let alone back to our homes, is slim as it is. The odds are even worse for you, since the only way in or out that we know is through an Exchange world that, right now, is probably being transformed into an armed camp. If you have any slight hope of getting back and reporting this to your own people, we'd better work together."

"You sure about this?" Jimmy asked him. "The way I read it, *both* of those bunches have hypnos. *You* may be immune, but *we* aren't."

"Join up with a bunch of religious fanatics? You have to be kidding!" Josef came back. "Maybe they're all priests who can't sin, but under their religion there's no sin involved when you're lying, cheating, stealing and backstabbing nonbelievers. No thanks. We might be able to make a deal with you, though—once we take care of these prayermongers. Those aren't soldiers or traders down there—they're the gods-be-damned Inquisition!"

"Cooperate with demon worshipers?" Manya shot back. "Never! That would be worse than death itself! It would imperil our souls!"

Gun Roh Chin, who was in no mood to die at the moment and, in his position, very likely to do so anyway, tried to calm things down. "I have some experience with the Mycohl, Captain, being a civilian ship commander like yourself and not a priest. I've also been in the Exchange. The Mycohl respect only power and strength; any sense of honor they have, when they have it, is only to each other. Even if disarmed, which would make them useless partners, the Corithian is a force unto itself. As for my people here, I might make some guarantees, but they wouldn't be binding on the Holy Ones with me, who have their own inflexible mission."

Tris Lankur looked around at the others. "Any comments or suggestions?"

"I'm afraid I must go along with them," the Durquist said. "If there were a way around them, I'd say walk around and leave them to each other. They certainly seem to deserve each other."

Modra thought for a moment. "The Durquist's right. What we have most of all is a roadblock up there. On the other hand, we've been going crazy worrying that our power levels would run out. You realize how much power those two groups must have used coming at each other, even if only two are dead?"

"Good point," Lankur acknowledged. "McCray?"

Jimmy scanned the top of the hill with instruments. "I could probably pot at least one of them right now. Two if they start going at the Miz below."

"So? That just gives the Mizlaplanians, with their superior telepath and hypno to boot, a free hand," the captain responded.

"Not what I mean. In fact, their telepath right now is explainin' my meaning before I can say this to you. They can't get the Mizlaplanians unless we let them. Even that metal horror they have with them can be melted into scrap if we get our sights on it. They can keep us off for a while, but we've half again their power reserves. So they all sit in the rain just like us and glower at each other until Hell freezes, or they run out of power or get desperate, or they take off and live to fight another day."

Tris Lankur nodded. "What about it, Mycohl? Twenty minutes to get off that hilltop and make your way on. You've got the lead now; whatever's ahead is yours first, for all the good it'll do you. Then the Mizlaplanians move up and get the same margin. Then we're going to move in. Any moves against us, in the rear, now or in the future, and we'll intervene on the side of the other one. It's not perfect, but at least it may get us all out of the rain."

There was silence for a moment, and Jimmy said, "Their telepaths are explainin' to them how it can be verified. I don't like it, but, all things considered, it gets us moving."

The Mizlaplanians, and most particularly Gun Roh Chin, were all for the idea. Suddenly, Chin looked around. "Where is Morok?"

"Here," came the voice of the Lord High Inquisitor of the Arm of the Gods. "I've fallen halfway down. I'm afraid I've twisted, perhaps broken, something in my left leg or foot."

"We will come and get you, My Lord!" Krisha called to him. "I am certain that the Exchange people will allow it!"

"No!" he responded. "At this point I am a burden to the

Arm, and we do not know what is ahead. You must leave me here on my own until I can find a way to repair my leg and become mobile. Otherwise, caring for me will surely cause the rest of you to die."

"But, Holy One, we cannot leave you here!" she argued. "Particularly not *here*. Besides, right now I am blocking them from even knowing that you are there. If I leave, the Exchange telepath will find you."

"This will not be the first time I was left behind, nor the first time I have had that problem," he told her. "I *do* have certain Talents of my own to cover such problems as you suggest. You might be surprised. I might well be able to catch up with you later. Now it is my command that you go as soon as you are told you can safely do so. Krisha, I pass the sword of the Arm to you until such time as I can reclaim it. You cannot refuse me."

And she could not, for obedience was one of the cardinal provisions of ordination in the faith. Tearfully, she responded, "Very well, Holy Father. I obey."

"All right, we agree," Josef sent back to the Exchange team. "But we want an hour's start. It's slippery and dangerous up here and the best ways are flooded."

Tris Lankur sighed. Another long period in the mud. "All right. One hour."

"Ah! Team Two passes Team One in the Quintara Marathon!" Jimmy McCray said cynically. "They take a one-hour lead over Team Two, and who knows how long over Team Three, in dead last, as usual."

"It's a hell of a race, McCray," Modra sighed. "We don't even know where the finish line is—or if there *is* a finish line, short of death."

"Oh, it's simple," the telepath replied. "This is a race where third place might be the place to be, since, obviously, whoever is left alive at the end wins."

Up top, Tobrush caught the term and the holographic image it aroused in the mind of Stryke and the Durquist. *"Quintara,"* he said.

"Huh? What's that you said?" Josef asked, irritated at having to abandon a perfect trap.

"The demons. That's what they call them. The leader is half

Terran and half machine. Apparently he directly tapped the records from the place, even though almost all had been destroyed. The last words his counterpart said back in the first station before the demon ripped it apart was 'The Quintara—they still run!' ''

"What a bunch of bullshit!" Kalia snapped. "We ought'a just take out the Mizzies and take the rest on and be done with it. We'll have to do it sooner or later."

"Later is better in this case," Josef responded. "Besides, I am leader here. Your place is not to question but to obey."

"Yeah? Well, Your Leadership, you already led us into this hole and almost got us all killed. Maybe you ain't cut out for leadin' this kind of thing."

He turned quickly and faced her, eyes blazing, unavoidable. "Do you want me to enforce my leadership?" he asked in a dangerous tone of voice.

She felt the hypno power seeping into her mind, closing off control. "No, no. I'll go. Don't be so damned touchy!"

"I believe we should take full advantage of the hour," Desreth put in. "This does us no good here, now."

"I agree," Tobrush put in. "Did your alternate route indicate any idea of where the next station might be?"

"No, but if they are equidistant, than we have a good day and a half's journey yet."

Josef shook his head. "Uh-huh. And we don't even know this time if we're going in the right direction."

Well under an hour later, Krisha was able to say, "They're gone. Out of my range, anyway, which means out of shooting range as well."

"Why don't we just get going again?" Manya asked, irritated not only at letting the hated ones pass them but also not a little put off by Morok handing the leadership role to Krisha, of all people, instead of her. She, too, had to obey, but there was nothing in the vows about liking it, or preventing criticism.

"We will wait the full period," Krisha responded, knowing how Manya felt and feeling sorry for her that she did. This was the *last* thing the telepath wanted, either, and she would have gladly surrendered authority to Manya if she could. Captain Chin, of course, could not lead, not being under the vows, but, like Morok, she intended to defer to his own experience and wisdom where possible. "Even if it wouldn't be a good idea to show the Exchange people we keep our word, which it is, I want to give Morok all the time I can shield him to find a place where he will not be detected."

So it's "Morok" already, Manya thought sourly. *How quickly the mantle of leadership passes.* She knew that Krisha could read her mind, but she didn't care a bit.

While they passed the time, Krisha, under some questioning from Chin, explained her newfound attitudes and the reasons for them. He was impressed, and understood her. He wondered, though, if she could *keep* refusing temptations. For all her rebelliousness, she'd led, overall, a very sheltered life. This was, in fact, her first journey outside the well-regulated Empire in which she'd been born, and her first encounter with enemy aliens outside her own turf.

Still, Morok had believed, and trusted her, and Morok was no fool. He wouldn't even bet against the old fellow catching them somehow, although it was difficult to see how.

"It's time," he told them. "Move up carefully—that's still slippery and exposed as well. We've also got to remember that we're the outnumbered ones now, and the Corithian is undetectable except by instruments—and then only with luck. I wouldn't put it past them to leave the thing somewhere along the route to snare us."

"Their leader might," Krisha acknowledged, "but that girl—I don't know if any of them can completely control her. She's so sick inside, so full of hate, and she is not one to be put off carrying out her own revenge for Manya's wounds that she carries on her face. No, I fear more that the girl has no fear at all; left to herself, she would free a demon with *nothing* promised in return except our own deaths."

"Well, let's go, then," Manya grumbled.

Krisha nodded, then paused. "I can no longer hear Morok's thoughts. I do not understand, if he is too crippled to walk or climb, how he can have gotten that far away, though. Still, if I cannot hear him, neither can the ones behind us." She sighed. "At the moment, I can see no choice for us. We have but one mission, and until it is done all else is secondary. We must kill all of the Mycohl, no matter what the cost. They are the only ones of this group likely to eventually release the Dark Ones."

Gun Roh Chin went to Savin's limp, twisted body and removed the dead Mesok's utility and power packs. "We'll need all we can get the next time we face the Corithian," he explained.

Jimmy McCray walked around the small ruins, frowning.

"You want to get some dry sleep here, like they did?" Modra asked Lankur.

"I don't think so. I know we're all in, and I'm not in any big hurry, but I just don't want to get trapped in here like they did, just in case somebody bright got the idea to double back. Still, I wanted a look at these things. Durquist?"

"Fascinating," the star-shaped creature responded. "*Very* ancient—at least five or six thousand years. I couldn't be more precise without some samples and my lab. What astonishes me is that I have seen such ruins before, on many other worlds. Home worlds, not colonized ones, that is. They usually had some astronomical bearings to them, and were some sort of temples. Since the Quintara seem a bit too advanced for this, I would suspect that this is not theirs, and that implies that, at least at one time, somebody else lived on this dunghole of a world."

"What's eating you, McCray?" Lankur asked. "You've walked around that dead body on the stone a dozen times."

"Just thinking, but it's not the body, it's what's under it that interests me. The Durquist's right—I've seen pictures of these in ancient books. Back before our people ran smack into the Three Empires and got gobbled up by all of them, as it were, we found a few worlds with these things as well, and there were references to older ones back on the ancient home world of our ancestors. This is the first one I've actually seen, though. I've been tryin' to figure out what's nagging at me mind on this one."

"I don't see how you could tell much," Modra commented. "After all the years, these rocks have been worn into shapes the builders never thought of. And that ugly monster on top doesn't make seeing the detail any easier. It just gives me the creeps."

Suddenly he had it. "It's not the shape of the top, lass—it's the supporting posts here. The two front ones are quite a bit closer together than the rear ones, and why three in the rear, with one out so it almost pointed to the river?''

''Maybe that was what was required to hold the thing up,'' the Durquist suggested practically.

Jimmy, however, didn't hear. ''If we assume the capstone at one time was shaped deliberately, then it would be a pentagon. Five-sided. A pentagon or—of course! Of course! A *pentagram*!''

''A what?'' the Durquist asked.

''A pentagram. Naturally. In the old legends, you used a pentagram when you were gonna invoke a demon spirit. 'Twas said they couldn't cross them for some reason. I'll bet that if the post holes were measured they'd be exact. You make a pentagram by drawing a five-pointed star and then connecting the points. The pentagon shape alone won't do it. If the demon is invoked inside, he's trapped there and essentially at the mercy of those who called him. If *you're* inside one and a demon comes to call, it can't get to you. If that holds up here, it means that either they worshiped the demons and called them up somehow here, or they used this central place to come to find some protection.''

''Superstitious rot,'' the Durquist mumbled.

''Maybe not,'' Tris Lankur replied. ''It's an ancient religious power symbol to a lot of Terran groups, and I'm sure I've seen it elsewhere as well. We don't know how the dimensionality works, and we certainly don't know the potential power and technology of the Quintara. When we say 'dimensions,' though, we're really using a mathematical model to make comprehensible something not really clear. Suppose—just suppose—that certain geometrical shapes are needed for some reason. That they cut through if you know how to do it, or provide insulation. We didn't see all of any station. Suppose *they* are pentagonal? We don't know what's in the bases of those imprisoning pillars. McCray's pentagrams, perhaps? Or some even more powerful geometrical shape our ancestors never lucked into? It's possible. McCray, can you lay out a pentagram for us if you had to? A really exact one?''

''I suppose so. If the suit computer can calculate the distance from here to the top, it certainly can measure some simple straight lines, if I had something to draw them with. If it wasn't raining like hell, it could be done with a stick in the dirt or a piece of chalky rock.''

''Well, we'll keep it in mind as a possible protection when we can do it. I'm also resolved to take a *much* closer look if we see any more imprisoned Quintara, too, no matter what the risk. Any race that can just walk through a solid wall like it's a piece of paper isn't going to be held by that stuff so easily shattered by gunfire. Something else is holding them there—something that the shattering undoes. I want to know what.''

''In the meantime, let's go if we're going,'' Modra suggested. ''This place is a place of death.''

They continued on up, the shale providing something almost like steps to reach the top where the deadliest part of the battle had been fought. Jimmy McCray wanted to examine the larger ruins for a moment, and, feeling safer, they felt they could afford to. The truth was, most of them wanted rest more than they wanted to move on, but, without some cover, the beating rain on their helmets was almost like drumbeats, bad enough awake.

''Looks like the same sort of folks,'' the telepath commented. ''Maybe the same people built it. Hard to say. At a guess, though, even though it's in worse shape than the one below, I'd guess this one was newer. It's more exposed to the weather, which would account for its more worn shape.''

''What makes you believe it is newer?'' the Durquist asked him.

''The altar in the center. Below, we've got a probable pentagram. That's a protection. This one—no pentagram, no likely shape of that sort. If you look at the old altar, it's got grooves in it and down to the floor, where there's another channeling that probably took the runoff over the cliff when the thing was whole, same as it's doin' as much as is left with the rainwater. This, I think, is a sacrificial altar. Those grooves took the blood or whatever the folks here had inside 'em away.''

''Frankly, McCray, I believe your imagination is running wild,'' the Durquist responded. ''You see some ancient ruins, built by a people no longer here and whose shape and very nature we can't even guess at, and thanks to an odd number of pillars you see a pentagram and thanks to erosion you see a sacrificial altar. All based upon some scary tales told you by your own religious leader in your childhood and a book you loved in school. Virtually *all* cultures tell those stories to their young, either to teach morality or, in some cases, just to scare unruly children into social conformity. The similarity of the Quintara to those ancient devils has brought back all those childhood fascinations and fears, and now you see it all vindicated. I will grant that the Quintara are the source of the nearly universal demon stories, and even that they're another of the Higher Races, like the Guardians, the Mycohl, and the Mizlaplan. They're dangerous—that's why someone or some group more powerful locked them away. But supernatural?''

''There's no reason why you aren't both right,'' Tris Lankur pointed out. ''Something that's supernatural is something nobody else has figured out how to do yet. The behavior of almost all the ancient gods and demons mirrors the cultures that created them. People create and develop gods in their own images. The relative consistency of the demons indicates a common source in reality, a source we now know. We also know that, while they can be pretty brutish, they had a well-developed technology beyond anything we currently understand and which is probably the source of their ancient power. I think all of us have been on worlds with very primitive and ignorant races who regarded *us* as supernatural. The demons themselves have their own kind of religion, as we've seen—they worship power. Power for its own sake. They *like* being gods. They enjoy it, even revel in it. If they have any higher agenda, we haven't seen any evidence of it. The clues are here—such a race would never accept anything but the very top ruler spot over all others. They'd be warlike, and war lovers, which might account for their high level of technology. You see what I mean?''

''You left out an important part,'' McCray commented.

''Oh?''

''There's two of 'em loose now, heading someplace important. Quintara or devils or both, if I suddenly found myself, maybe a low-rankin' demon in their hierarchy, suddenly loose in the old candy shop, I might be tempted to leave any possible competition behind and go for the center of power of the old days. Maybe gather up a few of the most trusted old boys who'll work just under 'em and be the rest of the gang. If it was the Big Three we know who put 'em here—the races that run things—they're obviously fat and lazy shadows of what they were. No match for these boys now, who have the same knowledge and fighting trim they did way back when. If we so-called lessers can't figure out a way to do 'em in somehow before they get all set up, then Higher Race or Princes of Darkness, it won't make a wee bit of difference. They'll take all ninety trillion of us in the Three Empires like fruit overripe and a bit rotten falls from the tree with a mild shake.''

The Durquist could not find an answer to that one.

Modra sighed. ''Well, there's no sign of shelter up here. Let's see what we can find further on. You keep those mental channels open, too, McCray. No telling where our friends up ahead will stop, either.''

''I'm not so worried about them, at least not yet,'' the telepath replied. ''They're so filled with killin' one another we won't be real targets until one of 'em makes it happen. Let's see if we can figure a way not to swim along this mountain ridge here and find someplace for a little rest.''

It wasn't easy going; without the properties of the suits, the odds were they would have all slipped off or slid off at one or another point, or worse. Deep grooves, like paths, perhaps worn down by all those who came up for the temples, existed, too filled with water to be useful but vital as indicators of a direction to follow.

Finally, though, they reached the end of the high ground and looked down upon an eerie forest; the first real life, such as it was, they'd had any evidence of here.

The trunks of the tree-like plants might have been mistaken for vast numbers of eroded pillars; twisted, rising well up into the air, a mixture of grays and browns whose exterior looked and felt very stone-like. They also were embedded not in soil but in apparently hard basalt with a tremendous amount of obsidian embedded within. Yet, from their tall tops, half as tall as the hillside, sprang massive, thick leafy growths like great panels of marbled dark blue and gray canvas, catching the rain and funneling it somehow into the center of the stony stalks.

''Certainly not photosynthesis or any similar process,'' the

Durquist commented. "Indeed, they appear silicon-based, although that might be deceiving."

"But what do they feed on?" Modra wondered. "No sun, no soil . . ."

"No animal life, either, thank heaven," McCray added.

"I wonder," the Durquist mused, "if the rain and whatever is below the bedrock could be enough for them. There must be a method for the water to recirculate as vapor into the air or we'd be in the midst of a sunny ocean. If all they need are minerals and water to mix them internally in order to grow and reproduce, the rain itself might bring them all they require, somehow. I am pretty sure the rain is harmless to us, but I've done no chemical analysis of it. Fascinating."

"I'm more interested in the fact that most of the hillside runoff seems to go into those cracks and crevices below," Lankur noted. "With the big leaves or collectors up there, it's likely to be, if not dry, at least habitable in there. Modra, McCray—you have any sense of our friends down there?"

The empath and the telepath each surveyed the scene. "Something *very* distant, nothing close," Modra replied.

"That's about it," Jimmy agreed. "The Miz probably managed to get a few hours' sleep back there at the ruins before bein' so rudely awakened, so they're probably in the best shape of all of us. Even so, they'll want to pick and choose how and when they hit the Mycohl crew and won't be spoilin' for a fight right off, I'd say. Nope—I'd guess that if we can use the forest for cover, it's pretty safe on this side."

Hopping over the cracks and crevices that collected the water proved a little difficult, particularly for Molly, whose feet really weren't designed for all this, but she was game. If those Quintara could do it, so could she.

Now, finally, they stood at the very edge of the forest. "Which way?" Modra wondered. "We probably won't even have telepathic clues in a little while."

"This may seem a little nuts," Jimmy McCray said, "but there are two trees next to each other, about thirty meters down, that look a wee bit different than the rest. *Shiny,* if you see what I mean."

They walked the distance and looked at them. They *were* different; the exterior of their twisted trunks was encased—not all the way, but in three bands of clear, weatherproof material.

"Sort'a like the stuff they stuck the big syns in," Molly noted. To her, the demons were variants of her own kind because that's what she could understand.

The Durquist's stalked eyes stared a moment. "You know, she's right. It *is* similar stuff," he said after an examination, a bit amazed. "Now, I don't presume to think the way another race and culture might think, but I can see only one possible reason for doing this—and only to two trees."

Modra nodded. "Trail markers." She walked between them and, within eyesight, about ten meters farther in, was another pair similarly marked. "That's how they do it—and how the others did it," she told them.

They went in but a little ways; it wasn't exactly dry underneath the forest canopy, but it wasn't a thundering rain, either. Rather, the thunder, even the screams and moans, seemed very distant and far above them, and everything was just simply wet.

"I'd say right here is the best place," Tris Lankur commented. "We have the trail, and shelter about as good as we can expect, but we're close enough to the edge of the forest that if it holds any ugly surprises, we can make a break for it. I'll stand guard again, the rest of you get some sleep. No telling when we'll have another chance at it."

They settled down, and within minutes Jimmy McCray, Molly, and the Durquist were all out to the world. Modra, however, stretched out as she was and, very tired, found it suddenly impossible to go to sleep. *Overtired,* she told herself, but it was more than that.

None of them, not even the telepath, could know how much her encounter with the demons had hurt her. Molly had wrenched her out and away by the single-mindedness of her simple outlook, something which had also insulated her to a degree. The demons, probably confused by Molly's mind and the odd readings they were getting, had ignored her, perhaps dismissing her. Still, the fact that Molly couldn't really comprehend what those bastards were doing to Modra's own psyche meant that she, too, didn't realize the full extent of injury.

The Quintara had multiple Talents, which was the age-old

definition of a Higher Race—although it remained to be seen
what, if any, Talents the mysterious Guardians of the Exchange, if they still existed, possessed. They had read her mind
for the source of her jumbled hurts and emotions, then
broadcast and amplified just the worst ones. That effect had
only been diminished by Molly and time; it hadn't by any
means receded to the level it had been before the attack, even
if she still could put on a tough front.

The fact that Tris was there, the walking corpse of the man
she felt she'd murdered by her own insensitivity to anyone and
anything but her own interests, so self-absorbed in her own ego
and troubles she'd never guessed the depth of his feelings and
reactions. Her, the empath! Choosing security over romance
was something she knew would hurt him, but she hardly
expected the kind of despair that resulted. He'd always been
too strong, too flip, too tough for all that.

There, in the eerie forest, she couldn't help but think back to
that last nightmarish time when they were together, clinging to
each other for security and sanity while under attack from
horrible forces, and which had frightened her enough that she
never wanted to do that again.

And for what? Here she was, the damage done, stuck in a
damned alien forest on some dark, dank, rotten world in the
empire of Hell, haunted by the ghost of the man she'd driven
to suicide.

For nothing.

She got up, yawned and stretched. Lankur looked up and
said, "Any problems?"

"Can't sleep," she told him. "I just need to stretch a bit."
She started walking slowly toward the edge of the forest.

"I wouldn't go back out there," he warned her. "I can't
guard everybody."

"That's all right. I'm not going out there, just to the edge. I
need to be alone for a few minutes." *How can I tell you I just
want to be out of sight of you for a few moments?* "It's all right.
I won't be long, and I can tell if somebody's lurking about.
Besides, we're on intercom."

He didn't like it, but he settled back, knowing he was unable
to prevent it.

She walked to the edge of the forest, then over a bit, so she was completely out of sight, and leaned on one of the trees, gazing out at that constant, unbelievable rain.

The weird sounds of this strange world were much lóuder here, possibly even amplified by some kind of echo effect bouncing them between the hills and the forest. They were kind of creepy, but she didn't want to turn the exterior sound off. The silence of all but her own breathing would be worse still.

She tried to imagine some ancient people coming through here in ritual processions to their great monuments up on high. What had become of them, she wondered? Did they die out after slavishly serving the Quintara? Did the Quintara grow bored and kill them off? Or was it, perhaps, just some sort of natural calamity, some great climatological change that swept away the old, familiar world that had supported them along with all the life in the chain, making way for this newer, duller, quieter life to take over? Was there, in fact, now a sun up there at all? It seemed that the light varied a bit, from gloomy to gloomier, but it was never pitch-dark and never bright as a true rainy day anywhere else she'd been.

McCray was a little too nuts on his childhood nightmares, but she couldn't help thinking along those lines as well. It matched her mood, even as it took her thoughts away from what she *really* didn't want to think about.

Tris—*Damn! Can't get around him!*—was wrong when he said the Durquist and McCray were talking about the same thing, no matter how reasonable it sounded. He and the Durquist were in tune, with their view of a very nasty and dangerous crew that was still understandable, comprehensible, rational in the civilized sense. McCray's childhood demons were more than that; even death didn't free you from them, but rather enslaved your mind, your spirit, your soul, whatever it was called, to them forever in some other plane. He was saying they were worse than tyrants, of which the universe still had plenty; that those shrieks and moans that howled through this terrible place were the cries of the damned in eternal torment. Perhaps even the souls of all the ones who'd given their souls on this world to the demons.

It was easy, looking out on the place, to imagine that those ancient builders were still here—just out of sight, just beyond their perception, in another, eternal continuum.

The idea, in spite of her own lack of belief in anything she couldn't see, hear, feel, or touch, gave her the creeps.

She thought she heard a different noise, not far off, sounding like a flag flapping in the brisk wind. It was oddly different, but she dismissed it as perhaps the sound of the great leaf-like collectors adjusting to the rain. She turned to look, but it was gone just as quickly, and she chided herself at getting *too* jumpy. She was simply too tired, and too depressed, and this place and McCray's talk of demons and pentagrams and rituals had fed on that.

She felt, rather than heard, someone behind her, and turned, expecting to see Tris coming to check on her.

Instead, she was staring suddenly into huge crimson ovals of eyes, eyes that seemed to drain her strength and her will but from which she could not turn or break contact. She was suddenly totally without thought or will of her own, and, while not a word was spoken, she found herself shutting off the suit intercom, then switching the suit radio to an upper, rarely used frequency and turning on both the personal scrambler and the translator.

"You have no thoughts, no fears, no worries, no cares," said a flat voice on the channel. "Your thoughts are only what I tell you they are. Your only purpose to existence is to help me in any way you can and obey my commands. You feel strength like you never have before, all through your body, and your mind is clear, alert, wide awake, without a trace of fatigue. You will now turn off your location transponder and help me into the forest but away from the marked path and your companions. You must save me and yourself from your companions. Your companions have all been taken over by the demons as they guarded or slept, and who now control them. You are the only one they did not get. Your only chance is to help me reach my people, and for you to join with us. Now—help me. Get me to a place where they cannot find us or the telepath locate us. I will need your help. My leg is injured. Come. Help me with your strength to escape the demon tools."

Unhesitatingly, she supported him on one side, and they made their way as quickly as possible into the dense stone forest.

.   .   .

Tris Lankur was suddenly aware that Modra had been away a very long time.

"Modra?" he called on the intercom. "Modra, come in."

He stood up now, concerned, and switched to the all-frequency call. "Modra? If you can hear me, please acknowledge."

No response.

He brought up the locator to get a fix on her transponder and found no result.

The all-frequency call had aroused the others. "Huh? What . . . ?" Jimmy McCray mumbled.

"Everybody up! Modra's gone!"

That brought them at least to wakefulness. "What do you mean, 'gone'?" the Durquist asked him tiredly.

"She couldn't sleep, walked off a little ways towards the edge of the forest, and suddenly she just wasn't there. No call acknowledge, no transponder, nothing. McCray—see if you can get a handle on her."

Jimmy yawned, trying to come to wakefulness, then cast a routine mental net. There was *something* there, heading slowly away, but it made no real sense. It seemed like there were *two* minds, then one, then a lot of crazy gibberish. "Grysta, I need more juice."

<Shit! Don't anybody get rest in this outfit? Oh, okay. . . .>

The amplification didn't do much for sense, but it did give him a fair idea that he wasn't dealing with Modra alone.

"It's Miz stuff, nutty stuff," he told the others. "Are we sure all four of them went up that hill before us?" He snapped his fingers. "Shit! It's that damned hypno of theirs!"

"I thought you said none of them were even close," Lankur shot back.

"They weren't! Not within a couple of hours of this place! I'd swear it!"

"Nevertheless, the creature is here," the Durquist pointed out, "and it took Modra."

"I blame myself a little for it," Tris Lankur sighed. "I let her get out of sight, violating a cardinal rule in these situations."

"No, we just underestimated them, I think," the Durquist consoled.

"Or overestimated ourselves," Jimmy added. "Look, I get the idea that the Miz is hurt—maybe back in the battle. Somehow, by some trick, he managed to avoid both Modra and my sweeps. I don't know how, but we all know by now that nothing's foolproof; there's a way to fool almost anything, man or machine. I think Modra was just a heaven-sent target of opportunity."

"Well, where are they going, man? And how do they know where they're going without coming through here to get the trail marker?" Tris pressed.

"I can't tell. You know it's not directional. If we get started after them, though, they can't be all *that* far away. How long was she gone before you noticed she was missing?"

"Twenty minutes. Maybe half an hour."

"Great!" grumped the Durquist. "You could go pretty far in that time in this jungle."

McCray shook his head. "No, he's injured, and she's all in, no matter how much his hypno power tells her to ignore it. They can't be more than a kilometer or so, but they're on the move."

"That may be true, but the only way we can locate her is through trial and error with you checking for amplitude," the Durquist pointed out. "If they're lost in this mess, it would just get *us* lost as well."

"The Durquist's right," Tris Lankur agreed. "We can't go barging around in this or we'll be in here forever. We've got to assume that either he knows where they're going or he'll eventually think to use Modra's empathic Talent to head for his companions ahead. In any case, we know where they're going, and we can assume that the Miz team is following this trail the same as we. Our best bet is to get moving fast along the markers here and try to get ahead of them. McCray will be able to warn us if we get close."

"Makes sense," the telepath agreed. "Have you figured out what we do if we catch him, though? He's a damned *hypno*!"

"*I'm* not bothered by a hypno, or any other Talent," Tris reminded him.

"True, but neither are you immune to being shot," the Durquist added. "I confess to an almost sneaking admiration for this fellow."

"I will admire him to death," Tris said evenly. "They broke their word and so have broken the peace, as well as weakening our team. In the last analysis, they are between the Mycohl and us. That makes them the meat in the sandwich, and I have every intention to chew them up and swallow them."

VAULT
OF THE
DREAMERS

"WHY DO WE PRESS ON TO THE POINT OF utter exhaustion?'' Tobrush asked, unable to fathom the single-mindedness of the Mycohl leader even after reading his mind. ''We must rest, or when they catch us we shall perish.''

''We should have waited in ambush for them within the stone forest,'' Desreth agreed. ''A threat removed is a concern no longer.''

In point of fact, even Josef was coming face to face with the realization that even he could go no longer. ''We know the way is marked,'' he pointed out, ''and that they will have to come this way. It is of no great concern where the next battle happens, so long as we pick the place and time. Now both the others are far behind us, looking nervously at every rock and dark place. Now we can find some cover and rest.'' He looked around. ''Does it *ever* stop raining, I wonder?''

''There is a waterfall or something that sounds like it ahead,'' Kalia said. ''You hear it?''

They stopped and grew still, and heard now the sound of distant, steady thunder, a deep rumbling that could only be some sort of massive overflow, far larger than the one at the scene of the first battle, and that one had been fairly impressive.

"From what we've seen on the way, it is likely that there will be more temples and ruins at such a falls," he said hopefully. "Perhaps it is there we'll find our shelter and rest."

The tremendous rumbling grew louder and louder as they approached, until it seemed to be beneath them, shaking the very ground. There was a slight rise ahead, and Kalia pointed.

"Look!" she shouted. "Smoke!"

"A volcano?" Josef mused. "It doesn't *feel* like a volcano. Let's see."

They mounted the rise and the sight they beheld was more breathtaking than any volcano they could imagine.

The area was a huge, horseshoe-shaped basin, perhaps four or five kilometers across, and over it dumped not only the great river they had been more or less following but other rivers and streams as well, combining into a solid sheet of water falling into a pit so deep they could not see bottom. The smoke rising from it seemed to be water vapor and spray created by the falls itself, swirling around and creating an ever-moving fog in the center of the thing.

"It looks like the biggest toilet in the universe," Kalia commented.

They just stood there for a few minutes, gaping at the sight. Finally Tobrush went over quite near the edge. "I hate to say this," the Julki shouted over the roar of the great falls, "but these two coated rocks sticking up here seem to say we're to jump in!"

Josef approached very near the edge, going through the two rock markers, and nervously looked at the point indicated. He stared for a moment, then made his way cautiously back up. "There's a kind of ramp there that seems to run along the rim to the left, going in back of the falls," he told them. "This area is made up of very hard rock, and it looks intact. It is perhaps two meters wide, and there is no depression or guardrail."

Kalia repeated his steps, although not quite so close to the edge, then came quickly back. "I don't like it!" she said, shouting against the roar. "It's bound to be slippery and very wet, and we have no idea where if anywhere it goes."

"Assuming it was our demons who built it, as might be

inferred from the coating on the markers, and not the temple builders,'' Tobrush said thoughtfully, ''and making the possibly erroneous assumption that our two fugitive demons came this way, I must assume it can be negotiated by any or all of us. You saw the suspended ones, with those big, thick cloven hooves. If such ones with hard, flat feet and top-heavy bodies can do it, there is no reason we all cannot. Assuming, that is, that they actually went that way. If not, and there is weathering and a lack of maintenance further on, we may be in deep trouble. There is a downward angle; getting out of there might be far more difficult than getting in.''

Josef nodded. ''I see no alternative but to try it, but I'm not about to attempt that without rest and sleep.'' He looked around. ''Well, if we can stand the noise, there's no end of shelter *here*.''

Built right into the rise were the most elaborate ruins yet. These looked less primitive and far less worn, perhaps because of their slight shelter by the rise or perhaps, too, because they were newer or made of much stronger rock. The complex went on in both directions as far as they could see; windows and doors carved out of the rock itself, looking at once crude and civilized.

''Let's see if we can find one that's reasonably dry on the inside, has two exits, and gives a view of this point,'' Josef suggested. ''Desreth—check out the few nearest us.''

The Corithian scuttled over and entered one of the misshapen doors, and was gone for quite some time. Getting nervous, Josef called the creature through the intercom. ''Desreth?''

''I am here,'' his voice responded, sounding odd and hollow. ''I believe you should take a look in here if you have some light. It is not at all what one might have expected.''

They went to the doorway and entered, one at a time, switching on their helmet lights. The rumbling from the great falls became more remote and spooky inside, but what was still there gave a constant, echoing roaring sound within.

Instead of being a series of small structures carved out of the rock wall, the complex proved to be one or perhaps more huge structures with many entrances. Part of it was certainly natural; it had the look and feel of natural caverns that were, possibly, lava tubes out of this region's ancient volcanic past, since there were no stalactites or other formations as such.

Inside, too, were ancient pits where obviously some kind of cooking or heating had been done for a common population, as well as other primitive structures. Here, too, along the stone walls and columns, was the first evidence of the people who had once lived here beyond their decaying ruins, in the shape of varicolored paintings and designs. They were at once both elaborate and crude, but they gave something of a picture of the place as it had been.

The folk themselves were bipeds, somewhat humanoid in appearance, but with odd, reptilian faces with pushed-in noses, and on their backs were large oval shapes that at first they took to be packs of some kind but which seemed so consistent that they finally decided that the shapes were growths, perhaps part of the body.

"Vestigial remnants of a shelled ancestry," Tobrush guessed, "like my own people. Hard to tell with all the drawings in two very flat dimensions, but it makes the most sense. The eyes are very large and bulging, and always drawn segmented into three parts, I note. One wonders what, and how, they saw. Certainly they had good color sense, even if very bad taste. Big, powerful hind legs, so they could run, shell remnant or not, and fairly fast—and from those oversized, clawed hands I would say that they did not embrace as a form of affection."

"But what did they *eat*?" Josef wanted to know. "I haven't seen a sign of anything edible yet." He wasn't just curious, but also thinking of just how many more days' rations they carried.

"From the pottery remnants and the fire pits, they cooked whatever it was," Tobrush noted. "With that face, and that jawline, I would doubt if they were meat-eaters, either."

"Those claws look pretty good for ripping flesh," Josef noted.

"In defense, I suppose, but I think more likely they were diggers. Tubers, roots, who can know? But the odds are they smelled out what they ate and then dug for it. The legs indicate they were built to cover a lot of ground in a hurry, yet they had settlements like this one. That in turn implies enemies from which their best defense was to outrun them."

Josef suddenly remembered the basics of defense himself.

"Desreth—cover the entrance with the best view of the trail to the edge," he ordered. "This is the best we're going to do to get some sleep."

Tobrush kept playing his light against the wall. "No eating scenes, or normal scenes of life here, but—wait a minute! Captain—I think you ought to look at this."

Josef came back over, suddenly feeling all the weariness of the journey, but he couldn't scold Tobrush after he saw the scene.

It was clearly the falls, in full two-dimensional glory, and all along the ledge the creatures were shown in great numbers prostrate before it. But it was in the falls, or, rather, in the mist of the falls, that the scene became eerie.

There was a shape depicted in the mist, a huge, menacing outline, of a great, broad horned head and neck rising up, almost filling the bowl.

Surrounding the scene were smaller scenes, almost frescoes, showing scenes of the creatures with horrendous devil masks, bodies garishly painted, and gruesome scenes of sacrifices performed at the edge of the falls and even, it appeared, self-mutilation. One showed the figure of a small child on its shell-like back, its mouth open as if crying out or screaming, as one of the painted and masked ones used a nasty-looking three-pronged knife-like tool and was clearly dismembering the hapless young one alive.

"Nothing we hadn't already figured out, except now we know who and what," Josef said at last, knowing his casual tone couldn't mask from the telepathic Julki his own feelings at the scene. He'd seen a lot of people slaughtered in his life, some senselessly and cruelly, often in staged fights to the death for the amusement of the nobility, or sometimes enemies of the Lords purposely and slowly tortured to death in public as object lessons. The Mycohl, however, always had a genuine purpose— entertainment, revenge, enforcement of discipline—but these scenes showed an entire culture, an entire race of people, whose entire lives revolved around such things. Blood to appease the demon-gods, and what had it gotten them? Where were they now?

Tobrush read his thoughts. "It is said that in the High Temples of the Lords of Qaamil, where high priests read the

Quiimish in its original and full form, that all of the dead are gathered, or collected, by the Princes of Darkness to serve them in all ways until the Great Judgment. Where does a whole culture, a whole race, a whole *world* go when it dies? Can a whole world die and be collected, too?''

"You expect me to sleep after *that* cheery thought?" Josef asked him, still staring at the reliefs.

"Of course. And so shall I. Even if this *is* the domain and plane of the dead, we are still alive and we cannot see them. Perhaps we can hear them, just a bit, because we are so close, but nothing more. We are here, but we are not yet collected. By getting some decent sleep and rising rested and refreshed, I fully intend to keep postponing that eventuality as much as possible."

"You old hypocrite! You never believed in any of that!"

"I do not say I believe it now," the Julki responded. "I merely state it as a hypothesis that fits the facts. *You* never believed it, either, except in the dark recesses of your unconscious mind where I cannot go, yet the idea unnerves you."

Josef sighed and walked back over near the doorway. His light, before he turned it off, fell on Kalia, who was already asleep, neither curious nor moved by all this. *She* believes it, he thought. In her limited, ignorant drol mind she believed every word of it, and it didn't bother her a bit.

"*She* doesn't have any problems with it, either," Tobrush commented. "Why, considering what we know so far, she'd fit right into the Dark Domain."

Josef sighed and nodded, then forced himself to turn to more mundane worries. "Desreth, if another team, most likely the Holy Horrors, gets here, they're almost certain to do what we did—head for the falls and not even see this place until after. Their telepath will probably warn them of something, but if they go past and you get a clear shot, hit them. Don't wait for us. Use your discretion but get maximum results."

"Understood," the Corithian responded. "We are into the hill, so they have no way to come up behind us, and it is quite a drop for them anywhere close but here. Suspicious or not, they will *have* to come between us and the falls. That will be most satisfactory."

· · ·

"Manya! Captain! Wake up! Wonderful news!"

Krisha might not have been able to contain herself, but her companions, who hadn't had the benefit of being unconscious and carried for many hours, had far different initial feelings.

Still, Gun Roh Chin managed to ask, "What is this about, Krisha?"

"Morok! He's *alive*! He's coming towards us now! Right through the stone forest!"

He stared at her blearily. "How could he get over the mountains? Are you sure you didn't nod off and dream this?"

"Quite sure! I can hear him now!"

Manya was no more trusting of her than was the captain. "Even if he managed somehow to get over the mountains, how can he be coming here, ahead of the heathens on the other side of this place? Granting the remote possibility of a miracle cure of his leg, this place is a maze unless the path is followed exactly, and we have our own location transponders off. You know that."

"He is being—assisted," she responded, more calmly. "He has the Exchange empath with him to home in on us. She is under his influence."

Gun Roh Chin sat back and sighed. He was glad to hear that the old comrade of so many past missions was all right, but he didn't like the idea of using a foreigner for the purpose. "Very lax of them," he muttered. "Sloppy."

Krisha frowned. "Aren't you happy?"

"At Morok's coming? Yes, overjoyed. But he used his Talent to kidnap her. I can't think of anything that would upset an Exchange exploiter team more than that. In that one act we've changed them from neutrals who got us out of a bad position into enemies who will never trust us or accept our word again."

"They're *heathen*!" Manya snapped. "Hence, they are incapable of making a true oath anyway. Remember that traitorous little witch who even violated the Treaty of Neutrality back on Medara? Besides, if I remember Krisha's description of them, the two females were both empaths, so we haven't diminished their Talents, nor did we harm her. When the Holy Father gets here, I can treat his leg with my kit and we can send her back to them."

He shook his head. "No, you don't understand them like I do. True, they are mercenaries to the core, but this guild in particular has a sense of honor between each other bordering on religion. They have to—they hire out to be dropped on newly discovered worlds just to find out what kills people there. If the team does not think and act in all the important ways as almost a single organism, they have very short careers."

This was one of the few times when he really wished Krisha could read his mind. Neither of them, and not even Morok, would believe the truth: if he had simply gone to them and asked for help, they would have given it. Exploiter teams were rather myopic in their view of others: they thought of the Arm as another team, and the Mycohl military unit as well. Their code would have required them to aid someone in distress, even a competitor, so long as it didn't cause them harm to do so, as this surely wouldn't. But, harm *their* team, treat *them* as an enemy, and you were in for it. It would be a concept totally lost and perhaps inconceivable to these clerics, and not something Krisha could have deduced from reading their own minds, either. You had to have been among them for a while, as he had once been, long ago.

There was nothing to do about it now, though. The damage had been done. As always, pragmatism came first.

"How far away are they, and about when do you expect them to get here?" he asked the telepath.

"Hard to say exactly, but certainly within an hour or two. Remember, an empath also has to use only amplitude to locate something, but I take from their minds that they have crossed the marked path and are making much better time straight for us now."

"What about the Exchange people?"

She shrugged. "Occasional thoughts and fragments only, but I know they are closing."

He got up and sighed. "If there is even a *chance* that the Exchange people can catch them, then we must go back and get them first, before they are overrun. Come—there is no time to lose. Knowing that he is a hypno with one of theirs in his power, they will shoot him down like a wild animal if they can."

About forty-five minutes of backtracking and Krisha said,

"We are very close—but so is the Exchange. I've thrown up a block sufficient to cover all of us, even His Holiness, but that won't stop them. They *know* he's got to be on the trail."

They quickened their pace, and within five more minutes came upon the Stargin and his Terran helper. He looked less than great, mostly hopping on one of those huge, clawed feet of his while holding the other up, with Modra supporting him under that arm. The High Inquisitor was wearing his instrument pack but had his environment suit tied around his body. The rain was beading and running off his oily, tiny feathers, but he still looked waterlogged.

"Blessings on you all!" he called, sounding all in.

"No time for anything, even pleasantries," the captain responded. "Everybody, off the trail, into the forest here. Go back as far as you can, without regard for getting lost. I'm going to stay close up here, and with Krisha and the empath you'll be able to home in precisely on my transponder, which I am activating now. *Go!* I'm a null—they won't detect me."

"But they'll know we're very close by my block!" the telepath reminded him.

"Close does not count. And get back up here when I call you just as fast as you can. Not withstanding the Holy Father, we'll have to stay close or they'll figure out we're behind them. Now—go!"

With Krisha now helping Morok out, they moved quickly back into the forest and out of sight.

Gun Roh Chin took a position where he could barely see the road but not be seen, or so he hoped. He tried scanning, but they were using scramblers and he got a bunch of electronic nonsense.

In just a few minutes, the Exchange team passed. It was the first time he'd actually laid eyes on them, and although the sight of the Durquist startled him a bit—he'd never seen anything quite like it before—it was the fourth member of the team that gave him his real scare. The skintight environment suits left no doubt that the remaining female not only wasn't human—at least not *quite*—but that she had goat-like legs. For a moment, he thought they had a demon with them, and now he wasn't sure just *what* the creature was.

And then, just before they would have gone out of sight, the group stopped, and the lithe little Terran who must be the telepath started looking around, obviously trying a scan.

Indeed, Jimmy McCray was getting very, very confused. "We should be right on top of 'em!" he insisted. "The girl is *strong,* the strongest I ever came across, but it's almost like they were skulking right by in the wood, or rocks, or whatever, as it were. Durquist, watch our back!"

"I have had one eye on our back all along," the creature responded, showing one stalked eye forward, the other back.

"Stay on scramble," Tris Lankur warned. "I'm gonna give them a call if they're that close." If one of them was dumb enough to answer, they might get a fix. He hoped the Durquist didn't also get that idea; his own mind was immune to telepathy, McCray could block his, and probably Grysta's, and Molly didn't have those kind of smarts, but the Durquist would be an open book.

"This is Exchange calling the Mizlaplan team," Lankur called. "Please acknowledge."

He waited, got no response, and tried it several more times. He sighed. "Well, they aren't going to fall for it. All right, then, it's one way." He turned back to the open channel on the translator.

"This is the Exchange. You might be able to block, but you can't hide forever or get too far from us and you know it. We demand the immediate return of our abducted member and the surrender of your team to our authority along with all weapons. In addition to violating our space, you have now committed a major crime against us."

Gun Roh Chin sighed and pulled his energy pistol. They might be great on primitive alien worlds, but they were rank amateurs in this sort of thing. Keeping the weapon on manual, so their own defensive systems wouldn't see a lock on and throw up deflectors, he took careful aim and fired at maximum stun.

The bolt hit them square at a distance of under thirty meters, and all of the Exchange team went down. The leader, though, fell only to his knees and then seemed to recover, the pistol coming up, the targeting system tracking the initial shot.

Chin cursed under his breath, remembering that one of them was a cymol. He aimed again, using target lock, narrowed the beam, and struck Lankur alone dead on. The figure fell back and collapsed.

The Mizlaplanian knew that Lankur's brain and some suit control would still be active, but he'd still be effectively paralyzed. "Everyone! Quickly!" he called back to Krisha and the rest. "Move back to me. Let me move within here well ahead of them and then join on me quickly! I've bought us a little time, no more."

"You *shot* them!" Krisha responded, amazed. "Did you really have to do that?"

"Believe me, it was the only way," he assured her. "And we may have to do even worse later. Are you moving?"

"Yes, but—"

"No 'buts.' That wasn't an opening round of negotiations the cymol was giving us, it was an ultimatum. Are you ready to surrender all of us and your weapons to an Exchange team?"

"Unthinkable!" Manya shot back, and she really spoke for all of them. As Gun Roh Chin understood, a priest would die before surrendering to a nonbeliever. Although one could eventually rationalize almost anything, *that* wasn't really open to interpretation. They could cooperate, certainly, but never surrender. "And to an abomination, a machine man? The very thought is the highest heresy."

"Well, at the very least, they would insist on us turning over the Holy Father as well as their person, and I told you what they'd do to a hypno who had already committed such an act on one of their own. These teams, out of the jurisdiction of civil authority, act by their own very austere code. Also, watch what you say and keep off the open channels. The fact that I've incapacitated the cymol doesn't mean he isn't wide awake, and remember that their suits are thought-controlled, like ours."

He met them just out of sight of the fallen team, on the marked trail.

Krisha glanced over at Modra, who was standing almost statue-like next to Morok and herself. "What about *her*?"

"She stays with us. Holy One, you'll have to be creative to free her up for action, but she must remain totally and completely under your influence. We've lost our empath and she's an empath, which is handy. Also, no matter how delicate she might look, if she's one of a team like that, she's tough and a dead shot—and she's got far more power reserves in her suit and weapon than we have.''

"I—I really had not intended all this," Morok commented, seeming confused by all this. "I had thought at least we would let her go back to her people."

"With all due respect, Holiness, this is *my* territory," the captain replied bluntly. "All we'd do is have *five* people instead of four in back of us who won't make that kind of mistake again."

"I—I could command her to mislead them. Delay them, trip them up."

"The telepath would figure it almost immediately, and if he didn't the cymol would assume it. They're like supercomputers inside real bodies. No, now that the damage is done, we use what we have. We need her, and she gives us an edge, and as long as she's with us she's a hostage. They won't do any sort of all-out attack so long as she's alive and in reasonable condition. How's your leg? We won't make any speed this way and they'll be smelling blood when they come out of it.''

"A bad sprain. No break that I could find," Manya told him. "I gave him a shot for the pain and another for temporary strength, but he really should not walk on it more than he absolutely must."

"I will do what I must," Morok assured them. "I got this far."

"Uh—yeah," the captain nodded. "So long as we're moving, how *did* you get this far?"

"I had no choice," the High Inquisitor replied. "I *thought* I could fly on this world, and I did. I removed my suit and tied it around me and then I jumped off the cliff into the river valley. It was a near thing; I came very close to dropping into the river before I caught a thermal that took me up. Not, unfortunately, high enough to go over the mountain, so I had to fly along the river until the mountains ended, praying that it was a fairly straight shot. I came in on the other side because I couldn't hope to cross this distance. The rain was keeping me too low, and I had no idea where to go. I spotted the tree markers and landed as high on the mountain as I could and waited, hoping I'd beaten you around. Alas, I had not, and I had no real hope of following in this mess. I found a weather-polished piece of rock, which allowed me to do a little trade-secret self-hypnosis, which helped the pain. Then I waited, trying to decide what to do next, when the Exchange team came along.''

The captain nodded. ''And when you saw her come out for some reason, and realized after a while she was alone, you flew down and surprised her.''

''Yes, exactly. I could not believe she was alone, but she just kept standing there, staring out. I didn't want to do it, but I felt that I had no other choice, and her separation and exposure seemed a miracle.''

''Well, we'll need some more miracles ahead,'' Gun Roh Chin told him. ''Otherwise, we shall just have to continue making it up as we go along.''

They continued on until it was clear that Morok could not continue without some more medical help. Manya's medical kit was very limited, of course, being more of a diagnostic computer and container/mixer for various antibiotics and painkillers that would work on the races of the Arm. You had to know what you were doing, though; a simple salve that would do wonders for, say, Morok, might be caustic or even deadly to Krisha.

Using bandages and a few strips of hard plastic improvised from some of the utility pack reinforcing rods, she managed to rig a primitive splint. She wasn't happy with it, but it was the best that she could do and she knew it. Gun Roh Chin had often reflected to himself that, were it not for the Gnoll's competence at so many things, it might have been impossible to stand her.

''Get your suit back on full if you can,'' she instructed him. ''It will sense the problem and help reinforce it.''

''I will manage,'' he assured her. ''Now bring the girl here. If we're to keep her, we want her as whole as we can make her.''

They brought Modra to him, and he gazed into her own eyes. ''Now, listen to me,'' he commanded, although in a soft voice. ''In a minute or two, I am going to bring you to full and complete wakefulness. When I do, this is what you will remember: you will see a scene where you begin to walk back from your sojourn to join your comrades, only to see dark, demonic things have descended upon them. Their sight is loathsome, the spawn of demons, and your empathic Talent left no doubt that these were pure evil. Appalled and helpless, you watched as those creatures melted into and entered the bodies of your companions. You know now that they are possessed by evil and are not their own masters. They will pretend to be as they were, but you know now that they are actually now ruled by creatures and driven to deceive and kill all the others. Can you remember it?''

"Yes," she said, gasping.

"You ran from them as they came for you," Morok went on, "and almost literally bumped into me. You know I am a hypno, but that I used that Talent to calm you and convince you that I was not an enemy but rather one who needed help. We have now come to this point and are together, but you are the sole survivor of your group. Your undead companions come only with malice and murder on their minds for us. Because of this, you will join with us, not as one of us, but as the sole remaining representative of the Exchange, who must get back somehow and warn your people. You will decide to join us of your own will after I awaken you. Do you understand?''

"Yes, I understand," she responded.

"She has a horrid imagination," Krisha noted. "The scene you described is, in her mind, so graphic I can barely stand to look at it myself. I think it will take. It must. I sense that the Exchange team is beginning to recover.''

"Very well," Morok replied. "Awaken now!''

Modra awakened with a start and looked around. "You did a hypno on me!" she accused the Stargin.

"I'm sorry. You were in such a panic I had no choice," he told her. "I also needed aid to cross the stone forest. Your erstwhile companions pursue us from behind now; the Mycohl are ahead. You are welcome to come along with us, but we are in a very bad position.''

She looked at them. Even through the helmets, she could see the others with reasonable clarity. The dark-skinned girl was a real beauty; the smaller woman looked like some witch or other fairy creature out of her childhood fairy tales, while the dark, Oriental-looking man was small but very strong looking. She was surprised that two, and maybe the gnome, too—it was hard to tell—were Terrans. It was always hard to think of people sharing your common ancestry as aliens and enemies.

She nodded. "I guess I have no choice," she told them. "I've never met the Mycohl, but I know that their religion has demons as good guys, and I've met a pair of demons and seen their work. But no more hypno jobs on me! I'm nobody's plaything, understand?"

"I give you my solemn word as a priest that I will do nothing at all to change the way you are right now," Morok said slyly.

Gun Roh Chin suppressed a grin. "I am Captain Chin, the non-cleric of the group," he told her. "The pretty one over there is Krisha, our telepath and security officer. This is Manya, of the Gnoll, one of our many other races, and our science and medical officer. Our leader with the commanding way about him is Morok. And I think we'd better let all the other pleasantries go for now, since we need to open up some distance and find some kind of fortified shelter ahead where there will be more than one way out this time. I fear we may well have to battle your old comrades."

She fought back tears. "That's all right. They aren't—my team—any more."

Chin switched to private one-on-one with the other Mizla-planians for a moment. "We must protect you, Holy One," he noted. "Without you to keep renewing this, we'll be enemies again a day or two later."

"Then find me a way to rest this leg," Morok responded.

Enlarged by one, they pressed on, now out of the stone forest, toward the distance, where other enemies awaited.

"How far away, Tobrush?" Josef asked the telepath.

"Hard to tell, that telepath's so strong. I can't understand why, if she could have blocked them all at any time, she didn't block them back on the entry world. In any case, they are certainly no more than an hour behind now. They've done a good job of catching up to us. Odd, too—the block's very good all around, but I swear that there are more of them than there were. I have a definite sense of a fifth presence that doesn't quite belong and which the telepath still hasn't fully compensated for. The language, the thought pattern, is different than the others."

"You think the Exchange teamed up with the Mizzies?" Kalia asked. "We could take 'em *all* out from *this* position!"

Oddly, it was Desreth who doubted. "We have spied on Exchange exploiter teams before. They are often loaded with almost anything they can imagine they might need, including thought-programmable mobile explosives. Tobrush, did you not also say that one of them was a cyborg of some sort?"

"Yes, they call them cymols. Unreadable as Corithians, but I got the information from the minds of the others."

"Captain, it was I who first suggested we take them out," Desreth noted. "Now I recommend that we do not. Just one of those explosives, directed in here, would bring this whole place down upon us, and even if we got them all in one volley, this cyborg could still direct fire into here. If it were just the Mizlaplan, then it would make sense to remain and finish it, but we should know much more about where the Exchange loyalties now lie before taking them all on. You have all had sleep, food, and water. It is best we go now if we are going down that falls trail. If they are so close, it is almost inevitable that they will camp here as we did. A sure lead is certainly worth more than the possibility of being outgunned and buried alive."

Josef sighed. "All right. I hate to abandon such a perfect position, and the fight has to continue at some point, but I agree with you for now. We've got the lead—we should keep it."

"Oh, not *again*!" Kalia sulked. "Must we always run from fights unless the enemy agrees to lie down and submit to execution?"

"In this case, I'm with you in my desire to have done with it," Josef told her, "but this isn't just a personal thing. This is duty now."

"Shit! We're most likely gonna die anyway! Why not chance it here?"

"Because," Tobrush put in, "then we'd never really know what this was all about. I am prepared to die if need be—my oath commands it—but not unless it need be, and certainly not without some answers."

Josef nodded, to himself rather than to Tobrush. That was really about the size of things. "Whatever those ancient people worshiped was connected to these falls, and the pit at the bottom," he said. "I have no intention of dying at the top of it, like *they* did. Let's go!"

The trail cut into the side of the falls was steeper than it looked, but there were also previously unnoticed handholds, a bit high up but usable, at least to Josef and Kalia, and to Desreth as well if the Corithian wanted to shoot a tentacle to them.

By the time they were at the falls itself they were already more than twenty meters below the rim; entering the falls from the side, they went through a curtain of water and then were behind the great volume of water, damp but reasonably dry.

"I gotta admit, this is weird," Kalia commented. "We're outta the rain 'cause the roof's all water!"

"Look at the trail and handholds!" Tobrush called to them. They all looked, and, slowly, eerily, the trail and holds were softly glowing.

"Did we turn on the lights or are we expected?" Josef wondered aloud.

"Whatever, it's a little late to back out now," she noted.

"I wonder if this can be seen from the rim?" Tobrush put in. "I was thinking of the effect it would have on a very primitive people to see ribbons of glowing light rising from below through the falls. If you also had some bright light, or perhaps even fire, it would impress the hell out of them."

"Or into them," Josef shot back. "At least this shows we're on the right trail, as it were. If something or somebody came up this way often enough to warrant a lighting system, they had to come from *somewhere*."

"Hey! It looks like we're comin' to the end up there!" Kalia pointed. "And we're not even out from under the whole falls!"

"No! It's a switchback!" Josef responded. "Now we go back the way we came and down more."

"If this thing goes down to the bottom, we had all better check flotation gear," Tobrush noted worriedly. "There had better be an 'exit' sign there before we reach the water level!"

"Hmmm . . . Let's not worry about that unless we have to," Josef said, thinking about just how long it was back and just how exposed they'd be coming back up. "What happens if we run into more demons like that first pair?"

"They are the demigods, the creators of us and our worlds," Kalia argued. "We should free them and worship them and they will be the powers to slay all our enemies!"

"If we could make a deal, I might agree with you on that, too," Josef admitted. "Unfortunately, I think we're considered no better than toys or pets to them. That's the impression I got, anyway. Anybody in this group want to be some other life form's pet or plaything? Particularly *you*, Kalia. I'd think that going back to being somebody's slave, if you were lucky, would be the *last* thing you'd want."

"But this is different! They are gods!"

"Which means that they have more power and knowledge than we have," Tobrush put in. "Why were you originally a plaything of the rich and powerful on your home world? Same thing, isn't it? The only thing you'd do is add somebody higher up to the top of the ruling heap; you would still remain on the bottom."

That stopped her. "I—I had never thought of it like that before," she admitted.

"The big problem," the telepath continued, "is their mental power. They had me cold back there—it took Robakuk to get me out of there. We don't have Robakuk any more."

Josef thought about that. "Desreth, Kalia, I'm going to give you both an order that is *not* to be countermanded under any conditions. If Tobrush moves to free a demon, kill him."

"Now, *wait* a minute!" the Julki exclaimed.

"Sorry, Tobrush. If they can beat you and take you over, we haven't any choice. If they *know* that any of us will absolutely do it, and with Desreth you won't even have the advantage of warning, they might try dealing instead, or at least keep you free. It's the only insurance I know."

"Um—thank you, I think. If I come up with a more palatable alternative, I shall assuredly give it to you at once, though. Still, I would count on nothing for certain in this place. Sooner or later, even if this works, we are going to meet one not imprisoned or contained. I had the very strong impression that, freed of all constraint, their mental powers are almost godlike. I should certainly love to know who imprisoned them, and how."

"Yeah," Josef sighed. "And if they're still around, do we want to meet *them*, either? Uh-oh."

They stopped at the next switchback, the fourth. It was difficult to say just how far their descent had been, but their best estimate was that they were now better than a kilometer below the surface and *very* close to where the water struck bottom, throwing up the massive spray and mist. That, however, wasn't the problem.

The path simply ended. No switchback, nothing. It just seemed to end, about ten meters above the water.

"*Now* what do we do?" Kalia asked, staring at the dead end.

"Scan the end of the trail," Desreth suggested. "I believe you will find the results quite interesting."

Josef turned all of his instrumentation on. The helmet now became a screen, with the entire forward area electronically scanned and analyzed. There were no surprises except right where the path ended; there the thing simply refused to lock, but showed a massive, irregular burst of energy.

Analysis was refused for insufficient data.

He switched the screen off and fed the information to the others. "Ideas, anybody?"

"I hardly think that the demons would like living in that paradise above surrounded by all those primitives," Tobrush said carefully. "If they were only here now and again, they wouldn't want any of the most daring, curious, or fanatical going where they weren't wanted."

"You think it's an illusion, then?"

"I haven't the faintest idea. Unfortunately, I can think of only one way to find out for certain. Any volunteers?"

Desreth went right to the edge. "I shall see if I can place an extension into the area and tell if anything is truly there without going over." A slender tendril oozed out of the body as if it were made of liquid encased in some metallic plastic and reached forward. The end of the tentacle vanished in mid-air.

"I am at the limit of my extension," the Corithian told them. "There is no sensation or measurable difference, but the humidity is down to only a fraction of what it was. Measurements indicate an artificial, enclosed place."

"Never mind the weather report," Tobrush said irritatedly. "Is there a *floor*?"

"I believe so. My confidence factor is sufficient for me to try it." And, without a word, the Corithian scuttled forward and vanished completely.

"Well? Where is it? Why doesn't it come back?" Kalia wanted to know.

"I have no idea," Josef responded, "but feel free to find out for yourself. As for me, I'm willing to put it to the test myself. Weapons at the ready." He sucked in his breath, then let it out slowly. "I've never walked over a cliff before."

"Bullshit!" she responded. "There's nobody in there of the natural world, and what good are guns against *them*?" And, with that, she stepped off and into the nothing ahead of him. Keeping his own pistol out, he followed her. Tobrush, suddenly alone, rushed after them almost without thinking, and only as the Julki went over the edge into nothingness did it suddenly think, *"What* am I *doing?"*

There was no time for a lengthy panic, however, by any of them. They were all standing there, together, on a very solid floor, trying to take in what they now saw before them.

The area was enormous; only with the aid of their suit magnification could they see the other side of the great circular concourse, and their instruments refused to consistently calculate its true size. The highly polished floor reflected their features, and within it ran ribbons of gold that shone like bright lights, creating elaborate geometrical patterns.

The room, or chamber, more properly, had walls composed of similar panels, about two meters across by three high, each also outlined by the golden light and each also embossed with a singular pattern which appeared much like a golden five-pointed star whose points were connected by straight lines, then also circled point to point.

Josef looked up, and saw that the panels seemed to rise as far as the eye could see.

In the center was an entire series of demon station entrances, maybe hundreds of them, one next to the other, angled up to the floor level.

Tobrush was so relieved to be *anywhere* that it took a few minutes before the telepath grew both curious enough and confident enough to move around. It was the empathic Kalia, however, who voiced the Julki's comments before the words could rise and form in its own mouth.

"They're all here," she breathed. "Demons . . . Hundreds, maybe thousands of them . . . One behind each and every one of those doors . . ."

Josef suddenly felt all the hair on his body tingle. "Those panels are *doors*?"

"Evidently," Tobrush responded. "I doubt if there's a back way out of them."

"How can you stand it in here if they're all in there?" the leader asked, both curious and nervous.

"They're not like the others. Or, rather, I think they *are* like the others, only not awakened to consciousness."

"They're not aware of us, then?"

"In a sense, yes. But they believe that we are dreams. After all this, I suspect they have a hard time telling the difference."

"Where's Desreth?" Josef asked, frowning.

"Here," the Corithian replied from far over toward the stations. "I could not return. Look around and tell me how you arrived."

Josef turned and saw only more of the same panels and symbols. There seemed no door, no way in or out except through the center stations; no break at all in the wall.

"As you can see, failing another coming through while I took bearings, I had no way of knowing where the portal is."

Josef nodded and peered nervously around. *Thousands* of them!

"I suggest that, no matter how tempting it is to explore this place, we move through rather quickly," Tobrush said, at least as nervous as Josef. "I have the most uncomfortable feeling that some of them are arriving at decisions on what is reality and what is not."

"Yeah," he responded dryly. "But which one? Are we at the center now? Is this the main station where they go to their other worlds, or is there more? And, if more, which of those maybe couple of hundred stations do we use?"

"I have the distinct feeling that this is nowhere near bottom," the Julki told him. "The picture I seem to get is of a race numbering as many as the stars themselves. These are—please, let us find or choose some way out! The more I probe, the more aware they become!"

"All right. Desreth? Any ideas?"

"Not yet, but let us walk around. There might be some hint," the Corithian said.

Tobrush was so torn between the collection of information

and fear of the creatures that it was impossible for the telepath to stop talking.

"These—none of them—are even very high up or very important," the Julki told them. "To this race, these folk who seem to have powers approaching godhood, are little more than drols. Low-class workers. This is a mere *work team*! Laborers, no more!"

That got Josef. "Laborers? A work team? All these of this power? Then . . . what are the higher classes? Their masters?"

"I cannot say. The concepts, the visions, are beyond me. I can only tell you that they are . . . still further on."

"Anything on which one of these damned stations to take?"

"I get the impression that it doesn't matter. The rule seems constant. So long as we go left out of any straightaway, we . . . *descend,* as it were."

"Descend? Towards what? Where?"

"I cannot tell you. The holograms are really confusing. It could be a city, or a great castle, or a central control room, or any one of a hundred other things. It might be all of them. Not that the stations don't go different places—they do. But there's some sort of differences in authority, perhaps clans or bosses or some sort of hierarchical system, that governs them. The only thing clear is that to descend towards the core you go left out of any station. To go anywhere else, you go right."

Josef sighed. "Then, even without any trail, we just pick one and it's the right one?"

"That is the impression I get."

He sighed. "Well, at least it'll take the pressure off our backs. The odds of either of the other teams picking the one we do is slim to none."

"That is some compensation," the Julki agreed. "At least until we get to where all leftward paths lead. So, please, pick one. They are growing more and more aware, and I have no idea how much longer I can hold out. I keep getting the same thought."

"What thought?"

" '*Our time is almost upon us again.*' "

Josef halted before one of the crystal-like openings. "Here. It's as good a choice as any, with no other clues."

"Fine with me," Tobrush agreed. "I notice that even Kalia

is having second thoughts about freeing *this* mob. Still, I at least can understand now why those two free demons didn't break out their companions.''

''Huh? Why?''

''They want to make sure that *they* are the ones, the only ones, to get credit for freeing the boss.''

Josef shivered, and looked at the others. ''Any objections to this one?''

''It is sufficiently random,'' Desreth commented. ''There is no clue as to which is which in any event.''

''Okay—through and now! And remember my orders on freeing any station managers!''

One by one, they entered the station and were gone from the holding place. And, all around it, the vast horde sighed and drifted back to their strange, endless dreams.

MORALITY
AND HONOR
IN HADES

HE WAS SOMEWHERE DEEP IN A DARK WELL, neck deep in blood, the stench everywhere, reaching out, clutching at anything in order to climb out. But the well was filled with monsters and unspeakable things; he reached for what felt like a limb and found that it was instead a severed arm. Tentacles oozed from the sides and tried to wrap themselves around him, and wherever they touched, it was like acid, burning his flesh and filling the claustrophobic enclosure with the added stench of burning flesh.

Bloody faces also lined the walls: familiar faces of comrades from past expeditions who'd died, often in horrible ways. Some were calling.

"Hello, Jimmy! Knew you'd get here sooner or later! Give you a hand?" And then a disembodied, bloody hand would shoot out and grab his throat and begin to squeeze. . . .

A new head—Tris Lankur's—materialized out of the ooze and opened its eyes and looked at him and said, "Sorry. Lost my head a while back. Now I lost my body, too. This provokes a fascinating quantitative problem for a rationalist, you know, particularly when one is a machine. It's because I've got brains, you see." And, with that, the top of his head popped off and the brain, which seemed both real and made of some kind of metal, began oozing out of the skull and enlarging itself until it threatened to fill the airspace remaining and choke him.

"Sweet Jesus! Have mercy on me!" he screamed, or tried to, but the blood, as thick as porridge, moved into his mouth and made him choke on the words.

Father McGuire's voice suddenly came to him from a great distance. "I'm sorry, but Jesus isn't in right now. However, if you leave your name and your identification number, and if you didn't desert Him and break your word to Him, He'll get back to you sooner or later. . . ."

"Jimmy!" It was Sister Margaret, floating there as radiant as always. She reached out her hand to him and he reached for it, but when he touched her, her body began a rapid and loathsome decay, until it was but a rotted, bloated, obscene corpse, covered by masses of living, squirming maggots that began to drop off her and onto him.

<Jimmy! Jimmy! Come out of it, Jimmy! I've done all that I can to minimize shock, but there are limits! You must *wake up!>*

"That's all I needed," he groaned in his horrible torture pit. "Even here I can't get rid of her!"

<C'mon, Jimmy, you bastard! Fight it!>

"Oh, shut up, Grysta!" he moaned, but then he noticed that, when she talked to him, the horrors moved back a bit, the blood level went down.

<You jerk! You dummy! You asshole! You took a stun hit full in the chest from close range! You wake up and now or you'll go where you already seem to think you are!>

She kept at him, cursing, cajoling, threatening, and, slowly, feeling like he was in deep ocean water and fighting his way to the surface, he finally came to consciousness.

"What . . . ?" he said aloud, still confused and disoriented, and not a little bit shaken.

<You got shot, stupid! They left the null on the trail and he nailed all of you with a heavy stun before you knew what hit you!>

"How long have I been out?"

<What do I look like? A clock? Pretty long, I think. Several minutes.>

"How do you know what happened?"

<He came up after he nailed all of you. Lankur wasn't all the way out so he had to hit him again. I didn't really see him, but I felt his presence and I heard him come up and heard the extra shot.>

Jimmy struggled to a sitting position and groaned. This *hurt*, hurt worse than he could remember ever hurting in his whole life. He was shaken, too; the visions of his delirium were still very much with him and seemed very, very real.

He went over to Molly first, not only because she was his responsibility, but because he hadn't the slightest idea how to judge the condition of a Durquist *or* a cymol, so there wasn't much he could do about them until they came around.

At first he was afraid she was dead; there seemed even less than usual in that pretty mind. But when he pulled her to a sitting position, supporting her, and kept saying her name over and over she smiled slightly and began coming around. Finally she opened her eyes, shook her head rapidly from side to side, and groaned at the sudden pain and dizziness. "Jimmy? What happened?"

"We all got shot," he told her. "Come on! On your feet! I know just what you feel like, but the more you move around, the quicker it wears off."

He got her up, then looked next at the Durquist. The creature was limp, and, in its environment suit, flattened by total relaxation, he looked less like a living being and more like some deflated carnival balloon.

"Durquist! Snap out of it and get in motion!" he yelled through the intercom. "Come on! Up and at 'em!"

<Just a few more minutes, Mother,> the Durquist's mind responded.

"Mother my ass!" the telepath snapped. "I may be host to a Morgh, but I'll be damned if I'm gonna be Mommie to a Durquist!"

Feeling almost back to normal except for a headache and some tingling in the extremities, Jimmy and Molly tried to raise the Durquist, and at least resulted in shaking him. Broad tentacles flexed, the eyes popped up, and the Durquist said, "I am really beginning to regret coming along on this trip."

"Well, time to see if the one who talked us into it is still among the living, or whatever cymols are," McCray responded.

"Functional," came an eerie, emotionless voice in the intercom that caused them all to look nervously around. "Restoring biologic interface. Checklist running. Completed."

Tris Lankur suddenly sat up, then slowly got to his feet, but in a jerky, nonhuman way. In the suit, the impression of not a human being but a mechanical man was almost absolute.

"Well, I'll be cursed!" swore the Durquist, staring. "He really *is* a robot!"

"I am directing biological interface manually," said Lankur in that weird, mechanical voice. "I am functional, but direct linkage to biologically stored data not fully operable."

"He got real problem," Molly commented needlessly.

Jimmy couldn't help but think of his nightmare and of the metallic, swelling brain of the pilot.

"Status reports on other units?" the cymol asked.

"We're all right—I think," Jimmy told him—it—whatever. "You're the one that's worse for wear."

"Second shot produced some tissue damage and electrical linkage shorts," the cymol explained. "Essential data intact, but am unable to access Terran simulation mode. Pre-cymol mode memories, habit patterns, not present."

<Jeez! Lookit the way he moves!> Grysta commented. *<He's a real walking corpse now!>*

Jimmy found the sight of the cymol stripped of his humanity to be very unsettling, but there were more pressing matters. "How functional overall are you?" he asked. "Can you make the distance? Can you fight if you have to and hit what you aim at?"

"Full control. Limits and reflexive actions impossible to predict, but no random or uncontrolled actions will occur. However, sensory and tactile feedback to brain is not functional at this time."

"You mean you can't feel pain?" McCray asked him.

"I mean I can feel nothing. But the biological unit appears to function as I direct."

<Uh-oh!> Grysta commented. *<Anybody bring any diapers? Otherwise he's gonna get pretty ripe real soon!>*

As usual, Jimmy ignored her. "Durquist?"

"It will have to do," the Durquist responded. "It is particularly painful for me to see him in this condition, since I was with him for so long, but, from a practical sense, it's far better than broken legs or puncture wounds or the like. What about our treacherous priests?"

Jimmy did a scan. "Ahead, of course. I think they made real time. Either that or we were out a lot longer than Grysta thinks we were. Still, I get the odd impression that they stopped somewhere ahead. If I were them, I'd want to get as far away from us as I could and as fast as possible."

"Haste makes for mistakes," the Durquist commented. "Let them stop and worry about us for a bit. Still, I would like to close and see if we can find some shelter from this interminable rain. How are you, by the way? From the angle, I'd say you got the full force of the first shot."

"I dreamt I died and went to Hell," the telepath said slowly. "Then I woke up and found I was already there." He looked at the stiff, jerky body of Tris Lankur.

<You sure he's still on our side?> Grysta asked a bit nervously.

The fact was, he wasn't sure any more. He wasn't sure of anything except that they were in the middle of a miserable world of gloom and constant, heavy rain, and he didn't know why he was there or how the hell to get out.

Listening to those omnipresent shrieks and moans, though, and still with vivid memories of his dreams, he definitely decided that he didn't want to die right now, no matter how miserable he was.

"Let's close on them," he said at last. "I want them to know we're there."

It took them less than an hour along the obsidian-encrusted black rock trail before they were very close indeed. McCray climbed almost to the edge of the trail and looked out at the great falls. Still, when Tris and Molly both made to keep walking, he stopped them. "They're there. Waiting for us, most likely," he warned them. "There's no cover for us down there on the edge of the falls, either."

The Durquist agreed. "If there is some overhang or ruins right against the side here, that's where I'd be. Waiting for us to step out and be shot right over those falls."

"This unit, McCray, and Durquist have two directional grenades each. Enemy does not or it would have used them in first battle," Lankur noted.

"But Modra's with them!" the Durquist reminded him. "We'd get her, too!"

"No logical way to recover Modra," the cymol responded. "Probabilities of doing so under this situation very small. Modra now just makes the Mizlaplan invaders the strongest group. Logical to eliminate them all. Advantage then returns to us."

"But that's *Modra* down there! Modra!" the Durquist exclaimed, appalled. Even Jimmy McCray, the newcomer, had problems with this kind of logic.

"Getting the bastards who screwed us is one thing," he said evenly, trying to hold his temper, "but I draw the line at the murder of one of our own."

"Without that action, a stalemate results and the Mycohl go on unencumbered by default," the cymol pointed out. "We cannot proceed without being ambushed by the Mizlaplanians. Mizlaplanians cannot proceed because we have a clear field of fire from this point. A stalemate is unacceptable so long as a third enemy group is involved and ahead of us. We have the means to resolve the stalemate. Not using those means violates all logic."

"It means nothing to you that she's one of our own, kidnapped against her will?" Jimmy pressed.

"The Exchange has approximately thirty trillion citizens. Of those, close to two point five trillion are Terrans. What is one more or less to the maintenance of order and harmony?"

"I assume that same logic applies to us," the Durquist noted.

"Of course."

"This explains a lot about the quality of life of the bulk of people in the Exchange," Jimmy McCray noted dryly, in the low, barely heard whisper he generally used only to talk to Grysta. "Grysta was right—you're not on our side any more. Somehow, I don't think you ever really were."

"Waiting is pointless. They are sheltered, we are exposed," the cymol commented.

"Hold, cymol—before you act!" the Durquist called icily, edging up to the man who'd once been his friend and captain.

"Yes?"

"What is the basic philosophical difference between you and your masters and the Quintara?"

"The question has no relevancy."

"It does to me. Very much so."

"Very well. The Guardians believe that the whole is far greater than the parts that compose it and provides the greatest good for the greatest number of people. The Quintara believe that the whole exists to serve themselves."

"Then, in the smaller sense, the team, which is us, has interests that outweigh the interests of a part of it, namely Modra. Somehow, *this* 'part' sees little practical difference to himself in that attitude. I cannot allow what you propose to happen."

"You have no vote. I act by the authority of the Guardians themselves as an officer of the Exchange. You elected to come with me; I did not order it."

"I am not at all sure there was much of a choice," the Durquist noted, "although, if there were, I would still have come because the *team* came. *All* of the team. Me, McCray, even Molly, and, yes, Modra. And I must wonder when you propose such a horrible violation of our codes if in fact there isn't still some little bit of Tris Lankur in there, perhaps the bitter, hating part, rationalized by the mechanical part, that seeks not what is right, or just, but revenge. She killed you, turned you into *this,* and now *you* would take *her* life in exchange!"

The vacant-eyed jerky body did not respond, but instead walked just to the edge, where the path went steeply down to the bedrock below. One of the Durquist's eyes swiveled to Jimmy McCray, who stared back at it and just nodded silently.

The cymol took instrument readings, totally ignoring the others behind him. "Range forty point two meters to the right, inside the cliff in some kind of cave or dwelling," Lankur reported to no one in particular. He reached into his pouch and removed a small black object, which hummed to life and then emitted a high-pitched, steady, whistling tone.

The Durquist stood, a bizarre caricature of a biped, and walked up right behind the cymol. Without hesitation, the "right" tentacle swung back, then loosed itself forward,

striking the cymol almost directly on his ass with such force
that the man was literally propelled into the air and came down
a good four meters on the bedrock below.

They could hear the yells of the Mizlaplanians below at the
sudden appearance of the cymol, and Jimmy, pistol in hand,
walked up and stood next to the Durquist, watching.

Lankur had landed limply, like a rag doll tossed from a
window, but now, slowly, he stood up and began walking in
that jerky, zombie-like way a few steps, then bent down and
retrieved the small guided grenade where it had fallen.

"Shall we just shoot the bastard and have done with it?" the
Durquist asked.

"No, let them do it," Jimmy responded. "If they can't take
him out, they don't deserve to."

Below, in the cliff dwelling, Krisha had been idly monitoring
the Exchange team that hadn't really paid much attention,
counting on her old instincts to flag anything really dangerous.
The cold hatred of the Durquist had masked some of his
thoughts, and, while she alerted the others and knew something
was going to happen, she wasn't quite sure what. Tris Lankur's
sudden arrival on the flat rock below was, therefore, only
slightly less of a surprise to her than to the others; by the time
she had sensed what was to happen from the Durquist's mind
and cried out, it had already happened.

"My God! It's Tris!" Modra cried, and then watched,
suddenly horrified, as the zombie-like motions of the animated
corpse in and of itself reinforced Morok's fanciful hypnotic
scenario. An old pro with a natural fear of being around a
hypno, she'd believed, but never fully accepted, the visions of
her comrades being killed and their bodies possessed. Now
here was the proof of it, and resolved the last doubts in her
mind.

"That's a programmable grenade he's got!" she warned
them. "It'll blow this whole place down if he launches it!"

"Then shoot, Modra! Shoot! You've got the best angle!"
Gun Roh Chin shouted.

She lifted her pistol but could not do it. No matter what the
sight, no matter what the horror in front of her, she simply
could not kill Tris. Not again.

Lethal bursts from Manya and Morok, who had a lesser

angle but still a sufficient one, struck the cymol full on. There was a sudden, shattering explosion that deafened them and brought down pieces of rock upon them as the terrible sound reverberated through the ruins.

The concussion knocked Jimmy backward into Molly, and they both tumbled in a heap as a small black cloud rose from the bedrock ahead. The Durquist merely flipped back to all five points and otherwise stood his ground, then slowly rose again on two of them. Jimmy picked himself up and made certain Molly was all right, then walked back forward to where the Durquist still watched.

There was very little left. The grenade had already left Tris Lankur's hands when the bolts struck, but as its route was in the direct line of fire they had gotten it no more than a meter from him, still in the air, and it had blown, ripping through the blue environment suit as if it were paper and then through the still all too fragile human body, spraying blood and body parts all over, even into the falls itself, as well as some luminescent yellowish fluid that must have fed the cymol part.

Eerily, the moans and shrieks and distant screams that were such a part of the background noise of this place that they'd almost been tuned out by the others, rose in volume for a while until they almost drowned out not only the rain but even the falls, before slipping back to their normal levels.

"Too bad we couldn't get his supply kit and power pack," Jimmy McCray said dryly, looking at the scene.

The Durquist was thinking along different lines. He was . . . remembering.

"He was a good man, once," the star creature commented. "One of the best. He clawed himself up out of a stinking little ball of dirt where all they did was wallow in the dry mud and sands and have as many starving kids as they could before they died very young. He was wild, reckless sometimes, the taker of incredible risks because that's how he rose to where he was, and he just never understood that everyone else wasn't like him. I think that's why Modra never considered bonding with him, even though she loved him. She knew that, sooner or later, he'd take one chance too many. I think she even married that other fellow mostly to make sure we didn't go broke and that Tris wouldn't lose his ship. Now it's over for him."

<Awww . . . That's so sad . . . !> Grysta commented sympathetically.

Jimmy McCray sighed. "Well, at least she didn't do *that*. Their telepath was so startled at all this she dropped her guard for a moment. Modra had a shot but couldn't take it. Couldn't bring herself to take it."

"I am glad for that," the Durquist replied. "She will never accept that his end came from his own immaturity, which was necessary for him to survive and get where he did, and not her direct action. His ego just couldn't handle a defeat, even so personal a one."

McCray shrugged. "Well, it leaves us a gun short, and no matter what I thought of his solution, he was right about the stalemate, and by saying that we're not going to get Modra back any time soon, either. That quick peek I had at her shows her expertly redone by their hypno; she thinks we're all dead and possessed by demonic spirits out to kill them all. After seeing Lankur, there, she's got no reason to doubt it, either."

"It *does* make things a bit complex," the Durquist agreed. "Do you suppose we could offer an amnesty and another head start if they cleared the fog in Modra's head and sent her back to us?"

"How could we know?" Jimmy asked him. "The telepath's powerful enough to screw up my monitoring, and I sure wouldn't trust a hypno in my sight. They certainly haven't proven trustworthy so far, and our sentiments, no matter how genuinely transmitted, may change, leaving them in the middle."

<Together we could break that telepath and you know it,> Grysta put in.

He wasn't so sure about that. But what if they could? That wouldn't get Modra back whole, and it wouldn't break the hypno, which was his real worry.

Finally the Durquist said, "Why don't we just offer them a straight way out? Modra is as safe with them as with us, and, so far, all our danger has been in front of us. Let them keep her for a while and go. We've got the power advantage, and I got the distinct impression that the hypno's injured—that might explain the kidnapping. I wouldn't bet very much on the chances of an injured man surviving very long if they push on, tough old veteran and hypno or not, and if the hypno goes, things suddenly become *very* much in our favor."

Jimmy thought it over. "Just get rid of the roadblock again?"

"That's about it. I shouldn't like the thought of the Mycohl making some kind of deal with our horned friends unencumbered, then just sitting back and waiting for all of us."

"All right—I'll make them an offer," Jimmy said, and sent, *<We can sit it out forever or work things out now as a compromise.>*

<How do you suggest we do it?> Krisha asked him.

<I've no love for sitting out here in the wet. I've had enough of it. We will backtrack for one hour. You move out and along the way, or pick some way if you haven't decided where to go. Then we head back. No tricks, no traps, or it's war.>

<We have an injured man. He needs more rest than he's gotten. Much more.>

<This is not a negotiation,> Jimmy responded. *<All grievances committed against us have been by you. We've done nothing to harm you, and, indeed, we helped you the one time you needed help. You repaid us with betrayal. We can hardly trust your word to us that you won't shoot as we go past, now can we?>*

Krisha found herself in a real dilemma. Morok was already back on the stone floor asleep, and the better for it. She'd heard the comments about him, and knew that they were counting on Morok's death and had no interest in helping him to heal. She really needed to discuss things, but couldn't do it openly. To do so would suddenly confuse Modra, who thought her remaining comrades were demonic beings.

<Wait a moment. I need to talk to someone,> she managed.

"I don't think they're going for it," Jimmy told the Durquist. He frowned, thinking for a moment. "Grysta? Do you think we could manage enough power to do what she does—at least to block out the Durquist as well, and Molly, too?"

<Why bother with Molly?> Grysta asked him. *<There's got to be something there before it's worth blocking out.>*

"Because Molly has ears, which is why this is even a lower voice than usual. I want a way where that telepath can't pick up a conversation between the Durquist and me. Nor thoughts about it afterwards.''

<*Hmmm . . . Yeah, I think so. But how will we know for sure if we manage it or not? With her block, I mean.*>

"You leave that to me. I can feel her probes and I'll know if she gets through."

He suddenly heard Krisha call him in his mind.

<*Sorry,*> she told him, <*but that is no solution. After the Holy Father is rested and better, then, perhaps. Until then, it seems to me that you have no choice but to stay up there and get wet. We know you won't mount an attack on us. Otherwise, you killed your man for nothing.*>

Jimmy smiled to himself. <*All right, lass. On your own head be what happens from now on. At least you saved me two hours' futile walk.*> He sighed. "Grysta—let's try the block right now. And maintain it until we no longer need it. No lapses or we might all be dead."

<*Uh—dead? I'm not sure I like this.*>

"Just do it, you little worm! You were born to sit and rot, but I was not!"

<*Okay, okay. Don't get so upset! Try it—now!*>

Below, Krisha was startled to find that the blind spot where Jimmy McCray was abruptly widened, blotting out all of the Exchange team. It was so sudden and unexpected, and so powerful, she grew nervous. What had happened was simply not possible, not without supernatural aid, which is what she believed increased her own power. She felt by now that she knew McCray's power and limits as well as any telepath knows another, and here, suddenly, was this massive surge.

She tried probing against it, attempting to break through, but it was impassive, a wall of white noise whenever she tried to read any of them. She looked over at Gun Roh Chin. "The enemy has suddenly gone dark on me! I'm not getting a thing! I don't understand it, but I don't like it."

Neither did the captain, weary as he was. "Wake the others and assume fully armed stations," he told her. "I still feel certain we have a level of safety, but I never like surprises or underestimate an enemy."

The Durquist, too, was a bit surprised, but pleased. "No one can hear us?"

"Nobody. The trouble is, if she mounts a concerted attack against me, it might weaken, and not even I know how long I can hold this." He stood and pointed to the falls. "Use your magnification. You see those markers there, kind of nubs but a bit shiny, leading right to the edge?"

"Yes, I see them. They *look* like the way to go, but it would be very comforting to know there isn't a sheer drop there."

"Look over at the falls itself, just a tiny corner on this side before the cascade starts. A sliver of a trail. I'm willing to bet my life on it."

"You propose going by them? How? I'll not collapse that roof!"

"I understand that," McCray told him, "but I'm not talking any kill. It *will*, however, be as risky for them as for us, if we don't do the figures exactly right. Fair's fair. We're taking most of the risk, and it's only right that some of it be shared."

"All right, then, what have you got in mind?"

After more than an hour, things began settling back to normal in the Mizlaplanian camp. There was only so much time you could keep yourself on the alert, particularly when the only thing that had happened to cause it was the enemy's sudden ability to block itself out.

They still had their hostage, and considering Krisha had overheard the entire debate that had led to Lankur's ultimate death, there was little concern that the remaining enemy above would really try and wipe them out. There was as well the knowledge that the only way through that was worth anything at all was right to those falls and down, and that area was in perfect view of their guns.

Modra Stryke had suffered not at all from seeing Lankur finally blown to pieces; instead, oddly, she felt much better, as if some load had been lifted from her shoulders. Tris was really gone; she was sorry about that, but it had been none of her doing *this* time. Not that it really mattered about that; the important fact was that he'd been killed in the act of trying to kill not just these people but *her*. If there was any clearer break with what was and with what might have been, she couldn't conceive of it.

She was also getting to know the Mizlaplanians; enough to

know that she kind of liked them as individuals, but found their value system, their beliefs, their very status disturbing. They were the most enslaved people she had ever met, yet they considered the enslavement and the totalitarian nature of their homeland to be free.

Krisha in particular bothered her; the dark beauty had just about everything a woman could want—looks, brains, capability—and here she was, a virgin priestess, celibate, bound to a monastic lifestyle except when defending the faith such as now. It seemed such a total waste.

At least they didn't try and convert her. She got the idea that almost any way to convert was okay with these people, but that doing it by hypno power was heresy of the worst sort. There was little likelihood they could convert her, in any event; to do so with her empathic abilities would mean automatic commitment to the priesthood. She wondered how, if all the Talents were celibate, and sterilized, priests and priestesses, they didn't run out of Talents. Discovering that most, including Morok and Manya, had been laboratory-bred from reproductive material taken from their parents at ordination, solved that mystery but didn't make it look like a wagon she would ever want to climb aboard.

Still, it was tough being an empath in this company. They *all* believed; they were all absolutely convinced of the truth of their faith and that their gods sat on their shoulders and directed their moves. When they prayed, particularly together, the rapturous joy and total emotional conviction flowing through them was so overpowering it almost sucked her in in spite of it all. That kind of certainty, of genuine comfort and joy, in a place and situation like this, was damned seductive.

She was aware, too, that her presence disturbed them. She was a shade of gray trapped in the midst of a group of people who saw only black and white.

Captain Chin was different, or at least he seemed so. The only one who was, really. She would have guessed his primary occupation without having to be told it; commercial skippers tended to have the same sort of look and manner no matter what the race or nationality. He radiated the power that only those in command feel; Tris had once had that kind of feel to him, too.

And he was worldly. Over there, far from everyone else, leaning on the crude cutout of a window and looking out at the rain, the glow from his second cigar attested to that. He alone had been outside the Mizlaplan before, to both Mycohl and the Exchange. Only the fact that he was a null, unreadable except by the most basic of observations, kept the real Gun Roh Chin something of a cipher. She felt certain he was totally loyal to his system and these people, yet she wasn't at all certain he believed any of it.

She went over to him, seeking some kind of comfort in the dark, no matter how different he might have been.

"I can't understand why they don't use the other grenades," she said, looking out. "We're wide open here."

"I think they can't program them properly," he responded slickly, glad he'd had a little time to think of that one. "That's why the one had to expose himself. I think we're safe here. It's when we have to move that we have real problems."

"I know the others think that this is part of a real Hell, where the sinners of the universe are sent. Do you believe that?"

Chin shrugged, but he was thankful to be off the subject of questions he had to lie about. "Manya, and I believe Krish, now, believe it. Morok does, too, deep down, but he would prefer not to."

"And you?"

"What did your people think?" he asked, sidestepping the question.

"Only Jimmy McCray, our telepath, thought that way. He was a very strange little man, too new to the crew for me to really get to know him the way I knew all the others. He was raised totally within one of the ancient religions of Old Earth, and had pretty much a tragic life, I think, and never really shook it."

"McCray," the captain repeated. "English? No. Irish?"

She was surprised. "That's what he said his background was. They have a couple of worlds of their own, preserving very much their old culture, very pastoral, I'm told—and very dull."

"You wouldn't like a little pastoral dullness right now?"

She smiled. "Maybe right now. My own upbringing was a little pastoral itself, and I hated it. I was the youngest of eleven kids, and the only one who wanted out of that life."

Gun Roh Chin chuckled. "Eleven! That is one thing we Terrans do with expertness. My own ancient culture was never very good at fighting. It kept losing wars to conqueror after conqueror. But we retained our culture and we retained our own belief in the superiority of that culture, and we bred and we bred and we intermarried with all the conquerors and, with infinite patience, one day there weren't any conquerors any more. Just us and a few added freshenings of the genetic pool. Now *all* Terrans, no matter where their part of humanity wound up and under what rule, have become my people. Not physically, but in the most basic sense. We can't interbreed with all those other races, of course, but we can outbreed them. We are already the largest single race in *any* of the Three Empires. Did you know that?"

"No," she admitted. "I hadn't realized that."

"Just look at the ones here. For your Exchange, there is you, this McCray, and the late Captain Lankur. Here, it's Krish and myself, and then there is the Mycohl captain and the woman with him. That's almost half of everyone who got here. You see what I mean? Give us a few more centuries and we will be the majority of everyone in all three empires. Now, in spite of we few here, the bulk of Terrans are coolies—sorry, an ancient term. The bottom of the ladder, socially and politically. We grow the food, we haul, we do the other races' laundry. One day, those races who now see us as little more than a faceless sea of workers will have to deal with a weight of numbers too great to ignore or suppress."

"You sound like a revolutionary," she noted. "Is that what you are behind your mysterious wall?"

"Not in the usual sense of the word. What threat am I? Or you? I merely state facts. It isn't really something all of us planned, you know, but you have to look at the competition. Manya's people have an amazing camouflage ability that helped protect them and raise them above all the others on their planet. Morok's people can fly. Savin's people were arboreal night dwellers who could be still as death for ages and had uncanny balance and even more uncanny eyes. We're about the weakest, softest, least able people to ever climb to the top of the ladder. We're no smarter than they are, even collectively, yet our sheer lack of attributes and our vulnerability has bred a race of survivors. Given enough time, we're the most insidious threat to all the other races ever born. I fear that when that finally becomes obvious to others, there will be pogroms in the Mycohl and Exchange to trim us back to size.''

''But not in the Mizlaplan?''

He shook his head. ''No, not in my region. It's the religion, you see. It puts everybody on an absolutely equal footing. Among my people, we are simply a class, a state of incarnation, and to the Holy Ones who bring the Word and keep the faith there's no difference between a Terran and a six-legged, silicon-based, ammonia-breathing Jabuk, so we'll not be barred from ordination or command or high office.''

''Still, you never feel stultified? Closed in by the rigid system?''

''Not really. You have to know the history of my people to fully understand that, though. The thing is, I've seen all three systems. They all work, but only ours works with no master races, no rich and poor, no major social tensions. Practicality says that there are only three possible systems right now— perhaps four if we count these demons, and we can see their idea of society in the crude paintings on these very walls. I consider the alternatives, and I am content.''

''I don't think I could ever accept your system,'' she told him honestly. ''I've never been in the Mycohl but I've heard about their system and it's pretty ugly overall. In the Exchange, if you're good enough, you can go all the way.''

He nodded. ''Unfortunately, very few are good enough. For the bulk of people in the Exchange, life at the bottom is as bad as life as a Mycohlian drol; most of the worlds are left to neglect or bled to death by the kings of transport and trade. An evolutionary monarchy is no more just for the masses than a hereditary one.''

She sighed. ''Maybe, but—''

At that moment there was a shrill, screaming sound, and then a tremendous explosion not far outside their dwelling rocked the place, knocking them down and causing a lot of rock to fall from the ceiling all around them.

''What—?'' Krisha and the others seemed to cry at once, and just as they regained their footing a second explosion rocked them and knocked them down again.

Modra, certain that the demon forces were now coming to get them, had her pistol out and struggled to the window to fire at anything out there that moved, but there was at that moment yet another explosion, knocking her back again and shaking so much loose inside the cliff dwelling that parts of it threatened collapse.

Finally, with the third major explosion, it was over, and they struggled to the front, all awake now, and peered out through the black smoke.

"They are making for the trail!" Manya shouted. "They are trying to pass us by, leave us here!"

Chin and Krisha ducked out their respective doors and fired a few wide volleys into the smoke, apparently hitting nothing. The smoke was beginning to clear now, and for a brief moment they saw the head of someone, possibly Molly, vanish below the rim of the falls.

"They *have* passed us!" Chin shouted. "To the rim! We might be able to knock them off that path before they get under the falls and we lose them!"

Modra was confused. "Why would they want to pass us? What is going on here?"

Morok, moving slowly, came up beside her. "Obviously they have decided that we are no longer a threat, child; perhaps our killing of one of them caused them to pause and reflect. At any rate, they now run towards their dark masters." His eyes seemed to shine right through her even in the darkness. "That is the answer," he said flatly.

Krisha and the captain had gotten about halfway to the rim of the falls when they heard another whistling sound. Both immediately started reversing themselves and, seeing they weren't going to make it, flattened against the rock. The bomb exploded just over the point where the trail met the rim, knocking some of the rock into the chasm below.

"Captain! Are you all right?"

"Yes, Krisha, I have survived as usual, except for the bruises I will have hitting this rock so hard and fast."

"How many of those bombs do they *have,* anyway?" she asked, getting to her feet.

"*Ouch!* Judging from Modra's pack, I'd say they've shot their load," he assured her, then, suddenly, he stopped and smacked his right fist into his left palm. "How stupid of me! Of course!"

"What?"

"Modra! She's still got her two! We can blow them off that wall even if they *are* behind the falls!"

She sighed. "No, Captain. Let them go."

"What? But they're wide open right now!"

"Captain—Morok, too, has thought of this. He thought of it when the cymol tried his attack on us. We could have killed them with Modra's bombs at that time. They were as vulnerable up there as we were inside."

"But—"

"Captain, they are not something one can use without a bit of training, and they require an Exchange suit to program. Are we murderers? Can we retain any moral superiority if we, by hypno powers, cause Modra to murder her own people? Particularly since, as their telepath pointed out to me, *we*, not they, violated our word?"

"Um. I see what you mean." He sighed. "All right, then, I suppose we deserve this, in a sense. But I have the oddest feeling we're in some sort of race, and we're losing."

"Funny. Their telepath said the same thing. The Quintara Marathon, he called it."

Chin gave a dry chuckle, calming down. "The Quintara Marathon. As good a name as any. But, the fact remains, if we're in some sort of race, we started off first, well in the lead in this run to who knows where. Now we're third. About the only way we can do any worse is to go backwards."

She nodded, well aware of that herself. "I guess we'd better get back and see what the Holy Father decides to do now. Much of this is dependent on his condition."

"You go ahead," he told her. "I'm going to risk a peek over the side, now that I'm fairly certain that there are no more big bangs coming. I want to see what sort of damage they did to that trail head. If they blew several meters off, then the matter is academic unless someone brought along a ladder or a rope."

He walked over, still very cautious, then took a look. It wasn't great—for the first two meters it was going to be pretty hairy going, with only a small part of the trail width present.

Still, they weren't marooned—not yet, anyway. He put his instruments on and tried to find them, finally locating the group well down in the chasm, far behind the falls, and barely out of range.

He walked slowly back toward the cliff dwelling, only now starting to feel those coming bruises, and found them huddled together.

"You *cannot* go, Holiness!" Manya was saying firmly. "You need at least a full sleep and could use far more! Your body needs time to repair itself!"

"Well, I cannot stay here behind—not again," he responded. "I had to leave you once, but now there is no chance of my catching you at a later date. We can all use many hours of sleep, Manya, but I refuse to believe that a mere few more hours will do what two weeks in a hospital would. If we wait here much longer, even the trail will be cold. We might as well not be here—and only the gods themselves know how far ahead the cursed Mycohl are by now, looking for the best deal from the demonic horde. If we do not go now, then why are we here at all? Why did Savin die? No, we go—providing, that is, that the captain tells us it is still possible."

"It's possible, Holiness, but it won't be easy the first six or seven meters. And with that leg . . ."

"I will remove my suit again, and pass it down to someone who makes it to solid footing," the Stargin replied. "Then I will do what I did before and fly to the safer part of the trail, where I can then reclaim my suit and join the rest of you. Overall, I am probably safer on that ledge than any of you."

Krisha suddenly gasped, and all attention turned to her.

"What is the matter, child?" Morok asked. "I assure you that—"

"No, no, Holy Father!" she responded. "I just now lost them! Completely lost them. I get no sense of anyone else on this entire world except for us. No blocks, no shields, no probes, nothing. They're *gone*!"

Gun Roh Chin sighed. "Well, maybe that means that we are finally going to get out of this damnable rain."

It had not been easy, but having had the Exchange team precede them down a trail with no detours, it wasn't as difficult for the Mizlaplanian group to accept the fact that what looked like the end of the trail was some kind of trick. Still, none of them stepped through the portal without a little heart palpitation and a case of nerves.

The great hall of the demons gave them pause and did nothing for the nerves. Once she'd established that none of the Exchange team remained in the area, Krisha decided to waste no concentration and personal energy on shielding the whole group. Still, it was impossible not to get much the same data as the other telepaths had from the assembled and stored demonic horde.

Modra stared at the design on each of the door panels. "McCray was right," she commented. "Pentagrams."

"Huh? What's that?" the captain asked.

"That symbol. I don't know what the circle means, but the five-pointed star with the tips connected with straight lines is a pentagram, or so Jimmy McCray said. An ancient symbol that was supposed to keep demons in, or out, depending on where you were. And these gold light strips in the floor—I can't make out the design, but I'll bet it's not just ornamental. They thought that the geometric shapes somehow proved to be barriers to the demons. Some of the old ruins we passed through early on had them."

"Demonic geometry," Chin commented, shaking his head in wonder. "Another rule to file away. And maybe some measure of protection if we can remember at least the one shape."

"Let's get out of here," Krisha urged. "I feel like they're all going to wake up and start in on us any minute."

Morok nodded. "She's right. If these designs are some sort of geometric means of imprisonment, then we're breaking them every time we stand in one or cross a line. I have heard of such things. They are taught to exorcists of the Inquisition. Let us get out of here."

Modra nodded, feeling it, too, and also feeling that forbidding, almost overwhelming sense of pure evil coming from all around her. Still, she stared at all the possible exits in the center. "Which one?" she asked them.

Gun Roh Chin smiled and pointed down. "Somebody didn't wipe their feet and tracked up this nice, clean floor," he said.

It was brightly polished, except in one area, where there were clear impressions of treads from boots formed by residue picked up on the trail.

He led, and they followed. It wasn't a consistent trail, but enough people had been through here that there were enough. "That one," he told them, pointing. "If we want to keep chasing them, that is."

"We are chasing the Mycohl," Manya reminded him. "We want to catch them, not avoid them."

"Well, it's a good bet that everybody went through this one," Chin noted. "I don't see any other trail so well scuffed up."

"Let's go, then," Krisha urged. "They are beginning to wake up, and they all seem to be thinking the same thing. They're saying, *'It's almost time. It's almost our time again.'*" She shivered.

"Maybe this one will be a desert," Modra suggested hopefully, and they stepped through.

The pattern was the same as for all the other stations, including the demonic pair in the center chamber.

<Welcome,> they said to Krisha. *<You are not the first to pass this way.>*

<And none of the others freed you, I notice,> she came back, bracing herself for their assault.

It didn't come. Instead, they said, *<It is of no importance. It is almost our time again, when we shall rule and reign.>*

"Something is different," she told the others. "They don't care if they are freed or not. They act like they expect to be free without strings or deals almost any moment."

"I think I like that less than an attack," Morok commented. "I just can't say why."

Gun Roh Chin nodded. "I have the feeling that we're missing something important. Something we don't know, something, perhaps, we *can't* know, but I get the oddest feeling that someone, *something,* is laughing behind our backs."

"Well, if they don't mind us going on, I don't see why we should linger," Morok said.

<Go. We shall remember you when our time comes, and it will come soon.>

Krisha shivered and almost beat the others out.

They approached the other side of the gate with relief that, at least, they were finally out of that terrible, drenched, dead world.

They stepped out, and were all but overcome by the sudden stench of sulfur and brimstone.

FIRE BURN
AND CAULDRON
BUBBLE

IT WAS A WORLD OF DARKNESS, AS IF THEY WERE inside some impossibly deep, impenetrable cavern, yet there was light enough to see—not from any sky, but from the massive lakes of boiling, bubbling, hissing lava that formed small lakes within the darkness, occasionally spilling over and forming rivers of the stuff.

Environment suits closed automatically; air refresheners kicked into action, clearing the outside atmosphere, thick with the fumes of hydrogen sulfide and other foul-smelling compounds, and the air-conditioning kicked in, mercifully cooling them in a matter of minutes from the sixty-plus degrees centigrade outside temperature to a far more comfortable level.

"This isn't good at all," Josef commented, looking at his power levels and computing the drain rate to compensate for this place. "What is your energy reading, Kalia? Tobrush?"

"Thirty-seven hours," Kalia reported.

"Thirty-eight, give or take a bit, here," Tobrush added.

"Well, I get closer to thirty-five," he told them. "It's taken us almost forty hours to get from station to station the last couple of worlds, and we didn't have to face anything like this.

These suits were never designed for lava, and even if they held, the power needed to sustain us inside would drain these things like water over that falls back there.''

"We could go back in,'' Kalia suggested. ''Take one of the other routes.''

"We're going to have to,'' he responded. ''I don't care if the demons can make it through in just those basic clothes they wear or not, it's a cinch *we* can't. Desreth? What about you?''

"It is perfectly tolerable to me here,'' the Corithian answered, ''but were I to have to go into the lava, I would dissolve. I would prefer another route myself.''

"That settles it. Everybody back in. Quickly! We don't want any more energy drain than we have to have!''

They re-entered the station with some relief, switching off the protection circuitry, then went through the first cavern to the demon chamber in the center. As they did, they stopped, dumbfounded.

The demons had turned around somehow and were now facing them.

"Tobrush? Ask them what's going on here,'' Josef called nervously.

<You cannot back up this way,> the demons told them. *<No matter what, you will have to exit as you did. To return to the Dispatch Center, exit and turn to your right, then proceed to the station that you find there and enter.>*

<You mean—once anyone is committed to a destination, they are truly committed to go there?> the telepath responded, appalled at the idea.

<Not anyone, no. But you must. You seek the Keep, the City on the Edge of Chaos, which is at the center and the boundary of all and of nothing. This is the only way for you now. All other routes lead to meaningless elsewheres.>

Tobrush reported this to Josef, who was hardly in a mood to believe them, yet dared not disbelieve them. He didn't even bother to ask them how far it was to the next station; there was no way he could believe them on that answer, either.

"Past them and out!'' he ordered. ''We'll soon see if this is some kind of trick.''

They went into the rear chamber and out, and found themselves in the same, dark, horribly hot place.

"Anybody? We can't spend a lot of time debating this.''

"We are clearly in their power as to choosing our destination once we stepped into the station," Tobrush pointed out. "We are going to wind up here no matter what. We either camp out in there and wait for the suits to run out anyway, or we try it."

"Tobrush is right!" Kalia responded. "If we are to die, let us die in the attempt, not in surrender! They are testing us! What is the purpose to a test if you cannot pass it?"

"I agree," Desreth added. "We have always been at the mercy of this system. In point of fact, the distance between the second and third stations was only eighty percent of the true distance between the first and second. It simply took as long because we had to fight and to rest. Now we are in the lead, without enemies ahead. If this is, perhaps, sixty percent of the distance, it can be done in under thirty hours."

"All right," Josef sighed, internally groaning at the idea of even thirty hours in this place without any prolonged rest, but knowing that it was necessary to do so. "At least we are trained for this kind of forced march. The others are not."

They turned left and started off. "The Exchange team probably has fifty or sixty hours minimum, without having to do those battles," Tobrush noted. "And I keep wondering if it gets worse from here. First unending monotony, then unending rain, then unending fire. I just wish there was better lighting here, not only to recharge these suits but also to better see where we're going."

"Too bad we can't convert this heat," Josef commented wistfully.

Tobrush took him seriously. "There might be a way to do just that, with some reprogramming," the telepath told him. "The suits aren't really designed to use it, so it would have low efficiency, but something is better than nothing, and at worst it would take the pressure off the air-conditioning. I'll work on it."

"Do that," the leader urged. "You've got thirty hours to solve it. In the meantime, anybody see anything that might be some sort of trail?"

"Unlikely," Desreth came back. "The black material upon which we walk is basically rock granules, tiny pieces of obsidian, and volcanic ash and dust. Anything that went through a place as dynamic as this one is would soon have anything, from tracks to trails, covered up."

"Well," Josef sighed, "we're on a rise between two lava lakes right now, so if we're going left, there's no choice of routes."

"Yeah, but what if that lava came through and ripped out the route after those demons went by?" Kalia asked them.

"Let's not think of that," Josef told her.

Desreth was more optimistic. "This is a known, established route. They have a station to it. You don't build things along consistent rules like they do without taking that into consideration."

They all hoped that the Corithian was right. Complex transport routes throughout the galaxy were maintained not only by building them right in the first place but also by constant maintenance. They'd seen little sign of maintenance machinery along this route so far, and it had certainly been a very long time since a crew had been by.

Still, with nothing to do except keep from sinking into or slipping down from the very loose gravel-like mound that was their only protection from the lava lakes, Josef couldn't help wondering just why this place—and the others, for that matter—were here at all. They reinforced his suspicion that the geometry of the dimensional walkways was not something that could be thoroughly planned. If you wanted to go from A to F, he mused, maybe that predetermined B, C, D, and E, whether you wanted to go there or even *should* go there or not.

There was something oddly reassuring in that concept. It brought them down a peg or two, in a way, to the level of other races, subject to fate and events beyond their control. Different, yes; alien, yes, but, in their own element and under their own rules, far closer to their own kind than even the demons probably liked to admit.

"There certainly has to be some control or design," Tobrush commented, reading his thoughts. "Otherwise they'd be wearing—and needing—environment suits of some kind as well."

He didn't like his more comfortable visions questioned. "Get back to your programming and stop eavesdropping," he snapped.

There were other things he didn't like that he preferred conventional theories to explain—if only he could come up with them.

For one thing, where were the stars? He could accept that,

perhaps, they were traveling great distances through dimensional folds, but at no point had they seen any stars or, indeed, clear sky at all. In fact, there'd been no light variations of any kind to even indicate rotation and revolution around a star. It was always twilight on the dull, flat world; always daylight, but through thick clouds that darkened the landscape, in the wet one. Here there was nothing but pitch-blackness overhead, as if the sky was not a sky at all, but some kind of black-painted roof.

The landscapes had certainly varied, along with temperature, humidity, even the gravity, to a smaller degree, but not the things that all his experience and training said should be here.

And no life, either, at least as they knew it; nothing, not a single plant or animal except those silicon trees that might or might not have been alive at all. Except for those ancient ruins and those wall paintings, in fact, there was no sign that any life had ever been in *any* of these places, even in the distant past.

It was almost as if they weren't on other worlds at all, but rather trapped inside some vast, impossibly huge set of museum tableaus, with the demons the guides and attendants.

"You seek the Keep, the City on the Edge of Chaos, which is at the center and the boundary of all and of nothing."

Did they? Did they indeed? Was that all the way down, if "down" was the right concept? And what did that demonic riddle mean? And why had this farther-in class of demons, equally trapped, been far more congenial and far less obstructionist than the earlier ones? It was almost as if the demons had expected them. They hadn't even tried to bargain or cajole or plead or demand their freedom. Why not?

Was it because they no longer felt as if they had to do so?

He wasn't sure he wouldn't have liked to keep the adversarial conditions of the first encounter; this was in its own way far more worrisome.

"Something moved in the lava pool to our right!" Kalia called suddenly, breaking his reverie.

"Impossible!" he snapped. "It's over twelve hundred degrees centigrade in that pool! Besides, we haven't seen anything alive in this crazy place except trapped demons."

"I saw something, I tell you! I swear it! It was big and black. . . ."

"Tobrush? Desreth?"

"I saw nothing," the telepath responded, "but I got the image from her mind as she saw it. It definitely looked like something that shouldn't have been there. Alive? I can't tell."

"Can we scan and come up with anything?" he asked, worried. In the *Quiimish,* the holiest scriptures of the Mycohl, the demons were the masters of the elements, one of which was fire.

"With what?" the telepath responded. "Nothing in our instrumentation pack or programming is designed to ferret out life in that sort of environment, and the thermals vary so much in moving lava that temperature scans are of no use, either."

"You ever hear of any kind of life that could exist under these conditions?"

"No," the Julki admitted, "but, then, until this trip, I had never spoken face to face with a living demon, either."

"It is difficult to tell crusting from anything else," Desreth put in. "I suggest we not attempt to solve this mystery but proceed with caution."

"Nothing else we can do," Josef admitted. Still, he would have preferred that Kalia not be spooked at this point. All it did was make the mood contagious.

Maybe, just maybe, he began to worry, being first in this trek to whatever was at the end wasn't such an envious position after all. Not, of course, that it made any difference—the odds of any of the others picking the same station as they'd randomly chosen were pretty slim.

That thought wasn't so comforting, either, even though their worst enemies were just behind them. If anything *did* live and lurk in here, there would be little chance of someone else diverting their attention.

Now they were *all* seeing things out of the corners of their eyes, just out of real sight. Even Desreth, who was emotionless, apparently fearless, and certainly had none of the psychological hang-ups conventional life suffered, seemed spooked as well. Every once in a while, the Corithian would suddenly stop and whirl around, stare for a second, then go on without a word.

It was going to be a long, long walk. . . .

"Sweet Jesus!" Jimmy swore. "We finally made it! Hell itself, fiery pits and all!"

<*Well, you said you'd take almost anything to be out of the rain,*> Grysta pointed out.

"Shut up, Grysta!" he snapped.

The Durquist was equally impressed. "This is going to be a mean one. Any sign of the Mycohl?"

"I'm not sure. Traces only. They must be many hours ahead of us. I'll respond to a probe, but I won't initiate one. We might be lucky and not tip them off that we're here."

Molly rarely said much, but she looked around at the burning, bubbling, hissing Hell and said, "This must be what folks on hot place live in."

It hadn't been but a week or so since they'd been working that place, via remote units, but it seemed such a lifetime away that neither Jimmy nor the Durquist had really thought about it.

"Huh! I think not, Molly," the telepath responded. "But it's a good point to keep in mind. We don't know what's ahead, but we've seen sentient life even worse than this."

"I just did the calculations, and we're fine if the next station isn't any farther than the past ones," the Durquist told them. "That's a stroke of luck in a place like this. The ones ahead and behind are a lot shorter on power than we are. Except Modra, of course, and her suit power packs are incompatible with theirs. Still, I think we ought to press on and quickly. The footing here looks less than great, and while the Mizlaplanians can't afford much of a battle, they're crazy enough to do it anyway."

McCray understood. The only one with the enemy to their rear who could afford a fight was Modra, and that would place them at a decided disadvantage.

They trudged along through the great lava pools and through wide expanses of black granular sand-like rock. It was only when they came to the necks, the narrow and dangerous areas between two bubbling, hissing pits, that they saw, or *thought* they saw, movement amidst the blood-red liquid rock.

"I see them," the Durquist told him, having the advantage of independent eyes that he could use, somehow, to look both forward and to the side without losing his step or balance. "They're in there, probably quite a number of them, but I can't give you a shape. They're not demons, though."

"I'm just wondering if and when they'll try and attack us," Jimmy said worriedly.

"I'm not sure they even know we're here, or, if they do, it might be because we're letting some of these rocks drop into the pools. They melt, of course, but it might set up some kind of vibration that either attracts or disturbs them. You get nothing from them?"

"Not on the t-band," the telepath replied.

"They hurt," Molly said simply.

The other two stopped, and Jimmy stared at her. "What?"

"They hurt. That's all."

"Uh—Molly. You haven't been *sending* to them, have you?"

"Just when they be close," she replied innocently. "Just tell them we not bad, we friends."

"You sent them *sympathy* for hurting? And how did they take it?"

"It make them sad so I stop."

The Durquist thought about that a moment, then asked, "Um, Molly—they didn't seem menacing, or hungry, or anything like that, did they?"

"No. I don't think they want to hurt us if that what you mean. Not like the big syns. Molly think they just want *out,* but can't get out. Hurt too much."

"Fascinating," the Durquist said, mostly to himself. "I wish there was some way to make contact with them. Of course, they could just be animals of some sort, without any sentience at all. What she said is consistent with that."

"Or lost souls, trapped in that lava for eternity," Jimmy McCray sighed. "Nothing we can do about it, though. Nothing we can do to contact them and find out for sure, either. It's very like the problem off the Hot Plant, only without a follow-up team. We simply have no common ground to establish communications beyond the empathic."

"Well, at least we know they're not apt to drag us down, at least not deliberately," the Durquist noted. "And it's *life* of some sort—the first we've really encountered except our demons. Not life as we know it, but life all the same. It may mean more of the same down the pike here."

"What kind of life would exist long in a medium that was painful to it?" the telepath mused.

"Oh, you know Molly. They are probably quite comfortable swimming down in that stuff, but when they try and come up to this relative air-conditioning, barely sixty to seventy percent of water boiling, it would be like absolute zero to us. They freeze and that hurts.''

McCray sighed. ''I hope you're right.'' He looked up ahead. ''We seem to be aiming to go up and between those two big hills. I hope we don't sink in when we start climbing.''

''Well, at least we know we're on the right track,'' the Durquist noted, looking at the sea of small black rocks ahead. ''That creature of theirs, the telepath, really plows up this stuff. I certainly hope they've picked right, since we're pretty slavishly following them.''

''I wouldn't worry much about that. I have a feeling these routes are laid out pretty consistently. Once you get the curve figured, it's simply a matter of keeping to it and following it around, or so it seems. We're closing on the Mycohl, by the way, but not by nearly as much as I'd have thought.''

The Durquist chuckled. ''I suspect that all eyes are on their power levels at this point. You can do wonders if the alternative is losing power, protection, and cooling in a place like this.''

''The Mizlaplanians are now in as well,'' Jimmy told the star creature. ''I have that block in back of me, perhaps two hours behind, no more.''

''Well, they've got the same problem, which puts pressure on us,'' the Durquist noted. ''I've been thinking that third isn't a bad position in all this after all. *Omph!* Tricky going up this slope!''

It *was* a difficult climb; although the hills weren't terribly high, they seemed to be composed almost entirely of the fine rock particles, causing them all to sink and have to really force themselves to keep going. Molly, in fact, had the least problem; for once her thin legs and wide hooves seemed to spread her weight better than the Terran or the Durquist.

Still, they all stopped at the top of the hill and looked down at a scene that was both unexpected and chilling.

''There's a *town* down there,'' said Jimmy McCray.

It was more than a town; more like a small city, and it certainly did not belong there, both because it was so out of place on this dismal, hot world and because nobody in their right mind would build a town just down a slope from an enormous, bubbling lava lake and on the edge of another huge caldera.

And yet, there it was—a complex of rectangular buildings, apparently made out of the same gray and black rock, almost filling the valley.

"What's *that*?" the telepath asked, pointing to a complicated series of coated, translucent tube and girder-like structures that extended from the lake at the top above the town down into a series of massive, windowless black buildings below.

"Some sort of flume," the Durquist guessed, then he had it. "It's an aqueduct! A series of channels that can be used to maintain a controlled flow."

Jimmy frowned. "A flow of *what*? What's it for?"

"At a guess, I'd say the location is no accident," the Durquist replied. "The coating might have a melting point well above the temperature of the lava, allowing some sort of sluice to open at the top, allowing liquid rock to pour, possibly at varying speeds."

"Why not just blow an opening in the crater wall?" the telepath asked. "It seems rather ridiculous to think of people going to all this trouble to transfer lava from one cauldron to another."

"You can be exceedingly dense at times," the Durquist noted. "There's no outlet. It flows into that complex over there, which has no roof but many structures in between. At a guess, I would say it's some sort of foundry. I will wager that the buildings it can flow into contain molds of some sort. The lava flows down, the speed controlled so as to vary the rate of cooling, and into the molds, where it will quickly cool, probably with the aid of other devices. It seems to us like the hard way to do that, but if you had a people who didn't find this air temperature particularly hot, you could make a great many building materials quickly and efficiently that way. Even statuary, although I suspect that the place primarily made stone blocks, perhaps columns, and the like."

"Who would do something like that? The demons?"

"I wouldn't try and guess. However, let's go down through there and see if there are any clues. That *does* appear to be the route, anyway."

Walking through the city produced a sense of double

paranoia; the doors and windows, black as pitch, seemed to represent all the menace that their minds had imagined from such a place, and there was the ever-mindful lava lake above.

"The average Durquist doorway is about one meter by two and a half," the Durquist noted, looking at the buildings. "They can be vertical or horizontal, of course, since it hardly matters to us, but they are pretty consistent in form. Your Terran doorways tend to always be rectangles, the higher edges forming the sides, because of your standard shape and bipedal restrictions. Take a look at the doorways of these huge blocks of apartments, which I assume they are. Workers' barracks, anyway."

They were essentially arches, two meters across by three high, but the side walls had a very slight but noticeable outward curve built into them on both sides about halfway to the ground.

"Not the Quintara," Jimmy decided almost at once. "Something else."

"Very good. But look up there, that slightly higher building at the end of the town. A bit fancier with the long stone columns—and apparently coated with the same material as the sluice. The twin front doors are both rectangles, about three meters high by two across, I'd say."

McCray nodded. "That was a demon house, then. The boss, most likely. I wonder if he coated the place out of fear that his workers might just accidentally on purpose poke a hole in that lake up there? Or if it was just precautionary?"

"Possibly both," the Durquist replied. "I wonder if we see here, in microcosm, what our future will be like if indeed the Quintara's 'time' comes again?"

Jimmy felt a cold shiver at that thought. "Still, it's pretty primitive, isn't it, for supposed demigods with access to technology we still haven't dreamed of as yet."

"I think it is deliberately so. The more I see of their works, the more I think I'm coming to understand them, at least in the basics. First, it's far easier to control a population where technology is kept strictly in the hands of the rulers. On the whole, the Mizlaplan restrict technology, I understand, classifying it into various levels, and you get only the level that's best for the interests of the Empire. The masses have next to none in the Mycohl, which still uses a lot of hand labor

that's just shy of slave labor, leaving the computers and air-
conditioning and such to the nobility, the military, and the
technocratic classes who work for them. The Exchange bans
most robots and robotics where possible, primarily to keep the
teeming masses employed at something. I think the Quintara
liked their subjects to be as ignorant and primitive as possible,
but for a different reason.''

McCray nodded. ''Because they like it that way. They love
playing God.''

''They live to exercise power, to dominate, for its own
sake,'' the Durquist agreed. ''Why? I suspect it's the only thing
they have. When you've got this much power, this much
knowledge, playing God becomes the only thing left to do.
They play games with everybody, and they play the games for
their own sake, their own entertainment, their own pleasure.
Isn't that what every god in any culture you've known can be
reduced down to? I seem to recall—didn't your own God get so
bored just creating pretty things that he created a worthy
opponent?''

''Uh, I suppose you *could* put it that way, yes.'' *And for
millions of years it seems like the opponent's been winning.*
''But ours, at least, had a reward at the end for even the lowliest
player who would do it His way and not the devil's,'' he
pointed out.

''Yes, in the end, that's the basic difference, I suppose. All
Durquist religions have gods of just about everything—every
tree, every leaf, every pebble and stone, everything. There are
so many shrines and so many things to pray to you can't walk
without tripping. You keep at it, being holy and perfect, and
you one day become a little god yourself, or so the system says.
I never saw much reward in becoming a leaf god or a stick god
myself, but they had power and you had to be nice to them in
any event because they might well have been your ancestors
once. If the Quintara live up to their legends, they promised
none of that. Serve them and you got rewarded here and now
with comforts and power and such; cross them and they sent
you slowly and nastily to oblivion. Not very pleasant, but an
easy enough concept to get across.''

<*We get to fly between the stars and become who we wish
when we die,*> Grysta told him.

The comment startled him. ''I never knew *Morghs* had a

religion." He *might* have known, of course, but he'd never asked her about that or a lot of other things.

<*I decided not to wait. I wanted to fly between the stars now, and I did. Of course, the price is that I can't find the Universal Consciousness, but flying around lookin' for it didn't seem like a nice way to spend eternity anyway.*>

"Well, if we're right, they're bloody consistent with their image," the telepath commented. "Even the Mycohl version, which is more benign, demanded human sacrifice, if I remember my comparative religions. I get the impression that they more admired the demons than really worshiped them, though. That may explain why they didn't free the pair who tried so hard on us. It's a rather common thing that slaves rarely lust for equality; what they really want is to reverse their positions."

They passed out of the city, neither anxious to explore it much for fear that they might just find something.

"Just out of curiosity," the Durquist said, "how do you know so much about other religions and demonology and pentagrams and the like, McCray? If that was a part of your religious education, you must have been raised in a very strange religion."

He smiled wanly. "All religions are very strange unless you're raised to take them for granted," he pointed out. "Let's just say that I had a greater interest in such things in my youth than was healthy. I've tried to get most of it out of my mind over the years, but it's all still there, and it seems to be coming in handy at the moment."

The Durquist wondered about that but didn't want to press it. If and when McCray was ready, he'd tell. Otherwise, it was none of the Durquist's business and he accepted that. Still, McCray occasionally dropped his veneer of the old pro, the cynical spacer, and revealed evidence of an education very much more advanced than the average spacer ever had, and in subjects pretty well off any practical track.

Even Grysta didn't know his real background, as much as she knew about his biochemistry and other physiological things. He'd never gone home, and, since she'd united with him, he'd never run into anybody who'd known him before he was a spacer. She had repeatedly pumped him, but to no avail, and she loved him too much to inflict the pain that might bring it out of him.

"We've closed a bit more on the Mycohlians ahead," the telepath noted, changing the subject. "We're not close enough for me to read thoughts, but their telepath and I could probably exchange messages at this point. The Mizlaplanians have closed a bit on us, although not as much as our forward gain on the Mycohl."

"They're like us. No matter how far it is, we can't afford to rest. Not *here*. They've both got power problems, and we've got enemies at the rear. I begin to wonder if any of us will really make it. There are physical limits, you know. None of us has had a lot of rest and even less solid sleep in quite a long time. I don't care how much power any of us have; if we can't all find someplace to slow down, even stop, we're going to be in such bad shape it won't take a demon to best us. Our own bodies will get us first."

Jimmy McCray nodded. "When I called this a marathon, I didn't think it would be literally so."

Kalia whirled again, pistol out. "If one of those bastards sticks its head up just once more, I'm gonna blow it clean off!"

"You will do no such thing!" Josef snapped. "For one thing, what makes you think you can even tickle something that lives in boiling liquid rock? Second, we're a lot more vulnerable than they are. What happens if you get them irritated and they decide to start splashing that molten crap at us? Your suit might protect you at the start, but we don't have the power or the time to dig you out of the solid rock that would encase you."

"Not to mention the fact that any shots strong enough to even have a prayer would do a nice job of wasting power, and, if they attacked, we'd be forced to waste ours as well. If you want to commit suicide so badly, just open your suit and start walking around. Then we can use your power pack and remaining supplies, too. I will not allow you to include *us* in your death wish."

"Allow! Try and stop me, you overgrown slug!" She whirled, pistol flying to her hand, to aim not at any of the lava creatures but rather at Tobrush.

It was impossible to make a surprise move on a telepath, and the Julki's suit was specially formulated to allow its tendrils to come through the material while maintaining a seal. Dozens of thin, wire-like tendrils shot out even as she moved on Tobrush, wrapping themselves around her arm and her pistol and squeezing tightly.

"Stop it! Both of you!" Josef roared. "If we keep this up, we won't need enemies! We'll do ourselves in! We're just tired, that's all, and tired people make mistakes. You are a military unit, and you were trained to be tough and take it. Remember that!"

Tobrush saw in Kalia's mind that she was no longer a threat and released her just short of cutting through her suit. She shook her wrist to get some circulation back in it and then rubbed it. Still, she glared angrily, not at Tobrush, but at Josef.

"Military unit!" she spat. "*Whose* military? Where are we? Where are they? *You* crossed the border and got us stuck here, Lieutenant Hypno! All on your own you decided to invade, and here we are! You hypnos are so arrogant and self-centered! It's *you* who included *us* in your suicide pact!"

A Mycohlian never apologized for power, either to others or to themselves; that was Rule Number One. "An officer *assumes* responsibility," he told her. "He is expected to act on his own initiative when faced with a situation not covered by the book. He alone answers for that initiative, not you. Your job is to carry out my orders. You walk when I tell you to walk. You fire when I tell you to fire and at what I tell you to fire at. And you do not fire or openly challenge me, whether you agree with me or not. *You* decided to take the offer to enter the military, and you took an oath. You lifted yourself up from whoring in the muck with the drols. Now you pay for it. This is the second time I have had to remind you of this. *I will not remind you again.*"

She glared at him with a fury bordering on hatred, but she turned and started walking again.

"I think we made it," called Desreth, scouting ahead. "I detect a telltale station discontinuity ahead, perhaps an hour's walk, no more."

"Either this better have a good deal of light energy for a recharge or it better be the last one," Tobrush commented. "None of us have sufficient power for another circuit, even smaller than this one. If it is not exactly what we need, Desreth will be pressing on alone."

•   •   •

"Where are you going, Captain?" Morok called, as Gun Roh Chin broke from the main group and began walking briskly over to the foundry building.

"I want to see what they were making here," came the reply. "Please press on; I will only be a few minutes and will catch up."

"What difference can it make now?" Krisha asked him. "Whoever built this place is long gone, perhaps ages ago."

Chin didn't answer, but vanished into the huge open-topped building. They all stopped, waiting for him, even if they couldn't afford the time. They were so tired that any excuse was one that just had to be taken.

"Are you all right, Captain?" Morok called at last.

"Yes, yes," Chin replied. "I—*umph!*—ah . . . Yes, I almost suspected as much. I'll be out in a minute, no more."

He emerged seeming quite pleased with himself, which drove the others crazy with curiosity.

"What's in there?" Modra asked him.

"Yes, what?" Manya chimed in.

"Just molds," he told them. "Most are devoted to blocks such as the ones you see on the buildings here, of course, but there were some others. The rock is nothing special; common igneous type, of the granite-basalt family."

"You didn't have to go in there to figure that all out," Krisha noted.

"No, but some of the molds were—interesting. You remember the ruins in the rain world?"

"Yes, so?"

"That's where the rock was created for them. You only had to put together the various molds and apply the sort of logic used in solving a child's puzzle to see how they were created."

"You mean—those primitives in the wall paintings came all the way *here* to make their temples?" Morok asked, stunned. "But they would have had to descend those falls as we did, know the trick to them, and pass through the transfer room to this very spot! I find that unlikely."

"I find that impossible to believe, myself," the captain agreed. "No, the temple blocks were made here and then transported there by another party. It is unlikely that those people could have survived here without a technology far higher than they obviously attained, or were permitted to attain.''

"Then the demons brought their own temples?" Modra asked, puzzled as they all were.

"I'm not sure. I think from the design of these buildings that they were more likely the masters pushing a third party to do the work, but they *did* bring the things through and they probably also at least supervised their construction. There are also molds there for statuary and gargoyle-like decorations, although we saw no sign of those back in the rain world, suggesting that this place, and perhaps many other such places in this world, supplied a lot more worlds than just the one back there, at least with templates for all that.''

"Indeed? And what were these statues and smaller figures?" Morok asked him.

"It was difficult to tell them in detail, sitting as they were, and with as little time as I allowed myself, but some were undoubtedly demon figures and demonic faces of one sort or another. Some looked a bit large or too oddly shaped for that, though, suggesting that the demon wasn't the only figure they made. It would have been interesting to see what some of them were, but I suspect we'd recognize few or even none of them. Still, I would also suspect that *some* cultures in the Mizlaplan, or Mycohl, or the Exchange, would know them as figures of mythology and legend.''

"You are suggesting, then, that this world was some kind of workshop where the demons created their monstrous blasphemies for the rest of the universe?" Manya put in.

"I think so. I am on my way to working out a theory of this place—I mean all of it, from the very entrance in our own universe on—and, so far, nothing contradicts it.''

"Indeed? And what is the theory?" Morok asked him, genuinely curious.

"Holiness, it is only partially complete, and I may be totally wrong, so I don't want to suggest it and gain your derision. It is such a totally bizarre concept I want to be absolutely certain first—and, frankly, it would do none of us a bit of good if it were right. Or harm, either. Leave it for now as a personal academic exercise to relieve the tedium until I can prove some of it.''

They all wanted to hear it, but Morok and Krisha, in particular, knew that to push Chin before he was ready was fruitless. He had a million ways of disobeying even a command without ever once violating law, scripture, or civility.

"Very well, then," Morok sighed. "Let's get moving, then."

"How is your leg?" Manya asked him.

"Not good," he admitted, "but I will do what I must for as long as I can. There is no other solution." This was not the first time he'd wished he could lie to the faithful, but he could not.

Wearily, they got back up and started walking once more, but not a one of them didn't wish that they had joined the captain and seen what he had seen. All had the idea that he wasn't telling something, something else he'd seen, and that he was much farther along in solving this mystery than they were.

The next time one of the strange lava creatures that so disturbed them, and particularly disturbed the empathic Modra, made its almost-seen appearance, Krisha jumped as always but held up.

"The poor things are in such pain," Modra commented. "It's so great you can almost cut it with a knife. To live in *that*, in pain and some fear—that is truly Hell."

There *was* fear there, but, with the expertness of her Talent, she knew it wasn't fear of them. That would have been understandable, and at least would have taken one element of puzzlement away.

"I wonder what they are?" Krisha mused. "How could they live like that, in pain?"

"They are possibly the mutated descendants of the people who worked this place for the demons," Gun Roh Chin suggested. "And their fear might be that their old masters are coming back. Certainly the demons now believe that they are all to be freed very soon. I wish I knew why they thought that, by the way. Or, the creatures might just be some kind of animal life, probably not native to here, that got here somehow and adapted as well as they could. There is no way to know for sure, unless we learn it elsewhere."

"They are the damned," Manya said flatly, "getting exactly what they deserve."

· · ·

Kalia stood atop a blackened, ash-covered mound looking down at the sight and said, acidly, "All right, *sir,* so what kind of decision will you make now?"

They were facing an enormous black igneous intrusion on the other side, a mountain of frozen rippled glass; and to one side, stacked as neatly as logs waiting for the mill, were a good dozen mammoth crystal buildings of the Quintara. Inside the center of the black, shiny hill, to the immediate left of the great crystal stack, was an equally massive opening large enough to stick one of the would-be stations through, descending into the blackness.

Josef frowned. "Those can't all be stations, can they?"

"Dormant ones," Desreth responded.

"Or ones yet to be activated," Tobrush added. "Look at the *size* of them, though! They go on and on! Five hundred meters, perhaps? More?"

They weren't uniform, except that they were clearly huge single crystals of the same unknown quartz-like mineral. Out of their half-buried state, and stacked as they were, it was easy to see none too subtle differences in coloration, length, and diameter.

"More unsettling is the question of who or what could stack those things so neatly like that," Josef commented. "The kind of field machinery we'd require in this near-average gravity would be impressive to see as well. You see any signs of machinery for hoisting and lifting? You see any signs that anything of that sort was *ever* here?"

"What do the supernatural need of such things?" Kalia asked scornfully. "As you are fond of pointing out, the rules are different here."

Josef gestured to them and they made their way down to the enormous pile and then walked along the side of the stack. Although the sheer size of the things dwarfed them to mere specks, they still seemed smaller than any of them would have expected.

"Feel that?" Tobrush asked the other Talents. "They're inactive, but every once in a while there's a resonance that produces that odd, dizzy sort of feeling you get when concentrating on the active ones."

Josef nodded. "They must be just on the edge of stability. Somehow, they are set to vibrating and the resonances cause them to fold again and again inside and outside the dimensions.''

"Who cares how it's done?" Kalia asked impatiently. "Do we go in the cave or do we walk around?"

That was a point of practicality they soon faced, for it was possible to walk around the great obsidian hill to the left as well as directly inside the cavern. Josef was well aware that the power levels were reaching critical lows; if he made a mistake, they would have no way to retrace, and getting lost in the cave was not an appetizing way to go. "Tobrush?" he called. "You're the one measuring the spiral."

"It could be either inside the cave or on the other side," the telepath admitted. "That depends on how far back the hill runs. I believe with my heat conversion program we could risk looking on the other side first, but, as much as I hate to tell you this, we have company coming."

"Huh? What?"

"The Exchange group. Smaller, I think. Missing more than one member if I interpret what I'm getting correctly, but they've still got their telepath. I calculate that if we guess wrong, there is a better than even chance that by the time we got back to this point to try the alternative they'd have the hill in back and we'd be perfect targets. Not to mention the fact that we have little energy left for a shooting spree, while they have a great deal of luxury in that department."

Josef shook his head in wonder. "How could they pick the same station we did? It defies logic!"

"Maybe we just tracked up the floor back there," Kalia suggested.

"It doesn't matter now," the hypno sighed. "Desreth, make speed and go around to the left until you are convinced that it's not the way, or that it is. Give us the word and head back. If it's in the cave, we'll go on ahead. Let the Exchange people go through and then follow when you're clear. If it is around, we will come to you with all speed."

"I will do what I can," the Corithian responded and scuttled off.

Josef turned to Tobrush. "I want progress reports. Give us at least five minutes warning so we can pick a route if we have to." He sighed wearily. "At least we don't have the Holy Horrors to deal with."

"I think we might," Tobrush replied. "I am able to pick up only one of the minds in the Exchange group at this point—the Durquist—and while I can't pull anything detailed from his mind, which works rather oddly inside, he just asked the telepath how far behind them the Mizlaplanians were."

Josef smacked his fist into his other palm hard in frustration. "Damn! We don't even get one tiny little break in this! How'd they get ahead of the Mizzies, anyway?"

"I'm not certain, but I get the impression that one of their number is being held by the Mizlaplanians. The thoughts when the Holy Ones come up are bitter enough that I suspect that, right now, they hate the Mizzies more than we do. We only hate them as a group; they have a specific grudge against *this* particular bunch. Might I suggest we may have an opportunity here for an alliance? We've done nothing at all to make them hostile towards us except on general principles, and general principles aren't very practical here right how. If we somehow get out of this, such cooperation might smooth over a lot of difficulties. If we don't, what do our nationalities and loyalties matter? And, of course, if they later prove a liability, I believe at this point we outnumber them, and close, surprise physical battle favors us with our military training."

"All good arguments," he agreed. "Still, they wanted us to surrender our weapons and authority, and I can't do that. It would have to be mutual respect or nothing. Maybe in a little bit we'll be forced to deal, but, right now, when they've got the guns and we effectively haven't, I'd like to keep us a little apart and in the lead. Still, if the Mizzies attack them, we'll go to their aid. We owe them that."

"As you wish."

"Desreth?" Josef called. "What's the situation with you?"

"It is a very large hill," the Corithian responded, "and the path grows ever narrower as a lava lake pushes in. It has to be the cave, Lieutenant. If this small rock bridge holds out at all, I can see no place within range that the station could lie."

Josef sighed wearily. "All right, it's the cave, then. Desreth, hold back. You heard that both the other groups are here with us?"

"I heard."

"Let them pass. Both of them, if you have to. Avoid battle unless there is no other way. Keep on this channel and we'll exchange positions when we get to the other side. If there is no way to recharge there, we're finished anyway. Just wait and use your own discretion after with the Exchange people, who will probably be the only survivors. If we get a charge, then we'll have them between us and perhaps we can do something nasty.''

''I understand. Go. I shall make do.''

Josef got up painfully, every muscle in his body pleading for rest, his mind sluggish. ''Let's go in the furnace and find that station,'' he said wearily.

After going in barely ten meters, they were on instruments to find their way around. In many ways, the inside of the extrusion was reminiscent of the chambers of the stations, and sweeps of the cave walls indicated the presence of the mineral from which the stations were made embedded throughout the glassine rock.

''Odd,'' Tobrush remarked. ''The normal rule just about everywhere is, the slower rock cools, the larger the crystals. Obsidian is formed by near-instant cooling, hence, glassy and no crystals. The largest crystals are always deep underground. Yet, here, we have substantial major crystallization with the obsidian.''

Josef shivered. ''You feel it, Tobrush? That same otherworldly sensation, all around.''

''I do indeed. It suggests that perhaps the properties within the chemistry of the obsidian could create the crystals. If there was enough resonance and the properties were already potentially present when it was still a liquid, that might explain it. Parts of the rock *are* cooling slowly—in other-dimensional space. If we go deep enough, it's entirely possible we will find crystals the size of the ones outside. They might well not have grown them; they might just have mined them.''

''We're going down, that's for sure,'' Josef agreed. ''I show close to a fifteen-degree inclination right now.''

''Temperature's going down, too,'' the Julki noted. ''Now instead of being Hell, it's closer to being hot as hell.''

''What does your suit reserve read?'' Josef asked. ''You, too, Kalia.''

''I've got about ninety minutes,'' she reported back.

''One point nine,'' Tobrush put in. ''I didn't do as much shooting.''

"I've got even a little less than Kalia," he told them. "We'd better get down to something manageable soon."

"Look!" Kalia called suddenly. "There's a light up ahead!"

There was a narrowing and slight bending of the passage, and, when they rounded that bend, they entered an enormous chamber, perhaps kilometers across. It was a place of spectacular, unreal beauty; the entire area was festooned with crystals, all shimmering and glowing, proving a dull but acceptable light level.

"The mother lode," Josef breathed. "The place where they all come from."

"Makes me dizzy and my head hurts," Kalia complained. "You mean they dug all the stations and all outta here? How'd they get 'em out, then? Not through the way we just come in."

She had a point. Although the crystals were of all sizes, from mammoth ones down to fairly small ones of only a meter or two, none of the ones the size of the stack they'd walked past outside could have possibly fitted through the linking passage, particularly around that bend.

"The temperature here is just a bit under thirty-eight degrees centigrade," Tobrush noted. "Atmosphere is very dry but otherwise a decent balance, and we have illumination. I suggest we shut down all but maintenance on the suits and disengage the helmets."

Josef nodded, feeling very light-headed, almost giddy. *I'm more tired than even I thought,* he told himself, dismissing the feelings on that basis.

"Pretty colors," Kalia said, in an odd, almost childlike voice. She stood there and began looking all around in wonder.

Tobrush, too, felt disoriented, as if the great cavern were beginning to move, to spin around. "Josef," the Julki called. "We've reached our limit, I fear. I dislike stopping in this place, but I don't think we can realistically go on any more."

"I know what you mean," he managed, putting his hand on a log-sized crystal sticking out of the cavern floor. "Still, this might be the perfect place. We can shut down power, so we won't lose anything, and we can get some sleep behind some of the bigger crystals, like those over there. Tobrush, if your Talent's as shorted out as mine in here, then even that Mizzie telepath couldn't tell we were here."

"I was about to suggest the same thing," the Julki responded. "I can barely tell that *you* are here and we are bare meters apart."

Wearily, unable to tell up from down or right from left, they gathered behind a larger set of crystal growths, shut down the suits, and just lay there, exhausted, unthinking, as the entire cavern seemed to revolve and swirl about them.

Molly stumbled and almost fell. Jimmy caught her, but with difficulty; he wasn't feeling too steady himself.

"It's the crystals," the Durquist managed, not too great himself even though he'd felt none of the effect from the stations. "They're resonating at every and any frequency and causing all sorts of effects which our exhaustion only magnifies. We've got to get through this cavern and fast!"

"Can't," Jimmy gasped. He accidentally let go of Molly and she slipped to the floor, then was unable to get up.

<*Don't ask me for help,*> Grysta put in. <*I'm getting the weirdest sensations I ever got in my life.*>

The Durquist had the most command, having the least sensitivity, but even if he could have made it out, which he didn't know, he couldn't take the others with him.

"We'll just have to find some cover, then, and to hell with the others," the star creature commented. "At least in here nobody's going to tell if we're around or not. I feel so damned *tired*! Maybe if we can just get some sleep we can fight these effects."

It made no logical sense, since it was obvious that the crystals were causing most of the problem, but they couldn't argue. They picked a spot, managing to crawl to it, and were all pretty well out cold within moments.

Even Gun Roh Chin felt it, although it was manageable to him. More like an anesthetic, a hypnotic numbness that seemed to lay hold of his mind and body and make them even less cooperative than they already were.

"We *must* keep on!" he urged the others, who were in far worse shape than he. "We can't stay here! It'll kill us, or drive us mad! *Think*! All of you! *Fight it*!"

"No use," Morok gasped. "I—" The Stargin collapsed, utterly, lying there just staring dully at the great crystals all around. Krisha found the whole place spinning and it became impossible to stand; she collapsed, totally disoriented, unable to even think.

Modra felt almost the same effect and collapsed within seconds of Krisha. Manya began praying loudly and turning around in a mad sort of dance, until she, too, collapsed.

With a massive effort, Gun Roh Chin managed to drag them, one by one, behind one of the larger floor growths, worrying that they might not be the only ones so affected in this place. Then, one by one, he powered down their suits and opened their helmets, conserving what he could.

I've got to get them out of here, he told himself, frantic. *This place is a death trap.* But, first, he just *had* to get some sleep. . . .

Twenty minutes later, Desreth came through, cautiously, examining and cataloging as it went along from one side to the other. Some of its senses were dulled in this place, others didn't work right, but the Corithian felt no other effects from the vast cavern and it never once occurred to the creature that anyone else might have a quite different reaction.

It passed the unconscious Mizlaplanians, not sensing them at all, then the Exchange, and, finally, its fellow Mycohlians, and never once suspected that they were there.

Consequently, Desreth the Corithian passed to the other side and walked out of the great cavern, looking for the rest of its companions.

WARRIORS
OF THE
CRYSTAL SPHERES

SLEEP ENHANCED RATHER THAN DIMMED THE sensations that bombarded their minds; unrestrained by will, they fell through space, through time, and through realms where none born of their universe dreamed existed. Their minds, untrained and unable to perceive the levels and layers now open to them directly, translated them into holograms that they could comprehend.

They were flying, soaring over a vast one-dimensional grid of dull, glowing green strands creating squares filled with equally dull glowing yellow; it twisted and became two-dimensional, and they were now between grids, the upper the same sickly green on yellow, the lower a fuzzy yellow on green, and, between them, tiny pinpoints of light in uncounted numbers around which the great pattern twisted and weaved in snake-like manner.

I'm dreaming, they all thought, at one point or another along the long flight. And yet—and yet, they did not dream alone.

The first to hear the voices, the many, many voices, were the telepaths, of course, but, after a while, the others began hearing them, too, as they soared, bright moths flitting in and out through an endless series of multicolored and twisting grids.

At one point they all tried twisting and turning, if only to see
what each other looked like in this bizarre environment, but, no
matter how fast the turn or how they swooped this way and
that, the others were always just out of sight, just out of reach,
their relative positions sensed rather than directly perceived,
except, perhaps, as lights flickering and burning in the darkness.

<Holy Ones, Mothers of Angels, Father to Universes, hear
my prayer and protect this humble . . .>

<Hey! You! Shut Up! How dare you pray in my dream?>

<Who are you who would blaspheme amongst the Holy
Spheres?>

<Oh, fuck you! Your Father to Universes was a rapist and
your Mothers of Angels were whores!>

<Peace be to all of you!> came a saintly male voice. <Why
must we battle even here?>

<Oh, shut up!> both women came back simultaneously, and
started in on each other again.

<Grysta! Grysta! Where are you?> Jimmy called.

<Here. Beside you, not on you, Jimmy,> she responded in a
gentle, almost awestruck tone she'd never used before. <I'm
free, Jimmy! I'm finally free!>

< You're free! You're the one that's been on my back all
these years!>

<Trapped there, you mean! A whole life, Jimmy, seen
through another's eyes, felt through another's nervous system,
filtered through somebody else's experiences, unable to communicate with others except through the one!>

It startled him. He'd never thought of that before, never
thought that this obvious truth might in fact be a greater
frustration to such a being than its attachment to him might
have made him feel.

<But, we're just dreaming, Grysta! Maybe we are talkin' to
each other, maybe not, but it's just a dream.>

<Uh-uh. I thought so right off, but I never dreamed before,
and not anything like this, anyway. Don't you get it, Jimmy?
Don't you get it yet? We're dead! We're dead and flyin'
through the universe of night lookin' for the Cosmic Whole,
just like the legends said!>

<Nonsense!> came a thought from the Durquist, apparently
hearing them both. <We are lying there on the floor of that

cave and the resonances from the raw crystals are turning our minds to mush.>

<Sweet Jesus, Durquist!> Jimmy swore. *<Can't you even have a religious experience in my dream?>*

<Your *dream! You, my dear sir, are in my dream and I'll thank you to obey the rules my mind insists upon establishing.>*

<There's a whole bunch'a folks here for just a dream,> Molly noted. *<Dumb old dream, too. Lots'a folks and no sex.>*

<Has anyone except the little parasite considered the idea that perhaps none of us are dreaming in the conventional sense?> Tobrush asked. *< It could well be that the crystals in the main chamber have sensitized all of us to the entire Talent band, which opens up the strong possibility that an empath and a who knows what are having an impossible telepathic fight over prayer and god right now.>*

<Parasite! I'll have you know I was a symbiotic organism, you Mycohlian slug!> Grysta came back.

<Tobrush?> Josef called. *<If you're right, then what the hell are we seeing?>*

<That which we cannot sense or see,> the Julki responded. *<Look ahead! See how the grids warp and bend. To look between them is to see what cannot and should not ever be seen!>*

And Josef looked, and perceived that, within the intricate folds and bends of the energy fabric were pockets of darkness, and within the dark there dwelt horrible things, dangerous things, consciousnesses which lurked and leered and gibbered, and yes, reasoned and cajoled as well.

There were pure evils: evils with every shape, evils with no shape, a purity of evil so absolute that what civilization perceived as the meaning of that word seemed a laughable concept, and beside which even the Quintara paled into bland nothingness.

And yet he knew them. They *all* knew them, for they had all encountered their broad shadows through the length and breadth of the galaxy, and within themselves, as well, and all whom they had known.

Here indeed were the elder gods and ancient dev̶̶̶ universe, as ancient at least as that vast field of gal̶ supergalaxies, omnipresent even to the edge of the c̶ places that would never be visited by any from the Three Empires. And here, too, was everything ever done by the most, and the least, in their names.

They tore at the newcomers; lashed out with whips of coal-black energy against the cosmic tartan, seeking them, promising all beyond which the demon offers were but nothing.

The lights are stars, Jimmy thought, his fear of the dark things still not dimming his awe and wonder at the rest. He swooped down toward the lights to test his theory and discovered to his shock that they were not stars at all.

They were galaxies.

Galaxies moving in circular patterns around a common point of darkness or a blaze of brilliance, and, in turn, these supergalaxies moved in their own circular orbits around still larger and more distant points. . . .

What could hold and pull even mega-galaxies as they also flew apart from one another into the void, still fleeing after all these billions of years from the great explosion that had created them?

There was no time, no space, in this place, for one point was as close or as far as any other to them, and as alien. This was the place into which the great crystals folded and unfolded, linking any spot with any other, as the perfect resonances of the great crystals made them One in this place, which was not of the universe they knew, yet at once was all of it.

That was what the Operators did; those Quintara imprisoned in their near-transparent mausoleums could subtly alter the resonances, reshape the folds, so that any point of exit was the same as another, that any crystal could become any other, for they all joined in this one, bizarre plane.

This, then, had been no random journey; this had been a guided tour.

<Modra! Modra! Swing this way!>

<Durquist? But it can't be you! You're dead!>

<No deader than you, although at this point I'm beginning to have my doubts about both of us. Their hypno did it to you! It was a trick!>

The truth broke through the spell that had held her in the other plane, but not here, where all were equal.

<My God! Tris—>

<Long dead. They killed only a corpse that, shorn of its pretty veneer, deserved burial.>

<McCray? And Molly?>

<Here, somewhere. We're all here. All the teams, all the survivors, somehow, together in this place. Watch it!*>*

The fabric rippled from below and from a hidden pocket spidery tentacles of perfect blackness outlined in bright electric yellow lashed out for her. She swerved at the Durquist's warning cry and barely missed being snared.

<That one didn't even bother to radiate its thoughts,> she noted. *<Durquist? Where are we? What is this place? What are those—things—that seek us out?>*

<I have no idea, but I believe that this might well be the t-band as a visible place, a place we can normally only touch here and there. It may well be the place through which our space drives travel, circumventing the speed limit of light, which is why so many of the early spacer families were sensitized to it and gained access to at least a tiny part of its power. Our bodies lay sleeping, but bodies are fragile things bound to the four-dimensional universe. Surrounded by the crystals, our minds are sensitized to this plane and freed to roam it, unfettered by any of the physical laws of the universe we know and which bind us.>

He paused a moment, admiring his own poetic leaps, then added, *<Of course, that might be all crap, and this something else entirely.>*

<It is *you!>* Modra exclaimed happily. Only the Durquist would find it impossible not to be cynical about even himself.

<Of course it is,> he responded. *<I've never been anyone else.>*

The patterns took a sudden bend and intertwined, creating a near tunnel-like effect, going what seemed to be *down,* if that word had any real meaning here.

<Where is this taking us?> she cried fearfully, noting that the place of darkness now seemed to fill the great voids in the helix-like energy tartan, making it harder and harder to dodge their grasp. *<It grows narrower, too! There is no way to forever dodge those loathsome presences! If nothing else, it ends below where all is darkness!>*

<It is the city!> Kalia cried out to them. *<The great city in*

the center and on the edge of nothingness! It is just as the Master said!>

<Pull up! Go back!> Tobrush warned. *<You cannot make the city! The darkness is too close, the presences will take you and eat you alive for eternity if you try for it now!>*

It was a beautiful, if strange, alien city that lay before them, just below the narrowest points. Multi-level, in a broad spiral just as the helix itself was a spiral, its great buildings and broad avenues seen in outline via the colors of the tartans, and rising through all the levels a great and perfect pyramid outlined in shining gold.

<I fear nothing!> Kalia exclaimed, but on this plane all were empaths, as all were telepaths and all the other great powers known as Talents and more besides, and they knew that even Kalia feared that darkness.

<That isn't true!> Josef shot back desperately. *<You fear showing your fear to us by turning back with us! You fear showing any weakness! But it is not weakness to hold and turn back! It is no more a weakness to do that than to seek cover in a gun battle! And being swallowed up by those things lurking there purely out of pride is like exposing yourself to a clear shot by an enemy! Don't let fear drive you to attempt the unattainable! Turn back!>*

Blackness tinged with crackling energy reached out for her, not on one side but on *all* sides, and it was with great difficulty and skill that she maneuvered through them and managed a curve and was now heading back toward the top of the helix.

Still, slight tendrils of the evil lightly brushed her, and the shock of the power she felt just in that brush, of the near omnipotence those presences represented, was like an ultimate seduction, and for just a moment she wavered, before continuing on up.

Jimmy McCray felt the Mycohlians pass him, as a chill wind rippling through his soul.

<There it is, Jimmy!> Grysta called excitedly. *<The Center of the Universe! It's beautiful!>*

He pulled up hard when he saw the city below and the path to it. *<No, Grysta! It's not heaven, it's Satan's city! It is great Dis at the center of Hell itself! You can not reach it! Not* this *way! This* way is eternal damnation!>*

<Oh, bullshit, Jimmy! If I fly fast and straight enough I can

make it! I'm not gonna go back, Jimmy! I can't go back! I can't!>

<No, Grysta, you can't! If you die, I die! And I'll not die yet, not here! You owe me that much at least!>

<Come with me, then! We can make it! We'll be together then! Not as we were, but as two wholes, apart! Listen to Them*, Jimmy! Hear* Their *whispered promises! They swear it!>*

<No, Grysta! They lie! They are the root of all lies.>

His pleas were unanswered. *<I can't go back, Jimmy! I just can't! Not now, not when I'm free for the first time in my existence. You always did say you wanted to be free of me. You won't die. Not if I'm not there to hold on!>*

<Grysta! No! I'd rather still have you than to see you do this! I'll do anything you want! Just turn now! It's almost too late!>

<Love ya, Jimmy! Love ya! Goodbye!>

He couldn't tell if she made it or not, for suddenly he found himself being pulled violently backward at impossible speeds, passing them, passing them all, and screaming, screaming. . . .

Modra felt his intense agony as Jimmy passed; they all did.

<That was McCray!> the Durquist shouted to her. *<Pull up! I'm going back—he needs me. Follow along! If we can get back before your new friends do, you might be able to escape them! They must be in the crystal cave as well!>*

<I'm with you!> she called back. *<If we can get back all the way!>*

<We've got to!> he replied. *<We were* shown *this, just as we were* shown *the rest! What purpose was it to bring us here if we cannot return?>* He wished he was as confident of that as he was trying to sound.

<Who was that who went through? Was it Molly?>

<No, not Molly. It was that thing he always talked to. The parasite. I—I haven't sensed Molly much at all since the beginning. I don't know where she is. Poor thing! She wouldn't have the sense to have any control in here!>

The Mizlaplanians were beginning to ask the same questions about one of their own.

<Where is the captain?> Morok asked. *<Where is Chin?>*

Krisha tried to contact him with a mental net and failed. *<I*

don't know. I sensed him with us at the beginning, but not after. I hope he wasn't too curious for his own good!>

<There is nothing we can do for him in any case,> Manya noted. *<The others seem to be trying a return from this place where even the gods do not look. Our prayers are returned mocked, as travesties, the evil ones beckon to us, and we alone are responsible for our immortal souls! We must return if we can!>*

Morok had a sudden realization that Chin wasn't the only one missing. *<Where is Modra? She was down and then she darted off on her own!>*

<I sensed her going back,> Krisha told him. *<I believe that your Talent could no longer hold her in here.>*

<Blast! All of us must be in that one great cave!> Morok realized suddenly. *<She's trying to beat us—me—back. She knows too much now to maintain the fiction we have kept up to this point. I will have to blank her memory completely—if I get the chance.>*

Krisha suddenly sped up, going away from the city. *<But can we get back, Holy One, where we were?>*

<We must! We must find the way!>

<And quickly, too,> Manya added. *<Now the others know we are all in the same place. If any of them awaken and find our entranced forms, we will have no bodies to re-enter!>*

<We will know the way,> Morok told her. *<We need only do as we have and follow the others. And they—they are following that scream.>*

Jimmy McCray was still screaming, only now, suddenly, it was with the enveloping, agonizing pain.

"Hurry, girl! We've got to get him out of that suit! You know how? The controls aren't the same as mine!"

She nodded, stricken by the waves of agony coming from Jimmy. "Molly know. Push these in this way like *this.*"

The telepath's suit suddenly swelled up, then collapsed like oversized baggy clothing, and from that it was easy to pull apart the pieces, although he was still screaming and writhing in pain, forcing Gun Roh Chin to hold him down while Molly pulled him out.

"Put him on his side there! *Hold him!* Oh, by the gods and their holy angels!"

Jimmy McCray's back was a sea of blood, and in the center, awash in it, was a gruesome grub-like thing perhaps twenty centimeters long, covered in thin brown and gray hair or fur on its upper side. For a moment, Chin didn't know what to do; it was unlike anything in his experience. "Do you know what this thing is?" he asked her.

"Grysta. She live on his blood long time. Jimmy say if Grysta die, he die, too."

He poked at it with a finger, thankful for the protection of the suit. "I don't know if it's alive or dead, but I'd say it's dead. At any rate, we have to get it off him if we can. Clearly we can't do anything without that, and he's certainly in agony now, and if we can't get beyond this monstrosity to sterilize and seal the wound he'll die from lack of blood anyway. I wish I knew whether to cut it out or pull it out or what." He sighed, stood up, and drew his pistol.

"No! No shoot Jimmy!" Molly screamed.

"Don't worry. It's going to be the lightest possible stun. Just enough to knock him out so we aren't fighting him. Stand back. It'll take away his pain so we can work."

Hesitantly, she let go of Jimmy and stood back, and Chin gave a minimal charge to the telepath, who stiffened once, then was still.

"Help me turn him all the way on his back," Chin ordered. "That won't hold him for long, so it's best we're done with this."

Bracing himself with a knee against Jimmy's back, he reached down with both hands and took hold of Grysta and tried pulling the creature straight off. The tiny form gave for a little bit, but did not come free, and he looked under and saw that the underside of the Morgh was not furry, but barren, and from the top, in the direction of the unconscious man's head, three tendrils emerged, two very much like veins or arteries, the third smaller and more wiry, and went into McCray's back.

"I don't dare go any further," he commented. "I'm going to have to cut them off and then cauterize them." He fumbled in Manya's medical kit, taken from her suit pack. He picked up the small powered scalpel, switched it on, and then took a deep breath and cut without any hesitation. The body of the Morgh came free and he tossed it aside. Leaving some of the tendrils out just a bit, he cauterized them with another of Manya's tools, then ran the sterilizer over the whole thing. Finally, he used some of McCray's own suit water to wash off as much blood as he could, then applied a bandage, and administered a strong pain shot. Finally, he got up and sighed. "I can't do any more for him," he said simply.

Molly was impressed. "You be doctor?"

"No, I'm a ship captain," he told her. "A captain often has to learn to do a lot of different things. At least he's a Terran, so I had some knowledge of what I was doing. If he'd been some other race, I don't know if we'd even have gotten this far. Certainly I wouldn't have known which shot to dial."

"The others. You think maybe they die, too?"

He shook his head. "I don't think so. At least not yet. Apparently this other creature *did* die, and the shock to his system yanked him back as well. The others . . . I don't know."

Molly turned suddenly. "Somebody else back. Molly hear noises."

He held up his hand. "Don't. We don't know who it is. If they're the Mycohl they're going to be pretty angry, but they're real killers, girl. If they're your people or mine, we'll reveal ourselves and deal with them."

In the main cave, Josef stirred, then opened his eyes and tried to sit up. He was still dizzy as hell. He checked his suit, and was alarmed to discover that it was completely switched off and just hung on him. He tried powering it up, but it wouldn't come on.

He pulled himself up to a sitting position as first Tobrush, then Kalia, stirred as well, and saw that their suits were collapsed, too.

<Son of a bitch! What's wrong with this suit?>

Josef felt a sudden energy shock. Kalia hadn't said a word as yet, and yet he'd heard her! Heard her thoughts, and also felt her anger.

He stared at her. *<Kalia? Can you understand me?>*

"Sure I can," she snapped, aloud. "What the fuck's wrong with the suit?"

<Fascinating,> Tobrush's thoughts came to them. *<We're still sensitized!>*

Kalia was still mad about the suit. "What are you two . . . ?" Suddenly her jaw dropped as she realized that she was the only one who'd actually *said* anything. *<Holy shit!>* she managed.

"I might suggest we all speak until you get more of the hang of it," Tobrush said as calmly as was practical. "Otherwise all our thoughts will be jumbled together and we won't be able to tell ourselves from the others."

"All right," Josef agreed, a little unnerved. Although he always knew that his surface thoughts were an open book to telepaths, it was easy to put that idea out of your mind. Somehow, now he felt as if his privacy had been forever violated. Telepaths were trained to block; he had no idea how that was done. He tried to force himself to practical matters. "Can you figure out what's wrong with the suits, Tobrush? Were we out so long we just ran out of power or what?"

The Julki examined the suits. "Offhand, I'd say not. If you check your power pack, you'll see that your power cube isn't there any more, I'll bet. Mine isn't. Someone, it appears, got here ahead of us."

"Damn!" He opened his mind in the chamber. "I don't sense anybody else here who's awake, though."

"No," the Julki agreed. "And I have experience. I don't expect we are going to be alone here for long, though, and I might point out we're now weaponless and without shields—and if they wake up as we did, they'll have no trouble locating and finishing us off."

Josef nodded, thinking along the same lines. "We might as well get out of the suits and remove the supply packs," he told them. "Then we'll have to get out of here and fast and pray that whatever's beyond isn't lethal."

Kalia wriggled out of her suit and reached back in and pulled out her knife. "I'm not without a weapon!" she announced proudly. "And neither are you, O Great Leader. And you, Tobrush, can poison anything with these bristles. I'd like to take the time to find that praying bitch who burned me and make sure she wanders in that place forever, tryin' to pray her rotted soul out!"

"We can't chance it," Josef told her. "I think I hear somebody else waking up over there, now. Let's move forward, out of this place, before these things start vibrating and suck us back again. Already I can feel the pull."

Kalia looked at the other two and sighed. "I wonder if I'm *ever* gonna get my crack at her? Particularly now, with me bare-ass naked and you wearin' only a jock strap. About the only thing we haven't got yet is freezin' cold, and we're sure ready for that, aren't we?''

''One step at a time,'' Josef cautioned. *<Still, I'd like to get my own hands on the bastard who took our power cubes.>*

Across the great cavern, Modra Stryke groaned and stirred and came to. *What a hell of a dream!* she thought, shivering.

<It's no dream, Modra. It was very real! Now get your tail over here before that hypno wakes up and nabs you again!>

She frowned. ''Durquist?'' she said aloud, her voice echoing slightly. The crystals stirred, and, feeling suddenly disoriented a bit, she stayed still.

<Yes, it's the Durquist. Don't shout, just stand up and quietly move towards the other end of the cave. I'll see you. And don't say anything aloud right now. For some reason, we can still talk telepathically.>

<It's the ones from the Exchange!> Tobrush's thought came not just to its companions but to Modra and the Durquist as well.

<Forget it! I can tell right now they've still got power. Let's move! I don't want them getting any more of our thoughts than they have,> Josef snapped.

Modra stopped dead in her tracks. *<Who was that?>*

<The Mycohl, I think. Ignore them for now. Here, I'm bipedal now. Can you see me?>

She looked around, then saw the familiar if somewhat grotesque form about thirty meters from her and immediately began walking as quickly as her vertigo allowed toward the Durquist. When she arrived, she looked around, puzzled. ''Where's McCray?'' she asked aloud.

''Gone. And Molly, too. I tried hailing them on the intercom but got no response. Anybody missing from the Mizzie party?''

She frowned. ''I—I didn't think to look.''

''Hmmm . . . Talking *does* help sort it out, so long as you don't talk loud enough to cause echoes and start the crystals resonating,'' he noted. ''This is quite odd. I always wondered what it was like to read minds and emotions, and now that I suddenly can, I'm not sure I like it. I wonder if we're hypnos, too?''

''Don't you find out on me!'' she responded nervously. ''I've had enough of *that* type for a while!''

"Don't worry. Still, I wonder if it's permanent, or if it'll fade once we clear this place?"

"Who can say? Who can say *anything* about this place now? Even now, I'm not sure we actually *went* someplace or if we simply had some kind of common dream influenced by these crystals and caused by this boosting of our Talents."

"I, too, wonder about that, but this is neither the time nor place to speculate. I feel like these things are going to start taking me off again if I don't get out of here."

She nodded. "Me, too. But what about Jimmy and Molly?"

"It would take hours to search this place, and I think it's dangerous to stay here. If they aren't already out, we'll give them a chance to get out and then wait a while—but not in here."

"You're right," she admitted, loath still to leave any member of a team. "All we'd do would be for both of us to look into Morok's eyes anyway. We can do more by following the Mycohl."

They made their way as quickly as possible to the far end of the great cavern. It appeared to have only one exit, as it had had only one entrance, and a very small and narrow exit at that.

The passage ran in a slight S-shaped curve for about fifteen meters, then opened up into a relatively smaller cave. They could feel the absence of the great crystals at once.

<*You still hear me?*> she shot to him.

<*I do. And I'm getting something else from over that way, although it's hard for me to tell just what.*> Both pistols came out.

"No shoot! No shoot!" they heard a familiar voice call to them.

"Molly?" Modra called.

"Hi, Modra! You all right now?"

"Yes, I'm all right. What—"

The guns had just been lowered when suddenly they came up again as they saw, next to Molly, the unmistakable yellow-gold suit of a Mizlaplanian.

"No, no!" Molly cried. "This be Chin! He help Jimmy!"

"Hello, Modra," the captain greeted them through the translator. "I see you snapped out of Morok's hold. In a way, I'm glad. I found it most—distasteful. I'm no threat, not now, I swear. You know me well enough by now to know my word is good. Please—come look at your man. I've done what I could.''

They hurried over, a bit wary, knowing Molly's innocence, but when they saw Jimmy lying there they both knew that Molly couldn't have done *that*.

"He had—something—a creature—on his back," Chin explained as best he could. "It was dead—I think. He was losing a lot of blood because of it. I got our medical kit and severed it and did what I could."

The Durquist went to Jimmy and began an examination with his own kit. Modra looked at the unlikely pair and asked, "What happened? How did the two of you ever come to be paired up?"

"I went into a terribly deep sleep," the captain told them. "Deep, but filled with odd nightmares that scared me as nothing has since I was a small child, but remote. They've all faded now already, all but the memory of the fear. I woke up on the cavern floor in there in a cold sweat. The girl, here, heard me and came over and was quite kind to me until I got my bearings again. At just about that time this fellow started screaming, and the whole place sounded very eerie and both of us got splitting headaches. We managed together to drag him out of here, where it was better, and, by that time, things had quieted down enough so that I was able to go back in and find the medical kit. The result you see here. I'm afraid I can't tell you any more than that, except that she told me she'd woke up with the same kind of bad dreams and had been trying to wake someone else up ever since."

Molly nodded. "Nobody move. Molly thought you all dead."

<The captain is a null,> Modra explained silently to the Durquist, finding this form of communication sometimes had its advantages.

<That might explain it,> the Durquist responded. <He was there, all right, for a while, but without the ability to receive the Talents, which even an ordinary no-Talent person has, he had no frame of reference. His mind balked, and he just had nightmares.>

<But Molly's on the band. She's an empath. Why did she even come out of it quicker than he did?>

<Impossible to know. At a guess, I think you have to

*remember that she's not really organic in the same sense we
are. She's basically a preprogrammed machine with some
freedom of thought and independence of action—thank heaven!
She just simply wasn't equipped for the trip.>*

"The Mycohl came through a few minutes ago," the captain
remarked, chuckling. "They didn't say anything, but they were
pretty mad, I think. You see, in the time between waking up
and this poor fellow starting to scream, we had a little time and
I found the Mycohl. I removed their power cubes and threw
them randomly back toward the entrance. They might still be in
front, but they're naked savages, without power or weapons,
and without suit protection. If the next world is worse than the
last one, as I have every reason to expect, they're probably
dead already."

The Durquist finished his examination and replaced the
bandage. "As good a job as anyone could do. Thank you,
Captain. You didn't have to do this."

He shrugged. "I thought I owed it to you all. Now, unless
you wish to take *me* hostage, I'd better take the kit and get back
to my own people. I assume they'll be coming around soon if
not now, and one or more of them might need something, too.
Be careful with him for a while, if you can. He's lost a fair
amount of blood and will be weak, and I don't know what will
happen when the pain shot wears off."

"I have some painkillers if need be," the Durquist assured
him. "Go back to your people, Captain. Consider us even."

The captain gave them a casual Mizlaplanian salute and left.

As soon as he was out of sight and they could no longer hear
his footsteps, Molly said, "We got to go right now!"

"I don't think the captain will betray us, somehow," Modra
assured her. "And I'd feel better if we saw how McCray was
before moving him any more."

"No, no! You not understand. When I see Chin take little
thing from red suits and they go off, I know what he do. So I
go over to *his* suits, do same thing. Think maybe if you only
one with suit, you be boss, not slave."

Modra's mouth hung open and, for a brief moment, they all
stood there, almost like statues. Suddenly she said, "Molly,
grab him under one arm. I'll take the other. Somehow, we'll
drag him out. Durquist, you make damned sure that captain
doesn't come back with his gun out!"

It wasn't that easy to do; the way was fairly long and very dark, but Jimmy was small and light and the two women were very well motivated to do whatever they had to do.

<Well, at least we don't have to worry much about an ambush,> the Durquist commented. *<And if the captain's right about wherever this is going, we're not going to have to worry about anybody but him, either. And, somehow, I think we can work with him.>*

The captain didn't have to wait for any of his people to wake up to realize he'd been had. He only had to look at the collapsed suits to know that he had gravely underestimated that girl. Maybe she *was* some kind of junior demon after all, he thought sourly.

But, no, he told himself sadly. This was *his* fault, and his alone, for even putting the idea in her head. He'd probably killed them all by his stupidity, and he'd have to atone for that.

The awakening was much like the others had been: the sudden shock of realizing that they were all reading each other's thoughts and emotions, the secondary realization that they had no power, and confusion. The one thing the others hadn't had was Captain Chin there.

"Wait a minute! You mean you're *all* telepaths now?"

"And empaths, and perhaps a lot more we don't know about yet," Morok told him. "I must admit it's something of a shock."

Chin immediately thought of the Mycohl, and of Modra and the Durquist. Them, too? Why should it be selective?

He sighed. "Well, since you cannot read my mind or feel my deepest remorse, I must tell you about the suits," he began, and proceeded to tell much, although not all, of the story. "Modra was already outside our influence and with her companion," he concluded. "It was either try and kill them all—and it was three to one against me—or do them a service and hope for the best. I chose the latter, although I did not, I assure you, know about *this* at the time."

"Captain, I cannot but forgive your lapse," the Stargin told him. "You did your best. In any case, they will not take us as ogres or monsters. Modra knows us, for one thing, and now you helped their man. As to the suits—how many hours of power do you have left, Captain?"

He hadn't even thought of that. "Three point four hours, Holiness."

"Precisely. And ours were at least as low."

He thought of something. "I still have Savin's module," he reminded them. "That's got over forty hours left on it! You take it! It'll power one of the suits! And, of course, my power can at least give a few hours to another of you."

He was answered mostly with silence, an occasional "No, but . . ." or grunt or gesture being the only other punctuation. He was beginning to feel very left out of things.

"This is much too confusing!" Morok exclaimed at last. "We must train ourselves to speak in the old ways. Krisha knows how to do this; we do not. So many rapid-fire thoughts and half-thoughts fill my mind I can hardly think!"

"The Holy One is correct, as always," Manya agreed, much to Chin's relief. "I, for one, need to focus. But the fact remains: you must take Savin's power supply, Holy Father. You are our leader and guide in all things."

"No," he responded. "We must face it, my children. My leg is not getting any better, and there is a limit to how long I can fool myself about the pain. Nothing, but nothing, must keep at least one of us from attaining our primary goal. Krisha, you were second only to Savin in weapons skills, which are the primary skills needed right now. You must take Savin's power. As for the captain's, I fear it is irrelevant. What is three hours in *this* place? You might as well keep your suit on, Captain. The skills that Manya is best at would take more practical power than you have. Now—help me out of this bag of useless rags."

Manya said nothing, although her thoughts were plain to the other two priests. She felt she was entitled to Chin's power, both by her position and ordination, and because it had been, after all, the captain's own inexcusable lapse that had caused the crisis. On the other hand, with a firm belief in her own perfection, she knew it was her duty to sacrifice.

And, as the Holy One had pointed out, three hours wasn't enough to get upset about losing. She had always thought that she would go, one day, as a martyr to the faith. Perhaps this was the time.

Krisha took Savin's power module and inserted it in the pack, then reactivated her suit, as Morok and Manya, the latter a bit surly about it, got out of theirs. Chin was amused to note that, while most members of the Holy Orders wore little or nothing under their robes or, in this case, suits, Manya had on a complete black body stocking. Still, shorn of her suit and without the flowing robes she wore otherwise, she now looked far less Terran than she otherwise seemed to; among other more subtle features, the large single breast with the multiple overlarge nipples, now apparent, giving her a decidedly other-race cast.

"Manya, don't forget the supply pack and medikit—I put it down over there," Chin reminded her. "I'll carry your pack, Holy Father."

Morok looked around nervously at the great cavern festooned with glowing crystals. "Let us get out of this place, no matter what awaits outside. At least we can no worse than die beyond. In here, I sense there are far worse fates."

They all sensed that, and there was little argument on the point. In a few minutes, they made the far end and the passage to the smaller cave beyond, where Chin and Molly had ministered to Jimmy McCray. The captain drew his pistol and said, "Let me go in first. I don't underestimate the Exchange people, but I don't want to overestimate them, either. The fellow was in very bad shape; they might well still be there."

Krisha stopped him. "No, I will go. Then Manya and the Holy Father will also know what is there before any of us step inside, and I have far more power if it comes to shooting."

She knew before she entered the outer cavern, though, that the others were gone, and as soon as *she* knew it, so did the other two sensitized people behind, and they quickly joined her.

They did not realize how much tension and pressure upon them was being caused by the crystals until they were out of there. It was as if a giant weight was lifted from their shoulders at the same time a cloud lifted from their minds.

"I suggest we wait here a bit," the captain said. "They'll be carrying an injured and probably still unconscious man and that will slow them. If you can read each other's thoughts and feelings, then they can read yours as well."

"Agreed," Morok said wearily, settling down to rest his leg. Chin was no doctor, but you didn't need much training to see the difference in the two long, spindly legs, and realize that the leader of the Holy Arm was in far worse shape than his manner implied.

"We'll give them another fifteen minutes or so," he suggested, knowing that every delay would help a little. "While we wait, can you tell me what you saw in your common dreams?"

Krisha shook her head slowly from side to side. "That's the real problem. I *can't* remember clearly—or, maybe, I don't want to. I remember that we were all flying, somehow, in some sort of space unlike any I've ever seen before, and that we were surrounded by horrible, graphic evil. But I can't clearly sort out or remember just what it looked or felt like, and the evil that was so clear and so absolute then is just blackness now."

"We were being pulled towards a city, I remember that," Morok added. "Still, beyond a fleeting glimpse of the city in the distance, set out around a great nothingness, I can add nothing to Krisha's account. It is as if there are no words, not even concepts, to explain the medium we were in, and that the mind rebels and shuts out the specifics of the evils embedded within it."

Even the usually absolutist Manya agreed on that. "It was the place from which all evil in the universe comes," she told him. "As if the worst evils any of us could imagine were just pale shadows of the true evils that lived there."

"I do remember that the city was beautiful, if menacing," Krisha put in. "It beckoned with a cold, multicolored beauty, yet it was unreachable. The evil was too close in around it to be able to make it through."

"That cavern back there, and even its bizarre mental effects, are in some way the source of the demons' power," the captain said firmly. "I would bet on it. You all came out of the experience mutated—changed, more powerful, more sensitized to all the power this whole Quintara complex represents. It opened your minds so you all, from us to the Mycohl to the Exchange, who could receive those bands, shared a common nightmare that forms the experience."

Krisha once again shook off the captain's comments. "No, no. It was no nightmare—we are all certain of that. It was *real*. It was, somehow, a very real place, where only the mind and soul could go. The evils, and the city, too, are real, Captain. We were simply seeing them in a different, alien way."

Chin reserved judgment on what was real and what was not, not having had the experience himself but in the most elementary, and brief, sort of way, but he was willing to go along with it as a working hypothesis. "If so, then we might suspect that the city that you saw is our ultimate destination. A city surrounded by and guarded by evil and in turn surrounding nothingness. *That* would be a most interesting city to visit, if we are capable of understanding what is there." He sighed and got up. "I believe it's time we found out what's next."

Krisha nodded, and she and Chin helped Morok unsteadily to his feet.

"The worst thing is," the Grand Inquisitor sighed, "we still don't know if this is indeed the correct way out of this place."

The route still led down, or so it seemed, and perhaps it had the leftward curve and perhaps it didn't; it was nearly impossible to tell for sure. Still, the glow from the smaller crystals embedded within the rock all around them continued to provide a dim but serviceable light.

<There's a cool breeze flowing in from somewhere ahead,> Josef thought to himself, not for the first time forgetting that his surface thoughts, at least, were no longer just his own.

<Just so long as it doesn't get too cool,> Tobrush responded. <I keep having this fear that after fire comes ice.>

<Yeah, and we ain't exactly dressed for the part,> Kalia put in.

There was a sudden leftward shift ahead, and they all sensed instantly that, beyond that bend, was someone, *something,* that was aware, that knew they were coming, that waited for them.

Without Tobrush's handy psychological ability to rationalize almost anything convincingly to himself, Josef could not forget those presences within the strange place they'd been carried to by the crystal cavern. The memories lurked just out of reach in his mind—and thankfully so, he knew—but their effect on him remained very real. Still, even the other two had been affected by it, as they stopped before making that turn and looked at him.

"Well?" Kalia asked aloud. "Do we go or not?"

He shrugged. "We have a choice?"

They went on, rounding the curve, then stopped again, somewhat overwhelmed by the sight that met their eyes.

The passage ended in a gate much like the energy barrier for the stations, but larger, *much* larger, and, this time, it was flanked by the figures of two *enormous* demons, one five meters high at least but perfectly proportioned, the other perhaps half a meter shorter but no less grand. Instead of the plain and somewhat primitive dress of the others, these two wore robes and capes of the deepest purple; their clawed fingers were adorned with great rings of gold and precious gems of fantastic size. The one on the left, slightly larger than the other, had not the short, sharp horns of the previous demons but great, curled ram's horns coming from his head, the other mere bumps, like rounded buttons, but had a plume of deep purple hair even darker than the garments running from the brow between the bumps far back until it was swallowed in the folds of the cape.

Neither was encased in anything, but they stood in the center of a glowing, perfect design that appeared as if it were built in somehow to the cave floor: the pentagram inside a circle.

Although they radiated power that might be taken as evil in a strength far beyond the ones previously encountered, it seemed to pale beyond what they had experienced, and half-forgotten, from the helix. Oddly, it made them much easier to deal with.

<*Welcome,*> they said, speaking in the male-female unison of the others, as if they were one creature but two organisms. <*We are pleased that so many of you made it to this point.*>

Josef felt he had nothing to lose by showing bravado. "Who are you?" he asked aloud, his voice echoing a bit. "What is this place?"

<*You already know who we are,*> they responded. <*We are Quintara, whom your Holy Ones call demons, or devils or a million other terms. It has been eons since we last walked among you, yet your people still remember us, and, although we have not been present in the flesh, we have been among you and with you all during this time. We have nudged and prodded where we could, but we have waited long and patiently for you to finally arrive here.*>

<*You knew we were coming all along?*> Tobrush asked, being literal as usual.

<*Not you, specifically, until our station was discovered and until it was possible to arrange probability to bring represen-*

tatives from your Three Empires together here, in competition.>

<Then it was chance that brought us to you,> the Julki said, finally glad to have settled a point.

<Chance for you specifically; you were in the right place at the right time. If not you, another group would have been.>

"But what *is* this place? All of it? And why were we drawn here?" Josef demanded to know.

<This is the Greatest Empire, the Inner Empire, which borders upon all points in your universe simultaneously, yet is a part of all and none. From us sprang all the worlds and races of the universe, not merely your tiny Three Empires, which, as large as they are, are but dust specks compared to the glorious whole of the universe. We gave birth to you all, and then withdrew, awaiting the time when our children would develop to a point where they could come to us. Those who came first, and could get this far, would be set above all the others in the universe. Only one thing remains. You must liberate us, all of us, of your own free will.>

"Why do you need liberating if you are what you say?" Tobrush asked them, speaking aloud as well. "Who is it that imprisoned you here?"

<Why, we ourselves did this. Your own logic should tell you that no conqueror or enemy would leave us thus and all this in place when they had us at their mercy. It was necessary to restrain all of us, lest we be too tempted to stop the experiment, or more actively interfere in it. It is necessary that you free us because only that act, having seen what you have seen and knowing what you know, shows true trust in us.>

"We don't yet possess that sort of trust and you know it," Josef countered. "Nor do your answers clearly explain all this, while the only physical evidence we have of what fate befalls someone who liberates you is a mass of decaying bodies."

<The answers you seek, and the proofs as well, lie yet beyond,> the demons told them. *<Remember the Great Helix?>*

"We remember," Josef responded uneasily.

<Now it is time for you to walk that road again in life. Beyond this gate lies the physical representation of what you have already been through. At the other side lies the city, and within the city lies Chaos Keep. To enter the city of the Quintara is to become like us; to become like us is to know.>

"Know? Know what?" Tobrush cried out.

The demons ignored the question. *<You are the first. Leave everything you now have here. Take nothing in but yourselves. We shall ensure a level playing field. All that you require is provided. As with the crystal plane, it is a journey of choices, not of needs.>*

Josef held up his pack. "This is food, water, medicine. We're not going into an unknown place without at least *that*."

<If you refuse our advice, you will suffer for it. Trust us, and you will reach the city. To not do so risks failure. You are not the first races to find us, merely the first of your own groups. The others did not trust us. The others are no more, and they doomed their own people to be the subjects when our time comes again. Trust only us to reach the city. Only by trusting us will you reach the end of the quest and reap uncounted rewards. The others approach. Do what you will, but you must go.>

It was more an emotional than a thought process that Kalia went through, but she dropped everything she was carrying, even her knife, and then walked forward.

<I didn't expect to live beyond this point anyway,> Tobrush commented, and did the same.

Josef hesitated, weighing the options, then stepped through, still carrying his knife and his pack. At the point where he touched the gate but could still see the demons out of the corner of his eye, he saw them flicker slightly, and frowned.

Projections, he thought. *They aren't even really here at all.*

Jimmy had come around, but he had a high fever and enough pain that only strong medicine would bring it down to livable levels, and he wasn't really all there yet. Still, balancing on both Modra and Molly, he managed to do some of his own walking.

Modra and the Durquist both felt the presences, but aside from shifting to allow Modra to draw her pistol with her free hand, they did not really hesitate. As the ones who'd come before had also decided, there wasn't any other choice.

<Welcome. We are pleased so many of you made it to this point,> the demons said, again opening a discussion that did not differ much either in questions asked nor answers given from the Mycohlians' experience.

<You must leave the suits, and everything else manufactured that you have, here,> the demons warned them at last.

"We'll not give up the only advantage we have left!" Modra told them firmly.

<You must. We have promised a level playing field.>

"Your reputation, punctuated by what your people did to our research team, says that *you* never like a level field," the Durquist pointed out.

<True, but it is not against us that you play. Does a game piece play the owner of the game? If you refuse, you will discover that you have not gained any advantage, only exposed yourself to danger that could cost you everything at the very time when you might yet win. But the choice is yours—it is a part of the game.>

Modra pointed to Jimmy. "That's not level. He needs medicine and the support the suit gives."

<Have him eat and drink of what is beyond, and bathe him in the waters you find there,> the demons instructed. *<It will restore him.>*

"We'll take our chances," Modra insisted.

<Consider what you do. If you are not among those at Chaos Keep, you condemn not only yourselves but your entire people, your entire Empire, to eternal slavery. No one can stand against you with us at your side. No one can stand against us and not fall.>

"I do not recall asking to play," the Durquist commented.

<If an answer is irrelevant to what is, why bother to ask it?> the demons retorted.

Jimmy came around for a bit, stared at the demons like a drunken man, then looked down at their feet and pointed. "Ha! The Seal of Solomon! You're still bound, you horny bastards!" And then he sank back once more into a semi-stupor.

"If they're held as McCray says, there's nothing stopping us from just walking past this pair," the Durquist noted.

Modra nodded. "I'm not in the mood for debating right now, and the Mizzies have to be right on our tails, and I wouldn't give a rat's ass for McCray's chances if Chin gets one shot at us. Let's go."

She and Molly grabbed Jimmy, and, together, they all walked through the gate.

The Mizlaplanians, slowed by Morok's wound, were just about ten minutes behind them.

They got the same greeting, but Manya in particular was having none of it.

"Princes of Darkness, you have nothing to say to us!" she declared.

The demons seemed unimpressed. *<Trust in your gods and die, then,>* they responded calmly. *<For your gods are false, your Holy Angels nothing but your masters to keep you in bondage, and all your sacrifice merely wastes what life is all about and yields the same corruption as one who has yielded to all the pleasures of life. The Mizlaplanians created your entire pitiful religion and its boring, passive totalitarian system as a defense against us, but the tragedy is yours, not ours, for it was all futile and wasted. We have little hope for brainwashed automatons like you. Go now and die right off, in pain and agony, so that we need not be bothered any more by your stupidity!>*

There hardly seemed much point to waiting around, although Gun Roh Chin regretted that he wasn't able to ask them some questions.

THE
GARDEN OF
THE GODS

IT WAS TYPICAL OF THE INSANE LOGIC THEY HAD
been experiencing up to this point that they had entered in a
cave and descended, yet emerged from it near the top of a hill,
looking out over a landscape that was as breathtaking as it was
bizarre.

It was a green place; almost every shade of green was
represented in the grasses, trees, and shrubs that covered the
land to the horizon, and while the exact taxonomy of the plants
might have been unfamiliar, their basic shapes and forms
seemed comfortably familiar.

What gave it its extremely alien feel was the sudden
realization that, while the landscape was brightly lit, as if a day
in springtime, there was no sun and no shadows—indeed, no
sense of where the light source was coming from was present
at all.

The sky in fact was dark, but, again, there was a strangeness
even to its darkness, as if they were looking not at a night sky
but rather up and out of some vast window, a single, flat pane
that sloped down toward the horizon, and through which could
be seen the brilliant colors and bright shapes of what might
have been a galactic cluster.

<Beautiful,> Kalia thought. *<Beautiful but strange.>*

<Manicured,> Josef thought, taking in the whole scene.

<Eh? What's that?> Tobrush asked him.

"Manicured," he said aloud. "Like the formal gardens of some great Lord. Even the trees are shaped, deliberately so, if you just look at them, and the shrubs and hedges are nicely trimmed. All but that first, flat, featureless world we entered has been a dynamic landscape left to develop according to its nature. This is artificial and well maintained, not left over the centuries to go wild. I wonder how it is maintained, and by who?"

"I have been wondering all along," the Julki commented, "whether these places are always here or are being created expressly for us. If we assume a race, or races, as advanced over us as we are over the microbe, almost anything they can routinely do would seem like magic to us, as what we do is magic to lesser cultures."

"I just had an odd thought," Josef commented, still staring at the beauty before them. "For all their mental prowess, these Quintara seem very much in the mainstream of life as we know it. Possibly one cut above us, as are our masters the Mycohl, or the Guardians of the Exchange, or whatever the Holy Horrors call their angels, but, in most ways, they don't even seem *that* far above us. Certainly not supernatural. You noticed, I assume, that the pair back there were projections?"

"Yes, it seemed so," Tobrush agreed. "Oh, I see your point. Certainly not the kind of race and culture to have evolved the kind of power we've been seeing."

Josef nodded. "Almost as if they were a people who blundered, perhaps quite by accident, into someone else's master control room, and who, through trial and error and pushing buttons, figured out, somehow, how to operate the thing without actually understanding how it worked. Not gods, but, intoxicated by the power, playing gods."

"Indeed. And, if that's so, then where is the control room?"

Josef pointed at the horizon over to the left of them, where there was a distinct glow against the darkness. "The city," he replied. "The city seen in the mass hallucination or whatever it was back in the crystal chamber. How was it put to us? 'At the center of everything and on the edge of nothing.'"

"Something like that. Well, the only thing we gain by

standing here is the likelihood that the Exchange group will come in behind us. I think we'd better go down there.''

Josef nodded. "Still, they promised us a level playing field here.''

"I'll put no stock in their promises," Tobrush maintained. "They've lied right along, I think. Perhaps, by this point, they're even lying to themselves.''

Josef pointed to the vastness of the garden. "You notice the straight lines on the hedgerows? They form patterns, which grow increasingly complex and dense as you go in.''

"A maze, perhaps?" the Julki suggested. "The sort of thing one sets up in animal experiments?''

Josef sighed. "Usually they're decorative when they're in a formal garden, but I have the uneasy feeling that you might be right. Still, as you say, there is nothing to be gained and much to be lost by staying here. Let's go down.''

The grassy hillside ended in a line of neatly trimmed and well-spaced trees.

"There is no path," Kalia noted. "No sign this time of which way to go.''

Josef looked behind them at the way they'd come. "Tobrush, if you were a little lighter and less bulky there'd be no way they could find out where we enter this thing. As it is, that matted grass you leave gives a perfect trail.''

"Then we will give them several," the Julki told him, and set back out up the hill. Partway up, Tobrush turned and came down to the trees twenty or thirty meters from them. Hurrying, the path was again retraced and, in a matter of minutes, there were at least six possibilities, ending with a center trail. They walked over to the Julki, who said, "Now let them choose.''

Josef thought a moment. "If I were tracking *them*, I'd be consistent and take the leftmost trail. We'll go in here. It may not make any difference in the long run, but it'll give us some breathing room.''

They walked into the forest, and after about a hundred and fifty meters the trees and layout changed. "I hear a stream over that way," Kalia said, pointing a bit to the left. "And, look! These are fruit trees of some kind! See?''

The trees were definitely arranged as a sort of grove, and the fruit, while unfamiliar and oddly shaped, looked quite similar to tropical fruits he and Kalia, at least, had known.

"Do you think they're safe to eat?" Josef wondered.

"As you keep saying, O Great Leader, what choice have we got?" she retorted, then jumped, grabbed a branch, and allowed gravity to bring it and her back down. Josef picked a few, and she let go. They were as large as a melon, but more shaped like squash, no two exactly alike, with thin skins of mixed yellow and pink.

Using his thumbnail, Josef scored one along the center and then broke it open. It was pulpy inside, a pale pink citrus-like consistency surrounding a bright red core. He smelled it, and it smelled sweet, almost perfumy.

Kalia took half a fruit and then said, "Well, *I* will trust them," and started digging out the inside and eating it. *<Incredibly sweet, almost like liquid sugar,>* she thought and continued on.

"If it is that high in sugar, it might also serve for me," Tobrush commented, shooting tendrils up to a nearby tree and bringing one of the fruits down to it, then shoving it whole into a cavity below its eyes.

<What the hell,> Josef thought, staring at his half. *<I expected to be dead by now anyway.>* He ate some of the pulp, hesitantly at first, then continued on when he saw that he wasn't getting sudden nausea.

It was much *too* sweet for his taste, almost like chewy syrup, but it seemed quite filling.

"I wish I had my instruments here," Tobrush commented. "I believe there is some sort of natural fermentation inside the fruit. I can tell that there is some alcoholic content."

Neither Josef nor Kalia could taste anything alcoholic about it, but the sweetness so overwhelmed everything else it might well have been true. After two or three of them, though, Kalia, at least, began to feel light-headed and slightly dizzy. "Woo! They got a little kick to 'em!" she exclaimed. "I think I better stop."

"Let's find that stream," Josef suggested, and they walked toward the sound of gurgling water.

The stream wasn't very cold, but it was clear and, again, looked safe, and appeared to be no more than a meter deep at its worst. Josef bent down and cupped his hands and drank some of the water, trying to get the sweetness out of his mouth, while Kalia went into the water and splashed around for a bit, then lay down in the deepest part and totally immersed herself. Getting back up, she seemed pleased. "First bath I've had in *ages,*" she told nobody in particular.

Josef watched her, tempted to join in, while Tobrush rolled down the side of the creek about ten meters, curious about something that might or might not be there. "Josef! Come up here!" the Julki called at last.

"What's the problem, Tobrush?" he called, walking slowly to join the creature.

"Tracks. I originally thought it was where something was dragged, but now I see it's a large, heavy body that passed. The tracks look familiar?"

Josef saw six heavy but irregular depressions, three on each side, making a progression to and into the stream. "Desreth! Somehow I'd almost forgotten about Desreth." He turned and looked across the stream. "And there! You can see where it came out of the water." He straightened up and called to Kalia. "C'mon, Kalia! We're going to find Desreth!"

She came down to them still in the water, splashing it like a little kid at a picnic. "Best I felt since that witch bitch burned me!" she enthused. "Now, what's this about old Metal Pants?"

They waded into the water, came up on the other side, and proceeded on into the trees. These, too, were in organized groves. The shorter, thicker ones on the left had banana-like stalks of a blue fruit, and the ones starting just beyond to their right were taller and ramrod straight and had fruit something like violet-colored apples.

"Have you noticed something odd about this garden?" Tobrush asked as they followed the tracks of the Corithian. "Other than the obvious, I mean?"

"Like what?" Josef responded.

"No insects or anything obviously in the role of insect, and no wind. No clouds, either, to give them steady water. It is deathly still and quiet here, more like a greenhouse than a true garden. If these plants pollinate in any one of the eleven known ways other than budding, it's done artificially."

Josef nodded, understanding the point at once. Somewhere around here, someone, or something, was the gardener.

The Corithian's tracks faded in and out, but, since they knew just what to look for, it wasn't difficult to follow the trail, nor, they suspected, was it intended to be. The one Mycohlian the others in back of them still didn't want to find was Desreth, but to the Mycohlians he represented as much as all their e-suits and pistols put together.

The groves, or orchards, or whatever they were, ended abruptly after a while, and the land opened into a broad meadow perhaps two kilometers across, carpeted with thick blue-green grass interspersed with thousands of multicolored flowers. On the other side, forming an effective wall four to five meters tall, was the beginning of the maze.

<I can't explain, but there's something I don't like about this area,> Kalia said in the new nonverbal way, as if she was afraid someone, or something, else might overhear. *<It's wide open for much too big an area. If we got caught in the middle of it, there'd be no place to run.>*

The others felt it, too, but it was not merely the openness of the meadow but something else, something indefinable.

But the tracks went straight ahead, and, after giving the area a very close going-over, they started out as well, but spread out, in spite of the fact that they really had nothing to hide behind, nothing to fight with unless Josef wanted to throw his pack at whatever it was, and nowhere to run.

About halfway across, they spotted a low, dull, coppery form standing on the field. "Desreth!" Josef yelled in his best, booming command voice. "Desreth—wait! It's us!"

They began to run toward the Corithian, who just seemed to stand there and wait for them to come. Kalia reached Desreth first, and stopped, standing a bit off, just staring. Josef and Tobrush both backed off and slowed as they joined her.

The Corithian looked frozen, but, more important, there were black marks all over as if it had been in some kind of fire, although what sort of fire could harm Desreth?

"Is it—dead?" Kalia asked nervously. Up until now she had simply never thought that a Corithian *could* die, short of being melted down by concentrated energy fire.

Tobrush circled slowly around the still form, making a thorough visual check. On the opposite side he spotted a slim, sharp tentacle emerging from the Corithian's body. It, too, was still, but Desreth had used it, perhaps with its last tiny bit of energy and will, to write something in the ground in the ideographic language of the Empire.

<Clouds?> Josef read, stooping. He looked up at the black roof of the place through which, dully, shone the brilliance of the star field. "What clouds?"

Kalia, too, scanned the sky, and suddenly she pointed to the distance to her left and said, "Maybe *that's* what Desreth meant!"

The other two turned and saw a small, white fluffy cloud in the distance. Suddenly, it moved—not as a cloud moved, but more like some sort of aircraft. No, that wasn't right, either. No aircraft ever sped up and then came to a sudden, complete stop like that cloud was doing, nor made right-angle turns at full speed.

<I don't know about you two,> Kalia sent, *<but in about one second I'm gonna run like hell!>*

"Scatter!" Josef shouted, and all three began making for the hedge, which was still a good kilometer away, in a widening pattern so that none of them were close enough to be taken with a single shot.

The cloud seemed to sense them and suddenly rushed to their position, stopped instantly, and its bottom layer began to darken, while the center of the darkness took on a bright glow.

Suddenly a bolt of white-hot lightning shot from it and struck the ground just behind Josef, who began to run in a zigzag pattern. About ten seconds after the first bolt, a second shot out, this time barely missing him, filling the air with thunder and the crackle of pure energy.

<Josef! The pack! Drop the pack and keep running! Drop it now!> Tobrush sent frantically.

Josef didn't stop to question. He flung the pack out and immediately started running away from it, still zigzagging. A third bolt shot out and struck the pack before it had hit the ground, enveloping it in a blue-white field of energy that crackled and hissed, and then the entire thing was a ball of superheated flame.

The cloud then started off, coming right over Josef, who slipped and fell, then lay there, bracing for the end.

The cloud kept going, its underside already becoming once again a nice, even, fluffy white. After a moment, he watched it go, turn, and head out over the orchards. It darkened again, but without the glow, and they saw rain begin falling from it as it moved slowly in a preordained pattern.

Josef was shaken, but he got up and walked as close as he dared to the pack. The energy bolt that had struck it was more powerful than any lightning *he'd* ever seen; the thing was literally melted into a blackened shape that bore no clue as to what it had been.

He allowed himself a big sigh of relief. *<When they say nothing, they mean it, don't they?>*

<The Mizlaplanian might well have done us a favor back in the cave,> Tobrush noted. *<How would you like to be wearing an e-suit out here? And I think we all would have if we'd still had them.>*

<The demons told the truth,> Kalia noted with some satisfaction. *<They said we'd all be even in here, and I think we will be. We might even have some barbecued enemies if we're lucky.>*

Josef nodded, still shaken. *<But why Desreth?>*

<The thing is obviously a gardening tool, a robot of some sort, doing double duty as a security guard,> Tobrush guessed. *<I would suspect that it is programmed to eliminate all non-living things. Apparently, for some reason, Corithians do not meet its predetermined definitions for same.>*

Trying to get himself back together, Josef said, "Well, let's see if we can find an opening in that hedge wall."

"Did you hear that?"

"I—I *think* so, Durquist," Modra responded. "I got a picture of some kind of overhead thing shooting at somebody's suit pack. That and a lot of fear and confusion. Much of the rest were words I couldn't understand, but the emotions came through with the mind-pictures."

The Durquist surveyed the horizon. "There is a cloud over there, acting very unnaturally. It appears to be watering something. Let's get into the trees in a hurry. I have no rational basis for it, but something tells me that whatever else it does, it won't do it in the trees."

"Don't scan it!" Modra ordered. "If it's hostile, we don't want to draw attention to ourselves."

They didn't even try to figure out which path the Mycohlians had taken; they wanted to get under some kind of protection and fast.

"I thought I saw another one of the things coming in slowly

from the left, towards the glow,'' the Durquist noted. ''This
may be tricky.''

Molly was oblivious to both the telepathically intercepted
messages, which she was incapable of receiving, and of the
potential danger the clouds represented. ''Boss syns say give
Jimmy bath,'' she noted. ''Molly not see where.''

''Huh? I hear water or something over that way,'' Modra
said, snapping back a bit to reality.

They saw the fruit groves and orchards but did not immediately stop for them; they still had food synthetics in their suits
and they weren't sure what would happen if the aerial watering
can up there didn't like snackers. That brought them rather
quickly to the stream, which Molly was convinced was what
the demons had meant. She got Jimmy out of his suit and then
removed hers as well, and took him gently out into the water.

Modra watched her and said, ''You know, sometimes I
almost envy her. She's like a little child who can't grow up, no
matter what that body's for, and everything's so simple to her.
She doesn't seem to have any ego and just about no idea what's
going on, yet she's devoted and just wants to help.

''No matter what medicinal properties are in that very
ordinary-looking water, she doesn't even seem to realize that
any modern medical patch is going to give a wound as much of
a seal as a suit. What she's doing is meaningless, except in her
simple way.''

But when she immersed Jimmy, face up, in the deepest part
of the stream, his head suddenly came up and cried out,
''*Ouch! Damn* that hurts!'' Molly dutifully pushed him back
under, showing her considerable strength. Empathically, all
three of them felt at least some of that pain, but when he went
under again it seemed to genuinely lessen.

Modra pointed. ''Look! That's the patch, floating downstream! It's come off!''

''Must not have been put on right,'' the Durquist said. ''Still,
it seems to be helping him.''

Modra nodded. ''I think I'm gonna get out of this suit and
take a dip in that stream myself. I feel like the filth of ages is
upon me.''

''You think that's wise?''

She shrugged. ''If we could hear the Mycohl, mentally,
anyway, then I can hear the Mizzies when they come through

as well—if those demons let them through. That'll be plenty of warning."

"Suit yourself."

She collapsed the suit and wriggled out of it, then walked, naked, into the stream, which, at its greatest depth, was only a bit above her waist. She headed immediately for Molly, if only to rescue Jimmy McCray.

"Molly! Enough! He has to breathe!"

As soon as the syn let go, Jimmy's head came up, gasping and choking, and there was a sudden flood of thoughts, curses, and expletives the quality of which even Modra had never encountered before.

"All right! All right! No more, Molly!" he yelled, and sat up. Modra waded over to him.

"Let's see your back, McCray," she said.

He shook his head, frowned, and looked over at her. "Huh? Modra? How'd *you* get back?" His mind also added an automatic, typically male, and very positive analysis of her upper anatomy which, she realized, he didn't know she could now hear.

"Long story. I'll tell you later. Let's see your back."

He turned and she moved to look at it and gasped. The back still looked bad, with the cauterizing creating ugly and discolored bumps and scars, but the parasite's three tendrils had shriveled to almost nothing and seemed in the process of dropping off him. There was no blood, though, and no raw wounds as she might have expected. Indeed, while it was ugly to look at, it appeared to be an old wound, perhaps months old or better.

<That must be one hell of a medical patch the Mizzies have,> the Durquist commented.

Jimmy McCray frowned. "What the devil? How'd *he* know? He's way over there!" He had seen his own back through Modra's eyes and felt her astonishment, something that was just now registering on him.

<I'd hoped not to tell you this right away, but whatever happened made almost all of us telepathic, and I do mean all *of us. Everybody except Molly and Captain Chin of the Mizzies. It also appears to have turned everybody into empaths as well, and we're not sure what else, so you're not the only one out of a job.>*

He sighed. *<Will you open your mind to me? Just relax and let me dig a bit. I won't peer into your private areas, I swear. It's just the easiest and fastest way to bring me up to date, and the Durquist's mind beyond the immediate conscious level is too bizarre to make much sense.>*

<My mind is labyrinthine? You should have to bear the random thoughts of Terrans!>

<Uh, I think I've just been insulted,> Modra noted good-humoredly. *<Still, all right. I'm new at this, so I couldn't really resist much anyway.>*

<Just settle down in this nice water and relax,> he told her. *<Won't take a minute.>*

And it didn't, although it was a *very* odd sensation, and somewhat dizzying, as memories flooded back through her mind and then just as quickly were back where they should have been. Legend always said that the last moment of your life was something like this, although he wasn't going that far back—she thought. It wasn't possible to keep track of the rapid flow.

Finally he nodded. "That's it," he told her. "That really helped. Thank you for your trust."

She shrugged. "We've got the power, yes, but we really don't have any solid control over it or know how to use it, just as your empathic abilities are going to be pretty unrestrained for a while. I have a feeling, though, that if I don't learn how to control this mind-reading business and ever get back to the real universe, I'll go nuts."

"Many people do," he told her. "And nobody's sure about the rest of us, including us. It's sort of like always being at a huge party where a hundred people are all speaking at the same time. You have to train yourself to tune out all the background noise, or, at least, keep it down to a dull roar you can ignore, while concentrating on the person you want to talk to. That's not as easy as it sounds, but you have to master it before you can learn even the basics of blocking. Until you can block, you're an open book to anyone, particularly ones like me with a lot of training and experience, who can 'read' you."

She nodded. "That bothers me a little. It's why the Durquist and I have continued to just speak normally when possible. It seems to focus things."

It was, however, now apparent to her what a "block" felt

like, at least. Although she could read Jimmy McCray's thoughts, she could read only what he wanted or allowed her to read, and that wasn't an awful lot more than if he were speaking aloud. He was still as much of a cipher as ever.

''All the pain's out of my back and gut,'' he told her, answering her earlier question. ''It's still in other places not so easy to heal.''

She felt the enormous sadness and sense of loss he was feeling, and it puzzled her. ''I thought you'd sell your soul to be rid of her.''

He nodded. ''I might well have, and yet, now that she's gone, it's as if I was married and my wife had suddenly died, somehow.''

''You married,'' Molly pointed out. ''You marry Molly!''

''That's true, I did,'' he responded. ''And I don't know how I'd feel if I lost you, too.'' He switched to telepathy, mostly to spare Molly's feelings.

<You see,> he told Modra, *<I didn't want Grysta, would never have consented to her, but, once she was there, and started takin' on the kind of personality she did, she wasn't just a pain in the back, as it were. She was—well, closer to me than anyone else could ever come. It's rather bizarre because, well, I hated her control, we fought all the time, but she was, well, the closest friend I ever had in the world. My only friend for many years, in fact. And, the truth was, I wasn't just a host to her, either. I could take out all my frustrations, my fears, my worst and blackest thoughts on her and she'd give as good as she got. In a way, it's very odd. I wallowed so much in self-pity about her bein' there, it never once occurred to me that she was as frustrated as I was, livin' a life vicariously, as it were, but never directly. She was bright and inquisitive and she could only interact with anything and anyone secondhand. It was drivin' her nuts, as it would you or me, and I was so self-absorbed I never even noticed!>*

Modra looked at him, a serious expression on her face and perhaps the start of a tear in one eye. *<I think, maybe, I know more about how you feel than you think.>*

He felt suddenly very foolish. *<I'm sorry. I'll stop this, which does neither of us any good anyway. Remember, I never knew Tris—before.>*

She smiled at him and then turned away and went a bit

downstream, and, in spite of her face being out of his sight, he knew she was softly crying. He turned to Molly. "You want to help her? I'll be all right now."

"No," Modra said aloud. "That's all right. I think maybe those tears were months overdue."

<Who's that?>

The thought went through all three of them and galvanized them into sudden action.

"Saints preserve us! It's the damned Mizzies!" Jimmy McCray shouted. "That telepath's already put the block on, soon as she sensed us, but without Grysta to amplify, I can't block much of you two any more!"

"Durquist!" Modra called. "Grab the suits and come across. No time to put them on now! We need to put some distance between ourselves and them!"

Using one point of his star to gather up the three suits, the Durquist started across as they all made for the opposite shore.

Krisha, leading the Mizlaplanians down the hill, got so excited that she allowed her own thoughts to get to McCray. Either that, Jimmy thought as he ran, or she was deliberately leaking the thoughts to keep the pressure on.

<We caught them not far from us, and all but one out of their suits!> she shouted. *<Manya, stay here and see to His Holiness. Captain—if we hurry we can catch them before they can stop and dress and reactivate their suits! That makes it two to one!>*

Gun Roh Chin had little against the Exchange people, but it didn't matter. If the Mizlaplan wound up with only one gun and suit and the rest had none, then that put them in a superb bargaining position.

<Can't we stop and get armed?> Modra called.

<They're gaining!> Jimmy came back. *<We need to find a place where the Durquist can cover us until we can change.>*

Without warning, they broke out into the broad, vast, flower-filled meadow.

"Shit! This isn't gonna do us any good at all!" McCray shouted. "Durquist! Give us our suits and we'll try and get 'em on before they get here, slim a hope as that may be. Give us cover fire to keep 'em back!"

"Get in back of me!" the Durquist shouted back. Tossing the suits back into the field, where they landed, scattered, he got down on three points and used the other two to draw and hold his gun.

Jimmy, still weak and out of shape, slipped on the slick grass, then tried to pick himself up again. As he did, a massive bolt of energy from above shot down and fried the suit nearest him. He dropped and rolled and saw one of the clouds almost directly above them. It began to glow again, and he shouted, "Molly! Modra! Stay away from the damned suits! Flatten on the ground!"

A second bolt caught the second suit only meters from Modra, who felt the searing heat and tried to scramble away. A panicked Molly shouted, "Look! In back of you! 'Nother one!"

Modra suddenly had a terrible thought. "Durquist! Get back in the trees! Get back in the trees or take the suit off at once!"

The Durquist did neither, instead whirling with a speed that belied its shape and firing directly up and into the cloud with full sustained power.

It appeared to have no effect on the cloud, which glowed and then sent a thunderous bolt at the third empty suit, destroying it.

The Durquist gave up and made for the trees. It looked as if he were going to make it, but suddenly the dull gold suits of the captain and Krisha appeared at the edge of the forest and he reflexively paused.

A bolt from the first cloud struck him full on, enveloping him in that terrible heat and flame. All four onlookers heard the crackling and felt and heard the mental death agony which was mercifully short.

And, just like that, the Durquist just wasn't there any more, only a smoldering, liquid goo giving off acrid black smoke.

"Durquist!" Modra screamed, tears welling up inside her. *"Noooo . . . !"*

Jimmy McCray was conscious of the fact that the two clouds were still poised up there. "Modra! Molly! Tears later! Run for it! Out into the field!" He got up and grabbed Modra, dragging her to her feet.

The explosions shocked the two Mizlaplanians, who were suddenly aware of how exposed they both were to the clouds as well.

"They're waiting for us!" Krisha told him. "For some reason, they won't blast into the trees."

Chin, still shaken, nonetheless was the pragmatist, as always. "We could still take all three of them down with a wide stun from here."

"No! Those *things* might interpret it as an attack and blast us anyway. Besides, they're all naked and defenseless now. Wasn't that the point?"

He sighed. "I suppose it was." He looked at the smoldering piles. "Suddenly I feel more naked inside this suit than I would out of it, though. Notice how they took no notice of the three. It was the suits they were after, nothing more."

She nodded. "I know just what you mean. Let's go back to the others. I'm afraid we've got a hard decision to make."

She was silent and tight-lipped on the way back, and he finally asked, "Feeling guilty? Like you killed the Exchange creature for nothing?"

She nodded. "Something like that. Those weren't the real enemies."

"Don't be. You didn't kill the creature—you saved the lives of the other three."

"Huh?"

"If we hadn't rushed them, they'd have all donned their suits and then proceeded with all speed for that very spot. The odds are very good the clouds or whatever they really are would have nailed all or at least almost all of them before they realized what hit them." He sighed. "I must say that the little fellow has made a recovery I can only call miraculous. A few hours ago he was in agony and severe shock and near death, with tremendous loss of blood. Now, suddenly, he's running, diving, and ducking. I must be a much better doctor than I thought."

They returned to find Manya by the side of the stream and Morok soaking in it. Both had received multiple, if confusing, versions of the events.

Morok was sympathetic, but, "The captain's right, you know, Krisha. We probably saved the others. The problem is, while we have the only working suits and weapons at this point, they do us little good. I saw the meadow in the mental images. There is simply no way we are going to get across with them on."

Krisha nodded. "Whatever they are, they are programmed to stop anyone taking anything from outside past that point."

"They are lesser demonic spirits guarding the gates to the capital of Hell," Manya insisted. "Why won't you face facts and accept the tenets of your faith? Were we not all permitted to *see* the absolute evil that underlies this place?"

"Not all of us," Chin reminded her. "I wish, though, that I hadn't been so clever with the power modules on the Mycohl suits now. They would never have crossed that space without them, and that would have ended the problem."

"How could you know?" Morok asked.

"You should have just slit their throats while they were in the trance!" Manya snapped. "*That* would have solved the problem then and there!"

The captain sighed. "Perhaps I am not resolute enough. It's probably true what you say, and I freely admit that the thought crossed my mind. If the Mycohl succeed and serve the demons, I will carry that thought with me for the rest of my probably very short life, and the responsibility for it as a black stain on my soul. Still, I was trained as a soldier, and in a fight I'll do whatever is my duty. I discovered, on this journey, that I could not be a murderer. No matter what, I just don't have it in me."

"You are a good man, Gun Roh Chin," Morok assured him. "Stay that way. And, Manya, you must remember that these Mycohl are not demons; they are people, just like us, and they believe as they do and act as they do because they were raised in an evil and predatory culture. They didn't choose their positions, any more than we chose ours. The sin of the evil ones is that they are as they are by choice and by rebellion."

"If a pet animal is cruelly tortured and trained to be a vicious killer, it, too, has no choice," Manya responded. "But you destroy the mad pet, which will kill anyway, no matter whose fault it is."

Krisha was too upset to let this continue. "All of this is meaningless! What someone should or should not have done is hindsight. If they are not demons, neither are we gods. There have been mistakes enough to go around this time! The only question we have is how to move forward, and when, and the others, naked or not, are proceeding while we debate philosophical points!"

Even Manya seemed to sense that she'd gone a bit too far. "How is your leg, Holy Father?" she asked.

"Oddly, much better," he responded. "It's a bit stiff, but I'd swear that the swelling's gone down to almost nothing." He got up on both feet and Manya was startled to see the degree of improvement.

"Amazing," she breathed, inspecting the leg. "There must be some remarkable curative in the water."

"That might explain the little fellow," Chin commented. "And I was patting myself on the back. Oh, well . . . At least we will outnumber the Exchange, whose weaponry and power we no longer have to fear, and have equal numbers with the Mycohl, and if that mess of hedges is as confusing on the ground as it appeared from above, we might well be able to make this a closer competition yet. I do, however, wish we still had more of an edge. That Corithian could take all of us in a matter of seconds."

Morok flexed his wings. "Perhaps I can fly over it, guide the rest of you," he suggested. "There is little risk now that no one on the ground can shoot me down. The conditions here feel favorable in the basics, although it will have to be a series of short flights with me doing most of the work, since there's essentially no wind here and, therefore, no thermals to ride."

"Those *things* are up there, too," Krisha warned him. "I think you're best off staying on the ground."

"Perhaps. We'll see. They might only guard that perimeter. Once beyond it, it might well be safe."

Gun Roh Chin deactivated his suit and got out of it. "I feel a bit self-conscious and modest," he told them, genuinely a bit embarrassed, "but there is no other way."

Krisha sighed and did the same. "I suppose I am destined to leave this life with nothing more than I took in," she commented dryly. Still, she *did* feel self-conscious, not around the other two, who were both of other races and also priests, but in front of Gun Roh Chin.

"You look—superb," the captain assured her, once more happy that his mind could not be read and not a little worried that his animal lusts might well be beyond disguise from this point.

Manya alone retained her body stocking, and they began to walk to the clearing. At the clearing, however, they saw the two clouds, still there, now moving back and forth in their impossible manner as if guarding a picket line.

Seeing them for the first time in person, as it were, and also seeing the scorched remains of the earlier attack, Manya felt suddenly less confident. "I wonder if it is—anything?" she said nervously.

"You must trust in the gods and your own wisdom, Sister Manya," Morok responded. "I cannot guide you in this."

She sighed. "I would be a target they would love an excuse to attack," she said at last. "I will not give them an excuse until I can give as good as I get." And, with that, she removed everything.

And, with that, they started off across the meadow.

The clouds moved in their rapid, unnatural fashion, and seemed to be inspecting them. All four of them looked up nervously from time to time as they went past the remains of the Durquist and the suits of the others, and across. The clouds did nothing.

After half an hour or so, they spotted and diverted to the carcass of the Corithian. That, too, was nerve-wracking, all expecting the thing to come to life again and attack them as they stood there, defenseless, but it was soon clear that the creature was dead.

"*That* is a relief," the captain commented. "Now it's four-three-three, and all of us equally vulnerable."

They walked on and received another comforting sign as the clouds zipped away at fantastic speed and finally resumed their watering jobs far off.

"Apparently, being more than halfway across, they've decided we're no threat any more," Morok noted. "Still, I would expect they'd be back in a real hurry if any of us reversed direction."

Eventually, they reached the hedge wall. "Interesting," Krisha commented. "I can't pick them up. Be on your guard—I'm going to lower the block for just a moment."

They waited, trying to keep their minds as clear as possible, and, from far off, they received snippets of mental conversation. Then, just as suddenly, it was gone again.

"That's that," she said at last. "In there, if they can't hear us, we can't hear them. That poses a problem I'll have to experiment in dealing with, since they'll all be able to sense our block, and, therefore, have a fair idea of our position even if they can't get anything. On the other hand, we'll be blind to them unless the empathic or other abilities show up stronger and more controlled than they have so far. I'm just going to have to lift it now and then get bearings on them, and, when I do, we'll be wide open to them. I simply can't teach you all to individually block under these circumstances."

"Do what you must," Morok told her. He looked up and down. "I would say that a more pressing problem is deciding how to get *in* there."

Gun Roh Chin gave a wan smile. "How else?" he asked rhetorically. "We go left until we find it. *They* did."

It was about an hour's walk down, and appeared to be the *only* one, at least as far as they could tell.

They were immediately met by a choice of two directions to travel. "I assume we keep on the leftward track if we can, or until the rule proves to have exceptions," the captain noted. "I have a feeling, though, that it's not going to be *quite* that simple."

It wasn't. The second opening inward proved to have an obstacle to leftward travel about thirty meters down that unnerved them just to look at it.

It didn't really block the passage, but it took up about half of it, and it was an enormous statue in what appeared to be black marble. The figure itself was monstrous: a great creature full of tentacles and claws and ugly things that ripped and tore, and it radiated its ugliness and, yes, its evil, to Terrans and non-Terrans alike.

Except, of course, to Gun Roh Chin, who saw only the aesthetic ugliness of the statue.

"Why do you hesitate?" he asked them, genuinely curious. "It's just a carving."

They walked down the path slowly, with the captain in the lead, and as they drew closer to it Krisha suddenly shouted, "Hold it!"

He stopped, puzzled, and turned to her. "What is it?"

"That thing *moved*! I swear to you that it did!"

"There is a consciousness in that thing somewhere, Captain," Morok agreed. "I cannot explain it, but I can *feel* it."

Manya suddenly had an insight. "The great dream, the

colors, the evil things . . . It was a representation of this! The
evils there intersect here through the idols!''

''Nonsense,'' Chin said, but he didn't move forward. Now
he thought he'd seen some movement out of the corner of his
eye. *I'm being spooked by them,* he told himself. Still, they all
definitely had attributes that he lacked, and at least one
important piece of this puzzle was theirs that was denied him.
If Krisha had said she was reading the mind of someone one
row over, he would never have doubted her. Why should he
doubt them now? Still, he needed some more proof before
breaking precedent in this place.

Wait a second! Maybe there *was* a way. ''Krisha, try and
sense a mind in there,'' he asked her. ''If you can.''

She tensed and took a deep breath, then allowed the block to
drop as she stared at the hideous idol. Suddenly she started,
gasped, and brought it back up again. ''It's there!'' she told
them. ''I feel suddenly—unclean—just having touched minds
with it!''

''As do I,'' Manya agreed. ''The thing is *vile.*''

Morok looked a bit shaken, as if suppressed memories had
suddenly resurfaced. Still, he said, ''Krisha, you will have to
lower that block. Not when we are in the presence of such as
this, but at other times. It is the only way we can tell a clear
path.''

She nodded. ''But let us get away from this one, Holy
Father, before I do. *Ugh!* Disgusting!''

Chin frowned. ''But won't dropping the block give our
positions away to the others?''

''They have that now,'' she pointed out. ''And I fail to see
anything we can think that would assist them. They, after all,
already came this way. We might even get some clue as to what
is ahead.''

''All right, then,'' he agreed, ''we break precedent and go
right.''

''I fear that this route is highly perilous, more so than any
other to date for all its beauty,'' Morok commented. ''The way
through in the other plane was to steer the course between the
evils, but it was a relatively straight shot. This is twisted
beyond divining.''

''Yes,'' Krisha agreed. ''And, remember, so thick was the

evil and so narrow the way through at the city gates that none could pass without being snared.''

Jimmy McCray was having his first real taste of the disadvantages of being empathic. The darkness flowing out of Modra's very core was so strong and so heart-rending it was difficult for him to deal with more practical concerns.

"We *must* go on," he told her. "I lost everything long before I came to this place, and, after, I lost what little was left. But I found something, too, in this place. I found out that I really don't want to die, and that I want to find out the meaning of all this, find out who and what's behind it, and face the bastards."

She looked at him mournfully. "The only three people I ever really was close to are gone," she sighed. "One before you came aboard—the one you replaced, really. Then Tris, and now, finally, the Durquist. When I stepped aboard *Widow-maker* for the first time, it was *so* different. It was fun, it was a camaraderie I'd never known before, it was . . . life. For the first time, I was really *alive*. They were my family. I knew them better than I knew my own real family, and they knew me. Now they're gone. They're all gone. Oh, Tran's still alive somewhere, I suppose, back on the ship, but it's not the same."

"You have a husband, I believe," he pointed out.

She nodded. "I knew him for less than three weeks. I've been with *you* far longer than I've been with him. I married him on an impulse, in some ways to gain security and status, I guess—I'd just been pulled out a few weeks earlier from the most horrible experience I'd ever had in the field—until now—but, mostly, because he had money and position and he could save the team from going bankrupt. Most of all, I did it to save the team, keep everyone together. Now look what's happened! Tris blows his brains out, the Durquist is melted into goo, and I'm sitting here, stark naked, in the middle of a place I don't understand and that wants to finish me as well. And what if, by some miracle, I *did* get out, get back? To what? For what? It's all gone, now."

"There you are again," he told her in a stern tone of voice. "Wallowing, like I used to wallow. Oh! Woe is me! 'Twould be best if I were never born than to suffer this way. Well, it's crap. It was crap when I did it and it's crap when you do it. It'll destroy you, and you have enough other things to destroy you without having to give it more pushes. I may not have known you since you was a wee little girl, but I am part of this team. So is Molly. You hurt Lankur, yes, but you didn't kill him. He killed himself. You think that's normal behavior for someone who is lovesick and heartsick? It's not. You may want to, but you don't do it. You go on, and you find someone else. Maybe you take on the world, or get sloshed a lot, but you manage, and, sooner or later, you figure a way to something else. In truth, from what I'm hearing, you *did* make the wrong choice, since neither you nor Lankur were mature enough to make it together.''

His comments raised anger within her, and that was a start. He wouldn't be surprised if he got slapped before this was done, if he had to go that far, but this was survival.

''The Durquist, now—he's like you and me. We volunteered. We came because it was a team decision, a team vote if you will. Maybe it was a wrong vote, and maybe there wasn't another way out of there and maybe there was, but we didn't have to join this thing. I know at least the Durquist and I both felt that there was a quick way out. Goin' right, perhaps, all the time. It was a problem we could work on once we got the system, but it was a problem we never actually *did* work on because we weren't going to leave the team. We got warned about the clouds, whatever they are. The demons at the gate warned us, and we got confirmation from the Mycohl. If we're too bloody stupid to listen to two warnings, then terrible things are gonna happen—not because of fate, or even the Quintara, damn their hides, but because we're so damned full of ourselves we don't listen and we make mistakes. And, in this business, mistakes kill and it's only blind luck that saved us. You know bloody well the Durquist would never have taken off that suit or dropped that gun. He was a solid rationalist with faith only in what he could see, touch—or wear. He went well, defending the team and doin' his duty. I'll not cry for that. I may regret, and I may wish it hadn't happened, but I won't cry for that honorable a death.''

She stared at him, more puzzled than angry now. This was a new Jimmy McCray, one she hadn't met, or, perhaps, hadn't noticed before. ''You sound like a cross between the old Tris

Lankur and one of those Mizzie priests back there,'' she noted. ''Just what do you want of me?''

''Nothing,'' he said firmly. ''Nothing except the same sort of team support that I'd give you. Somewhere in this mess there is an explanation for all this. Whatever those researchers unlocked, it's powerful beyond anything we could imagine, and it's damned dangerous. Whoever, whatever is behind this, it knows about us. Not just we individuals, but *everything*—our people, our worlds, our past and present. That's what those demons were doing before and after ravaging the place. They were standin' there, quiet and playin' dead, while they telepathically got all the information they needed from the researchers' own minds, right up to our current level of knowledge. When they were freed, or caused themselves to be freed—we'll never know the answer to that one—they finished off the ones they didn't need any more and then they went for that cymol and they read out all the data in her robot mind. Then they finished off everybody as easy as you please and came in here to report that information to somebody. They know more about us and our civilizations than we do.

''But we—the remnants of the three teams still going here—we, now, are the only ones who know about them.''

She nodded. ''But they could have killed us at any time,'' she pointed out. ''Why go through all this?''

''Why, indeed? The Mycohl and your Mizzie friends aren't dummies, either. The ones that make it through will be the survivors. Perhaps we'll consider the dead the lucky ones when those of us who *do* survive get to the answers, but I'll give no one the satisfaction of killin' me until I face them down. You and me, we're well suited for this. We got nothin' left to lose.''

Modra gave him a wry sort of smile, and Molly leaned over and whispered in his ear, ''Jimmy gonna marry her, too?''

He laughed, possibly the first laugh he'd had in ages. ''She's already spoken for, my dear,'' he responded, getting to his feet, then helping Modra up as well.

He made a grand gesture, pointing off in an essentially random direction.

''All right, me lovely beauties. The finish line's right over there someplace, more or less, and all we have to do is sneak past some ugly buggers to reach it. What's past is past. We start again right here, right now. No power in Heaven or Hell can withstand an Irishman with a beautiful woman on each arm, but, if something could, what a way for an Irishman to go!''

"Oh, shut up, Jimmy!'' both the women responded, almost in unison.

The city was ancient; so ancient that no calendar devised by any of the folk of real space had any meaning at all here.

Its broad avenues and tall, sleek structures were silent as a tomb, untrod and uninhabited for thousands upon thousands of years. And yet, within the Great Pyramid that was the centerpiece and heart of this great, silent city, sleepers stirred, black wings flexed, and an excitement ran through the place where the Princes stood.

<They come!> cried the thoughts of all of them. <*After so long, they come at last! Soon now, very soon, they will take the keys to Chaos itself and bring forth our new age, our new time. We grow stronger and stronger, and with the passing of inconsequential moments, our liberation is at hand. Soon we will embark upon our greatest adventure, as our Master had foretold so long ago, and, this time, the Gates of Heaven shall not prevail against us!*>